LOOK
INTO MY
EYES

Annie Mars

DEDICATION

For Mum,
We both see the world a little lopsided.

CONTENTS

PROLOGUE

"Doctor Sage," someone called as he made his way down the hall, but he kept walking. "Doctor Sage," the voice called once more, prompting him to stop and look back. It was Jete Finnerty, a junior researcher at the lab.

"Yes?" he responded, turning to face Finnerty, who was half running, half tripping over himself to keep up. Sage sighed. It was increasingly hard to find discreet and independent assistants these days. Nonetheless, Finnerty's work remained dependable, which was what truly mattered.

Well, uh… You see, Doctor Sage," Finnerty swiped and tapped furiously at the tablet he was carrying.

"Spit it out man," Sage cried. There was only so much snivelling that he was able to take from the likes of the young researcher. If he did not get the man speaking now, he would be sputtering and stuttering for the next ten minutes. Brilliant as he was, his ability to report or even to move from one place to another at speed was greatly impaired.

Jete Finnerty looked up from the tablet and pushed his glasses, back up. "Ah, yes," he said before going back to fiddling with the tablet. "The animal tests have provided results finally."

Results. Results would be a good thing unless they were not satisfactory results, but he needed something to prove that all his hard work and innovation had finally paid off. He had to contain his excitement at Finnerty's words. It would not do for one of the junior lab members to see his giddiness at the prospect of positive results.

"And what results would those be?" He was trying to be patient. He really was.

"Fire. Everything the rat looked at erupted in flames." Finally, he held up the tablet and presented Sage with the footage he had been looking for all along. "It works, Sir. It really works."

Sage rubbed his chin as he stared at the docile rat on the screen. It opened its eyes and blinked. Stretched its little legs and stood up. The blinking stopped as its attention was caught by the food bowl in the corner of the cage. The rat approached it, but suddenly the bowl burst into flames. Scared, the rat scampered around and more things in the cage started to erupt around it.

Sage was mesmerized by the footage. "It works," He breathed out. His life's work. They had succeeded. Excitement bubbled up inside the man.

Finnerty nodded, a grin threatening to emerge on his pursed lips. "It works." His glasses slid down his nose again.

Sage looked away from the footage of the rat's last moments as it was consumed in a fire of its own making. He looked at Finnerty, ignoring it as the younger man pushed his glasses back up his nose again. "What else do we have in the works?"

"We haven't woken up the uh… Stone or frost eyed rats yet… But they're next," he explained. "As these are physical results caused by focus, we want to wait on the other options, such as the control and telekinetics until we have a more sentient subject."

Sage rocked back on his heels as he rubbed his chin. "It's about time we moved the schedule up then. Yes, I think we need to move everything up." He turned and walked away from the researcher without another word. He had preparations to make, subjects to secure and history to make. Where was that one promising looking subject he had been following? Yarm. She was in Yarm. Perhaps it was time to head there. Everything was coming together ever so nicely.

1

"And we can see from the scans that things will only continue to deteriorate…" The Eye Doctor kept on talking, but I wasn't listening. I just could not find it in me to continue listening after those first few words. I had been having a hard time seeing the board in class. A hard time seeing what was right in front of me as well. Easy fix in some places. Get some glasses. I just needed glasses, but not here. Not in Yarm, not with so many migrants from Eriden where the low-visioned were left to wither and find a way to muddle through life until something finally put them out of their misery. I didn't know much of the history of the war-torn country. History's not my best subject in school, but the one thing I do know, is that opinions changed as they came. In Epreah, Nostines, Susweassau and beyond, such a thing like glasses would be met with jokes and light-hearted teasing like 'Four Eyes,' not that I wanted to deal with the 'four eyes' taunts at school either, but it would be better than this continual blurriness that was becoming my day to day and my eventual downfall as a Sightless. It could be worse I suppose, I could be Eyeless.

My mother and the Doctor were still talking. Mother was asking questions, and he was saying things that I was not listening to and to be honest, I thought that my mother probably wasn't listening either. I knew what my mother was thinking and ultimately hearing behind every word the doctor said.

Blind. I was going blind. By the end of the year, before I even turned sixteen, I would likely be blind. For life. Irreversible. How would I go to school? How would I get a job? How was I going to live? Would my friends want anything to do with me when I was blind? No, they wouldn't be caught dead with a Sightless. How would my mother cope with my being blind? How useless would I become? What would become of my life from this point on? Pity? Derision? I didn't know. I didn't want to know.

I would always be 'the blind girl' wherever I went and there was nothing I could do about it. That much I had caught before I had zoned out. Blind. Forever blind. Always trapped in a darkness that I would never be able to escape. I closed my eyes and let the black emptiness engulf me. I wondered how I would live like this every single day.

Suddenly, I was being shaken. "Come on. We're leaving." My mother declared. Leaving? When had the appointment finished? How much had I missed while off imagining the eternal darkness?

"Hold on a minute," The doctor said. "I want to take one more look." He came over from around his desk and inspected my eyes with a torch once more, before slipping a small bottle wrapped in thick paper into my hand. I looked at him curiously, but he just looked awkwardly towards my mother, hovering over me. I understood. Mother had been her usual, delightful self.

My mother almost hauled me out of the chair, and I followed obediently, not really sure what was happening anymore. I couldn't find the willpower to object or disobey. I would soon be wholly reliant on her for everything while she suffered the social disgrace of my existence.

Ok, maybe not everything. I knew that in other places Sightless people lived perfectly happy lives and did all the things sighted people did… But… I was only fifteen! I did not want to lose the light. I wanted to finish school. I wanted to get a job. I wanted to get out this house… Maybe I just wanted too much.

2

Doctor Erol Gruda leaned back in his chair as the girl left with her mother. If one could even call that woman a mother given her attitude. He picked up the file and looked over the girl's details again. Her eyesight would only get worse, and it was degrading at a rapid rate, faster than he had initially predicted. Doctor Gruda thought it might have to do with the mother not doing as she was told. Not letting the girl have access to medicines and aides that would have supported her eyesight for longer. There was nothing he could do about that now. Anything to do with eyesight was so complicated with people.

Damn that Eridenti influence. Yarm used to be such an educated country and now the people were as shallow and narrow-minded as their Eridenti neighbours, with their tragic views on sight issues. Realistically, there was no reason that girl and any other child like her should have their lives snatched away from them so unfairly by something that's not even their fault, but parents overcome with shame or outdated views held their children back for fear of being thought less of, because he highly doubted that the mother's only concern was financial. He'd tried going over alternative routes to treatment with her when the girl had first been diagnosed to no avail.

Well, if she wasn't going to do anything to help her daughter, maybe he still could, before the girl lost her sight completely and was hidden away from the world as some sort of horrible secret. It had only been a short while ago that a representative from Sage Laboratories had made the rounds, promoting a new trial, something supposed to completely reverse the kind of degradation that led to full blindness. Where was that card he'd been left? And the prospectus, he needed to make sure the girl really did meet all the requirements.

He pushed papers around on his desk. He really needed to take the time to tidy up, but there were so many patients these days, there was little time for much else than consultations and practical treatments. He was lucky if he got any reading on the latest research done. There was a stack of medical journals on the bureau to the side of his office, the top one with a picture of Nelson Sage himself in his state-of-the-art laboratory, looking for all the world as though he was the man who was going to fix everything.

Erol Gruda hoped so, at least, for that girl.

His hand fell on the prospectus, and he pulled it forward, setting it beside the girl's file. It might be her only chance at a normal life if she continued to live in Yarm.

The girl was the right age. Her prognosis fit with the parameters. His fingers tapped on the card of a Ms Reavis as he read. He felt himself getting excited. The published results to date were promising.

But how to get that obstinate woman to agree to let her daughter take part? Well, he could cross that bridge when it came to that. First, he needed to let them know he had a promising candidate for their study and see if he could get her a place.

As he dialled the number on Ms Reavis's card, his eyes scanned the girl's file again and something caught his attention. A secondary contact. Perhaps the girl's father? Maybe there was a way to get the girl involved after all, that wouldn't involve the mother. It wasn't entirely ethical, but as long as that girl got the treatment she needed, Doctor Gruda would be able to sleep soundly at night.

The dial tone changed to a crackling silence before a voice spoke. "Sage Laboratories, Ms Reavis speaking."

"Ms Reavis, my name is Doctor Erol Gruda, and I would like to talk to you about Test Program Three Nine Three Seven. I believe I have a suitable candidate for your trial stage."

3

Nelson Sage frowned as noticed Jete Finnerty push his glasses back up his nose. He was pacing the room, working his way through his thoughts. They were so close to achieving his lifelong goals. The girl being prepped in the next room was just the beginning. Yet, that little act of indulgence from the younger researcher irked him. If only he'd let Sage do the corrective surgery.

The boy was always fiddling with those glasses, but he was Suseassaun and didn't seem to feel as though they made him less than. No, he had this deluded idea that those ridiculous pieces of glass before his eyes made him look more intelligent. It was positively ridiculous. He should do something about the boy and his imperfect sight. For now, though, he needed to focus. He resumed pacing. What was taking so long? How long did it take to operate and remove the useless eyes from the girl? He stopped before the viewing window and watched the procedure.

"Tell me about her," Sage said, startling the young researcher. He dropped the tablet he was carrying, then hurriedly dropped to his knees to retrieve it. The man was a colossal fool. Perhaps he had bigger issues than his lack of eyesight in that he seemed completely incapable of using his limbs with any sense of aptitude.

"Uhh," the boy said, standing, readjusting his glasses once more and trying to locate the requisite information. "Minetta Ishani, eighteen years old. She wasn't born without sight, but contracted Meier Rutger Syndrome as an infant which permanently affected her eyesight, leaving them clouded over with a film of hardened mucus, which they were unable to remove." Meier Rutger Syndrome was a precarious illness, which was often mistreated as liver disease when the eyes went yellow. Failure to treat for Meier Rutger's meant that the person was likely to permanently lose their eyesight because the film that coated the eyes, turning them yellow. The residue thickened and solidified until it was unable to be removed. Caught early, medication could clear up the disease, caught moderately advanced, operating would potentially remove the film, clearing the eyes up again. Cases like the Minetta Ishani, that were left too late and in a region with little to no sufficient medical treatment were left permanently blinded and even if operated on, there was no removing the hardened shell that encased the eye as the entire eye withered and died within the casing. "She was left untreated for upwards of two years and by the time she was seen by a specialist, it was too late.

"So, she's never seen the blue skies of day as far as she recalls," Sage said reverently. "Won't this be a gift for her then?"

"Umm..." Jete murmured hesitantly. "Yes?"

"What else? Lab work? Any traces of the illness left in her blood stream?" Meier Rutger also lingered in the bloodstream. For short term survivors, it built an immunity into their systems over time, but for long term sufferers, it meant the constant threat of it reoccurring over time.

"Aside from her obvious issues with her sight, the remnants of the illness appear dormant, though there are traces of it," Finnerty explained.

"Hopefully this won't negatively impact the plans for the next stage, but at this point, we have no data to indicate what might occur."

Sage nodded as the young man spoke. "Fine, as soon as she's out of surgery come and find me." Then Sage turned and left the room.

Jete watched him go, breathing a sigh of relief as the older man disappeared. As brilliant as Sage was, Jete did not like the man.

4

Sage had to wait before the surgeons declared the incisions healed enough for Minetta Ishani to progress to the next stage of the experiment. During that time, Doctor Nelson Sage tuned his attention to other projects. He had another of his projects transferred to the lab, not wanting to take time away in case his experiment was ready sooner than anticipated.

This one, if it worked, would make a perfect military scout, able to see for miles without risk of getting spotted or shot at. Those Shiuran bastards wouldn't know what was preventing them from launching their attacks. One of these, attached to every unit would make the Eridenti military almost unbeatable.

He stepped out onto the roof of the lab where they were all waiting for him, including the subject, a young girl The experiment, for some reason, seemed to work better on females, though there were a few successful cases with male subjects. Except, they also had a tendency to escape. The girl was standing there, medical gauze wrapped around her eyes. The stark whiteness of the gauze contrasted against her dark, rich skin and wild brown curls that were only barely constrained by the bandages.

Sage nodded to the line of researchers. His son stood in line beside Jete Finnerty, both of them with a clipboard in hand to take real time data and observations. That morning, he had come into the laboratory, dressed in the same dark slacks and pale shirt that the other junior researchers wore. His father had wanted him there. He was glad that he had decided that today was the day for his son to become involved. He didn't believe any longer that the university had anything of importance to teach his son that he couldn't learn from being in the middle of authentic, important, revolutionary research.

There had also been some muttered cursing about morals and ethics, but the younger man had taken his father at his word and shown up. He could think for himself. He knew what was right and what was for the betterment of Eriden. He didn't need any out of touch professor babbling on about subject rights and undue and unforeseen consequences.

He could see his son, brimming with excitement. Sage often talked about his research at home and how it would impact not only Eriden, but one day, all of the Continent. The boy looked from the girl to his father and Sage nodded. It was time.

"Located in the distance, are several targets. I want you to locate them and read what was written on them. Understand?" he said to the girl.

She nodded hesitantly. "Ok..."

"Good," he said, then he held his hand out. Jete jumped forward, proffering a pair of scissors to the man. Sage took them, and almost reverently, cut the bandages from the girl's eyes. As they fell away, the girl gave a cry of agony and raised her hands to cover her eyes. "Take a moment to adjust to the brightness of the day."

"Perhaps this should have been started in a darkened room," the young man said, looking to his father. "Allow her to adjust to light and then start the tests."

"What Birdie here has, are not like your eyes or mine or anything you've seen before outside of the animal kingdom. Her vision will extend kilometres further, like a predator in the sky able to locate a tiny morsel of food, scurrying along the ground. Light will not affect her in the same way it does those of us with perfect vision." The young man didn't look convinced, especially given the girl's reaction. Sage pulled the girl's hands away from her eyes. "Look," he ordered.

She did so and screamed. Her hands went for her face, tearing at it. "My eyes! What have you done?" Her head tuned from side to side wildly, like an animal trying to escape. She looked towards the young man, and he could almost see the way her eyes seemed to change, and she screamed again, still trying to claw at her face. Large men grabbed for her, pulling her blood-stained hands away from her face. Then, she seemed to sway, disoriented, before turning and vomiting all over her captors, heaving up everything that had been in her stomach.

"Can you see?" he asked the girl. When she didn't respond, too busy trying to breath, Sage reached out to her, took her chin in his hand and made her look at him. "Can you see?"

Terror filled the girl's entire face. "Pores, nose hairs, follicles." She pushed out at him, trying to push him away. "Get away!" she begged.

Sage put his own hand to his forehead. "We will try this again another day. Get her out of here."

5

My mother was on the phone with my father. I don't know what she thought he would do about this situation. I didn't want to listen anyway. I didn't care what he had to say. He had left us years ago for another woman. We had been left with a house that mum could not afford to keep payments up for and a mountain of debt. The idea of needing glasses had already been an inconvenience, and my mother had spent the entire car ride home going on and on about the aides the doctor had mentioned for me to begin getting used to them and how there was no way any child of hers would be caught using sight aides.

Yeah... I felt like going back there to the Doctor's office and telling him that there was no chance of my ever using any of those things. We could barely afford the roof over our heads and food to eat, even if my mother could deal with the shame of my condition. Now, my mother was on the phone yelling at my father. Somehow, this was all his fault. Well, maybe it was or maybe it was hers. It was apparently a genetic condition, but what did I know? I had barely listened during the appointment.

"I just don't know what to do with her," my mother was saying in her high, whiney voice. The one she pulled out whenever she wanted someone to have sympathy for her. Yeah, because she was the one going blind. This was ALL about her. "She's useless now."

I was supposed to get a part time job after school. Or preferably, next year when it was legal, drop out and get a fulltime job, help my mother pay the rent and the bills, because there was no help coming from anywhere else, especially not after mum had ruined the divorce decree meaning that dad was not liable to us for anything. As much as she whinged and whined that it was something my father had done, I knew it was her. I don't know what she did, but I knew she did something.

I guessed that I was now useless, to my mother at least, she was going to try and wheedle whatever she could out of my father for her own benefit, because it sure as hell would never go to my living a regular life. I didn't know how to go to school without my sight and without the ability to see, I was never going to get a minimum wage job. Yarm just didn't facilitate resources for the sightless.

"No. She is still your child. Just because you picked up with some floozy, doesn't mean you don't still have a responsibility to her. I let you get away with everything you put us through, but I cannot handle this! Not alone!"

I sighed as something my father said made her mother scream at him. When she became hysterical, it was impossible to understand anything she said. Her words rolled together and became incomprehensible. I kind of felt sorry for my father having to listen to it. Still, he could just hang up on her I guessed.

"Don't you dare!" My mother screamed. "The bastard! He hung up on me!"

I had spoken too soon. Of course, he would do that. I had never expected him to help. I didn't know why my mother had, but I had known better. "Mum…"

"No, don't. Do not stand up for him!"

I stared at her. I had never stood up for him. Ever. Whilst I disliked my mother, I disliked my father even more. Still, every time I tried to calm her down, it apparently came out as my defending him. "He was never going to help us. Especially not now that he's got that new baby."

"New baby?" My mother asked, her voice quiet, most likely from becoming hoarse, but maybe from shock.

"Yeah… The announcement went by on The Yarm Yarn a few days ago," I told her. "He's not going to help me." Then I braced for her reaction, and I wasn't disappointed.

"Baby?" Her voice was shrill, and she dragged the word out as though it was something offensive.

"A boy," I said softly. It was odd to think that I had a brother. I'd never met him and likely never would. I backed out of the room as she picked up a mug from the table and threw it against the wall. I heard it shatter as I darted up the stairs.

Later that night when dinner was finished, I backed off spending time with my mother and went back to my room. I told her that I had homework to do, which my mother no longer saw the point in. Neither did I really. As my mother said, "what was I ever going to use it for now?" but I needed to be alone. I had not had the chance before that appointment The one that had led to the end of the world as I had known it and afterwards… Well, that was something else altogether

I turned all the lights in my room on, knowing it would reflect in the power bill, but the bright light helped me see better and I took the bottle that the doctor had secreted into my hand from my bag. I extracted the note from around the bottle. It was handwritten in large, easy to read writing. The note said that the eye drops would clear up my vision for short periods of time. I was not to waste it, as it was unlikely my mother would allow me more. I could only imagine her arguments, something along the lines of, "It's not like money to buy the stuff grows on trees," or "What if you get caught using that or I get caught buying it? Absolutely not!"

I took a deep breath as I looked around my room. I knew my bedroom. I knew what everything was and where everything went. But now, everything had a tinge of blur to it. Nothing had an edge but instead bled into one another. The pictures on the walls were nothing but fuzzy patches of colour and when I caught a glance of myself in the mirror, I could see myself.

Sort of.

I could see the person staring back, but the face had no definition. I touched my face. I could feel my mouth and my nose. My eyes, but what I knew them to look like from before my sight got bad, that was not there. A point of colour where my eyes should be. My traitors, my enemies. Not just one of them, but both of them. I decided then and there, I needed to look at my own face for what might be the one of the last times, before even the eye drops would not be enough to salvage any sight. It was my own face. I had every right to see it.

I unscrewed the little bottle of eye drops. Here went nothing. I leaned my head back and squeezed two drops in. I blinked as the cool liquid touched my eye and reached out blindly for a tissue. There was a box somewhere on the table beside the bed. Finding it, I pressed the tissue to my eye and waited. I repeated the process on the other side.

With everything done, I was surprised to find myself unable to open my eyes. I wanted to, or did I? Maybe I was afraid of there being no difference. Or even more afraid of being able to see clearly, knowing just how soon it would all be gone.

Deep breath. Eyes open. A simple instruction that my brain was sending to my body. Finally, they opened, and I was confronted with my ceiling. Not that bad of a view of a plain white ceiling with a light in the centre of it, but not what I had been thinking about looking at. If I could see clearly, I really should not be wasting it on the ceiling.

I looked forward and faced the mirror. My face stared back at me. I could actually see my eyes and the greyish blue colour, ocean that they were, just like the clouds on a stormy day. My curved eyebrows, long eye lashes. The definition of each strand of hair. I took my hair out from the tie and let it fall around my face. It was getting darker. I remembered when I was younger, my hair had been this golden blonde and now, it was looking dusky and closer to a mousy brown. It was an odd feeling, looking at everything so clearly and running the tips of my fingers over the contours of my face.

7

"Today marks the culmination of years of hard work and dedication from each and every person here," Sage said, stepping to the middle of the laboratory. Finnerty and another worker were transferring the girl from the gurney she'd been transferred in on to a large, clear sided tub with a sleek seat that would curve around her body. "Your expertise and enthusiasm have been pivotal in bringing us to this point. Today, we see the final stage of our project and the beginning of a new world for Eriden and the whole continent." He turned to Finnerty. "Are we ready?"

The young man adjusted his glasses and nodded. "We are."

Sage walked to the prone girl, she was still sedated as she had been since her surgery, allowing her body to heal without complications. "Let's take a look then."

Finnerty carefully picked up a thin pair of scissors and situated them at the edge of the bandages that encircled the majority of the girl's head, keeping her eyes covered. He snipped in slow, gentle cut, peeling away the bandages until all that was left were two small circles of gauze pressed against the eyes. Before proceeding further, Finnerty looked up at Sage, awaiting any further instructions. A reverent hush came over the room, interrupted only by the beeping and bleeping of machines. Sage nodded and Finnerty lifted the first patch.

The bandage was clean, which was expected given the healing time and regular changes. Carefully, and full of hope, Finnerty removed the second one, frowning at the dirty, yellow-brown discharge that spoiled the bandage.

Sage stepped up beside the girl, extracted a pen torch from his pocket and pulled back the girl's eye lid to look inside. The empty eye socket was deep, red and irritated on the edge, but in the centre lay a small pool of the yellowy brown discharge. "There's a buildup in this eye. Let's clean that out."

"We could postpone," a woman said from a nearby station.

"No, we will continue. She's been given the all clear. This discharge was not there at last inspection," Sage said. "It's likely remnants of her battle with Meier Rutger Syndrome. There's nothing there for it to infect anymore though. We will proceed."

The discharge was cleared out of the empty socket and then cleared out and cleansed further. "Ready," Finnerty announced.

Sage leaned over and pulled a trolley over to sit beside him. Atop it was a small pedestal, which cradled two objects that seemed to have difficulties deciding if they were triangular or circular. They were mostly white, except for the centre, which was black. The aim was to do these up better, but they'd only been able to make the moulds the day before, so they'd forgone decorating the eyes with a realistic looking irises. When this worked, he would make more, so many more.

He lifted the first of the tiny objects in fingers. With his free hand, he manipulated the girl's eye lids, revealing the hollow space beneath and with some awkwardness, placed the object inside. He then repeated the process with the other side.

Then he stepped back.

"Now what?" one of the onlookers asked.

"We wait," Sage said. "Finnerty, lift the sedation."

Carefully, the young man injected a serum into the girl's arm. She started to stir, groaning as he started to awake from her weeklong sleep. Her eyes fluttered and Sage leaned in eagerly. The pure black spots in the centre of the eyes were disturbing to look at, but he smiled down at the girl. "Hello."

The girl blinked again. "Hello?" she slurred out.

"Minnetta, what can you see?" he asked.

"See?" she slurred.

"Light?" Colours?" He smiled brightly, "my face?"

She shook her head. "Nothing... I can't see anything. I never have."

As soon as he reached his office, Nelson Sage slammed the doors closed behind himself. He leaned back against them, trying to remember to breath. He reached into his pockets and stared down at the little porcelain prosthetics. He'd ripped the porcelain eyes from the subject's face before storming from the lab, leaving her screaming in his wake.

Angrily, he tossed the tiny objects against the wall. They clattered with tiny thuds to the carpeted floor. Frustration welled within him. He stalked across the room, ready to pick the prosthetic eyes from the floor, but just staring at them, lying there, it made it all real. He had failed. He had never left any thought for the prospect of failing and now, he was faced with starting all over again.

He let out a primordial bellow, thrashing his arms over his desk, sending papers, tablets, pens and the phone flying across the room. He stood there, heaving for breath in the aftermath as his rage ebbed and flowed. He wanted to throw more things, hear the satisfying cracking and shattering of something breaking, but he restrained himself as he heard a knock on the door.

He took one more deep breath, steadying himself. He was about to call for the person to enter, then realised that he couldn't let anyone see his office in such a state of disarray. Sighing, he turned, straightening his lab coat before opening the door. "What?" he barked, not bothering to check who it was before speaking.

Finnerty stood there, tablet in hand as usual. "Doctor Sage?" he asked hesitantly, far more attune to the doctor's moods than most people were. "We... uhh... umm... what I mean is... We're..."

"Yes? What is it Finnerty? Just spit it out already."

"We're wondering if you want to complete the prosthetics or redo the chemical preparation of the girl," Finnerty said, his words rushing together. The way Sage hovered in his doorway, blocking all sight of the interior office made him nervous and he shuffled his feet awkwardly as he looked down at his tablet, after anything to look at except for his boss.

"Neither," Sage scowled. Having seen the girl, he already knew what was wrong. There was no coming back from what was wrong with the girl. He should never have done this with her, but how was he to have known? "The fluid buildup was from her battle with Meier Rutger's. It won't make a difference what we do. Not with her. The Meier Rutger's will just continue to infect the sockets, eventually encapsulating the prosthetics. Get rid of her and-," he cut himself off, a thought occurring to him and he stalked back across the room to his desk. He picked up the file put together by his recruiter and read over the details once more. The girl in this one was in Yarm. It wasn't Eriden, but Meier Rutger's was almost unheard of in Yarm and better yet, the girl's father was originally from Erihall, meaning that genetically, she might be exactly what he was looking for. He held the file out to Finnerty. "Get me this one. Everything you need is there."

It was a few weeks later when I came home from school and found my father sitting at our kitchen table talking with my mother. I stopped short in the doorway between the hall and the kitchen when I saw him. I dropped my bag and stared. I couldn't help it. My father had not been in our house, well, this house, ever. It seemed so incongruous that my father, who I remembered always being so clean cut with perfect hair and expensive suits would sit at our dingy little table, one leg crossed over the other, his fingers tapping against the tabletop as he watched my mother. I could remember when he'd tried for a beard, it had been hard and scratchy when I had gone to kiss him on the cheek. He was clean shaven now. His new wife must have convinced him that the beard was a bad idea.

"Hi…" I said softly. I had to admit, I was very unsure of what was happening right now. The last time my father had even been mentioned had been that night after we had returned from the Doctor's office.

"Your father came by with some news." I looked at my mother. She seemed calm… And my father was in the same room. What was going on? He must have brought the most amazing news in the whole world for her not to be screaming at him. For some reason, the way they were staring at me made me incredibly uneasy.

My father moved the chair next to him out. "Come and sit down," he said, and I looked at my mother. Yes, I looked at my mother for permission before sitting down next to my own father. I did not need the rest of the night to be all about her feelings of betrayal because she thought I sided with him. I tentatively thought about taking a different chair just to be difficult, but decided it was too much effort.

"What is it?" I asked, looking from one to the other.

"I've been doing some research since your mother called the other week. Asking around, looking for anything that would help your situation," I frowned. My situation. He made it sound like I had gone and done something stupid and gotten myself into this situation from mere bad decisions.

"My situation?" I asked him.

"Yes, the doctor's prognosis. It is unfortunate that we're here, but we are." What was he implying? What did he think was happening? I could help but think that, if I had not been in that doctor's appointment, I honestly would now be thinking that I was pregnant or something.

"I'm going blind, dad. You can say it," I told him. "And no one asked you to take a break from your oh so busy life and do anything." Ok, maybe I was a little annoyed. I had not seen my father in months and now he shows up talking about me as if I was an embarrassment. It was bad enough having my own mother constantly bemoaning the increasing cost of my care to anyone and everyone who would listen, but now this? "Don't act as though this is my fault. I didn't cause this. I didn't ask for this. I'm not some screwed up kid who did something dumb and is looking to her parents to clean it up for her."

"Don't-" My father started, but I didn't want to hear it. How dare he insinuate that this was all my fault. Even my mother hadn't stooped that low.

"What? Don't talk to you that way? You chose to stop being my dad. You chose to leave us. And now you come in here and act as though we're an inconvenience to you. Well, I never asked you to," I went on. "I didn't want you to come. I didn't want your help."

"Just listen to him," My mother said. "He might be on to something..." My mother, encouraging me to listen to my father... Ok, that was new. I guess that I could listen. It had to be good if my father had won my mother over.

My father sat up straighter in his chair and looked at me. "I found a trial."

A Trial. It all came down to a trial. I sighed. I didn't know how I felt about being a guinea pig, but the more my father talked about this trial he had found, the more confident he sounded that the trial would work and so against my better judgment, I agreed to go meet with the people in charge.

10

My father arranged everything. I don't know why or even how, but he did. He set the date and the time, even checked it with my mother and me. There was an unusual amount of courtesy going on between the two and it made me nervous. Then, on the day of the appointment, he showed up at the house. He drove us into the city, to the office where the people from the medical research lab were holding their interviews or the trials itself. I wasn't really sure. The one thing my father did not do, was explain anything to me. I didn't even know how he'd found this trial, and I didn't even know if I wanted to be there. As scared as I was of going blind, I didn't like the idea of being some sort of guinea pig or lab rat.

It was an awkward car ride. Neither my mother or I said much and just let my father go on and on about how wonderful he thought the trial would be. I would sign up and get selected. I would see again. Or better yet not actually go completely blind.

We parked out front a small office building. I personally did not see any cutting-edge medical trials actually happening on site. My father had spent the entire drive over trying to sell it to us though, as though my mother wasn't already excited enough about the prospect of my not going blind. Mainly because then it wouldn't cost her anything else in the long run, I guessed.

The waiting room was sparse and still looked like an office. An office in a small office building. It didn't even smell like the science labs at school, and I was pretty good with smells now. Something didn't feel right.

When we were finally led through to an office, a man stood from behind his desk, shook hands with my father, then my mother and to my annoyance, ignored me. Well, ok, if it was going to be one of 'those' parent conferences.

"Yes, nice to meet you, Doctor Sage," I said holding out my hand to him. I was going blind, not deaf. He looked at me surprised, perhaps overly so that I was able to locate him. I was not blind yet. He tentatively took my hand and shook it, while returning the greeting. He then directed us to seats. I sat between my estranged parents and waited to be talked about as though I didn't exist.

Doctor Sage seemed to direct all his attention at my father. It was like my mother, and I were not even there and when I tried to ask a question, I was told in not so many words, to let the grownups sort everything out.

I listened. I waited. I wasn't going to zone out this time, not like I had with Doctor Gruda. I should never have let my mother take charge there and allow myself to be ignorant of what was happening. I didn't like what I was hearing. Something didn't feel right, but I couldn't put my finger on it. There was a lot of grandiose talk, big, impressive words being thrown about, along with numbers that supposedly meant something, but I didn't know what. Then, when I asked for actual results – Science class remember? – I was ignored and assured that everything was great.

I was going to be great. They just needed a blood sample to see if I matched the criteria for their trial, and they'd get back to us very shortly.

11

Nelson Sage watched as the family left the office, the giddy feeling of success bubbling within him once more. He hadn't felt that since the failure with Minetta Ishani. He knew, just from looking at the girl and her medical records that she was perfect. When he'd looked into her dying eyes, he'd been certain. Her medical records were free from any sign of Meier Rutgers, as were her parents. Her age was suitable. The mother was a Yarm native, but the father, as he'd already known was a transplant from Erihall itself. There was a good chance, he carried the genetic traits required, without the being a carrier for Meier Rutgers. On top of all the positive signs for eligibility, the parents were willing, particularly the mother, just as Ms Reavis had said their doctor had indicted. The girl though… She was another story.

Sage walked to the window of the office and looked down at the parking lot. The three of them were leaving. The mother and father talking animatedly while the girl followed along. She stopped and looked up at him. There was no way she could have known he was watching and no way she could see him now, not with the state of her eyesight being what it was. He was sure of that. She was capable of getting around, but not of spotting him watching her. Hands behind his back, he waited. In the corner of the room, with the open portable testing kit, one of Sage's researchers was testing the sample the girl had provided at her parent's urging.

She was curious and perhaps a little too inquisitive, too headstrong, but that could be dealt with. Sage had no doubts that the results would match. He would have that girl, and she would make his life's work a reality. Of that, he was sure.

Doubt crept in slowly. He'd been sure about the last one too, but that hadn't worked out. Even the scout prototype hadn't worked entirely. Well, no, she'd worked just fine, except she'd disappeared when they'd disposed of Minetta Ishani. She wouldn't be the first one to escape, but he knew how to make it work and he had found a way to make sure that the test subjects never attempted to escape again.

The car the family arrived in drove away. He watched until the car turned out of sight and, Sage turned back to watch the test. "And what have we, Mr. Finnerty?"

"Just one more moment Sir," Finnerty said as he tapped away at the tablet computer attached to the equipment. Sage paced the length of the room before the window. Waiting was not one of his strong suits. Finnerty looked up. "She's a match."

Sage stopped and walked over to the man. "How much of a match?"

"She's not like the others Sir. She's a one hundred percent genetic match for the model you created," Finnerty assured him as he handed over the tablet. "With no sign of Meier Rutger's or other potential virus's that could impact the trial process."

Sage stared at the results. He had known it in his bones that she was perfect. The perfect subject for the perfect plan. Preparations. Preparations had to be made.

12

A knock at our front door that night was a surprise. My father had left, and my mother had been so enamoured with that Doctor Sage, that it seemed to escape her that he had ignored both of us during most of the meeting. He had given me the creeps, but she kept talking about all the things he had said about fixing me. I knew that I didn't want to go blind, but something about that man and the trial made me feel as though it might be the better option.

"I'll get it," I told my mother, leaving her to finish cooking dinner. I padded down the front hall in my socks. Life was not great, but I could manage without that weird trial that my father had found. I opened the door and there, even if his face wasn't all that clear, I could see it was Doctor Sage.

"Oh…" I said.

I was surprised. I hadn't expected him to show up at the house and it was only a few hours after we had left his office. They could not already know whether or not I was a match for their study, could they?

"Doctor Sage," I said, plastering a smile on my face.

"Hello." This time, he held out his hand to me. He must have learned from our first meeting. "Are your parents' home?"

"Mum's cooking dinner," I said, standing in the doorway, blocking his entrance. Why was he there? A phone call to say whether I was in or out would have sufficed. Really? So, what did he want? "Why are you here?"

"I have good news," he said, standing there, looking like he was getting irritated with me. Why would that be? "So, your mother or your father?"

"You could just tell me," I tried, but Sage shook his head and asked for my parents once more. I scowled but held the door open for him. "Come in," I lead him through to the living room. "Have a seat," I said stiffly. "I'll go get her."

I walked into the kitchen and looked at mum "Who is it?" she asked.

"It's Doctor Sage."

My mother whirled around. "What?" She asked, brushing her hands against her jeans. "Here? Now? Did he say anything?"

I shrugged. "He asked for you and Dad, but indicated that he had good news." Whatever that means, I thought. "He refused to tell me anything."

"Ok, Ok. This is a good thing," my mother said, brushing her hair back and checking her reflection in the glass of the microwave. "Come on," she said turning the stove top off and hustling me out of the kitchen and into the living room.

"Doctor Sage," Mum said walking over to him. "Thank you so much for coming. I hope you're here for good news and not to let us down gently." She beamed at him, and I leaned against the wall and crossed my arms over my chest. I did not think I was going to like this one bit. "It is wonderful news indeed. Your daughter is a perfect match for our trial."

"A perfect match?" My mother asked breathlessly.

"Oh, yes. Between her own medical records and the tests, we ran. We are certain that the trial will be an absolute success for her. I was hoping to talk to you and your husband about moving her to our facility to begin the trial.

"Oh, we're not-" my mother started, no doubt wanting to correct him on her marital status, but who cared about that? What was this about moving me to some facility?

"What?" I cried, cutting my mother off. "Move me to your facility?"

Sage looked at me and I felt a shiver run down my spine. I wondered what I would see if his face was clearer. "Yes, it's a residential trial at this time. That will allow us to fully monitor your wellbeing and ensure that everything is going to plan."

"That sounds as though you have thought of everything," my mother said, and I could not believe her. She actually thought that this was a good idea?

"Why wasn't this mentioned at the meeting earlier? What about school?" I pressed.

Sage smiled. Or at least I was sure he smiled. "I've found that people shy away from even applying to trials that advertise being a residential program. So, we bring that up once people know that they're a match, leave the choice in their hands, but now with some knowledge at their disposal. As for your education, we will ensure that it will continue."

"When would you want her to start?" My mother asked.

"Mum!" I cried. "How about asking if I even want to do this?"

She looked at me incredulously. "Of course, you do. Doctor Sage is promising to save your sight. Without it, what could you ever be?"

"Any number of things! Blind people live perfectly happy, independent lives, mum!" I think.

"But you don't have to be a 'blind person' now," my mother said. "Because Doctor Sage will fix you."

"Mum!"

"It's ok," Sage said. "I understand your hesitancy. You're young. You have your friends, your life. You don't want to give up those things. But think about how much better everything will be when the trial is successful," He turned to my mother. "Well, we could get your daughter situated tonight and begin tomorrow if you consent."

And so, against my protestations, my mother consented to me going into Doctor Sage's residential trial program.

13

Sebastian had seen the girl brought in. Unlike previously, there weren't any other projects running at the same time, just continuation on the projects still ongoing. Also different from the last one was the propensity to refer to this one by her case number than by name. No matter where he looked, he couldn't find it. Perhaps they were yet to file anything about her. He would need to keep looking. All he knew was that to date, no one had used a name to refer to her. Were they trying to distance themselves from her? Dehumanise her? He didn't know, but he could feel that something was wrong with how the experiments and trials were progressing. This girl was different from the others that had come before her. In the beginning, she had talked confidently, telling Finnerty in no uncertain terms that she did not want to be there and that it was about time someone started listening to her instead of her parents. She was fiery. She was electric. She was everything he wasn't. He'd been entranced.

In the time since her arrival though, he'd not been able to see her again, except from a distance. When he had been near her, she'd seemed different. She hated the guards. Sebastian wasn't all that enthralled by them either. They were gruff, uneducated men that his father kept around only for handling unruly subjects. That wasn't what was odd though, it had been the change in her. Her fiery personality had disappeared; her demeanour had become almost childlike and submissive.

Right now, he figured that he needed to ingratiate himself, be allowed to work near her, around her. Perhaps conduct some of the tests himself. Afterall, he was supposed to be getting hands on experience. Then he could be around her, try to get to know her.

He turned his attention back to the assignment that was supposed to be consuming his attention. Finals were any day now and he really needed this last one done before he could crack down on his exam studies. Maybe as soon as they were over, he could finally spend some time at the laboratory.

Where was that reference book he'd had only the day before? He scoured the desk, but as always, his father's desk was strewn with books and papers and journals and all the detritus an academic accumulates of the years. All of it just seemed to gather atop the desk rather than making their way to the many shelves or draws, where they could be arranged and catalogued with care.

His searching dislodged a stack of books, sending them sprawling to the floor. Sighing in frustration, Sebastian slid from the chair and started to gather them up. Amidst the array of project notes, textbooks and other things, he found an old notebook, bound in cracked leather. The brown cover was torn in several places, but at the centre of it, it had the initials 'N.S.F' embossed in peeling gold film.

His father's initials. He picked it up, kneeling, to rest against the floor as he flipped the book open. It was handwritten in stiff, solid handwriting that looked like his father's.

There's something going on. Something mother and father won't tell us. I don't know what, but Dom is worried, especially as his health continues to deteriorate.

Sebastian didn't know what it meant and flipped to an earlier page.

Dom won't wake up. It's been three weeks since the accident and nothing the so-called medical professionals do will wake him up. They say his body is healing and that until he wakes, we won't know the full extent of his injuries.

Who was Dom? The handwriting looked like his father's, but maybe it wasn't. He didn't have any aunts or uncles. He flipped to another page.

Dom woke up. Sebastian flipped to the next page, apparently that was all the update his father had time for that day. The next day, he continued with more. *Dom states that he can't see anything. I don't understand. Mother and father are worried, but it seems as though something else is bothering them, something bigger than Dom's injuries, but what could be bigger than Dom and his recovery?*

Sebastian sat back on his heels. He would need to read this diary, for that was what it seemed to be, some sort of diary or journal kept by his father when he'd been a boy, but why was it on his desk and who was Dom?

14

The beeping of an alarm woke me. With a sigh, I sat up. I blinked, but like every day there was just darkness. Everything has always been darkness, for as long as I can remember Whether I have my eyes open or closed. Whether the light is on or not. Whether it is night or day. Everything is always darkness. I was sure that this was so, because I could not recall having ever seen the light of day and yet... That didn't sit right with me. I was sure that I could not name the colours of a rainbow if I by chance was ever able to see it, even though I knew the names of the colours. Or could I? Maybe I could. It could not be possibly true that I had never known those things, right? I had to have come from somewhere. I could imagine the sky, trees, the ocean. I could see people and places in my imagination. Things I was sure that I had never laid eyes upon because I had always been here, but I could see them, oh so clearly in my imagination. Where had that imagination, my imagination, found these images? These ideas? Who were the people I saw? Where were the places that seemed to bring comfort? I had no idea. I craned my neck to the side, then to the other, stretching out the crook that had developed overnight.

I had mapped my room out in my head. I knew that if I stepped, one foot in front of another front one end to the other, the room was fourteen feet long and eleven feet wide. There was a bed under what I suspected to be a window. The wall felt as though it gave way to glass and during the day, I might feel warm if I stood in front of that space. Beside the bed was a dresser of some variety. It had two small drawers on the top level and two more, larger drawers beneath that. My food trays often waited upon that dresser, and I would sit upon the bed and eat, feeling my way across the tray, desperate to not spill or drop a single dish from it, because if I did, the consequences could be dire.

I had never even seen my own face. I knew that I had long hair. Brushing it was a pastime that kept me occupied for a short time every day. I had felt my face, my hair, my nose, my mouth, my ears and even my teeth. I knew the shape and feel of all these things intimately. I knew the shape and feel of everything in my room as though it was an extension of myself.

The thing that I felt the need to explore every day though, was my eyes. The empty holes in my face that did not hold so much as an unseeing eyeball. Maybe tomorrow there would be something there. They sure poked and prodded me and my empty eye sockets enough every day. Filling and unfilling the holes. Running test, after test, after test.

I looked forward to and dreaded test time. Test time meant interaction with other people, a departure from what felt like captivity in this room. People spoke to me, and I got to speak to them. That was not always a good thing because they did not always like my answers. They were rough and it was clear that they saw me as a commodity and not as a person. There was often talk about rats when I was around. I got the message though. I was a lab rat and nothing else. I was nothing and when I stopped being useful to them, I would be discarded. The only question then was whether I would still be alive when they decided to do away with me.

In all the time I had been here, in this place, and I really didn't know how long that had been, I still did not know what it was they wanted from me. They spoke in scientific jargon that boggled my brain. They asked me questions or spoke around me but never answered mine. My questions were not important. Something about not contaminating their data with my expectations. Whatever that meant. At the end of their testing, I was always taken back to the room, escorted by two guards… As though I was going to try and escape… Ok, so maybe I had tried – and failed – several times. Only so far, the blind girl could go without knowing her way around.

I learned though. How many steps did it take to get to the next turn out of my room, to the next turn to the elevator, from the elevator to the lab? From my room to wherever else they brought me. The place was big. I would make it one day. Until then, I would bide my time and learn the feel of every step of this place.

15

With exams over, Sebastian finally had time to turn his attention back to the journal. He had spent nights reading entries while in bed, but he hadn't been able to focus on it, not the way he wanted to. He flipped it open the next page he was up to. Dominic was coming home from the hospital.

Dom cries every night. He wants to see. He thinks that without his sight, he will be useless. Something else eats at him though, and I see him in conference with mother and father, but they fall silent whenever I enter a room.

The journal ended there, and Sebastian cursed himself for not remembering that he was almost at the end. He dropped the notebook to his bedside table and listened. The house was silent. Ever since the new girl had been brought into the laboratory, his father hadn't been around much, always working, as though around the clock. Tomorrow he would bring up starting work at the laboratory for the holidays. That would be good. Real world experience, just like his father wanted, except his father hadn't wanted him there since the last time. He'd been all for it a year ago, but now? Now he just kept brushing him off and disappearing to work on the new girl.

The house sounded silent. Well, he wasn't going to sleep anyway, not with that journal burning a hole into his subconscious. He got up. There would have to be more in his father's study.

He was certain that his father wasn't even home, but even so, he crept ever so quietly down the hall just in case he was sleeping in his room. He reached the door to the study and pressed himself against it, trying to muffle any noise that the click of the latch might make.

He stood in the darkened room. He knew that there was nothing like the journal on the bookshelves, so where would they be? In one of the locked cabinets? Well, he knew where the keys were. He went to the desk and pulled out the top drawer, extracting the keys to the cabinets. He took one more look around the room. If he were his father, where would he hide personal journals? Sebastian had to know what had happened to Dom. He'd lost his sight in an accident, something he was fairly certain the author of the journal, likely his own father, was responsible for.

He unlocked a cabinet, one that was visible from the desk, which could always be gazed upon with longing or intent. He grinned. He knew his father all too well. The cabinet was filled with brown leather journals, all in various states of disrepair. They had been thoroughly used, likely carried around everywhere as the author documented everything. He picked one up.

I beat Dom today. For real this time.

This one seemed to be earlier, before the accident, so Sebastian returned it to the shelf and picked up another that had been situated next to a gap, hopefully caused by the removal of the journal he already had in his possession.

University selections have begun. Dom seems morose, unable to settle on anything. Mother and father insist that he should continue to study the political sciences, but Dom argues that there's no point. He's of no use in that arena and even if what they say is true, what good would he be? I need to find out more about this, because it doesn't make any sense.

It seemed to be some time after the accident and Dom had still not regained his sight. He likely never would. As Sebastian read on, he discovered that the author had developed an obsession with eyes. He went into detail in some cases on the dissections he did on the eyes of animals. Sebastian had done dissection in class, but there was a cold, clinical tone to the writing in this journal that had nothing to do with the classroom of professionalism. Sebastian had no idea what had caused the accident, but the more Dom descended into his depression, the more the author seemed to become obsessed with eyes, going on to study both vision science and biology. Another thing Sebastian had been unable to ascertain though, was the secret the author's parents were hiding from him, and he spent the rest of the night going through the journals.

16

Echoing footsteps. Someone was coming. I had been right. The time had been very near. A little nearer than I had thought, but they were coming. I stood and walked to the wall, trying to hear the footsteps clearer. They were softer. Not the heavy boots of the guards. Something more refined like what the researchers wore. The other odd thing was that there was only one. Guards always moved in at least pairs and researchers were always flanked by guards. I wondered who was coming. There was no point in hiding or cowering from them. They would only drag me out of the room kicking and screaming if I did. I had tried various acts of rebellion in my time, from holding on to the bedframe as they tried to haul me out of the room, it was bolted to the floor apparently, to hiding under the bed or behind the door. Hiding behind the door had worked the best. I had hit the guard I'd called Butch over the head with my dinner tray and bolted from the room. I'd made it two levels down before I'd finally been cornered and caught. None of my attempts had ever succeeded, but I had also never seen, well, heard from Butch again. I'd tried less dramatic things too, like faking being sick or spitting in faces, in the end, submission had turned into my only route for survival, at least until I had a plan. Then, all bets were off.

The door rattled and clattered as whoever was coming in fiddled with their keys and the locks. It had three locks. I heard them every single time they came to get me. The door opened. Sound was how I lived my life. I listened to everything. Every word, every sound. I even knew their smells.

The door opened and I was overwhelmed by the new scent. He smelled... Clean. Like he had used some cologne or something. He'd definitely washed recently unlike the usual guards or at least he didn't engage in the same bad habits that they did. This one was something different. He was definitely not a guard, but he also didn't have the smell of antiseptic and laboratory all over him. Who was he? I was sure this new person was a man.

"You're new," I said. I heard his feet shuffle, followed by a gasp as though I'd startled him. I smirked.

"I am," a voice replied. Definitely male. It was light, comforting, gentle, younger than the others around this place.

"Who are you?" I asked, canting my head to the side in contemplation. I couldn't see him, but I could imagine him. He was skinny, with shiny hair and good clothes. I didn't know what colour hair he had, but I gave him a dark brown. It maybe even flopped into his eyes a little.

"Sebastian," the voice said coming closer. The door closed behind him and his footsteps approached me, bringing his clean, perfumed scent with him. I took a step backwards.

"No one around here gives names," I told him. "I don't even have a name. Just how new are you?"

A tray clattered on the dresser. "It's my first day."

How had I not smelled the food? Had the scent of this strange man really distracted me that much? "Trying to get yourself fired by being stupid then?" I asked, pressing myself against the wall.

He stood before me, his scent invading the air around me. I could feel him, the warmth of his body, his presence standing over me. "Is that any way to speak to the person baring your meal?" he asked in a low voice, which seemed more filled with intrigue than derision. Very strange.

17

Sebastian couldn't believe his luck. Not only had his father finally agreed to let him work for the lab again, but he'd also been able to meet the girl. He would need to search the files again for her name. Or he supposed he could ask his father the next time he saw him. He could bring her good news when he visited next. Would there be a next time? He hoped so.

She'd been everything he'd imagined. Fiery and fierce, her words cutting sharp even as she'd tried to blend into the wall, trying to appear unthreatening. He knew that wasn't true. She'd made several escape attempts, even if they'd failed. So where had he gotten the childlike and submissive idea from? The girl was just as he remembered her that first time, he'd seen her and yet... Something just seemed off about her.

How had she picked that he was new? Was he really that different from everyone else that she had contact with? Why hadn't she looked at him? Maybe that was just her appearing submissive even as she plotted. Something told him, that if he hadn't been so different from the usual guards that she might have tried something. Had he intrigued her as much she intrigued him?

He settled into the desk he'd been given for when he worked at the lab and pulled up the files on the girl that he could find. He'd wanted to do that earlier, but he'd not known her name, identifying number or room location. Not until he'd walked in and seen her. It had been about a year since the girl had been brought in and his father had become incredibly closed lipped about what he was doing, as though trying not to jinx his work.

He frowned as the file loaded. What had she meant by, *"No one around here gives names. I don't even have a name."* Of course she had to have a name. All he could find were the daily notes and even they only went back about a week. Where was the rest of it? Where was any of the information about her origins?

He read through what was there. Lots of data collected from tests, a genetic model that she seemed to match to a high degree. The file mentioned another name, someone who had matched the model at about 70% of what was desired. He clicked the link.

The file opened, showing two pictures. *Minetta Ishani*. The first pictured showed a girl with the crusted eyes of someone who suffered from a severe case of Meier Rutger's Syndrome. The second, showed the same girl with no eyes. It wasn't that surprising, that was common for survivors of Meier Rutger's, but it was an eerie sight. He went back to the mystery girl's file. She had no history of the disease. So, what were they doing to her?

He picked up his bag from under the desk and extracted the latest of the journals he'd been reading.

It might be possible to use sight to win the war.

War? There hadn't been war in Eriden for years, though he did know that his father had worked for the war office.

Subject 27 – Attempt to awaken latent abilities unsuccessful. Subject deceased.

There were dozens of entries just like that one, ending in death or permanent disability that were seemingly discarded. He looked back at the files and noted that Minetta Ishani's possessed a disposal date after her trial phase failed. What did disposal mean here? Returned home? No, disposal said something else to him. It meant nothing good.

Would that happen to the girl? Not if he could help it.

18

I tilted my head up. He felt taller than me. The strange man, Sebastian, had started coming every day. Most days, I did as I always did, pressing myself against the wall, but it had been a week of his daily visits and his attempts to engage me in conversation with him. What did he want? I didn't know, but maybe one good look at me would send him running. I didn't need a friend. He'd already gasped once at the sight of me. Others had balked at the sight of the eyeless girl before. It had sent them running. He gasped again and stepped back. His overwhelming presence withdrew a bit.

"Something the matter?" I asked with a smirk. At least, I hoped it was a smirk.

"You- Your..." He leaned down to really look at me. That was unexpected. No one ever wanted to get closer, not when I was in my room at least. "Your eyes," He murmured, but it wasn't a sound of disgust, it was, fascination? Was that what I was hearing?

It was interesting. He was interesting. He had not beaten me yet, had not yelled at me or poked at me or fed me strange tasting concoctions. If I spoke to the others like this, I would have at the very least had a slap across the face. Something to remind me of my place. "What? Never seen anyone without eyes before?" I asked, testing the waters so to speak. "Neither have I."

That was when he really surprised me. He laughed. It was the oddest thing I had ever experienced. I'd heard chuckles at not particularly funny jokes told in the research labs, the occasional full bellied laugh at some raunchy joke from the guards, but this man, this Sebastian... He wasn't like any of the others. I felt him lean in closer to have a closer look at my face. "No... I guess you haven't. And yes, you would be my first." I felt something brush against my cheek and I jerked away from the touch.

"Sorry," he said, backing away from me. "I should have asked."

I shook my head. "Why? No one else does." He said nothing though, so I changed the subject. "So..." I cocked my head to the side as if I was contemplating the tray he had brought in. "What's for lunch? The makings of a sandwich that I have to put together myself?"

There was silence for a moment as he shifted, stood and I guessed, inspected the tray. "How on earth do they expect you to deal with that?" He asked and it sounded as though he was genuinely curious.

"Oh, I am very adept at making sandwiches now," I pushed off the wall and finding him in my way, indicated for him to move. "If you're going to stay, can you get out of the way?"

"Right..." he said moving backwards. "May I sit?"

I looked over my shoulder to where I'd heard him. He wanted to stay? Why? Who was he that he thought he could suddenly change the way things worked? I shrugged. "You probably have more right to than I do," I said as I felt over the tray for where everything was. The bread. Some cheese. Little bowls with condiments. I stuck my little finger in each one and tasted the available range. I made my way over the rest of the ingredients, identifying each of the options and nodded to myself.

Behind me, Sebastian sat, and I was certain that he was watching my every move. Despite being difficult, especially if I dropped something, I found the routine of making a sandwich calming. I spread condiments, I layered ingredients, then feeling my way over the top of the bread, sliced two sandwiches in half. I turned to him with the plate, both sandwiches situated upon it. "Here," I said holding it out to him so that he could take a sandwich.

"Uh…" He was surprised. I could hear it, and I could imagine the face I had made up for him, looking at me with an open mouth and wide eyes. "Thank you. You didn't need to do that."

"Yeah, well… You're still here and it's rude to eat in front of other people," I said sitting back down on my bed, wondering where I had heard that or who had told me. Just another unanswerable question about my existence.

19

Nelson Sage scowled as he watched the video from the last round of tests. It had been bad enough when they'd been in the room, but here it was, a reminder that the boy was acting like a fool. Laughing and joking with the girl, which was no way to behave with a subject. It could totally invalidate his results, and he would not allow anything to get in the way of his success this time.

"There you are!" He exclaimed, spotting Sebastian walking past the open door to his office. "I was just going to come find you." He narrowed his gaze when he saw the tray of food he was carrying. "How often are you seeing the girl?"

"Daily. I bring her meals."

"All of them?"

Sebastian shrugged nonchalantly. "Usually just the midday meal."

"I hope that you're not getting attached to her," Sage said. "She's a research subject, not your friend or even your girlfriend. You must remember to maintain your professional distance."

"Professional distance? Like failing to record her name. Why doesn't she even know her name?" Sebastian asked. "How far have you gone in the name of professional distance?"

"The decision was made to make this a blind study, with no personal identifying data," Sage said.

"That's not how blind or double-blind studies work!" Sebastian exclaimed. "Father, you can't have a blind study. The girl is here. The girl knows her own fate."

"But does she?" Sage asked, walking back to his desk. "Maintain your distance, Sebastian. That's all I'm saying."

"What's her name?" Sebastian pressed.

"I don't know," he said and really, he didn't. Despite meeting with the girl and her parents back in Yarm, he couldn't remember her name and didn't feel as though it mattered now. Knowing it would only get in the way

When Sebastian left with the food. He made a decision. It was time to move up the trial date. They were just about ready anyway. He needed to finish this and begin the next phase before his son became overly attached to the girl.

He picked up the phone on his desk and dialled the extension for Finnerty's office. The young researcher picked up before the first ring had even rung through.

"Yes sir?" he asked.

"Are we ready to proceed to live trials with the girl?"

There was a sharp intake of breath on the other end of the receiver. "We can be sir. Is there a reason we're now hurrying? I thought we were taking this one slow."

Sage took a deep breath. It wouldn't do to let his frustration with Sebastian out on Finnerty. They had been going slow, but it had been a year, and he was ready to proceed, even if they weren't. They already knew the steps and the girl met all the markers that were required, far better than the last one. They were ready and if he couldn't ban Sebastian from seeing the girl, he would need to move this along.

"Finalise the requirements and get the prosthetics made. I want to begin at the end of the week."

"The end of the week?" Finnerty almost squeaked. "Yes sir."

Sage put the receiver down without saying anything further. This time, they would get it right. This time, they had done all the necessary testing. The prosthetics were already mostly made anyway. The moulds for the eyes had been finalised months ago and the work had been put in to making them appealing compared to his first attempt. This attempt would work and be ready to use straight away. He was certain of that.

20

The door, the one on the far side of the room from the bed was always kept locked. It always called to me, as though there was some other way to get it to open. In the first days that I could remember, I had felt every inch of the door. The frame, the seals, the handle, the locks. Its mere existence was always there, reminding me that there had to be more than this room and the laboratories. Every so now and again, I would check it after someone had been in, just to see if something had been changed or if it had been left open. Nothing ever changed with the door. Instead, I was only ever let out on certain occasions and if my reckoning of time was right, that would be happening very soon. These outings, they were a departure from the dreariness of every dark day, even if Sebastian's recurring visits brought a little light to my days, but the experiences always left me tired and in pain. My eyes would burn in the aftermath of their actions. Not that anyone ever cared, even if I complained. I no longer bothered complaining.

There were footsteps in the hall. Two pairs of heavy boots, lots of additional gear that weighted the wearers down, making their steps heavy. The door rattled and clattered with each of the locks, then swung open. There were two of them as I had guessed. Always the same two recently, at least since Butch's sudden departure. I knew the feel of each of their hands as well. The large, rough hands on my left. He never spoke. Maybe he couldn't. I don't know, but he had loud, heavy footsteps and hands that felt as though they would scratch me like sandpaper every time, he touched me. The other one always smelled. He smelled of cigarettes, sweat and wet dog.

I hated them both.

They were cruel and needlessly so. Sure, I had made a few escape attempts in the past, but hey, I'm still here, right? I had not made an attempt in months. It wasn't that I had given up, I just needed to plan. I needed to learn. I was biding my time. These two though, they liked to remind me of my place, remind me that I was not worth anything.

Scratchy, the one with hands like sandpaper, dragged me from where I had been sitting on my bed. "On your feet girl."

I stumbled as he hauled me up by my arm. I would feel the bruise there for sure. Instead of helping, he proceeded to drag me. My feet kept scrabbling, desperate to get upright and walk on my own two feet. I had to get on my feet before we reached the door to the room. Counting the steps from the room to wherever we were going was my plan. I had to know how to get from here to there. I couldn't rely on landmarks or maps to guide my way. I reached up and grabbed onto his arm. Then pushed myself to my feet as I felt his arm ready to shake me off.

"Let the girl walk," said the second guard said. I called him Stinky, because I wasn't sure if he had ever bathed in his life. "Don't want to explain again why she's scratched up." I felt him grab my other arm. Hmph. Now that I was up on my feet, he felt the need to get involved. Together they marched me out of the room.

We turned left and walked twenty steps. They slowed down for no one, and I figured it might wind up being a little more than twenty, especially since I was struggling to keep up with what I guessed to be their much larger strides. We turned right and walked thirty-three steps before they took me down a flight of stairs. Thirty-six steps.

"How'd that date go last night?" Stinky asked Scratchy.

"It was all going great, till she tells me I ain't coming home with her cause she's got kids at home," Scratchy said.

"A kid?" Stinky asked. "How old?"

"Not a kid, kids. Teenagers. Fourteen, fifteen, sixteen. Something like that," They turned us right at the end of the stairs.

"Damn. How old is she?"

One. Two. Three. Four. Five.

"Like thirty-five or something. She's a damned looker… But a bloody single mother… Who's got time for that baggage?"

Six. Seven. Eight. Nine. Ten.

"Especially one with a couple of kids that old already."

Eleven. Twelve. Thirteen. Fourteen. Fifteen.

"But man… You should see her!"

Sixteen. Seventeen. Eighteen. Nineteen. Twenty.

"The kids, mate. The kids."

"Teenagers though… Almost out of the house… Actually…" Scratchy paused for a thought. "Oldest girl's as blind as a bat without her gigantic glasses…" I felt sorry for the girl already. I'd heard the talk, how all of these people considered me and other people with no sight. I wanted to find a way to tell this girl to run, because something told me that Scratchy had plans for the girl.

Twenty-one. Twenty-two- We stopped and one of them, Stinky I think, typed something into a keypad. There was a beep and a click, then they pushed the door open and hauled me in. Noise. People moved and spoke, and machines hissed, mewled, beeped and whined. This room was a hub of noise and for some reason, I was grateful for it.

"You don't think?" Stinky asked, potentially thinking the same thing I thought Scratchy was thinking, but any further conversation was cut off.

"You're late," A harsh voice cut across the multiple conversations going on throughout the room. Oh. Him. That voice. So strict. So calm. So… In charge. It could only be Doctor Sage. He was the only one with any authority. "Get her strapped in. We're ready to begin."

Scratchy made to haul me up, but I stepped on his foot. "I can get up myself," I snapped. My rebellion lasted only a second before he backhanded me, sending me sprawling to the floor.

"What have I said about manhandling the test subjects?" the man in charge intervened. Doctor Sage, the man with the vision... or so he liked to say.

"Sorry Doctor Sage, but she-" Scratchy objected.

Sage didn't let Scratchy argue though. "I don't care, just get her situated.

By this time, I had already managed to get myself back to standing and I felt for the seat type thing. It was bad enough that they would strap me down, but I hated being lifted into it. I got their precaution though. I had used this time once to make a break for it and broke several pieces of their fancy machinery. I lifted myself up and laid back. I could get through this. I did every other time.

Someone approached from the side and wrapped the straps over my shoulders and my waist, holding my hands to my side. Then they strapped down my legs over my thighs and ankles.

The boss, Doctor Sage approached. He wore soft soled fancy shoes, similar to Sebastian's and not at all like the heavy clunkers the two security goons wore. "Are you ready girl?"

I looked towards the sound of his voice. "Ready for what?" I asked, wondering what he was on about this time? When was I ever ready for these tests that they did not explain to me? He always asked such senseless questions. It wasn't like they would stop what they were doing if I said no, but I would never say yes. That would be giving in. That would be accepting their actions. No, I never said no, and I also never said yes. I was just… resigned to the inevitability of it all.

Doctor Sage chuckled in that way he does that always sent a shiver down my spine. I imagined a strange, cruel smile gracing his lips as he did and a look in his eyes that would and most probably could instil fear in the person he stared at. "To see. To see girl," He exclaimed.

"Huh… Might be a bit hard without any eyes," I said. It was a sore point. I remembered the first time I had realised that my empty eye sockets were something strange and not something that everyone else had. The researchers had been talking about giving me new eyes, interchangeable eyes. It hadn't made any sense, but someone had made a comment about how awful I was to look at and I recalled the all-encompassing fear that had overcome me in that moment. After that, I tried to touch someone else's eyes. It was a researcher, and I had scared the woman half to death. Her fighting with me to stop had resulted in my scratching her eye. It was an accident, mere curiosity. I swear, but it was another reason I was strapped down when in the laboratory. While I had no memory of ever seeing, I realised after touching her eye, that it was an odd thing to touch your eyelids and feel nothing but loose flesh. To move your fingers further and feel the sticky wetness of the eye socket itself. I had heard the gasps from various guards or workers. I had heard the talk, but that day changed everything. I knew that they considered me a freak, but then, I considered myself one too.

But I was certain that I was a freak of their own making.

21

Sebastian slipped the last of the journals back into their place in the office. Dominic, his father's brother. Why had he never known that he had an uncle? It explained a lot about the research Sage had dedicated his life to, but it also opened up so many new questions.

Where was Dominic now?

Why be so secretive about everything?

Why not simply cure blindless and low vision?

What was all the rambling about Eriden and Shiura and thrones?

None of it made any sense. What could he work on next? He stood and turned on the spot, his feet turning ever so slightly with every step. The books on the bookshelves were the same old technical books he'd already read. He'd just retuned the last journal, what did that leave? Then his gaze fell upon the ugly metal towers behind his father's desk. The filing cabinets!

He could look over the old experiments and their results. The recent experiments had to have come from somewhere and maybe if he could trace his father's reasoning, he might be able to talk some sense into him, get him to revert back to medical science rather than this warfare-based project he seemed so determined on.

He tugged on the first drawer, but it held fast, and Sebastian cursed under his breath. It was locked. He looked over his shoulder towards the door. He didn't hear anything on the other side and sound, particularly footsteps echoed in this place, so he would hear anyone coming, but where would his father keep the key to the filing cabinets?

The desk drawer. He pulled the top one out and a ring of keys sat there in the corner of the drawer. So predictable. Sebastian tried the first key, but it didn't turn once in the lock, then tied another. The fourth one in, he finally got the drawer open. File after file with names on little tabs appeared before him. He scanned them, looking for the filing system used, alphabetically, by year it appeared, so he should, in theory be able to start at the beginning, with the first set of trials and work his way to now.

He pulled out all the files for the first year, dropping them onto the desk. They slid precariously, several almost toppling to the floor, but he managed to catch them before anything could happen. He sat in his father's chair and began to read. The first year's files went by quickly, as did the second and third. The early trials failed to improve or cure the visual ailments the subjects were afflicted with, but by the third year, Sage Laboratories were experiencing success with their work and the experiments became larger, bringing in more subjects, operating with double-blind conditions and they had been doing good. Then, the research had changed.

Sage Laboratories received a contract from the Eridenti government, and the research shifted from medical research to biological warfare. It didn't make sense. Shortly after that, the research stopped for a period because of a lab disaster at their primary site, killing many of the researchers and the subjects.

After two years, a new lab was operational, and the results were... Strange. Vision was restored to many subjects, but many were unable to live normal lives in the aftermath The subjects also went from being adults, to children, signed over by parents to trials that were meant to improve their quality of life. Sebastian started to take down notes, trying to get a handle on what changed and what the research really was.

- *Milo Pugh. Age 12. Vision restored and now boy who could read any language he laid eyes upon. (Deceased, Age 15)*
- *Lynn Everitt. Age 13. Vision restoration failed.*
- *Adrian Cavanah. Age 11. Vision restoration failed.*

- *Cecilia Rosheuvel. Age 11. Vision restored and now the girl who can see through walls. Location: Eri-Rhou.*
- *Kieran Fulford. Age 12. Vision restored and now able to move items by looking at them. Deceased.*
- *Rebecca Bakare. Age 14. Vision restored and now has a permanent laser from one eye. Deceased.*

The list went on and on, listing children who were either now dead, missing, in a worse position than before the trial or located in Eri-Rhou, the capital of Eriden.

- *Birdie Tsiuri. Age 17. Vision restored. Scout eyes capable of seeing up to several kilometres away. Exact distance unknown. Subject missing.*

He remembered that girl. He'd been there the day they'd tried to test her sight. He remembered her panic, fear and eventual illness as she was unable to control… the zoom? What was it Sage had said about her? That she would make a good scout.

He flipped through more names. There were so many.

Cassias Mikael Romeijn, Cordula Roslyn Liisi, Elijah William Aharon, Emanuele Weekes, Harvey Tilen-Das, Henryka Eirwen Bogdanov, Minetta Ishani, Sadie Marybeth Linton, Sameer Ilya Artz Notah, Sophie Elena, Trenton Matheus Kovac, Vera Tove, Vilma Calanthe.

And it went on, their ages from early teens until about eighteen. How could any of this be ethical? It wasn't, that Sebastian was sure of.

One file stood out from the others. The folder was orange, compared to the tan of the others, as though it had to be something special. It might have been a clerical error, but Sebastian didn't think so. The boy had been so young, younger than the others.

- *Noah Mercia. Age 7. Vision restored. Able to counter all others.*

What did it mean? He looked back over his list and frowned. Many of those abilities were uncontrollable according to the notes, resulting in damage and death. Was that why they'd created the boy? What about all the deceased subjects. While many died without additional notes, indicating to Sebastian that they'd died during their trials, many had died after what were supposed to have been successful trials. What was his father doing? And what was the girl they were now working on supposed to be?

22

For as long as I could remember, people would poke and prod at my face. They poured liquids into my empty sockets or gels that solidified. Sometimes the substances were soothing, at other times they burned. I wondered what it would be today. There seemed to be an air of anticipation and excitement all around me that wasn't usually there. It made me uncomfortable to say the least. I tried to follow the many murmured conversations going on around me, but there were too many to keep track of any one topic.

Until somebody nearby asked, "Are you going to do the honours sir?"

"Yes. I think I might," Doctor Sage said.

"Very well Doctor Sage, which one shall we choose?" Sage moved over to the last speaker and silence descended over the laboratory as he must have been inspecting something. Between the silence and despite my inability to see, I wasn't liking what was happening. This was different. Too different from normal. I felt the need to crane my neck in the direction he had walked, as though it would help me understand what was happing. I wanted to sigh, I wanted to scream, I wanted... I didn't know what I wanted. Most of my time here was always spent waiting. Listening to them talk in half whispers and broken sentences that meant something to them, but nothing to me.

"I think," Doctor Sage said, "We shall try these ones."

These what? I wondered. What were they going on about?

"Are you sure about that Doctor Sage?" Another person asked. "Should we not start with a more basic prosthesis?"

Prosthesis? A prosthetic eye? What the hell were they talking about? What was happening? And what did a 'more basic one' mean?

"We need to know that it works," Sage said eagerly "All of it. We need to know that all of it works."

"But we know that from the animal trials. The girl... You can't really want to give her that kind of power?" the other man protested.

Power? What kind of power? Sight? What else could there be? What were these people on about?

"I have chosen," Sage declared, stopping any further discussion on the matter. "This has never been about restoring the girl's eyesight. This," he paused to emphasise something to the people he was talking with, "This has always been our priority, our goal."

What goal? What about my sight? If they weren't giving me sight, then what were they doing? What was going on?

"Yes… But…" the same man tried to argue, but Sage was apparently in no mood to listen. His excitement was palpable and his goals… Whatever they were, were within reach. He would not be stopped.

"Enough. To your stations," Sage demanded. There was a mass movement of people as footsteps spread out around the room. Right, I guess this was happening then… Whatever 'this' was.

Doctor Sage, I could tell that it was him by his footfalls and the scent of whatever cologne he always wore, approached me again. "Ready to make history Girl?" History? Oh boy… I'd always suspected that he was some kind of madman, but now he was starting to show it.

I turned my head towards him, allowing him a good view of the empty eye sockets that always seemed to make other people recoil in horror. He stood firm. "Just do it," I said, "It's not like I get a say in the matter."

"Oh, I think you'll like the results girl. Now, stay still." With that command, he reached out for my empty left socket and pulled back the lid. He poured something cool and wet in. Saline from the smell and then I felt his other hand. It was holding something, trying to manoeuvre the hard object into the socket. Oh, God. What was this? What was he doing? "Blink." He instructed when he let go of my eyelid. I did as instructed. It felt odd. There was something there, filling that space that had always been empty. It was cold and round. Well, not entirely round, but it fitted the space in my face that was always empty.

Then he reached for the right eye lid and repeated the process. Suddenly there was something filling both eye sockets and it was weird. I wanted to reach up and touch my eyes, to feel what it was that they had done, but I was still strapped down. What colour were they? How did I look with eyes?

Suddenly, a burning, searing pain shot through my body. My face burned; the eyes that had just been implanted felt as though they were about to explode right out of my head. I screamed and struggled against my bonds. Pain seemed to radiate out from my eye sockets through my head and down to the tips of my fingers and toes. My body writhed as wave after wave of agony reverberated through me.

"Heart rate is skyrocketing." One panicked voice shouted over the machines.

"Her blood pressure is dangerously high." Another called.

"Brain waves indicate nothing but pain reactions."

"Open your eyes girl!" Sage demanded, his voice urgent, but lacking the same fear and panic his staff seemed to have. "Open your eyes!"

Their voices just kept yelling, to each other. At me. I couldn't keep track. It was everything I could do to squeeze my eyelids shut and try to contain the pain. It was agony and I ripped and kicked and struggled against the straps that held me down to the chair. The straps dug into my flesh, but I barely felt them through the pain shooting in waves through me.

My breathing, it was ragged, and every breath hurt. It was as though the mere movement caused by breathing ratcheted against my eyes and the impact was debilitating. They pulsed. Maybe in time with my heartbeat. I didn't know, I just wanted the pain to go away. I was no stranger to pain by this point in time, but I had never felt anything like this!

Another wave of pain rolled through me and my entire body arched, straining at the straps. Oh god, when would it end? It had to end, right? Something snapped, one of those restraints I thought and suddenly I was sitting upright. The strap around my chest and arms had broken. How had that happened? I looked around desperately, but I still could not see anything. Someone cried out as my hands searched desperately for the other straps. I had to escape. I had to get away from the pain.

"Get her restrained again!" Sage called. He was not as close anymore. The coward had run from me. Why? Why had he run? What was wrong with me?

I felt arms against me, trying to restrain me once more. I kicked and shoved and thrashed. My left foot tore free from the ties. Only fabric ties down there, they had never expected much from me in terms of escape from the testing chair. I kicked the attendant on my left, and he grunted in pain.

Finally, the all-encompassing pain started to subside, and I felt able to think. The waves of pain lessened, coming with less frequency and intensity. My hand moved when I willed it to and I thought that maybe, I could finally open my eyes. It was a sudden feeling, the need to look, to see, to take everything around me in. It was excruciating. I wanted, no, I needed to come out of the darkness, and I could not understand why. All I had ever known was darkness. Right? Sage had mentioned seeing, but I had not believed him. Why bother? He had his own agenda and what was sight in the long run if I was stuck in this place?

I forced myself to still and take five deep breaths. The pain was disappearing slowly, and I was free from the restraints. Despite the arms reaching for me, trying to hold me down, I was free.

All I had to do was open my eyes.

Open.

Come on. Open.

Open. Open. Open.

Open your god damned eyes!

23

I was screaming at myself. Screaming for myself to move two tiny parts of my body. Given how much my entire body had moved in the convulsions of pain, it shouldn't be that hard, but my eyes were still closed. Closed damn it. Why? Why would these two little parts of my body not move the way I wanted them to move?

Then everything went from interminable black to blinding white. Why? What was that?

Light. Oh god, everything was so bright. So, so bright. What was this? Was this what seeing was? Bright, white light. It was so bright it hurt. It burned even. My body hurt. The eyes hurt. Why was everything hurting? What had they done to me?

The bright white slowly started to fade away into colours. Blues, greens, greys, blacks, browns. I could identify colours. How could I do that? There were reds and yellows. Mainly on people's clothes, but there were colours, and I could identify them. I had always wondered if I would be able to attach the colour names to the colours themselves. I guess I could.

What did that mean?

The blobs of colour started to shift from blurry blobs to distinguishable shapes. They had definitive outlines, and I could distinguish shapes as people or machines. Two faces separately stared at me from above. Who were they? Was one of them that Doctor Sage guy, another researcher or were they the security guys, Stinky and Scratchy? Could I emblazon their faces on my mind to always remember them? Actually, why would I want to do that? I never wanted to know what Stinky and Scratchy looked like. Maybe they looked like ordinary people, like the way I imagined Sebastian to look rather than the hideously grotesque monsters I had envisaged for them.

I stared at the people above me as my body stilled. I stopped struggling, the pain fading and just… stared. They also seemed to take that as a moment of peace while I took them in. The man above me had clipped black hair and blue eyes. The blue shirt he wore under his white lab coat seemed to accentuate the colour of his eyes. The other one beside him was a mousy woman, with light brown hair, wire-frame glasses, and brown eyes. A mole was situated just to the upper left of her lips.

Something strange happened. I stared at one. It was the man at first, but his face started to change colour, from that healthy pink look to something grey and washed out. He stepped away and another took his place. A big, gruff man stepped up. As his hand touched my bare arm, I figured that he was Scratchy. Behind him, the other man started to scream, then as Scratchy's face started to also go that strange grey colour, he too started to scream. I was confused as to why he was the one screaming until I noticed that the strange grey parts of his face hadn't just changed colour, but those parts were… I didn't know, but they didn't move.

It was slow, but the greyness crawled along his cheek and then his nose. The scream stopped suddenly as his mouth seemed to freeze in a silent wail. He backed away from me in fright. I turned my head to follow his movements. Behind him, the young researcher with the blue eyes wasn't moving. More and more of the man I thought was Scratchy was turning grey. He stumbled, a grey hand crashed into the still form of the researcher, sending him tumbling to the ground. Scratchy shifted and collided into a bench. To my surprise and absolute horror, both men shattered. I couldn't see the researcher anymore, but as the solid, unmoving form of Scratchy fell, his horrified face looked up at me. His still and terrified face didn't even twitch as the rest of his body fell to the ground. The grey parts of his body shattered on impact. His legs, still 'flesh' I guessed, lay there twitching for another moment before they too became still. The woman above me screamed and an alarm started to wail around us, a flashing red light overlaying everything.

"GET HER!" Someone screamed.

"Get them out! Get them out!" People started to run, panicked as they sought for an exit.

I turned my head towards the person who had screamed and was confronted with what looked like a wall of muscle. Big, burly men and women, dressed in black, weapons at their sides. I focused on one. He screamed as my gaze met his.

"NO! Get her away from me! Get her away!" he screamed, breaking formation with the others in an attempt to flee from me. What was wrong with me? What had happened to Scratchy? What was happening to this man? I didn't understand.

I kicked my leg free from the last restraint and stood up. I was in the lab and not restrained. This was a first. I could see. This was also a first. I turned around on the spot, needing to see everything and everyone. In fear, people turned away from me, skittering away like rats from the light. Maybe they were thinking that if they were to look into my eyes, they too would become like the shattered men. How had that happened? Was it because they had looked at me? How could I see? What had Sage done to me?

"Where's the sedative?" someone cried, their voice shrill with fear.

"Hold her down," Sage ordered.

"Don't look at her," Another ordered, holding out a syringe of something, likely the sedative, to one of the bulky guards.

"You can't expect us to go near that monster?" the man wailed.

I took an unsteady step forward towards a huddled group of guards and researchers and they scattered. The man with the syringe, seeming to back away the fastest. They had done this to me, right? What had they expected to happen? What had happened to Scratchy and the other man? I searched for the one with the soft shoes, but while all the guards wore large, heavy boots, Doctor Sage was not the only one wearing soft soled shoes. Most of the lab coated researchers were too. I stumbled forward as another step seemed to sap my energy. I hadn't been this tired before I could, see? Was this a side effect? Or was it the lingering pain that was still sending jolts through my body? So, where was Doctor Sage? I was standing now, and I had best talk to him, right?

A shiny steel table turned that same dull, rough grey that the men had turned, along with a portion of the floor. So, it wasn't only people that turned grey? Interesting, but why were they turning grey? What did it mean? My bare feet stepped from the laboratory flooring to the grey floor I had somehow created. It was cold. So cold against my feet. What was this new material? I scraped the ball of my foot against the surface. Stone. It was stone. How had I turned the floor to stone? I thought about the two men who had shattered, the other people had run after seeing how the greyness crawled up the legs of tables and chairs. I looked over my shoulder to where the two shattered remains lay, the one pair of legs that were still flesh that was missing the upper body. I shivered. What had I done? I looked back to the group, realising that a swath of wall had turned to stone as I'd been looking around.

The group scattered, screaming in fear of what they had created. One man didn't run fast enough. He was scrambling to pick up a collection of paper and electronic tablets that he had dropped in his effort to escape, and the greyness started to crawl up his feet. A look of absolute terror overcame his face as he looked up at me.

"No. No. No. No." He cried, holding the tablets and papers he had tried to rescue close to his chest. I turned away from him. I didn't want to see what was happening. He wasn't Sage anyway. His whimpered cries had proven that. I knew Doctor Sage's voice. No way was he the boss. An older man stood near a computer. He watched me, a look of fascination and delight dancing across his face. Despite all the chaos, he was smiling, He was happy with what had happened here. At least two people were dead. Three, that last one with the papers held against him. He wasn't making a noise anymore. I approached the smiling man. I watched him as he turned to the computer, and I felt revulsion. Revulsion for him and most of all, revulsion for what he had turned me into. Send me back to my room. Throw away the key.

"What have you done to me?" I asked. My voice sounded almost… Hollow to my own ears. It wasn't shrill with the fear I felt or loud with the anger that was burning deep in my chest. It was just… hollow.

"Would someone please tie her back down," Sage said calmly. Why wasn't he turning to stone like the others? I heard tentative footsteps behind me, so I turned and looked in their direction. A corner of their lab coat started changing and they ran, pulling the garment from them and tossing it as far away as they could. What was this power? And why wasn't Doctor Sage as scared as everyone else?

"Doctor Sage," I said, and my voice still sounded strange to me.

He looked up finally. "Ah… I see." He canted his head to the side as though inspecting me. Why wasn't he changing? It made no sense.

"I see you," I told him, and I could. I was seeing for the first time in as long as I could remember, and I could see him. The old scientist before me with his gadgets and gizmos waiting to experiment on his little lab rat. Next to the computer he was working on was a case and in that case was something I had never in all my life expected to see. Eyes. Rows and rows of eyes. All different colours, but all the same size and shape. They stared up unseeing at the roof of the lab. Two of those little eyes were missing. I guessed that they were the ones currently filling my usually empty eye sockets.

What was this? What had they turned me into? The sight of those men shattering filled my mind again, followed by the look of terror on the last man's face as his had turned to stone. I swallowed hard. What was I?

"What have you done to me?" I asked slowly.

"Be a good girl and look down," he said coming out from behind the bench slowly, as though waiting for me to comply.

I was feeling defiant. I was stronger than his guards. They were all scared of me now. I wanted my freedom. "No." I said and took a step closer while looking right at him. He wore glasses unlike the others. Maybe that was why his face did not immediately start to turn? But I had seen this work on the floors and walls and clothes. That couldn't be the answer. The left side of his neck started to turn grey and somewhere in the deepest recesses of my heart, something rejoiced. What would it take to push this man over? To shatter him to smithereens like the guard. The grey started to track down his arm and he screamed, clutching at the limb that was turning to stone. And that feeling of joy I'd been feeling, turned to horror. What was I doing?

"Get her!" Sage screamed as he turned away from me, fear at what I was finally setting in as it started to affect him the same way as the others. He cradled his stone arm against his body as he backed away, realising that whatever had been protecting him, was no longer working.

"Kill her!" Someone else instructed from somewhere behind me.

That startled me and I paused. Kill me? Would they really? Their prized lab rat? Would they really kill me? The thought was terrifying. But all too possible. I was entirely at their mercy most of the time. It was only now, with these eyes that I had become a threat to them. Not only could I see, allowing me a freedom I had never known, but this ability to literally stop them in their tracks made me dangerous. Not only to them… What would happen if I did get out?

Sage's reaction though was instantaneous. "NO!" He cried, raising his stone hand to object "You will not kill her."

"She's too powerful like this," the same person that had suggested my death cried, holding up what looked to be a gun in my direction. "We can't control her like this."

Indecision struck me as they argued about my fate. If I continued after Sage, the other man would kill me. Regardless of his orders. I looked to where the tray of eyes was laid open, protected by whatever had protected Sage as he had stood behind the bench. All those eyes, different colours and designs. Did they all have abilities like these things I had in now? Something that could help me get out of here? If I could get my hands on them…

A sharp pain shot through the back of my head, and I stumbled forward. It was instant and debilitating. My legs collapsed under me as my body raced to catch up to the idea that someone had struck me on the head from behind.

"Sedate her! Now! Get those eyes out," I heard the calm voice of Sage demand. I was on the floor, and he was calm once more.

No, I thought. Those eyes were my only way out of here. You can't take them from me. No… Even if I'm a monster, I'd rather be free.

But a prick in my arm lead to darkness overcoming me as I slumped the rest of the way to the floor.

24

Sebastian ran into the lab, his feet skidding on… He looked down at the ground, gravel? Why was there gravel strewn across the floor of the lab? Wails of panic drew him from his contemplation and his gaze took in the whole lab. It was chaos. Stone was everywhere, including what looked to be, life size statues of people, shattered on the floor. The walls were swathed in rock hard stone as if some malevolent and powerful being had taken a paintbrush, turning everything grey in its wake. Machines that once hummed and buzzed and beeped either stood silent, half machine, half stone, while others sparked and fizzled.

"What happened?" he breathed out, standing in the doorway, frozen to the spot by the chaos playing out before him. He'd never seen anything like in his life.

"She's too dangerous!" an angry voice bellowed.

Sebastian looked towards the sound. He saw a guard standing before Doctor Sage, his irate face red and blotchy Sebastian almost froze for a moment when he looked at Sage. What was that on his face? Glasses? Not like the ones worn by Finnerty and a few others, but large, wide framed things that seemed to encompass half his face. Sebastian narrowed his gaze at the older man. No one in the labs wore protective eyewear. It was akin to wearing glasses and Finnerty was one of only a very select few that Sage tolerated.

"She's exactly what this war needs," Sage said, though to Sebastian, he sounded strained, as though he was injured. He hurried over to the two men.

"Not if you can't control her!" the guardsman bellowed.

Her? Sebastian looked around. Where was the girl? "What have you done?" He almost gasped out. Where was she? At this facility, she was the only research subject. Everything was focused on her. Sage had wanted no distractions for himself or his staff while working on her.

A gun was ratcheted and Sebastian jumped, his panic to find the girl multiplied. Where was she? She wasn't in the tank where the experiments took place. Then he saw the direction the guardsman pointed with his weapon, and he ran.

"NOO! He cried, running towards them, falling to his knees, and skidding to land beside her prone form. "You can't just kill her," He exclaimed, blocking her from the line of fire with his own body.

"Get out of the way!" The guardsman screamed, the gun waving wildly in his hand.

"Get her out of here!" Sage ordered, moving his body stiffly and awkwardly as he tried to indicate the direction they should go.

Sebastian scooped the girl into his arms, cradling her small form against his body. Her face looked red and inflamed, swollen around her eye sockets, which seemed to bear small, bloody scratches around the edges, as though someone had reached in and ripped her eyes out. Except they had done that months ago.

As he carried her through the lab, people shied away from them, cowering, and whimpering in fear at the mere sight of the unconscious girl. What had happened in this room?

The corridor outside was strangely silent after the chaos of the laboratory and Sebastian stumbled, the disorientation and the weight of the girl making him unbalanced. He leaned against the nearest wall, holding her against him, looking down at her still, but tormented face.

Heavy stomping feet coming towards them sent him hurrying down the corridor in the direction of her room. He laid her on her bed, settling the sheets around her before stroking her cheek. "I will figure out what happened."

One thing he did know, was that the girl needed out. It would be only a matter of time before one of them 'accidentally on purpose' did her in and he would not hang back and do nothing while that happened.

He backed out of the room, carefully locking the door behind him and adding another lock that only he had the key to. He knew that wouldn't hold for long, but he needed to something to make sure those brutes couldn't just barge in.

25

It was that same dream again. A woman was calling to me. I don't know how I knew it was me she was after because I never heard her mention a name, but my heart longed to follow the sound of her voice.

I would look, everywhere and I could see as clear as day, the rooms of the house. I knew every part of that house too. I walked confidently from room to room, looking for the source of the voice. Who was the woman calling to me? My mother? My grandmother? My sister? A friend? Some other woman important to my life before this place?

I had no idea who was calling to me or where they were, but I wanted so desperately to find them. I felt unwell and I wanted to be comforted. My head hurt. My eyes were straining.

I called out.

Surely, they would respond. The woman called something out again. A name, followed by, "What do you want for dinner?"

"Your… Your…." Your what? I didn't know who this person was or what they cooked. What food did I want to eat? Something I could see, that was for sure.

I stumbled. That was new. My vision blurred. Not as unusual. My head. It felt as though it was splitting in half. "Help!" I croaked out, but the woman just pottered around the kitchen, not noticing me anymore

"Wake up!" A hand was shaking my shoulder. "Come on, wake up!" The voice attached to the hand sounded anxious. Why?

I groaned. I hurt. I hurt everywhere, most of all, my head felt as though it was going to split in two. The back of my head throbbed and the front, around my eyes felt like I'd run into a wall. As I moved, I realised that the rest of my body also ached, nowhere near as badly as my head. Oh god, my head.

"Wha-." I tried to speak. I really did, but it just seemed too hard to form any words, and the effort seemed to send waves of agony through my skull that crashed like waves in my ears.

A form sat down next to me, the mattress dipping under his weight. Was I lying down? Apparently so. Maybe I was back in my room. "Come on. That's it," The voice coaxed. I recognised the voice. It wasn't the voice from my dream, but I recognised it. I could put a name to it.

"Se-," I tried. "Seb-," I swallowed, but speaking was hard. I couldn't even manage to say his name. My hand rubbed at my eyes and…

And… I wasn't sure whether to be relieved or dismayed. I tried to open my lids but knew that there was no point. I couldn't see anymore. They were gone.

"That's it," Sebastian crooned. "Come on. You can do it." He hauled me up to sitting and my head swam. In that moment, I was glad that I couldn't see, because I was sure the room would be spinning if I could. The thumping in my head continued to feel like ocean waves crashing upon a cliff side. "See, that's not so bad now-."

I slumped over sideways to the bed and rolled to where I knew the side of the bed was. This wasn't good. My chest felt tight, and I could feel something rising. Oh, I was not going to be able to keep it in. I could feel it bubbling up, threatening to overcome me. I don't know when the last time I ate was, but everything came up and in the aftermath of my retching, the smell consumed us.

"Ok…" Sebastian said good naturedly, "Maybe not so good. Ugh…" Sebastian reached over, and I felt a glass touch my hands as he held me up again. "Drink," He ordered. I did so, but I spat the water out over the floor along with the rest of my mess.

"Come on," Sebastian continued. "Let's get out of here."

He took the glass from my hand and put it back down, then picked me up. He was strong. Not at all how I had imagined him to be. He wasn't like Stinky or Scratchy, or like the lab technicians I had felt around me. I felt myself being carried away from the smell and that room. It was easier to breath the further we got from my bed.

"I..." I tried to speak. "I can..."

"No, you cannot walk on your own," Sebastian stated, "that knock to the head and the sedatives are doing a real number on you. Just stay still and I'll get everything sorted out, ok?"

I wasn't sure if after everything I still trusted Sebastian. He had come from nowhere, without explanation and aside from his visits to my room, I never noticed him around when I was having tests or other... experiments? But what other choice did I have? I was sightless again. I couldn't stand straight because my head hurt like nothing I had ever experienced before. With a sigh, I leaned my head against his shoulder and allowed him to carry me without complaint. Despite my mixed feelings about him, I felt oddly safe as I felt his arms tighten around me. For the first time that I could remember, I did not count the steps or the turns.

When Sebastian finally put me down on a chair, I was pretty sure I smelled the medical lab. Panic started to swell within me. "Why are we here?" I asked finding that my mouth was finally able to form the words my head thought of, but my voice sounded shaky. Was that my fear showing or the pain?

"I want a look at your head before we continue," Sebastian said. "Also, I'm concerned about the seizure you had when those glass eyes were put in. It's not what I would call a normal reaction." So, he knew what had happened. Had he been there? It's not like I would have recognised him if I had seen him, but… I didn't know what to think. How did he know?

"There's a normal reaction for that kind of thing?" I asked. The lab, the pain. It all came flooding back when he mentioned it. The fear in the eyes of the researchers. "I could see…" I breathed out almost reverently. Faces and colours and everything that had been in that room. Faces that feared me.

"Yes. That was a target goal which was successfully achieved," Sebastian said.

I looked down. It was pointless to move. I couldn't look him in the eyes the way I was now. I reached up and touched the empty and flaccid flesh of my eye sockets again. Nothing. The eyes were gone just as I had thought, but that was to be expected after what I had done right? What had I done? "I turned those people to stone…" I said softly. "I turned them to stone, and they fell."

I felt Sebastian's hand cover my own. "You were afraid. The seizure also prevented you from having any control over what happened."

"I killed him. He shattered into all those little pieces… And… And…" My chest constricted and it was hard to keep speaking. Hell, it was hard to take a breath. Oh god… I was a monster. Just like that one researcher had said. I was a monster. I killed a man, no, two men? Three? I tried to kill others. How many had I eventually killed?

"Hey," Sebastian said softly. "It's ok. You're ok."

"They're not," I said.

"Yes, people died. They died because of a poor decision," Sebastian said, "Not because of you."

"That does not mean that I had to be the one who killed them," I shot back. "Me. I killed them, and I don't even know how," I cried.

"Shh," Sebastian hissed, "I'll explain everything that I can in time. Your head will be fine. It was the sedatives that knocked you out, not the blow to the head," he paused. "I would like to put another set of eyes in-."

I cut him off. "No!" It was abrupt and I could think of no other answer to give him. If seeing meant that I would kill those around me. No, absolutely not."

"These ones are just for sight. Nothing else. Nothing extra. I promise. You need to be able to see for what comes next," Sebastian countered.

"The pain…"

"I know," Sebastian said. "I don't know why that is, but with any luck we can figure that out… You and me, hey?"

I liked the idea of being able to see. "I won't be able to kill anyone by looking at them?"

It took Sebastian a moment to respond, but I felt his body moving near me. Had he shook his head? I think he had. "No. These are purely sight related. As I said, what happened in the lab, that was poor judgment on Doctor Sage's behalf. He should have always started with these. I think he just wanted to jump to the end of his experiment." What did that mean? Was his purpose to turn me into a weapon, not to fix my sight?

I took a deep breath. "Ok."

27

The pain had not been as bad this time or maybe I had just been expecting it. The light in the immediate aftermath of opening my eyes was still a killer. Sebastian hurried to turn the lights in the room off, easing the burning sensation. I think that the pain was just going to be a thing if I ever changed them again. Maybe I would never have to take them out again. I could stay seeing forever. Or maybe I'd have to put them in each day, go through that pain, every single time until it became normal. I could live with that I supposed. I blinked several times and looked at Sebastian.

"Hi," he said.

"Hi," I replied. He was younger than I had expected. Maybe early twenties or even late teens, whereas everyone else I had seen or met had always seemed older. His hair was sandy brown, and his eyes were a deep chocolate brown that seemed to stare into my soul with concern. I swallowed and blinked. Biting my lip, I asked, "And you're sure…"

"Absolutely. These have nothing but sight," Sebastian reiterated.

"Why?"

"Why what?" He asked cocking his head to the side.

"The weird ones. The stone turning eyes and every other eye in that case… I saw it. There were heaps of them, all different kinds…" I was probably being rude, looking at everything but him, but seeing… I could see. Him and everything else in this room.

"That was…-" Sebastian paused. "That was Doctor Sage's ultimate goal. Eyes that could be weaponised and exchanged."

"So, I'm a weapon?" I asked.

"No, the eyes are a weapon," he said.

"Little difference… It rings the same as 'guns don't kill people, people kill people,' hollow and empty," I told him. "I could still see it you know, even in the darkness. The sight of those men shattering on the floor of the lab."

"It will haunt you," Sebastian confirmed. "As it should, but you were not at fault. They should never have started the test with those. They should have done it with these, ones that have no attack ability. Nothing but sight."

I nodded. Nothing was really making any sense and the last day or two had really thrown me for a loop. "Now what?" I asked finally.

"Now?" Sebastian asked. He turned, picked up a bag and handed it to me. "You get dressed into something more suitable." I looked into the bag and found jeans, t-shirt, and a jacket. I had no idea where he had gotten them or if they would fit, but something other than the clothes I currently wore. Something different with new textures. It would be good. I looked up at him and he blushed. "I'll uh… I'll wait outside," he said quickly and moved towards the door. As it closed, I stood up. I was still a bit wobbly between the head and the new eyes. Maybe I should have had him stay… But no, this was better. I stripped off the plain white tank top and the grey track pants that had been all I had known, although I had never known their colours until earlier in the lab.

He had bought a sports bra, the kind that you didn't need to know the size for to wear. I couldn't help but smile at that. It wasn't like I knew either. I slipped on a new long-sleeved shirt and then pulled on the jeans. I found socks and sneakers in the bag as well, then pulled on the jacket he had also added. Inside was still a beanie and some glasses.

"Sebastian?" I called out softly.

"Yes?" He called through the door. "You need anything?"

"I'm done."

The door opened and he came in. "Good. Good. Ummm… Come on…" He said walking across the room to another door. "We need to get you some stuff."

"What are you doing?" I asked him as I followed.

"There's a lot of descent amongst the workers who were in the lab… Several are thinking the whole project is too dangerous now… That you are too dangerous…"

Kill her! The cry echoed in my mind. "They want me dead."

Sebastian nodded. "Some do and, in the end, there will only be so much Doctor Sage can do to protect you."

"You want me to run," I said. "But where am I supposed to run to? I don't know anything about out there… I don't even know my own name…"

"I can't let them kill you," Sebastian said, opening the door of the room. "I won't let them."

They walked quickly through corridors, Sebastian constantly looking over his shoulder to make sure that the girl was following him. She seemed to be tarrying, looking at everything they passed from the holes in the linoleum floor to the posters on the walls and through the windows into empty room, labs and offices. He wanted to begrudge her that and hurry her on, but he supposed that she had only ever imagined what the walls of her prison looked like.

The institutional green of the walls or the bare doors with nothing but numbers upon them were commonplace for Sebastian. He was embarrassed to admit that even the corridors back at his university weren't all that different, just with more scuffs, more dirt, and more posters from student groups.

"Where are we going?" the girl asked.

Sebastian paused his progress only slightly as he thought of how to say what he needed to say. "I can't just let you out… You'd never make it. You'll need supplies, so come on." He pushed the door open to a room that said 'Storage' and took the girl's hand, pulling her inside after him. The racks that were against the walls were stacked high with what looked to be laboratory supplies. He picked up a bag. It looked heavily padded and had several rows of zippers.

"C'mere," he said softly, drawing her towards him by their clasped hands as he reached for the bag with his other. He paused, sucking in a startled breath as her body brushed up against his. Reluctantly, he let go of her hand, even as he leaned in closer to her. "This is every eye they made from the mould of your eyes. I don't know what all of them do but take them. They'll be your defence, and your bargaining chip should it ever come to that," He explained.

She stared at the bag for a moment and Sebastian wondered what she was thinking as she reached out tentatively and slowly drew the zipper back, until she could open the case. She stared at clear plastic pockets full of eyes. Even Sebastian couldn't keep his eyes from the startling sight within the case. He thought how remarkably creepy all those still eyes of different colours and designs staring back at you. Silence settled between them as she continued to stare at them, so he took the time to relish the feel of her against him. Maybe this was all a bad idea, maybe he should alter the plan.

"I don't need anything but the ones I have now," she finally said.

"You might," Sebastian said insistently. He stepped back from her and grabbed something that he'd tucked behind a box on a nearby shelf. He slipped it into the back of his belt.

"Is that a gun?" the girl asked in a loud whisper, sounding more horrified than Sebastian had anticipated.

He ignored the question and picked up a backpack that was stashed in the corner that looked to be bulging. Sebastian just hoped he'd managed to think of everything she might need. It had taken him almost an entire day to put everything together within it. He held it out to her. "There's a change of clothes, some food, money, enough space to put the pack of eyes..." He trailed off. "I don't think I have forgotten anything..."

The girl just stared at him. "I don't understand what you are doing."

"Getting you out of here. Between what they actually want you for and the opinions of the staff around here. You won't live long. So, you're leaving. This is as much as I can do. I have to stay and see this through, but you are going." Although, in the back of his mind, he was wondering if he was better off going with her. No, he'd made it this far and someone needed to stay behind and clear the way for her escape. He was doing the right thing. He was sure of it. He just hoped that everything worked out the way he hoped. She might be his only hope.

I eyed everything in the lab as Sebastian led me through the winding corridors. I could not help myself, despite the direness of the situation. I looked in every window, seeing the places that I had only ever counted my way by. The corridors were green, and the floor was a squeaky linoleum that was scuffed from the passage of time. Inside the rooms through the windows were labs full of big, impressive machines that were covered in screens and buttons and blinking lights. Where were the people? Were there others like me? The lab rats?

"What am I supposed to do out there?" I asked in a hushed voice as we walked.

He didn't look back at me. "Survive."

"I don't even know where home is," I told him.

"That's probably for the best. If you did, that would be the first place they'd look for you," he turned a corner and pushed through a door. "The fact that you don't have any memories of your past means that you won't go back to the familiar. You can't. They won't be able to predict your moves."

I took hold of his arm. "Sebastian… Why?"

"Why what?" he asked.

"Why don't I remember who I am?" I asked, slowing until we stood still.

Sebastian pulled me onwards. "He's found a way to wipe your memory, keep you pliable and content," Sebastian said. "Well, not all your memory, because you can walk, talk, identify things around you."

Another door and we were outside. I stopped. My feet just would not move. I could not remember having ever been outside of the laboratory building. The sun was low in the sky, evening was falling, and it would soon be dark. There were trees and the smell of everything assaulted my nostrils. There was nothing antiseptic about the smells of outside. I looked around blinking, trying to take everything in.

"But then how do I know that, oh I don't know, that that's a tree and its leaves are green?" I asked pointing at a large, thick trunked tree with dark green leaves. It reached high into a sky that was bright with the afternoon sun.

"Memory's not all one thing or even long term and short term. There's all the stuff you know, like facts about trees and then there's you. Everything that makes you who you are. Parents, events, friends, and that's different. He's found a way to wipe this second memory. All your sense of self. It's called Declarative Memory, and it holds every about you. The procedure leaves your Semantic Memory, your basic knowledge, and skills, completely intact."

"Even my name?" I whispered, trying to figure out what this meant. I hadn't always been here. I had had a life before. How long had I been here?

He nodded. "Even your name. Now you need to follow that path. It leads through the forest. Staff use it sometimes for exercise and whatnot... It leads to the road and there's a bus stop not far from the entrance to the path."

"A bus? How will I get on a bus?" I asked, still reeling from the revelation about my memory. Who was I?

"There's a bus card in the side pocket of the bag," he told me, handing it to me. "Go."

I looked at the path he indicated, then back at him. "Why aren't you coming?"

"Someone needs to stop them from following you," he said and started to walk inside.

I took two steps towards the path. This was crazy and insane. I had no idea how to do the most basic of things... Or did I? When Sebastian had mentioned the bus card, I could recall how to use one... But how could I?

I turned back to him. "Do you know my name?"

He shook his head. "I don't know... I'm sorry." An alarm starts to wail from inside and Sebastian looked back over his shoulder in a panic. He looked back at me, the worry evident on his face. "Be safe."

And that was that. He was gone. I stared at the door to the laboratory for a moment longer, he didn't come back, and my name didn't magically come to me. I turned and started to walk down the path Sebastian had told me to take. The bag was heavy, but I figured that that was a good thing... For now, anyway. I listened as the gravel crunched under my feet. Birds whistled in the trees, leaves rustled, and the wind blew. It was all so new and yet... so familiar. How was that possible? All around me was awash with colours that I had only imagined. The bright blue of the sky, the brilliant yellowy-orangey sun, the multitude of colours that made up the trees and the bushes. There was so much to take in.

Under the canopy of trees, the darkening night was almost black. I could see better than I had in as long as I could remember. The noise though, all those unfamiliar yet somewhat familiar sounds... My room had been silent, only the sounds of footsteps outside the door and the occasional wailing of alarms. It took maybe ten minutes to find the road that Sebastian had mentioned. I looked left and right, trying to spot the bus stop Sebastian had said was there.

Why was there a bus stop in the middle of the forest? What else was around here? Or did the lab have their very own bus stop? Did Sage have that much power at his disposal?

Not immediately laying eyes on anything that looked like a bus stop, I turned left. I don't know why, but it seemed like a good idea. I seemed to be doing a lot of things on a whim today. On the other side of the road were signs that pointed downside roads about other buildings located in this forest. Companies that had warehouses, factories, and training facilities out in the middle of nowhere. A shelter and a sign not far ahead. The sound of a vehicle coming.

Was it the bus? Or was it people looking for me? I ran for the bus shelter but stepped into the bushes behind it until I could see the vehicle. Large, a destination atop the windscreen. A bus. It was going someplace named Erihall. Erihall... A manufacturing city in Eriden, I thought. Unless it was something else. I wasn't really sure. It seemed as good as anywhere else. So, I stepped out of hiding and hailed the bus down.

The bus slowed and when it came to a stop out front of the little shelter, the doors hissed open.

"Where ya headed?" The driver asked.

"Erihall," I said with more confidence than I felt and clambered on board.

I found the bus card in the pocket Sebastian had indicated and tapped it against the machine, wondering again how I knew to do all this. Must have been that other memory Sebastian had mentioned.

"Take a seat," The driver said as he got the bus moving again. I stumbled as I walked, and the bus lurched into motion. Most of the seats were full of dead eyed people who looked as though they were just trying to make it through the day, not even eager to be going home after work.

I found an empty seat and sat, shrugging the bag off my back and hugging it close to me as the bus passed through the night. I made eye contact with no one, for fear that one of them might have worked at the lab or worse, that Sebastian had gotten it wrong, and these eyes could harm them.

30

Nelson Sage waved off the medics who poked and prodded at him, He didn't need their scans and tests to tell him that his left arm had been turned to stone. It had worked. Everything he had dreamed of and even after the disappointment of the last failure, it had worked. The girl had been perfect, everything he had ever wanted in a research subject.

He leaned back in his chair, cradling the solid stone arm against his chest to prevent its weight dragging on his shoulder. He let his lips curl in delight as he let his mind play over the events of the morning. Unlike the last girl, she had seen. She had seen him, and she had been able to activate the power present within the eyes. He looked at his desk where the case should have sat and frowned. Where was it? He leaned forward, scanned the top of his desk, but it wasn't there. It wasn't like the case was small.

"Stop!" he ordered and like magic, all movement and sound in the room ceased. "There was a large black case on this desk. Where is it? Which one of you moved it?"

Confused glances passed between the people milling in his office. The confused glances turned to slow shakes of the head, but Sage looked to their equipment, heavy padded bags full of medical equipment that had been brought in when they'd come to tend to him. "Search everything," he ordered.

Security personnel descended upon the bags like a pack of jackals, tearing them open and pulling packages and equipment and vials out, throwing them to the floor. Medics cried in protest, only to have other members of the security team hold them back.

Sage cringed at the mess. But only said, "Find it." Then he stood, his desk chair rattling backwards until it banged again at the wall of bookshelves that lines the far wall of his office. He stalked towards the doors without another word.

The quiet was the first thing to hit him as he stepped into the hall. Everything had been chaos as the team sought to undo the damage done by the girl and ascertain just how much she had done. They had lost three people but given what this girl would be able to do, he could live with that. They knew that they were working towards, a unified continent under one ruler, with Eriden at its centre. They all believed and if they didn't believe, then they believed in the science of what the girl could do.

His arm was heavy as he walked. He passed the break room where someone wept, obviously thinking that they were alone. Sage passed by the open doorway without a word. He needed to see the girl. They had sedated her, but it had been hours since the incident in the lab and perhaps she would be coming around.

He stopped in front of her door, taking a moment to readjust his arm before letting it go so that his good hand could unlock the door. It swung open and he stepped in tentatively. The girl had been known to make escape attempts, and he didn't think now would be any different if she was once again lucid.

Like the hall, the room was silent, and he frowned. "Girl?" he said.

He scanned the small space. There was nowhere to hide, even if she hid under the bed, he would be able to see her, but there was no one in the room. All he could see was a large puddle of vomit that appeared to have begun congealing on the floor, a gap in the puddle formation where someone might have been standing when it had happened.

He stepped back into the hall and hit the buzzer a few feet away. He couldn't believe it. The girl was gone. But how? She had been in no state after the sedation. Someone would have had to help her...

Unless...

No...

There had been talk about her being too dangerous, that the project should be terminated. He turned and fled the room; he had to find the girl before it was too late.

32

I stared out the window of the bus as it left the cover of the forest and into the city of Erihall. The buildings were tall and old but got smaller and newer as the bus moved through town. It was odd. I had the idea that old, small buildings should be on the outskirts and new, tall buildings should populate the city centre. Maybe I was wrong. What did I know anyway?

The bus depot in Erihall was dark and loud. People were everywhere, talking and yelling, announcements and footsteps and bags thumping against the floor. Oh god… I was going to go insane with all that noise. There were so many different things to look at too. The advertisements that blinked too brightly. The people with their rainbow of clothes and multitudes of hairstyles. I pushed past people, eager to get out of this chaotic place, but found that every time I chose a direction, a crowd of people would push me in another. There were so many people. How did anyone deal with this?

Out. I just wanted to get out. I found myself pushed up against a wall as a group of men in suits passed me by, not even realising that I was there. Leaflets bushed against my head, and one fell to the ground as a late comer rushed past where I was standing. In a moment of peace, I bent down and picked it up. The face of a small child stared back at me. The boy had sandy blond hair and piercing blue eyes. A little button nose and lips that curved into a toothy grin as he stared at the camera.

MISSING

Noah Mercia - Age 7
Last seen at around 4:30pm on Saturday 4 December 2010

I stared at the face of the little boy. The poster looked old. I turned around and looked at the notice board that the paper had fallen from.

Dates read until... What was today's date? I looked around for a newspaper something that presented the date. A large clock hung from the ceiling of the concourse. It rotated slowly, allowing everyone a chance to see it, no matter which direction they were coming from. It turned slowly in my direction. The time. To be expected, but what was it I had seen on the other side? I kept waiting, holding myself back against the wall to stay out of the way of the passing commuters. The clock rotated around again, and the date appeared. I looked down at the poster of Noah Mercia in my hands and back up. The boy had been missing for ten years.

Other young faces stared out from the board too. All with the word 'MISSING' highlighted above pictures of bright faced and smiling children. A girl with dark, curled ringlets, a dark-skinned boy with a cheeky grin. I pinned the picture of Noah back to the wall between those two and moved on. So many missing children in this town... That was never a good thing, was it? What kind of place had I come to?

I saw an exit sign and finally managed to find my way outside the building. More people wandered around outside. Cars – Taxis, pulled to a stop in front of a line of waiting people and one by one they got in. I saw another taxi with its advertising board lit up with the face of another missing child. I missed the date or the child's name, but it did make me wonder. I turned away from the people and the taxis and walked. I had no idea where to go, I guessed that I would just walk until I found somewhere.

Everywhere I looked there were people. Erihall was a bigger town than I had imagined. The out of the way nature of the laboratory and the other factories out in the forest had made me think that Erihall would be nothing more than village or small community, but it was more like a city. It was an odd city though. Almost every second person I passed wore dark glasses and walked with a sense of uncertainty that felt familiar to me. Another thing was the fact that many carried canes that they moved discreetly before them, as though searching for something that would obstruct their path. Others walked with their hands clasped firmly onto companions, human or canine.

Was half this town blind?

It seemed absurd. Blindness was not contagious. Was it? No, the mere thought was ridiculous. There were diseases that caused blindness, I was pretty sure of that. But still something so rampant that adults of all ages were affected? No, that was just too much on top of the number of missing children, wasn't it?

It was late and the sky was darkening as evening came, so I saw no children wandering the streets on their own. Those I did see, were clutching to the hands of parents as they proceeded with their errands.

I kept my head down. I felt as though being able to see here made me an oddity and I did not want that to be too obvious. A man, a hat perched askew on his head and dark glasses obscuring his eyes bumped into me as I stopped to decide which way to go.

"Sorry."

"Sorry."

We both spoke at the same time, but it gave me a chance to examine him further. He stood hunched as though expecting something bad to happen and his hand tightened until the skin of his knuckles turned white against the cane he carried. He hadn't seen me. I was sure of it.

"I should not have stopped so abruptly," I continued. "My apologies."

The man chuckled. "Never mind. Happens at least three times a day around here."

I stepped out of his way and the man bid goodbye to me as he walked on with a confidence I did not feel. What was this place? I passed a news stand closing up for the night. The board on one of the sides held dozens of missing persons posters. All of them children. I recognised some of the faces from the board at the bus depot. Was that why the only children I saw were held tightly by their parents?

I walked on. I did not think that Erihall was a place I should remain for long, but I also did not want to draw attention to myself. I knew that Sebastian had left some money in the bag, but I was not inclined to use it just yet. There would come a time when I had no choice. I should have found out when another bus left this town. I did not want to stay here, but I was long past the depot now and it would look strange if I turned back.

A street sign pointed towards a park, and I turned to follow the indicated direction. It had been strange how odd the walk through the forest had been, but at the same time, how comforting. I wanted to recapture that comfort. Maybe the park would do that for me.

33

Walks in the park were one of the few joys still left in Alma's life now that her granddaughter had gone off to boarding school. Every day looked much the same. Rise early, walk through the park and watch it come to life as spring blossomed. Then to watch it change again as everything started to change colour later in the year when autumn came. Then it was to the clinic. There was always too much work at the clinic. The rampaging blindness of Erihall's citizens left Alma and her colleagues in constant work.

She stopped at the start of her favourite path and took a deep breath of the crisp morning air. Letting the air fill her lungs, she smiled and took off at a quick pace. A fast walk around the park to get her blood pumping and ward off illness. It was just the thing her doctor insisted. No one else seemed to share her love of cool, crisp morning walks. Maybe it was a bad habit left over from her war days. A walk whenever you could, a walk no matter the temperature and the cool ones had always been the best because the Shiurans had been less likely to strike, too busy curled up in their blankets and around their heaters to worry about what the Erinians might be doing.

Something odd caught her attention as she passed the copse of juniper trees that always looked splendid in the early light. The old woman looked around before departing the path to explore the splash of colour that seemed to have inhabited the copse of trees. There were plenty of receptacles throughout the park for litter to be disposed of properly. She could not abide people who just did as they pleased, ruining the natural beauty of the park with their carelessness.

She stopped short as she realised what she had imagined to be litter turned out to be sneakers and that those sneakers adorned feet, attached to legs. She pushed through the trees with a renewed sense of purpose upon realising that she was looking at a person.

"Hello?" She said softly to the still figure. The woman bent down and touched the hand of what she hoped to be only a sleeping girl. The skin was cold to touch. She moved her hand to the girl's shoulder and shook. "Hello? Wake up!" She ordered.

Eyes as blue as the sky on a clear day blinked back at her groggily. "Wah?" The girl murmured, her voice slurred with sleep. "Where?"

"Are you ok?" The woman instantly considered how stupid that question was. The girl had slept outside amidst a copse of trees on a night that had nearly reached freezing. Of course, she was not ok.

The girl scrambled away from her. "Fine," she whispered hoarsely. "I'm fine."

"My name is Alma," The woman said holding out her hand to the girl. "What's yours?"

The girl looked around unsure. "I... Umm..." She started to stand up. She brushed off her jeans and picked up the bag she had been using as her pillow. "Thank you."

Alma cocked her head to the side. "Thank you is a most unusual name," she said with a soft smile. Like any teenager Alma had ever known, the girl frowned at her, apparently not finding any humour in the comment. "Yes... Well, my granddaughter does say that I'm not particularly funny."

"I don't have a name..." The girl finally said. "They just called me Girl."

Alma frowned and held her hand out to the girl again. "Well, every girl deserves an actual name. I don't know who 'they' are, but they don't sound like very nice people." A sound of gurgling reverberated through the tiny space between the trees. "Are you hungry?" Alma asked as the girl looked embarrassed.

"No," The girl replied instantly. Another stomach growl gave her away. "Yes..." she admitted.

Alma smiled gently. "How about I make some breakfast for the both of us?"

The girl didn't take Alma's hand, but she did follow her out of the copse of Juniper trees. Alma kept her eyes on the girl, afraid that if she looked away the girl would run off. The girl blinked as she emerged into the early morning sun, but Alma was watching the girl's face as she stepped into the sunlight and noticed something off about her.

"Your eyes…" She said softly. "They don't react to sunlight…"

34

I don't know why I did it, but I followed Alma home. It could quite possibly be the stupidest thing I've done in my life. Not that I remembered most of my life, but Sebastian had warned me to be careful, and this did not feel like careful. It felt reckless. Still, this woman seemed kind and, in some ways, reminded me of Sebastian in the way she took care of me.

Alma sat me down in the tidy kitchen of a big house that bordered the park where I had spent the night. First, she had sent me to the bathroom to clean-up though. I changed into the clothes Sebastian had left in my bag and walked out of the bathroom with my face and hands scrubbed, my hair brushed, and the old clothes wrapped in a ball in my arms.

"Come here. I'll just put them in the wash for you," Alma said as she bustled around the kitchen and into a side room, which I guessed to be a laundry. I followed her aimlessly, not knowing what I could or should do. "Sit, sit." Alma insisted.

"Why are you doing this?" I finally asked, curiosity getting the better of me.

Alma looked up at me after turning her washing machine on. "Many bad people in this town girl," I flinched when she called me Girl, even if I had told her that that was what everyone else called me, it stung to have this nice old lady call me Girl. I couldn't stand hearing her call me that, just like those people at the laboratory. She wasn't anything like them. "Can't have a young girl like you wandering around on her own."

I leaned against the door jam, wrapped my arms tightly around myself and watched as she operated the washing machine. "Umm… "

Alma looked up at me. "What is it?"

I worried my bottom lip with my teeth and shuffled my feet. What was wrong with me? Alma though, she just smiled warmly at me, waiting for me to speak. "Please… Don't call me Girl…" I looked away and murmured. "That's what they called me…" I guessed that this time, there would be further questions.

With a final push of a button, Alma finished with the washing machine and walked over to me. "Who are they?" She asked and I was right.

I shrugged. "The people… I… I don't know who they were…" Could I give Sage's name? Would that help or would that result in him finding me? I didn't know. I needed to get better at this if I was going to stay free.

Alma bustled past me, as if pretending not to hear me and I kind of appreciated that, but what if she called the Guarda? I wasn't sure that I was ready to talk about the facility and all that had happened there yet. What would happen if they found out about the men I had killed? Would I be locked up? There were so many things I didn't know, and too many things had changed, practically overnight and I had no idea what tomorrow would bring.

"So, what should I call you?" Alma asked going back to the stove where she had put food on that smelled fantastic.

I followed. Nothing else I could really do. I stood at the island bench and watched her. "I don't know."

"Well," Alma said brightly. "You're right. It just won't do as a name. But you're what, fifteen, sixteen, seventeen? Something like that, right?"

"I heard someone say that I was sixteen once…" I said, trying to be helpful.

"Ok, sixteen it is," Alma declared as she turned and started depositing toast, cooked in the fry pan, eggs, tomatoes and bacon on two plates. "You're not vegetarian, are you?" She suddenly asked.

I shook my head. "I eat what I'm given."

Alma nodded solemnly. She pushed one of the plates towards me and I dug in. It was too good to let go to waste, and it wasn't a sandwich. I could not remember the last time I had eaten anything other than a sandwich. We ate in silence, which I also appreciated.

When my plate was empty, Alma put her own cutlery down and looked at me. "How about Juniper?" I stared at her, not comprehending for a moment. "For a name," she elaborated. "You don't know your name and I found you in the juniper trees."

I beamed. I liked it. "I'm… Juniper," I tried it on, and I liked it. I really liked it.

35

I insisted on doing the dishes. It was the least I could do after Alma had taken me in, done my laundry and cooked me breakfast. Hell, she had even given me a name, and I kept repeating it to myself as I stacked the plates and carried them to the sink.

Juniper.

My name is Juniper.

Hi, I'm Juniper.

It was strange how the possession of one little word could suddenly make me feel human. Like I was worth something for the first time in my life. I turned my neck to look at Alma, who still sat at the bench watching me. "What about you?" I asked.

"What about me, love?" She asked back.

"Who are you, Alma?" I asked, curious about this woman who took early morning walks and allowed random stray girls to follow her home.

The old woman chuckled softly. "I'm a retired doctor. Well, mostly retired doctor. Erihall has a big need for medical professionals. Alma Corbyn-Fisher, I used to be in the Army… Long time ago…"

I paused with that. "The Army?" I asked. There had been a lot of talk at the facility about the military, and I had to wonder if I had made the wrong choice in trusting Alma Corbyn-Fisher. A doctor, a military officer, was she really someone I could trust? Maybe I should I run at the first opportunity I got.

"Oh, that was a long time ago," Alma said cheerily waving her hand, as though that would wave away the fear that now lurked within my chest. "A lifetime ago even. When the war was at its height and the work was about protecting our people. Healing our people. Then, I was happy to serve." Alma leaned back in her chair, looking almost wistful.

"What changed?" I asked curiously.

"Active combat stopped when Shiura was subjugated. All that remained were outliers and rebels who objected to Eridenti rule, and everything became about the side effects of attacks used to control the Shiurans. Then we had the soldiers captured from the other side who had had terrible experiments performed upon them…" Alma looked away from me and her gaze looked out one of her windows into the large, pretty garden outside. "Needless, irreversible hurt was being done on both sides all in the name of one-upping each other. I couldn't take it anymore. I had sworn to do no harm and what was being proposed was perhaps the most horrendous thing I had ever heard of."

I left the plate I was working on in the sink and turned to her. "What was it?"

"Oh, I'm still ordered to live by the laws of confidentiality and national security… So, I cannot tell you that, but Erihall… Erihall is my penance for the part I played before realising what was going on…"

The old woman was a curiosity. To me at least. Her ties to the military made me nervous though. Sage had always said that he was working for the Eridenti government, that I would be his greatest weapon. Was that the project that Alma could not speak of? Or were there other atrocities being committed against people in the name of this war I knew nothing about?

There were very few cars in Erihall I noticed as we walked. "I expected more driving or cars…" I said.

Alma looked at the quiet streets. "Cars are expensive, you'll find that those who do drive, usually have a bike." We walked on a few more steps and Alma continued. "Erihall has particularly few cars or bike riders because half the population is blind or has very poor eyesight."

It was evident as we walked, the same things I had noticed the night before. Service animals, canes and lots of dark tinted glasses on the people we passed. "What happened here?"

Alma clasped her hands behind her back as we walked and looked up at the sky. "Erihall was… During the war, a place of great invention," she started, almost wistfully. "Invention, progress, production…" She paused and looked down at me. "Now all the labs and factories are out in the woods, but in those days the factories, the laboratories, the warehouses, they were all in town. They were the town. It existed for the workers of those facilities. Military and civilian alike. As with any situation like that, a town sprung up, schools, hospitals, libraries, a community. Despite the war, a community flourished here in Erihall…"

Alma trailed off again and this time, when she didn't continue, lost in her own little world, I pushed, just a little. "What happened?"

Alma stopped walking and looked out into the distance. "Do you see that black structure?" She asked, pointing in the direction she wanted me to look. "The one that comes out over those buildings there."

I nodded. "Yes… It looks… Like a damaged building…"

Alma nodded. "It is," she agreed. "It used to be the largest employer of Erihall citizens. Military research, until an explosion destroyed the facility killing everyone who was there and many in the surrounding buildings."

I stared at her. "It was that bad?"

She nodded. "Come on," Alma said as she turned down one of the streets. "We can detour past the site if you want."

I thought about it for a moment and nodded. "Ok," I said.

As we walked, Alma continued. "Many people died. More than a hundred staff within the facility itself and hundreds more in the buildings surrounding it," she explained.

"What does that explosion have to do with the people going blind now?" I asked, I figured that the two were connected. They had to be, right?

"Very good. They are connected," Alma agreed. "Many of the survivors started suffering horrendous deformities to their eyes in the year immediately following the incident. The children and those first babies who were born, were born…" she trailed off before continuing. "It was hideous… Many were born without eyes."

I took a step backwards. With these things in my head I could see, I looked normal, but without the things Sage and his people had created for me, I was one of those hideous children without eyes. Was it from here that he had gotten me from? Was I maybe from Erihall? Had I been born to a parent whose family had suffered through the Erihall disaster? I didn't know and I probably never would.

We rounded a corner and were faced with a street that was as black as night. I stared at the debris still strewn across the road, the burned-out cars and the blackened buildings. But rising from the centre of everything was the wreckage of a building that had once done work for the military. The metal supports, twisted and malformed, reached towards the blue sky like the grim visage of a corpse reaching out from its grave.

"Why was it never torn down? The buildings fixed?" I asked quietly.

"In the beginning, it was because there was no one to tear it down. No one to do the work between the dead and the injured and the grieving," Alma explained, her voice low and almost reverent. "Since then, no one has dared… It serves as a reminder of the people we lost. Of the lives that were ruined."

Alma motioned for me to follow her, and I did so. We left the dark, devastated street and as we turned the corner, sunlight seemed to magically reappear. Life returned to the street, and it was as though nothing had ever happened in Erihall.

Two blocks away from the site of the disaster, Alma stopped and opened a door to an unsigned building. "Come on in," she said.

"What is this place?" I asked as I stepped inside. It was dark but clean. Chairs lined the walls and people waited. A man close to the door sat with a dog beside him and dark glasses perched on his nose, a woman talking at the counter held a cane clutched tightly in her hands. Another woman sat, flanked by two children, one who wore thick glasses and the other with a patch over her right eye. The mother held both children close to her and seemed to have tears in her eyes.

"It's a clinic for the sightless and near sightless," Alma said. "I don't know how much you've noticed, but despite the number of citizens with poor or no eyesight, there's little care or respect for them. Not anymore…"

I stared at her. "How is that possible?" I asked.

Alma walked through to the back of the large waiting area and keyed in a code for the door there, allowing me to follow her in. "The sighted are well regarded in the town, the less you can see, the lower down the food chain you go. If you wear glasses, you are a rung below the perfectly sighted. Blind, but with eyes or blind, missing eyes, I'm sure you can guess who ranks higher." I stared at her in horror. I thought then, of the man who had bumped into me. His apology had been instantaneous, even fearful, as though something might happen to him. "Finding out that you or your child is going blind… It's a near death sentence in Erihall… So, I work here, with some others providing care to those in need."

I looked back towards the waiting room. All those people. Half of this town and I was just like them. I took a deep breath. I would have to hide that fact. Even from Alma.

37

The Erihall bus station was bustling with activity as it was every morning. Sebastian spotted several people walking by with uniforms for Sage Laboratories and he ducked out of sight. It wouldn't do for word to get back that he was skulking around Erihall, especially after last night.

A bus headed into the industrial park pulled out of the station, passing him as he stepped out of his hiding place. The notice board beside him rustled as the bus billowed a gust of air, blowing the papers against their meagre attachments. One broke free and he caught it. A small boy smiled back at him.

"Noah Mercia, huh? Well, we'll just see about finding you, won't we?" he said, striding past a bin and tossing the flyer into it. He stalked out of the bus station. He had to find Noah Mercia, the boy was the answer to stopping all of this and he had to find the girl.

Or did he? If she had listened to him, she wouldn't be anywhere near Erihall. Perhaps she'd jumped another bus and was halfway to Eprea or anywhere else that wasn't right here.

Ok, that wasn't what he would hope for. The boy and the others, they would find her and through her, he would find them. Even if she didn't find them, or even if they didn't find her, because that was how it always seemed to work, at least she would be safe if she wasn't here. He needed her safe, even if nothing else worked out,

He would take a walk and then head into work. They would have spent the night searching the laboratory grounds and the forest in the immediate area around their grounds. They would likely be planning to expand their search into the city. Right now, they couldn't imagine the blind girl getting further than the grounds on her own, but eventually they would discover that she'd had help. He paused as he contemplated his actions. No one had noticed him gathering the resources he'd given her. They'd all been too crazed by the effects of the test. The case of eyes though, that had been sitting on Sage's desk, a busy room at the time as security and medics had ranted, raved, poked and prodded. He'd swept through the room, and no one had taken any notice of him, even as he'd given a report to Sage regarding the girl's condition upon her return to her room. Had anyone seen him swipe the case? He couldn't be certain. In the moment at least, no one had said anything. Perhaps he really had managed it right under their eyes.

After getting the girl out, he'd wiped all the security footage, ensuring that whoever found that would know for certain that it was an inside job, but it was unavoidable. Besides, no one would ever suspect him. He was above reproach, and Sage would never let them interrogate him. He just needed to make sure that Sage himself never suspected him. Maybe then, they would all stand a chance.

His walk had taken him towards the centre of town where a park dominated the large open space. At one end of the park, a hedge rose up, surrounding the large house. It was more of a mansion really. The sight was idyllic as long as you didn't look back in the other direction of town towards the remnants of the old disaster site. He should turn back, catch a bus into work and hope.

The gate opened and an older woman stepped out. She was smartly dressed and talking animatedly to someone. Sebastian started to turn away when the sight of the younger girl caught his attention. Dirty blond hair, swept up in a ponytail, atop light jeans and loose grey jacket. It was the girl. He started towards them.

Neither woman spotted him as they talked. The older woman seemed to be giving the girl a tour of the town as they headed somewhere. He stayed just out of sight, which meant that he couldn't hear what was being said, but he was surprised when he followed them to the site of the old lab disaster. He watched the girl eye the remnants of the structure in some sort of horrified awe.

They left, as though the site was just an idle curiosity and Sebastian continued to follow them before he finally figured out where they were going. He stopped short, horror creeping into his veins.

What was she doing? Sebastian cursed under his breath as he spotted the girl step into a clinic behind the older woman. Did she not understand what he'd meant? She had to get away from Erihall. The city would not be safe once Sage's security personnel moved beyond the laboratory grounds. He had to meet with her. He had to talk to her, get her to leave.

I left Alma to do her job. She had people whom she needed to care for, and I did not want to get in her way. As I was leaving the clinic, she called out to me and asked if I was going to come back to her house. The thought made me smile, somewhere to go, someone who would be waiting for me. I told her that yes, I would come back to her house and had asked what time she would be there. It all seemed so normal, and I liked it.

Despite Sebastian's warnings to be careful, I wanted to see more of Erihall. The ruins of the old laboratory interested me and this culture of perfect sightedness that I had managed to miss the night before in my own self-absorption, was something that I wanted to witness for myself.

Wandering through town, I found my way back to the site of the ruined lab. The blackened building, the ruined street. Something about it had called to me when Alma had taken me passed the disaster site and I wanted to see more. This time though, I didn't just go into the street. I walked up to the ruined building and looked inside. What chemicals had this building released to create the blindness that afflicted this town?

"I wouldn't go in there," A voice said from behind me, and I smiled when I turned to see who was standing there.

"How did you find me?" I asked beaming and running over to him.

"You weren't exactly discreet with the bus…" Sebastian walked past me to the building's entrance. "And… I kind of figured that something would lead you here…"

"Why?" I asked. I never had any idea that I would come here. Until Alma had shown it to me, I hadn't even known it existed. Now though, my curiosity was burning, and I wanted to explore.

He turned to look at me. "This was where Doctor Sage started his work. His wartime laboratory," He shrugged nonchalantly. "I thought if you discovered it's history, you would come here. I did not expect it to be so soon though."

I stepped up beside Sebastian and looked at the remnants. "He had something to do with the explosion?"

Sebastian shrugged. "I don't know. I know that many people thought he did, but he owns this town and there was nothing anyone could do to prove it." Somewhere inside the building a beam creaked, and I looked around for it. "I need you to listen to me. He *owns* this town."

I stepped further inside, wanting to see deeper into the site. "What do you mean owns the town?"

"He used to be the major employer of people here, in this lab… In the aftermath of the explosion, he paid for the rebuilding of this town. Employed new people at the facility you were in."

"Ok…" I drew the word out, trying to phrase a question, but not entirely sure what to say.

"They'll find you here," Sebastian pressed.

"How?" I asked stepping around what might have once been a reception counter.

"They live here. In this town, the people who want you dead. Everything is funded by him. The security systems are all owned by him. You can't stay in Erihall, and you absolutely cannot trust anyone." He followed me. "What are you doing?" he asked.

"Exploring," I told him. "Going where I want, when I want. I was held hostage for God only knows how long by Sage and his goons," I said without looking back, but I could hear Sebastian scrambling over debris to follow me in. "I'm going to find a way to stop him. Look around you. I'm not the first one he did this too. There must be others, right?" It irked me that I had been held, and I didn't even know for how long. Where were all the missing children? Some had been missing for years. Was Sage responsible for the missing children? Were they trapped just as I had been? Was I on one of those walls? Someone had to stop that man, and I had nowhere else to be.

"Then you really cannot trust anyone who works at those eye clinics," Sebastian said, and I whirled around. How did he know about Alma? He was blurry, so I blinked. My eyes felt funny. I rubbed at them and cringed. It was like I was rubbing dirt into them. "Oh… God…" I groaned.

"What?" Sebastian asked as he continued to follow me.

"Nothing," I said. I could deal with discomfort. "If Sage ran this place and things went so horribly wrong with it, then somewhere in here is the proof, right?"

"You think that hasn't been tried?" Sebastian clambered over a piece of rubble. He wasn't quite as nimble as I apparently was, but he followed diligently. "Investigators combed through everything back then. They tore apart his life and what was left of this place looking for something to hang on him until one day it all went away. Just like that, money came flowing into the town and all suspicion went away."

I stopped. There was a chair in the centre of what had once been a room. Maybe a lab, maybe an examination room, I didn't know. The chair was similar to the one I had been strapped to at the facility. Large, reclined, with the remnants of tough leather straps on it and a cradle to hold the subject's head still. I felt a shiver run through my body with that thing so close to me.

"Hey…" He said softly coming up beside me. "What is it?"

I pointed at the charred remains of the chair. "That… That thing…"

"Sage is obsessed with what eyes can do. He always has been" He touched my shoulder. "Come on. Let's get out of here."

I could still feel the grit from before in my eyes, but I didn't say anything. I would figure it out. I could not rely on Sebastian for everything.

Outside the building, we walked, side by side back to the main street. I was covered in dirt and ash and so was he. I smirked as I swiped at some ash on his shirt. "You're a mess."

Sebastian stopped walking and looked at me, then raised his hand to wipe at some dirt on my cheek. "You're one to speak." Unconsciously, I leaned into his touch. "Do you have somewhere to stay?"

I nodded. "Yeah. Of course, I do."

"Good. Just remember, you need to get out of town as soon as possible."

I started to turn down the street to return to Alma's place when I turned back to Sebastian. I had just spotted even more posters about missing children. He stood there, hands stuffed into his pants pockets staring at me. "What about all the children?" I asked motioning towards the sign.

Sebastian walked up to it and looked at the faces of the children displayed there. Some were old now; those children having been missing for years. Others were new and I was sure that those parents still had hopes of one day seeing their children again. It made me wonder once again, if I would one day come across my face, smiling back at me from a poster, with a name of my own and the details of someone who loved me.

"I don't know," Sebastian said, not looking at me. Was he lying to me? "All I know is that children have been disappearing from Erihall for as long as anyone can remember. But you need to get as far from Erihall as you can if you don't want to go back to the facility."

It is great and all that he suggested this, but I had no idea where to go. Sure, I could hop a bus at the station, but where would I go? I didn't know where was safe. So, while I wasn't exactly stuck, here in Erihall I had Alma, at least for a little while. I would, in time, figure it out where to go though.

I watched Sebastian walk away. If he was so eager for me to leave, why not tell me where to go? He was so insistent and yet... His help, now that I'd had time to sleep, and think was so... I didn't know. But surely, if he wanted me gone, there was more he could have done.

39

Alma's house was spacious and felt safe. The large garden, the brickwork of the main building, the cosy fireplaces within. The woman herself had a grandmotherly appeal that drew me in.

He owns this town. Sebastian's words echoed in my head as I lay in bed. *You absolutely cannot trust anyone.* I had never trusted anyone in my life except maybe Sebastian and despite the seriousness of his words, the seriousness of his tone when we spoke at the disaster site, I found myself unwilling to believe him. I could trust Alma... Couldn't I? And at the end, when I had asked about the children... I don't know why, but I was certain that Sebastian had lied to me. He knew more than he had said. *Children have been disappearing from Erihall for as long as anyone can remember.*

I rubbed at my eyes, and it hurt. I felt as though there was something else in there with the glass eye, rubbing against the interior socket. Rubbing at it hurt. Blinking hurt. I had gotten some sort of debris in there at the disaster site. Now what? I really did not want to take them out again. Putting them in hurt so much.

But it was more than the pain of putting them in that made me afraid to take them out. The idea of being sightless again, being stuck in the darkness in an unfamiliar environment. Then there was this town itself. The social hierarchy... To them, I would be an Eyeless. I would be nothing.

During the day, I had no idea what to do with myself. I had nothing to do with my time, so, I offered to help Alma at the clinic. I could clean or something and having something to do with my time would help distract me from the discomfort I was currently feeling. When I had looked in the mirror this morning, my eye sockets, both of them, had been red and inflamed. The edges of the lids look almost raw and ready to start bleeding, but I could not afford to deal with it around this woman or any person for that matter.

I also couldn't afford to take them out. What if I couldn't get them back in?

Tonight, I would lock myself in my room and figure something out. Until then, I would work as I had promised Alma. Plus, keeping myself inside this place would mean that no one would see me, right? I would be safe.

I dragged the mop and bucket through the sterile hall of the clinic and listened as people talked in the various rooms. In one, a woman wailed, her distress palpable throughout the entire clinic as silence settled for a moment as everyone took her distress in. Then, conversation returned as though it was a normal occurrence. Two minutes later a door opened, and a woman exited, followed by one of the doctors. She clutched a small child to her chest as she practically fled from the clinic.

I turned my head and went back to mopping. There was nothing the likes of me could do to help that woman and her child. What did I know about being blind in a society where you were looked down upon for it? The doctor shook his head and followed the woman's path to the reception hall where he called in his next patient.

This went on for most of the day, the in and out of doctors and patients. The doctors appearing uncaring of their charges and the patients distraught with whatever news they had been given. I, on the other hand listened to everything I could as I cleaned. I was caught off guard by just how much these people sounded like the researchers at the lab. Alma talked of her patients with compassion, but for these people, they had no care or maybe they had seen so many in their time that they no longer could care.

I kept rubbing at my eyes more and more frequently, desperate to stop and look away from anyone who entered the spaces I was working in. I had seen myself a few times and there was no denying how red the skin around my eyes and the sockets were now. The glass of the eyes was still a pristine white, but now when I looked in their reflective surface of the stainless-steel cabinetry, I was cleaning I thought I saw a smear of red. I dropped the washcloth and leaned against the nearest counter. I could resist this. I would not give in. Blood or no blood, I would resist.

I grabbed for the cloth again and made a few futile swipes at a stain but then dropped the cloth again.

Out.

I needed them out.

The first time anyone had taken them out, I had been unconscious. Knocked out after the first lab experiment. No one had come near me until Sebastian had orchestrated my escape. I had no idea how to get them out, but they needed to come out.

I touched my fingertips to the glass of my right eye. The lid brushed against the skin of my fingertip, and it burned. The glass shifted easily enough, and I leveraged it out, only scratching the interior of the eyelid a little. Relief flooded over me. The pain did not fully subside, but the relief was noticeable. With the loss of the right eye, I realised that I could still see out of the left. This was something new, I realised as I stared at the little piece of glass in my hand shaped and painted to look like an eye. I attempted to repeat the process on the left side and as the eye came away, the black overcame everything as my vision disappeared with the little pieces in my hands.

Gently, I prodded at the lids of my eye sockets, it stung as my fingers touched the raw and enflamed flesh.

"Juniper, when you're done in here-," Alma said as she came bustling in and I looked up at her, horror overcoming me, "Can you-." She stopped short. I can only assume that she had seen me. She hurried over. I could hear her footsteps coming closer until she was right in front of me. She took my face in her hands and looked at me. I hoped that I had read her right and that she was looking at me with those big eyes full of concern and not disgust, but I couldn't see her... "Your eyes are bleeding," she said simply.

"I know…" I whispered. "It hurts…" I told her. "It hurts…"

"Come on," Alma said and then her hand clasped around mine, closing my fingers around the glass eyes that I held there. She then took me by the arm and led me through to her office and workspace. She guided me over to a chair and sat me down. "May I see them?" she asked tapping my enclosed fist.

Shaking slightly, I opened my fingers to reveal them to her. She was going to reject me, wasn't she?

"These are amazing. They look just like real eyes…" She said in awe. "And you can see when you have them in?"

I nodded solemnly.

"I… How?" She asked.

I shook my head. "I don't know…"

I heard her put them down on the desk then felt her hands on my face. "Let me take a look at you," she said gently. "How long have you had them in for?"

I frowned. I really did not know exactly. Today, yesterday, the day before, "Maybe three days…" I said.

Alma's finger pulled at my lid to have a look at the socket. "I have never seen damage like this from an eye prosthetic," she said. "Well, maybe on those who also have hay fever… But still… When did it start?"

"Yesterday," I didn't bother mentioning the fact that I probably got something in it when I went back to the disaster site. There was no need to tell her everything.

There was a knock on the door. "Doctor Corbyn-Fisher?" A male voice questioned.

Alma shifted in her seat. "Yes, Derrick?"

"Mrs. Glasson is back and demanding to speak with you regarding her son," he paused. "She won't leave without seeing you."

"Do you mind?" She asked, squeezing my hand.

"Go," I said. "I'll be fine…. I'm used to this…" I'll admit, I did feel a little abandoned as Alma got up and left the room, but I was not her patient or her daughter or even her responsibility. These people, they were though, and I knew that. In frustration I rubbed at the empty eye sockets, hating the feel of them again, but the pain made me stop more than anything else.

I sighed and got up. I had been in Alma's office when I could see. I should be able to find my way around. Or at least I had hoped that I could until my thigh collided with the corner of what I supposed was her desk. "Crap. Crap, Crappidy, Crap!" I cried. It hurt like hell, so I felt that I was justified in my exclamation. Leaning against the desk, I curled my fingers around the edge and hated the sense of uselessness and frailty I felt in that moment. I had never hurt myself in the past when moving around. I couldn't do this, not when there was so much more to the world around me than just my room and the lab and… Oh what was I going to do?

40

"There!" dark curls whipped around to view the building as she pointed at it.

"Where?" The pale boy beside her asked, shading his eyes from the sun as though that would help him see what she was seeing. "I can't see anything Chouette."

Chouette stepped behind him, pushing at his shoulders until he faced the exact direction she meant. Then peering around him and pointed again. "There."

"It's a row of houses," he said.

"Not that one," Chouette insisted, pointing seemingly to one that might have been the third from the edge of the row or was it fourth? Maybe she was pointing at the second? He really didn't know. "It's a clinic."

"Are you sure?"

If she could have rolled her eyes, she would have, but as she couldn't, she stared at him, glowering darkly. "Am I sure?" she asked in a low, dangerous voice. "Am I sure?" She asked again, her voice louder this time, when he said nothing, instead backing away slightly, aware of his mistake.

"'I'm sorry!" he hurried out. "Let's go then."

"That's better," Chouette said, turning her head away from him to look back at the clinic building. "It looks busy today, so they should all be occupied."

"Let's go then," the boy said. He went back to his motorcycle and climbed on, waiting for Chouette to do the same behind him. They rode into Erihall, and as they rode, he pulled his hood up higher, not wanting to risk anyone recognising him. Chouette apparently had no such fears. Her dark curls blew in the wind as they rode. He for one, thought anyone who'd seen her once would remember that face and that hair.

"And here!" She announced as they rounded the corner and slowed before the clinic.

The boy looked around. The street was busy, pedestrians walking by, cars and trucks speeding through. There was a good likeliness that they would be spotted. "Let's park the bike elsewhere then come back and scout it out on foot."

"Kay," Chouette agreed. He drove around, looking for a secluded place to leave their bike. It wouldn't do for someone to notice it and report to anyone in authority. Amongst other issues, it wasn't registered, which under Eridenti laws, it was supposed to be. That could lead to some uncomfortable questions about them if it was reported. "We're a long way out here," Chouette observed as he finally stopped them in an alley, almost on the other side of Erihall from the clinic. "Don't you think that will make for a difficult escape? Are you sure you wouldn't rather just park out back and run for it?"

The boy shook his head. "No, we walk."

Chouette huffed and would have rolled her eyes again if she could have. "Fine. But don't come crying to me when we have to run all the way here!"

41

In the room next door, I heard something fall from a shelf and crash to the floor. The room next door to Alma's office was a storeroom. There should not have been anyone in there at this time. I moved quickly, but carefully, my hands out to catch for anything else I might bump into. The bruise on my thigh was going to be a beauty if I ever got to see it.

I opened the door to Alma's office and peered out. Crappidy Crap! I cursed at myself. What on earth was I going to see? I listened.

"You idiot!" A male voice that I did not recognise said, somewhat muffled. Maybe he had his head ducked into the other room.

"Sorry! Sorry!" A female voice replied. She was inside the storeroom. That, I was sure of.

"Just hurry up, Chouette," the male voice pleaded. "Someone probably heard that!"

I ducked back into Alma's office. What was happening? What was I going to do? What would Alma expect me to do? I leaned back against the open door, hiding myself in case either of the intruders looked out into the corridor. There was more rustling and rumbling from the storeroom as they searched for what they were after. Why break into a clinic? Were they anti-medical treatment for the vision impaired?

I tried to look around the office, cursing myself once more. I had already become too used to being able to see. I was relying only on my sight rather than anything else, especially my memory. It had been bright and sunny that morning and Alma had worn big, stylish sunglasses for their morning walk to the clinic. Where had she put them? On her desk? Or on the cabinet next to the coat rack where she'd put her bag? I sidled awkwardly over to the cabinet first, listening out to the sounds from the storeroom. Nothing. Then, cautiously I made my way over to Alma's desk, running my hands over it. I knocked over a tumbler of pens, knocked the mouse from the computer terminal onto the floor, along with several files, but no glasses.

They were still there, still in the storeroom, making off with the provisions the clinic needed. I had to do something. I had to, for Alma. How else was I ever going to repay her kindness? Not by letting thieves get away with the materials she needed. I moved towards the sounds. Dealing with my life by sound alone as something I was used to, but was I ready for what came next when these people looked at me?

"Can I help you?" I asked and instantly regretted it. What a stupid thing to do! This wasn't Stinky and Scratchy. These were thieves, who probably lived by their wits and grit and strength. What was I, except for an eyeless freak?

The male figure in front of me spun around and I could hear him take a step back from me. My eyes, they were startling for anyone I supposed. "What do you want, Eyeless?" He asked.

Eyeless? Not even at the facility had anyone ever called me that.

"Be nice!" The female voice said coming out of the room. "They have it hard enough in the towns. They don't need us adding to it."

"Get out of here!" I said.

I could feel them, particularly him, looking at me. "What ya gonna do about us?" He asked. "You're an Eyeless. Chouette, find what we're looking for." His voice didn't hold any derision though. So why were his words so cruel? I clenched my fists. Had I been this angry at anyone else other than the guards and the researchers? I didn't know, but his demeanour irritated me.

"Kay, Kay! I'm going," The female replied, and I heard her move back into the storeroom.

The male though, he grabbed my arm. Or at least he tried to. What was he trying to do?

Get off the line. The voice in my head instructed and I did. Block but not push. Block and draw. I stepped to the side ever so slightly, my own hand meeting his arms where my other arm had been moments ago. I felt him stumble as he moved with the added momentum I added into his grab. I heard him turn and I guessed that his face showed surprise. If I were him, I would have used that turn to begin my next attack. I lifted my arm and felt it brush against his. He gasped as I used his own attack to project him away from me. He thudded to the floor. I had the feeling that his response was not the right one, but like him, I was surprised by my actions. How did I know this?

"How?" He asked as he got up. "You… You're an Eyeless, how are you doing that?"

I shrugged. "I can hear you…" That wasn't right. "No," I admitted, startled. "I have no idea. I don't know anything about much. I didn't know that I could do that…"

"You're not-," He was cut off by shouting out in the main reception area. "Who's that?"

I shook my head. "I don't know… No one I know…" A sound echoed down the hall from the main reception area, and I gasped. "Alma!"

The boy grabbed my arm and held me, stopping me from running down the hall. "Where are you going?"

"That was a gunshot!" I cried.

Instead of arguing with me, he hauled me into the storeroom. Before either one of us could argue, the girl who had been searching in there spoke. "What the hell is happening?"

"Guards!" The boy declared.

"What guards?" I cried. "What the hell did you two bring down upon us?"

"What makes you think it was us?" The boy snapped, before asking the other girl, "Did you find it?"

"Who else?" I asked, shaking my arm out of his grasp.

"No!" Chouette answered. "Not yet."

"What are you looking for?" I asked as the girl continued to go through cabinets.

There was silence between them for a moment before the girl spoke. "A specific medicine… It's called… Amastrin." She went on to explain that a friend of theirs needed the medicine due to a nerve condition that had affected their eyesight, but even as that had been dealt with, still left them with bouts of exhaustion.

"Why not come into the clinic like everyone else?" I asked them. That's what the clinics were for, wasn't it?

42

A door slammed somewhere outside the storeroom and heavy footsteps marched down, passing the rows of doors. "Oh god!" Chouette whimpered and I heard a slight slap of flesh against flesh as the sound of the girl's fear was muted. I thought maybe she had clamped her hand over her own mouth to control herself.

"Hey, it's alright," The boy calmed her.

"The door closed?" I asked.

"Yeah," he said. "Course."

"What if they find us?" Chouette pressed, her voice trembling. "They'll send us back! They'll send us back, Noah!"

"Shh!" He assured her. "Won't let that happen."

I looked around, hating the fact that once again I could not see, but I had spent my morning in this room stocking it. I knew every cupboard somewhat. "See that big one in the far corner?" I asked them. "The metal grey cupboard?"

"Yeah," The boy, Noah, Chouette had called him. "What about it?"

"Supplies didn't come. It's mostly empty," I stated, as I felt my way past them and to the side of the room. I sent my hand over the surface of the door, looking for the handle. Neither one of them moved to help me and that was ok. I did not want or need their help. Plus, I was pretty sure that they were deciding whether or not to trust me. Finally, I manage to wrench the cupboard door open. "Get in."

"Come on," Noah said to the girl, and I heard them move into the cupboard. I started to close it on them.

"What about you?" Chouette asked.

Yes, what about me? I was a runaway from the nearby facility. I was probably wanted. What if they weren't after these two, but after me? It didn't matter those heavy footsteps were getting closer. "I belong here," I said pasting a brave smile on my face. "I-."

The boy's arm reached out and grabbed me again. "Get in, Eyeless. You have no rights out there." I stumbled in, falling half on him, and heard Chouette closing the doors. Just as they did, the door to the storeroom burst open.

"People say they saw a girl around here that matches the description," A harsh voice said.

"And I have already told you," That was Alma, "I have not seen anyone that looks like that. If I had, I would have told you."

I let out a breath I didn't realise I had been holding. Alma was alright, but were they looking for me or for the girl beside me? I didn't know enough. My heart hammered in my chest. Like Chouette, I had no inclination to go back to where I had come from. It felt so hard and heavy, that surely everyone could hear it. I had to bite my lip to keep from letting out a sound of fright.

"That girl is dangerous, and she stole classified research data," The harsh voice continued. "After killing dozens of people." Dozens? That couldn't be right... Could it? I knew that Scratchy and one of the researchers had shattered as they had fallen, but who else had died? Sage? Half of his upper body had turned to stone. No, an image came to mind of a young man, papers scattered around him, begging me to spare him. Yes, he'd died... but who else had I missed? I shivered, my body shaking at the realisation. What had I done? I clasped my hands over my mouth to muffle any potential wail of agony I might let out. I really was a monster.

They were looking at me. Even if I couldn't see them, I could feel it. Even if we were all too afraid to move or even breathe, I could feel their eyes on me. I just knew it. They thought I was a monster too.

"And we have your flyers. We will keep a look out for the girl," Alma assured them. The group turned out of the room and proceeded down the hall.

I trembled as one of the others pushed the cupboard doors open. "Damn," Chouette said as she crawled out. "They weren't after us."

The boy, he helped me out, guiding my hand as I stood up from the cramped confines of the cupboard with three people huddled in it. "They were talking about you, weren't they?"

I nodded. Why was he being nice? I was a monster.

"Where did you escape from?" he asked.

"Doesn't matter," I said, separating myself from them. It wasn't like I really knew where the laboratory was anyway. "I'm not going back!"

Noah scoffed. "Yeah right. You will if you hang around here for much longer. You heard the woman. They'll turn you in."

"No!" I cried. "That's Alma. She lied when she said she hadn't seen me. I'm staying with her!"

"That Alma woman…" Chouette said. "She works here, right?" I told her that, Alma did work there at the Clinic. "Well… That says it all, right?"

"All what?" I asked.

"She's bought and paid for by Sage Industries," Noah said. "All the clinics and their staff are. They sell their data and patient files to the researchers."

"And then the children go missing," Chouette finished.

I shook my head. "No! Not Alma." I said it, vehemently, but up until today, she had not known that I was blind. She had been curious that my eyes did not react to sunlight like they should, but she had not known that I was an Eyeless and now she also knew about the eyes… Or at least one pair. What would happen now?

"They tracked you here somehow," Chouette said. "How, if not her?"

I sighed. "I've been around here for the last couple of days…" I thought back to Sebastian's warning. "And I haven't exactly been discrete… Someone could have easily reported me… And Alma…"

I walked away from them, feeling my way to the door of the supply room. I put my ear up against the door and listened.

"Hear anything?" Noah asked.

"No…" I said softly. "Its… Its silent… Like there's nothing out there…" I thought about that. "It's weird… It's too still, too silent. I'm not hearing anything from the waiting room or any footsteps… Nothing."

"The waiting room is a ways off," Chouette started.

"I'm blind, not deaf! My ears are excellent," I shot back.

I felt one of them approach and settle next to me. The smell, the sense of largeness, of masculinity, told me that it was Noah. "A trap?" He asked.

I shrugged. "I don't know… But this place is never silent…"

"Noah," Chouette said. "We still have something to do here… Regardless of," She stopped midsentence, and I could imagine her looking at me, with intense meaning meant only for her companion.

"What are you looking for again?" I asked. She gave me the name of the medicine. I had to think about it. I had seen a lot of new things since I had started helping Alma at the clinic. "Top cabinet, right at the back of the room. On the right-hand side. Third shelf… I think… But definitely that cabinet." I had helped Alma unpack the few medicines that had arrived only the day before. Alma had complained how it was only half the order they had been expecting, but I was sure the bottles that we had placed there were what these two were after.

I could hear her rummaging around after opening the aforementioned cabinet and I went back to trying to listen outside. I could feel him beside me, but I wasn't sure if he was listening too or watching the girl.

Suddenly, there were heavy footsteps rushing past our door and the sound of someone crying out in pain. Alma? She was the only one who had gone by in the other direction earlier? Or had they found one of the other doctors, hiding in their office?

"Found it!" Chouette announced proudly. "Right-."

"Shh!" Noah and I hissed at the same time, and she was instantly still.

The waiting room doors crashed open, and more people cried out. There was shouting and I had to strain to hear.

"This is a picture of a dangerous criminal!" A male voice declared. I guessed that they were displaying to everyone a picture of me. "She has been spotted in the area around this clinic."

"No one has seen her," Alma's voice interjected. Common sense really, considering this was a sight clinic and the patients were mostly blind.

Another voice. One of the doctors I thought spoke up. "Yes, you have," he cried accusingly. "She was with you." The man had outed Alma and by extension, me.

And that was when all hell broke loose.

43

"They're all occupied," Chouette said coming over to us. "We should leave."

"I can't leave Alma!" I retorted. It would be easy to run away with these people, but Alma had been good to me. She'd been kind when nothing had made sense. I couldn't just leave her... Could I?

"How desperately do they want you back?" Noah asked. I stared in the direction of his voice. "If they think you're attached to her, then she is a bargaining chip. They won't kill her. They'll use her to draw you out."

"So, what are you suggesting? That I just leave here? Run?" I asked.

"Exactly," Chouette said, putting a hand on my shoulder. "Come and fight another day."

They were serious. Oh my god, they were serious about abandoning the only person to have ever shown me any kindness in my life. "I... I can't..."

"If you go out there now, they will kill her," Noah added. "Let's get out of here. Regroup with the others..."

"I need to get next door," I said and started to open the door.

"No!" Noah shouted in a loud whisper as he held the door closed with his body.

"I'm useless like this," I said. "If I get into the other room, I won't be as useless."

"We're getting out," Chouette said, siding with Noah. "With or without you-" She paused suddenly. "What's your name? Everyone calls me Chouette, and the big lout is Noah."

"Hey!" Noah protested.

"Juniper... Alma called me Juniper..." I said softly.

"With or without you, Juniper. Noah and I are leaving. We can't risk our friends and there ain't no way in hell that we're ever going back with those people either."

I looked towards them. "You know them?"

"Yeah," Noah said. "Let's just say that we escaped from a facility some time ago." Were they like me? Had they escaped from the same place? Or did Sage have other laboratories? What was special about these two then?

"Ok…" I said straightening myself up. "We can go to Alma's. Get my bag. I'll be useful to you if I get my bag."

A scream rang out from the waiting room area, followed by cries of fear from more than one person. "They're getting worse," Noah pointed out. "We've got to move while they're occupied."

I felt him open the door slightly. I guessed that he was peering down the hall. "Everyone's occupied restraining your friend and the patients," he said gravely. "Let's go." He grabbed my arm, perhaps a little rougher than I would have liked, but I wasn't getting out of there without him. "Stay close," he ordered.

Chouette was right behind me. I could feel her hand on my shoulder as we moved quietly, but quickly in the opposite direction of the waiting room. I couldn't help but turn my head in the direction of the waiting room, as though I could see or do something about what was happening in there.

I leaned over, closer to Noah. "There's a back door-."

"I know. It's how we got in."

He pushed it open, and the warmth of the sun and noise of the street hit me. We slid through like snakes, then waited for him to close it with an almost silent click. With that done, we all leaned back against the door, breathing hard. Apparently, I had not been the only one to hold my breath as we traversed the hall of the clinic.

"Where's your friend's place?" Noah asked.

"A few blocks over. On the edge of the big park," I said.

"That big wartime mansion?" Chouette asked.

I nodded. "Yeah…"

"I know the place," she continued. "Your Alma lives there… She's extremely well off…"

I shrugged. "I don't know… But she's been good to me and I'm going to get her back!"

Noah paused and fished something out of a bag he must have had with him. "Those eyes of yours are creepy out here. Put these on!" He ordered, then proceeded to place something over my face, tucking something plastic behind each of my ears as something else settled over the bridge of my nose.

"What is it?" I asked.

"Sunglasses. No one will be able to see your... Issue... With them on," he said. Great, now I could get glasses.

I was entirely at their mercy. I didn't know these people. What if this was all a trap? What if this was something else altogether? I didn't know, but now, I didn't have a choice but to trust them and if necessary, bide my time until I could think of something else. There was a lot of distance to cover, and I didn't know where I was going well enough to help. Stinky and Scratchy had usually half carried, half dragged me everywhere. I had no idea how we were going to make it to Alma's without me tripping over something.

44

Speed. There was nothing quite like speed and the open air all around her, that made Aubrey feel alive. The long stretches of open road before her were what she lived for and Libby, the old war era bike she rode, was her constant companion.

There had not been anyone on the road in hours, and she relished the freedom that riding gave her. It was a sense of aloneness and freedom that she didn't get when at school in the big city. She knew that her grandmother didn't want her around town most of the time, some sense of needing to protect her, but Aubrey missed home. Her own time, her own things.

She slowed her speed when she spotted Erihall in the distance. She knew from experience that more people would be riding bikes, pushing carts, or just walking, the nearer she got to the town. It wasn't even a minute later that a truck came hurtling out of the thick wooded cover to her left, almost clipping her. Aubrey turned, speeding onto the wrong side of the road, and raced past the careless truck who blew his horn at her, as though she had been the one in the wrong. She didn't even bother to look back at him as she made some distance between herself and the truck.

She came into main street and smiled as she noted everything that had not changed since her last visit. Nothing ever changed in Erihall. Nothing ever would in her opinion, but she was too young to remember the factory or the days of endless change that had followed the explosion of the building in the centre of town. Her grandmother talked of those days, talked of the terror and the fear that had engulfed the town. The deaths, the injuries. It was just history to Aubrey.

The streets were oddly occupied with troops though. Sage Security were everywhere, and they were checking everyone. She was stopped at a checkpoint that seemed hastily put together with two large personnel movers blocking the road so that only one vehicle at a time could pass after going through the men.

"ID," A man said, a large assault rifle slung over his shoulder.

Aubrey pointed to her stuff, attached to the back of Libby. "It's in my bag. I need to get it out for you," she said, trying not to sound as nervous as she felt. The gruff man nodded, and Aubrey kicked the stand down and set the old bike to standing. She then swung her leg over the back of the bike.

"There's no need to dismount," The gruff guard said, his hands inching closer to his weapon. Aubrey's chest was thumping, and she could hear the beat of her heart in her ears.

"I can't reach my ID from the seat." Then she proceeded to go through her bags. She knew it was in there somewhere. She opened one bag and quickly reclosed it before the security man could see it. Then opened the next and pulled out her ID wallet. "Here," she said holding it out to him. Behind her, a horn honked, and someone shouted in frustration.

The man stared at the ID for a long while, then at the girl. "Go on," he said.

She shoved her ID wallet into her back pocket and zipped the bag she had retrieved it from back up. Then casually, she walked back to her back and got on, started the engine back up and kicked the stand up. What the hell was going on in Erihall?

45

"What about the bike?" Chouette asked, as we walked along the street. We were attempting the 'three mates out for a stroll' look. I had no idea what she was talking about, but I guessed that the bike was how they had gotten into town and their desired mode of leaving.

"It might be better to leave it," Noah replied. "Look around. How many Sage Security guys do you see wandering around?"

"They're everywhere," the girl agreed. "But we need a way back to camp."

"We can come back for it?" Noah suggested.

"No," Chouette disagreed. "Like you said. Those guys are everywhere," She paused, thinking for a moment and we all came to a stop. I hated this. I had no idea what we were talking about. I couldn't see them. I couldn't see what they were talking about. "I'll go get the bike," Chouette suddenly said, disentangling herself from my arm and pushing me closer to Noah. "Do the 'two young lovers out for a stroll' instead of the 'mates' routine," She suggested. "I'll meet you at the mansion."

"Chouette," Noah said, he sounded serious too.

"I'll be fine. Go!" She ordered.

"What the hell just happened?" I asked as Noah resumed our path.

He chuckled. "Chouette got her way. Like always."

"Will she find Alma's house?" I asked as he snaked his arm around my shoulders, holding me close and guiding my direction as we moved.

"Everyone knows that house. That old mansion is as old as this town," He reassured me. "Come on. We weren't kidding, there are guards everywhere."

I let him lead me. I didn't know the way to Alma's house well enough to be of any use. I was, completely and utterly useless here. I had not done a single useful thing to help in our escape from the clinic. "I'm sorry," I said softly as we walked. He pulled me closer to his side as we passed other people walking in the street.

"For what?" Noah asked

"Everything," I said. "You could already be gone if it weren't for me," I said. Ok, so maybe I was feeling a little sorry for myself. The last few days of sight had been a treat, and I had been spoiled.

I felt him shrug against me. "And we could have just left you to your own fate," He replied, never slowing his step. "But that's not what we do," He added. We turned and it felt chilly in the new street we were walking down, like all the heat had vanished, probably with the sunlight. Were we going down an alleyway now? We stopped and he pushed my back against the wall. "Play along," He whispered in my ear, and I could feel his breath on my neck. It made me shiver. He stayed like that for another moment.

"Just two kids," A voice said from a few feet away, a snicker in his voice.

"Looks like that kid has more game than you, Marlin," a second voice added as they walked away. "Let them be."

Next to me, Noah breathed a sigh of relief, and we separated. "Glad that they're gone."

I took a deep breath and was surprised to find myself disappointed by the distance he had put between us now. I had never really been held by anyone, not unless you counted being restrained and tied down, then, yeah. That had happened heaps. But in kindness? In affection? Never. Not that I knew of anyway... And yeah, I know that Noah didn't actually like me either, he was just keeping us safe, but what the hell? A girl could dream right?

"Thanks," I said. "Quick thinking."

He took my hand and lead me towards the street again. "Well..." He didn't add anything else. Instead, we walked, hand in hand for a few steps, but I found myself unsteady and stumbling. Not used to this yet. Noah slowed down, then put his arm around my shoulders again. "You're not like most Eyeless. Usually, they know how to follow or be led."

"I'm more used to being dragged," I said. We turned again, this time onto what must have been a bright street. Maybe it only had buildings on one side, because I could feel the heat of the sun against my entire body. "That the park?" I asked.

"Yeah, not much farther to the house," he told me. He hurried us across the road and a few moments later I heard the familiar squeaking of Alma's side gate.

"That's it," I said. Before he could ask how I knew, I added. "The gate. It squeaks. Even in the wind."

"Right," he said. We walked through Alma's sweet-smelling garden.

"There's a back door along this side of the house. It leads straight into the kitchen," I told him. "I have the key," I shoved my hand into my back jeans pocket and pulled out the key that Alma had given me, allowing me to come and go as I pleased. I had no idea why she had done it, but I was glad.

"There's a bike in yard," Noah added, obviously relieved, but I wondered how Chouette could have made it there so quickly. "Chouette must be here already." I wasn't so sure.

"Should we go around the front," I asked, tentatively. "Let her in?"

Noah scoffed. "No one picks a lock like Chouette. She's inside."

I wanted to protest about Chouette breaking in, but what was the point? What was done was done and these people... They did not live inside the law. Whatever their story was, it was not one of happy families and perfect lives.

The door squeaked as Noah opened it, and lead me in. "Can you navigate around in here?" he asked.

I thought about it. I did not know the house well, but yeah, I could probably make it from the kitchen to my room easily enough. "Yeah, go find Chouette," I said. "I'll be fine..." I hoped that I sounded more confident than I felt because we had just escaped from Sage's security team, and everything seemed a little quiet and still in the house. Sure, that was what I loved about Alma's, but it was making me nervous now.

I moved forward, away from Noah and felt my way along the kitchen cabinets. I didn't hear any movement from him though. Was he watching me?

Feeling along the corners of the counters, I continued along the next side and when the kitchen cabinetry vanished, I knew that I was at the entryway to the stairs.

"You're painful to watch," Noah declared and in a few short strides he was behind me, grasping my elbow. "Come on," he said as he tried to assist me up the stairs.

I jerked away from him. Swiping out at him to prevent him touching me, the feel of him gripping me suddenly all too similar to the guards trying to push me along. I banged my hip against the counter.

"No," I hissed, "I can do it!" I promised. "I swear I can do it! Just give me a minute." Why did everyone always want to rush me? The walk in the street had been one thing, but here? I would not let him hurry me here, in a space I knew.

"Woah!" He cried, obviously surprised by my reaction. "I'm sorry. I didn't mean to scare you." I rubbed at my hip and felt ashamed of my reaction. I knew he wasn't planning on hauling me up the stairs like Stinky and Scratchy always had, but his sudden appearance, the grip on my elbow, it had all been too much combined with the darkness I was once again engulfed in. "Juniper?" He asked hesitantly when I did not respond.

"No..." I said, my voice shaking far more than I would have liked. "I'm sorry. I..." I wanted to explain. I really did, but where did one find the words to explain that you had always been hauled up and down stairs without any care about whether or not your feet touched the ground. "I..." I tried again but instead reached for the wall by the stairs. "My room is this way."

"Do you..." Noah asked slowly, "Um... Do you want me to...?" He let his voice drift off and I knew he was asking if yes, I did want the help.

I shook my head. "I can manage the stairs. Really, I can. But... Maybe upstairs, you could..."

"Gotchya," He agreed, and I could feel him two steps behind me, waiting patiently as I felt my way up.

A sound of something ratcheting echoed down the stairwell and Noah grabbed for me. "For two people breaking in," A female voice said, "You two sure make a lot of noise."

46

"Juniper, you didn't say anyone else lived here," Noah hissed in my ear, hot breath sliding over my skin.

"Alma never mentioned anyone else," I hissed back. "And I've been here a week." I thought about the noise I'd heard. Where had I heard that before. I didn't know, but it sounded familiar like… "She's holding a gun, isn't she?" The ratcheting sound. I was sure I knew it from somewhere. But where?

"Yeah," the female voice answered instead of Noah. She sounded young, like us, but cultured, like Alma.

"A pretty damned big one," Noah added, trying to sound funny even as nerves seemed to tinge his words. "And she looks real comfortable with it."

"How'd you get in?" The voice asked, "and how do you know my grandmother?"

I brightened. I knew who this was. "Alma mentioned you… You're Aubrey, you also don't think much of her sense of humour." Maybe if I made a connection with this person, she wouldn't shoot us? I could only hope.

"She's looking even more like she wants to shoot us," Noah reported as I head the girl shift her weight.

Oh, great. That hadn't worked. This was not good. "How do you know my grandmother?" she asked again.

"Alma is letting me stay here. I have a key," I said holding it up so that she could see it.

"And what, now you come in with your boyfriend while she's at work and rob her blind?" the gun wielding voice asked.

"Woah!" Noah protested, stepping away from me as far as he could on the stairs. "I only met the girl today!"

"Absolutely not!" I cried, pulling back as well, but I was already pushed back against the wall.

A window broke downstairs. "Crap!" Noah said. "Do you think they followed us here?"

I shook my head. "No, I think someone reported Alma and they're here looking for me."

"Reported her?" The voice asked. "What the hell have you done to my grandmother?" Two more windows broke and the sound of men in heavy armour entering the house echoed throughout the halls. They were screaming and shouting orders, even as they traipsed through the delicate rooms of alma's house.

"Sage Security," Noah told her. "Now you can point that gun at us, or you can help us. What's it going to be?"

"Wait!" I said. "You said the bike outside was yours, where the hell is Chouette?" I asked.

"That's my bike," the voice said. "I don't know this Chouette."

"And how could you not tell that it wasn't Chouette's bike?" I added, turning pointedly to where I'd heard Noah's voice coming from.

"I don't know," Noah said, and I could hear the concern in his voce, "and I only saw the wheel… I assumed! So, sue me!"

"Just great… Just bloody great, you assumed," I muttered, I cut myself off though to listen. "They're getting closer," I said, hearing footsteps. "I need to get my stuff from my room. Now!"

Noah pushed me up the stairs, apparently deciding to ignore the gun toting girl. "If you're going to defend your grandmother's house from there, that thing better be loaded."

The girl scoffed. "Of course, it's loaded. There's no point to an unloaded weapon," She paused. "Which room did my grandmother give you?"

"She… She called it the Park Room," I said. "It looks out over the park and-." The girl cut me off.

"I know it. Come on," The girl said, and Noah hurried me past her. "Third door on the left there," she told him, then an epic bang went off as thumping footsteps entered the kitchen area. "I'll hold them off."

Now Noah did drag me, and I let him. The idea of those men taking me back to the facility terrified me. Or worse, what if they didn't take me back? What if they just killed me like Sebastian had said some people wanted to do?

47

I heard the door slam shut behind us as Noah hurtled me into what I guessed was my room. It smelled right, but I had only been there a week, what did I really know? "What about the girl?" I asked turning towards him.

"She'll be fine," he told me. Did he really believe that? It wasn't like we knew her and it sounded as though she was seriously outnumbered. "You didn't see her gun." Outside the door, we heard the sound of her firing upon the intruders. Great, big blasts seemed to rattle the walls of the room.

Well, that was true. I felt my way along the dresser beside the door, I had to prove eventually that I was not useless. The dresser gave way to open air, and I was certain that I had left my backpack there. Where was it? Panic gripped at my chest, like a fist wrapping around my heart and squeezing as I reached around, my fingers grasping at empty air. My hand seemed to swing around aimlessly searching until I felt the material of the bag brush against my fingertips. The fist around my heart unclenched a bit.

"Got it!" I cried victoriously, trying not to reveal just how panicked I'd been that the bag wouldn't be there, as I hefted the bag up. "There should be some stuff on the bed and the side table. Can you grab them?" I unzipped the bag and fingered the soft case within. The one carrying the eyes. I could still envisage the look of all those eyeballs, lined up and staring up at the roof. If I recalled well, not many of them looked like normal eyes. There was a pause where we couldn't hear anything from the girl in the hall, then the gun went off again. Something thumped down the stairs with a rhythmic thud, thud, thud.

"Here," Noah said, and I reached out to grab the clothes and the few items Sebastian had gathered for me before sending me on my way. Before I had a chance to thank him though, there was a thump against the door. We paused, frozen to the spot.

"Hey guys!" The girl called and we both seemed to relax. I heard Noah breath out in relief beside me even as my muscles unclenched. "Coming in," She declared. Then the door swung open and as fast as she could she shoved it back closed with a slam. The sound of more people thudding against it came next and I could hear the door rattling in its frame.

Noah left my side, and the door stopped rattling as much. He must have been holding it closed with her. "What happened?" he breathed out, sounding as though he was staining against the onslaught of the intruders on the other side.

"Ran out of ammo," The girl declared. "And their helmets mean no hitting them on the head!" I heard the gun rattle, something loose on it? Was she shaking it? Demonstrating hitting someone on the head? I didn't know.

"What now?" Noah asked. "We're stuck in here and we can't afford to wait for Chouette to show up… If she even is…" His last comment stuck me. He was really worried about his friend. "I don't want her coming into a trap."

I made a decision. It was all my fault that we were here anyway. Alma was in trouble. Noah and Chouette were separated and maybe she was captured. We were definitely cornered with no escape route. The gun toting girl had been attacked in her grandmother's house. It was all because of me, or at least that was how it had sounded back at the clinic. I pulled the soft case out of the bag. This was totally going to suck.

48

"One of you, help me!" I cried. I really did not want to do this. I had no idea what would happen, but I couldn't think of another way out. Maybe if we got lucky, I could do a repeat of the laboratory... And not kill either of these two while I was at it... I swallowed hard and tried to calm my ponding heartbeat that was ricocheting through my head. I did not want to this, but... What other choice did I have?

"You," Noah told the girl. "I've got this. What are you doing Juniper?"

I ignored his question and instead focused on unzipping the case. The girl approached and as the case felt open, she gasped. "Holy moly…" She whispered. "That's… That's…" She seemed stumped for words. "What is that?"

"Hurry up, Juniper!" Noah cried from where he was holding the door closed against the onslaught of security men. "Where'd you…"

I held the case out to the girl. "Just give me two that look the same!" I ordered her. "Now!"

"But!" She cried. "I have no idea."

"Neither do I!" I told her. "I'm going on faith here and if we don't try something, we're all going to be dead. So, pick two that look the same!"

"Do it!" Noah yelled. "I hope you know what you're doing," He added in a softer voice.

"Me too," I said as the girl placed two glass eyes in my outstretched hand. I felt around the first one. I had never done this myself, so here went nothing. I slipped the first one into my right eye socket. The pain from earlier was still there and having something back in there stung, but that was nothing compared to what was coming next, I was sure of that. "Get behind Noah," I told the girl. "And Noah, get you and her behind the door when you open it." I stuck the left eye in.

Pain. White hot pain flashed from my eyes through the rest of my head and down my body to the tips of my fingers and further to the tips of my toes. I cried out, unable to bare the onslaught. My legs trembled and I felt them go weak as I fell against the bed.

"JUNIPER!" Noah cried.

"What's happening?" The girl cried.

I gasped for breath. "Nothing. Just what always happens," I said through clenched teeth. "Open the door!" I was holding my eyes closed for the moment of truth. I had no idea what these eyes were. Sebastian hadn't been able to tell me anything about the other sets, and I had no idea what the girl had given me, even if I had known what they were.

Men came stumbling in, screaming contradictory orders.

"On the floor."

"Hands in the air!"

"Don't move, or I'll shoot!"

I opened my eyes and light, and colour came flooding in again. The scratchiness from earlier was still there, but it was bearable. I focused on the soldiers and hoped like hell something useful happened. What had I done last time? I had just looked at them and boom, they had turned to stone? Or was there something else? I got up off the floor where I had fallen and walked towards them on trembling legs.

"Stop moving!" One of the soldiers cried.

"That's her!" Another called. "Don't shoot her!"

"Screw that!" Another said, "I was there in the lab!"

I tried to smile, something to unnerve them, but I think it may have come out more as a grimace the way even my lips trembled at the strain of trying to smile. "Look into my eyes," I said, coldly, then grimaced. That sounded so stupid and cavalier for what was going to happen... Assuming something happened.

Two of the soldiers did and suddenly, ice started to crawl along their bodies. Ice? I thought to myself. What the hell had Sage created? Those guys were being frozen where they stood. I bet if they fell, they would shatter just as the stone people had. I didn't want to find out, but more heavy footsteps were coming up the stairs.

"Now!" The girl cried and suddenly she struck one of the frozen men with the butt of the rifle she carried. I cringed and looked away, not wanting to see the result more than concern for hitting her. Hearing the sound of the breaking ice was bad enough. The ice and the arm she had struck shattered like glass. A man, only half frozen over screamed and I could hear the absolute terror in his voice before I turned to look at him again, tears in my eyes and streaming down my face.

Noah and the girl emerged fully from behind the door. I wanted time to look at them, but I couldn't risk them. My companions, the people who had helped save my life. I noted out of the corner of my eye that Noah was significantly taller than the girl, standing more than a head above her and her ridiculously long red hair that seemed to go on forever. It was so straight and reached all the way to her knees, even while tied back into the long ponytail she had it in. His skin was pale, not quite white, but very pale. Light, golden brown curls that would make any girl jealous swarmed around his shoulders but were kept from his eyes by a bandanna that he had tied for that purpose. Eyes as brown as chocolate stared back at me. I also noticed that the wall I had been focusing on, was turning to ice. Well, didn't that just suck? I could see, but at what cost?

"Crap!" Noah said, suddenly rubbing his arms as though he was cold. I glanced towards him suddenly, but that's when I realised that the dresser, the wall behind it and the floor in front of it were turning to ice. I cringed and looked away, but a great swath of ice spread cross the wall and the lamp and the bed frame as I looked around. He had looked me in the eyes. That was bad right? I covered my face with my hands. Extra protection for them.

"I'm sorry!" I cried out.

"Crap…" The girl breathed out as she stared at the popsicle soldiers. "What just happened?"

"That's what I'd like to know," Noah said walking over to me. He took one of my hands from my face and placed something in it. The sunglasses I had worn over here to ensure that no one noticed that I was an Eyeless. "That should counter it," he said, and I slid them on. "Come on," Noah urged when I still kept my eyes closed.

I shook my head. "I don't want to accidentally kill you or… or…"

"The glasses will prevent our eyes from directly meeting," Noah said softly in my ear. He seemed so confident. How could he be sure of that? "You're fine to look at us. I swear," And with that he gave my hand a squeeze.

"You don't know that," I whispered.

"I'm pretty sure of it," he said, all confidence and I had no idea why. Who was this guy? Glasses. Was that how Sage had survived back at the laboratory? His glasses had protected him?

I don't know why, but I trusted him and opened my eyes, looking at the wall of the room rather than at either of them. Out of the corner of my eye, I did see the girl tentatively poking at one of the iced men. "They're really encased in ice… This… This is…" She blanched as she looked down at the shattered one, the ice already beginning to melt into a disgusting puddle of water and bodily fluids.

I glanced back at Noah. "How did you know that would work?"

He shrugged nonchalantly. "It was a hunch."

I stared at him. "You risked your life and hers… On a hunch?"

I shook my head at his cocky grin and looked over at the red-haired girl. She was occupied inspecting the soldiers so there was little risk of looking her in the eyes, but was that what I needed? I glanced around the room at the swaths of ice. A connection of eyes obviously was not necessary. So, what did activate it? I knew it wasn't eye contact, no matter what he said. Just having my eyes open? That's what it felt like, but I had looked at Noah and the girl hadn't I? They'd gotten cold, but no ice had formed. Why?

I carefully looked at Noah, who was still beside me. Why was he being so nice? But as I looked at him, I saw him inspecting the case of eyes. He gingerly ran the tip of his left index finger over the protective film that held them in place in the pack. "You're one of Sage's experiments," he said. It was not a question. It was a statement of facts.

"Yes," I said softly.

"Sage's experiments?" The girl asked. "As in Nelson Sage? That rich whack job who owns most of the town?"

"Yeah," Noah said looking over his shoulder at her. She came over to us as a result, leaving her exploration of the soldiers alone. Her rifle clutched in her other hand.

"Grandma hates that man and his research," she said.

"No one can hate him more than I do," I said standing up. I took the case of eyes from Noah and zipped it shut. The glasses would do for now and maybe in that case there would be another set that would be suitable for everyday wear, where I wouldn't kill a person just be looking them in the eyes.

"Debatable," Noah said as I stuffed the case into my backpack. "Very debatable," he added.

"Don't suppose either of you want to tell me what just happened here?" The girl interrupted. "First, I'm checked while riding into town by those goons and now Grandma's house gets attacked... What is happening?"

I shook my head and explained about Alma letting me stay with her and work at the clinic. Then today, about the soldiers coming into the clinic and scaring everyone. "I think that they took her. One of those doctors told them that I was with her..."

The girl's calm demeanour changed to one of concern and maybe even a little fury. "And you just left her?"

"They'd have killed your grandmother in a heartbeat," Another voice said from the door- No the window. We all turned to see Chouette hauling herself inside.

"There's a door," Noah said stoically.

"Blocked by popsicle men," Chouette shot back. "Anyway, as I was saying. If we had let Juniper turn herself in like she had wanted, they'd have just killed your grandmother as a traitor or whatever charge they would have posed against her." Her feet touched the ground, and she stood up. She turned to look at Noah and me. "Who's the new girl anyway?"

"How did Chouette know we were in here?" I asked Noah.

"Scouting and surveillance are kind of her thing," Noah said before going over to stand between the two girls. It was comical really. Chouette was even shorter than the girl and Noah towered over both of them. She was as dark as Noah was fair, her hair just as curly. But dyed some impossible shade of orange that contrasted against her coffee-coloured skin. Her white clothes were stained from the climb up the side of the house, and she looked really put out by it. I saw her piercings over both eyes sparkle in the light coming through the window. She was such a contrast to Noah and even the girl. "Chouette's right," he said to the girl. They would have killed your grandmother right there and then. Now they have a bargaining chip."

"Who is she, Noah?" Chouette asked again.

"I'm Aubrey Walsh. This is my grandmother's house," The girl Aubrey said. She clutched her rifle a little tighter.

"What took you so long?" Noah asked.

"Well Aubrey Walsh," Chouette said, seemingly ignoring Noah. "There are even more Sage goons on their way here. Presumably to find Juniper. Noah and I are getting the hell out of here before they close the town off all together."

"What about my Gran?" Aubrey asked. "I can't leave her in their hands…"

"Absolutely not. I'll help you get her back," I told the girl. I had to. It was all my fault that Alma had been taken anyway.

Noah and Chouette looked at each other. "She's one of us," Noah said to Chouette. "Juniper, I mean."

She looked at me and I looked at her. These glasses really did stop me from freezing people to death. Great! Chouette's eyes widened. "Really?"

Noah nodded. "Oh… Yeah."

50

Somehow it all got decided that Aubrey and I would return with Noah and Chouette to their hideout. I have no idea how that happened, but it did and as soon as Aubrey had packed up her rifle, collected new ammo from a storage cupboard I'd never known existed, and repacked her bags, we were riding away from Alma's house. Noah and Chouette on one bike and Aubrey and I on the other.

"Isn't this the ultimate freedom?" Aubrey asked as I wrapped my arms tightly around her waist, fearing that if I slackened my grip even slightly, I would fall off.

"Yeah," I managed to get my mouth to say. Further words were not possible. The wind was blowing and the sound of the tires on the road were deafening. Then, despite the fact that I my eyes were apparently not real, and I wore dark tinted sunglasses, I kept my eyes firmly shut, fearing any debris that might fly in as we rode at what seemed to be breakneck speeds down the road.

In the beginning, it was slow getting out of Erihall. We had to stay to the backstreets and away from any of the checkpoints that Sage's security had set up. Aubrey led us expertly through small laneways and alleys that seemed almost forgotten, explaining that until she had started at her new school, she had lived her entire life in Erihall. The bike had been Alma's and she had taken Aubrey everywhere on it as soon as she was old enough to hold on, teaching her all of the little back ways one could use to get in and out of various areas without being noticed. Alma's foresight was probably the only thing that got us out of Erihall without getting caught.

Then, we were out on the open road. It seemed to go on forever and it didn't take long for us to no longer encounter anyone on the roads. Aubrey had ceded the leadership of our little troupe to Noah and Chouette after leaving the town and now we rode at high speed with nothing to stop us. Or make us slow down.

I could see Noah and Chouette were talking. Were they talking about Aubrey and me? They had been the ones to suggest we come with them, but what did that mean for us? For Alma? Had I made a mistake trusting them? Trusting Aubrey? Sebastian had said to trust nobody... So, what was I doing riding out of Erihall to who only knew where with these people?

After maybe an hour of riding, how far had we gone in that time? Noah turned his and Chouette's bike down a small road that probably would not have been noticed had we not seen him turn that direction. Aubrey followed and the gravel surface caused the bike to move uncertainly. I gripped her harder, not used to the sensations the drive was causing. Where the open road had been steady and fast, the gravel seemed to kick out or cause the bike to swerve uncertainly at times.

It felt like forever before Noah finally stopped and allowed Chouette to dismount from behind him. Aubrey pulled to a stop beside the small girl and we both dismounted. I am not ashamed to say that my legs were a little on the wobbly side. This was all new for me. Bikes and hidden camps and becoming a fugitive.

I stood there, not saying a word as I took in the overgrown site before me. The buildings looked old, partially destroyed, but there were signs of life. Movement behind a window, noise coming from somewhere to my left, the aromas of food cooking, the movement of a sentry atop the roof. It all spoke of life and routine off the beaten path.

"Welcome to Camp Sight," Noah said, turning towards Aubrey and me.

"Come on!" Chouette added. "Let's go meet everyone!"

51

"We need to expand," Sage said, pacing up and down the length of the conference room. Ms Reavis stared at his immobilised arm, held against his body, and supported by a sling. He moved awkwardly now, unable to fully turn his neck. Looking at him made her feel a little nauseous now, especially when she caught sight of the swath of grey that slipped from the neck of his shirt.

"Expand?" Sebastian asked, looking up from his notes. "Are you sure that's wise? The last experiment didn't go to plan, and you no longer have the protype."

Sage stopped his pacing abruptly, turning his whole body to face the younger man. "But it worked!" he said, the sheen of success glowing in his eyes. He waved at his arm, "this is proof that it worked.

"So are the three dead personnel," Finnerty added. "We had no control over her in that moment."

Sage slid awkwardly into his seat at the head of the table and after tapping at a keyboard, brought up the footage of the experiment. He fast forwarded the footage until the girl in the tank began to seize and then allowed it to play in real time.

"That there is the problem. If we can determine what caused the seizures, we'll be able to maintain full control of the situation the next time we do this."

"And how do you plan on doing that? We no longer have the girl. She's likely dead somewhere," Ms Reavis said, staring pointedly at the gruff, and oddly scented guard that stood at the door to the meeting room. He glared back at her, arms crossed over his chest.

Sebastian nodded along to what Ms Reavis said, his heart pounding in his chest. No one had figured out his part in the girl's escape and he'd done his best to perpetrate the rumour of her untimely demise at the hands of the guards. It hadn't worked, but maybe Ms Reavis was one of those who still believed the rumour, despite the fact that she had been spotted in Erihall. Guards had even been dispatched to try and retrieve her. Their failure to do so worried him. They claimed they never saw the girl. What if Ms Reavis was right, what if the girl was now dead? Then everything would be over.

"We still have all her blood work, and we are in the process of retrieving her," Sage insisted. Sebastian narrowed his eyes at the older man. Was that true? Did Sage know where she was?

"Even if we get the girl back," Finnerty intervened, "how are we going to expand? The first girl was a bust and this one... it was hard enough finding her. Where are we going to get enough subjects to find anyone to expand this project further?

"What we need now," Sage said, pointing at Finnerty, "is access to all the records from those clinics across Eriden and even into Yarm and the neighbouring countries."

"We're not going to get that," Ms Reavis stated. "We've tried and even when we do get it, it's limited. What we really need is direct access to all the potential subjects, preferably in one place."

"And how do you plan on getting parents to part with their children in such a way?" Finnerty asked. "We all know this works better with the younger candidates."

Ms Reavis looked smug as she turned her gaze from the young researcher to Sage. "I have an idea," she stated. "Something that will get us all the candidates we could possibly want, right where we want them."

Sage leaned forward, his arm thudding against the table as he did so. "Tell me everything."

CAMP SIGHT

52

Everyone turned out to not be everyone. Chouette managed to rustle up only two other residents, practically dragging them into a large area with a few couches, an old pool table and a couple of dining tables. Two boys, comically larger than Chouette were dragged in. Both boys were almost a foot taller than the girl, and yet they followed where she directed. They were maybe the same age as I was.

"Juniper, Aubrey. I would like you to meet Emrys. Our resident computer nerd," she said.

"Wizard," he said in a low voice. "Computer Wizard," the large square shaped glasses he wore showed off dark blue eyes set in the centre of his square face. Was it square? Or was it easy just to compare his face to his glasses? His nose was big, but it did nothing to stop the glasses from slipping down and I watched as he pushed them back up his nose. He eyed first me, then Aubrey. "Why are we letting new people in?"

"Because I said so," Noah said walking past. He looked away from the boy he had been speaking to and looked at the other one. "Kattie," he said tentatively as though he knew something we did not. "Oh, for crying out loud!" He suddenly cried as he jumped in surprise. "HATTIE! Put on some damned clothes!"

"Why?" A female voice asked out of nowhere. Where had that come from? I didn't see anyone else in the room.

"Because it's downright creepy that you wander around here like that! Kattie, reign her in already!" Noah ordered.

Someone began tugging on the jacket of the tall, dark-haired boy named Kattie. His narrow face and pointy chin were accentuated by his shaggy black hair. I saw the jacket being pulled from his skinny frame. "Gimme!" a female voice demanded.

"No!" Kattie cried, holding onto his jacket, trying to pull it tight around himself. "You've got your own. Go get your own!"

133

Aubrey and I, we just stared at each other and then the spectacle of the boy fighting a supposedly invisible force. If it were not for the fact that I had definitely heard another voice, I would have been certain that he was crazy... Or was I going crazy? I didn't know. Someone else was there, but was she... I mean... She couldn't be, right? Invisible?

"Kattie, just give her the coat for now," Chouette said. "Please!" The boy mumbled something about his life being so unfair and why did he have to be the only one who could see the girl and it wasn't his fault that she was so inappropriate. Finally, we were faced with Emrys, who had just watched the two in dismay, Kattie, who was still grumbling about his coat and Kattie's coat, hanging there in mid-air. The coat, Hattie, apparently, rushed towards us, empty arms outstretched.

"Hiya! Welcome to Camp Sight!" the voice coming from the empty air above the coat giggled. "Get it?" She cried excitedly. "It's like a camp site, but we all have sight issues and stuff so its Camp Sight! So, not S-I-T-E but S-I-G-H-T," She babbled on excitedly as suddenly those arms wrapped around Aubrey and myself, clashing us together with the very physical form under the coat.

"Hattie, they get it," Kattie said.

"It's so nice to meet you!" Hattie went on. "We don't get anyone new here very often and there's two of you! Two new friends!"

"Whatever," Emrys said turning away from the scene. "I'm going back to my work," he said sullenly.

Chouette laughed. "Yep. You'll both fit right in!" she declared.

Well, I didn't know about Aubrey, but I felt incredibly out of place.

"Everyone has sight issues?" Aubrey asked as Hattie was disentangled from us by Kattie. "How come? I mean almost everyone in Erihall has sight issues."

I got it though. I had been watching Chouette ever since the house. I hadn't noticed anything off about her back at the clinic because I myself had been unable to see, but now, as she engaged in her own environment, and I could see her clearly. She never moved her eyes. Everything she needed to look at, she moved her head. Hattie being invisible. Kattie's comments about being the only one who could see her. "You were all Sage's experiments."

"Just like you," Noah confirmed.

53

"I think," Aubrey said as she stuffed her mouth with food that Chouette had rustled up for us from somewhere, since it turned out that the group had just finished dinner. "That this is all," I lost the rest to her munching. I just nodded in agreement. It seemed the easiest thing to do. She ate with such a gusto that I almost envied her. She caught me staring. "Oh… I'm the 'not really rich kid' at school. You could say that that puts a target on my back." I had no idea what she was talking about.

"Not really rich kid?" I asked, incredulous. "What does that even mean? I've seen your grandmother's house. Compared to the rest of Erihall, it's a palace."

"Exactly," she said pointing at me with a half-eaten piece of bread. "My grandmother's. My dad, don't know if there even is one. I mean, there is a dad somewhere. I know where babies come from and all that, but it was always just me and mum. But mum died a few years ago and I went to live with Grandma." She stuck the piece of bread she'd been waving about in her mouth and chewed contentedly.

"I'm sorry," I said. I was, but I was also kind of jealous. Aubrey had this whole life that she could remember. People she had loved. People who had loved her. I didn't even know if such people existed for me. Was there anyone out there looking for me?

"Don't be," Aubrey said. "I'm over it. At least, if I tell myself that enough times it begins to feel true. What about you?"

How did I explain me? I didn't know, so I shrugged. "I have…" I sighed, what did I want to say? "All I remember is being in this facility," I told her. "Noah and Chouette, you can hear it in their voices that they care for each other. For the people here in this camp. Kattie and Hattie too, even as he yells at her, it's affectionately. I've never had anyone talk to me or about me like that… Or maybe I have, and I just don't remember them."

I looked over at her. She had finished her plate of food. Mine was still half full. Chouette had also located some pre-packaged cake bar thing, calling it our dessert. Aubrey was already ripping the packaging of hers open. She took a big bite and groaned in delight.

"Oh! I haven't had one of these since before mum died! They're always the first to go from the food stores at school."

I shook my head. Maybe food was her thing. Everyone had a thing, right? That thing that they loved above all else, that made them... them? She scrunched up the packaging and grinned.

"That was great!" I picked up mine and handed it to her. "Here," I said. "Have it."

Did I have a thing? That thing that had made me... Who? Who had I been before Girl? Before Juniper? I had no idea, and I had no idea of how to find out. Perhaps it wasn't worth looking back at whomever I was before the lab. Maybe I needed to look forward and discover who Juniper was.

Her eyes brightened. "Can I?"

"Sure," I said. "I'm full anyway." I was surprised to find that it was true. The meal had been a practical feast. I had always been careful not to eat too much at Alma's. I didn't want to put her out, especially since I didn't have much to offer her and now, I had gotten her in trouble to boot. And before Alma, food had always been sparse, and it had always been such a chore to consume.

She took it eagerly. "I don't remember the last time I had two!" She practically sung as she ripped the packet open. I just shook my head as I pushed my own plate away, content to watch her eat.

54

We walked back to the small room Chouette had offered us. She had apologised, asking if we minded sharing. It didn't bother me. It might be nice to have someone else in my space after so long. Aubrey herself had said she shared a room with three other girls back at school, so the idea of having only one person sounded fantastic.

The beds were simple, camp style cots with mismatched blankets and pillows covering them. My backpack was sitting where I had left it on one of the cots, while Aubrey's bag and rifle case were on the other. I went straight to my stuff and pulled out the clothes that Sebastian had found for me. It seemed like so long ago that he had gotten me out of that place. I wondered where he was right now. What he was doing. I pulled the case of eyes out and from behind me, heard Aubrey stop moving.

"Do they all do different things?" She asked.

I shrugged. "I guess so…" I wish that I still had the plain ones. The ones that were sight and sight alone. No killer abilities attached.

"Do you know what they do?" She asked, coming to stand beside me and look at the case as I unzipped it.

"No," I said. "I know one of them turns people to stone, but I don't remember which one it is. I never actually saw them…" I sat down on the bed beside the case and carefully took of the sunglasses that Noah had put on me back in Erihall. I had not taken them off for fear of hurting someone. But need to if I was going to try and sleep. Taking a deep breath for courage, I tenderly extracted one eye and then then other. I held them in my hand, weighing them. They were so small and yet, they did so much.

"But these pretty, ice blue ones turn people to ice," Aubrey said matter of factly. Were they pretty and blue? I didn't know. Like the stone ones, I had never seen them. "We should experiment with them. See what's what."

I nodded. "You're right, but I'd rather not call it 'experimenting' if you don't mind…" Then I thought about something else. "I don't want to hurt anyone though…"

"Right," Aubrey said with a nod. "No problem. Exploration then!" She said triumphantly, "And given what you did to the wall in the Park Room, I think we can test safely without hurting anyone…"

"Exploration," I agreed, wishing I felt as confident as she did. Something about being back in the darkness made me feel fragile and useless. I wasn't sure about anything; not like I had been only moments ago.

"You need some eye drops or something... They look really inflamed..." Aubrey said. I could feel the heat radiating off her body as she leaned in to get a better look.

"That's what Alma was going to do before everything happened," I said. "It's fine. I'll get used to it." I felt my fingers across the protective film, looking for the empty holes.

"Here, I'll do it," Aubrey said, her hand touching the one of mine holding the two little glass eyes.

I hesitated before turning my hand and letting them fall into her palm. "Thank you," I said softly.

I listened to the sounds of her fiddling with the case. Closing everything up. Then, she handed it to me. "Any time."

We went about our night-time routines as best as we could, trying not to get in each other's way. I changed my clothes, feeling my way through the items in my bag. It was different, learning the new space with someone there. I allowed Aubrey to escort me to a small privy and explain where everything was in relation to me and then back to our small room again.

As we felt ourselves ready to turn in for the night, we crawled into our respective beds. I took a moment, to let my fingers wander my empty eye sockets. Seeing had been so nice. It had felt like freedom to be able to see. Laying there, I found that I couldn't sleep, it wasn't half as silent as the facility had been. The forest around us made noise. People somewhere were talking, and I could have sworn that there was a small explosion too? There was also the sound of Aubrey breathing. A rhythmic, peaceful sound that comforted me.

"I'm sorry," I said suddenly. I had been feeling the need to say it for a while now and we were alone. Now was as good as time as any to apologise for getting her and her grandmother caught up in my mess, but the breathing from the other side of the room was even as though she was focusing heavily on maintaining her calm.

"Don't be," Aubrey said, though she sounded a little tense. "Gran knew what she was doing." I frowned and turned over in bed intending to look at her before I remembered that I couldn't see anything. I heard Aubrey turn over, the sheets rustling and the springs of the bed squeaking with her movement. "Get some sleep. Then we can get her back." Aubrey's breathing didn't even out, so I wondered if she had slept, even as I lay there trying to figure her out.

55

I was warm. The kind of warm you are when you're engulfed by another person. You're small and your mum or your dad pick you up and tell you that everything would be ok. They coo soothing words into your ear and because they are your world, you believe every single thing they say. It was a surprisingly familiar feeling to me. I could feel those arms, wrapped protectively around me. I was safe.

Cheering. Hugs. Slaps on the back of congratulations. Everything was right. Everything was good. Ushered out to do my best. Told that if I remembered my lessons everything would be ok, and I would win. No, not win, but that I would be fine. If I just remembered. Remembered what?

The lights are bright, and people everywhere are talking. Talking and looking at me. I am the centre of everyone's attention. I want to shy away. I want to run, but I can't. There's nowhere to go. There's the panel of judges? Examiners? Then someone steps up across from me. I can't see his face. We kneel. We bow to one another and then we fight. I show everyone who is watching, even as I wish they would all disappear, that I have remembered every lesson, even those I thought forgotten. He rolls away and stands. I haven't seen his face yet, but what does that matter, the next attack is coming. He has speed. I turn his momentum against him, and he goes flying across the mat towards the audience. Can't they see him coming towards them? He's going to fall right into the first row of gawkers, but they don't move. Then he crashes into them, and they shatter. Stone shards fall to the mat beneath our feet, and he stands back up, but I'm on top of him, moving to force his movements to my will. He comes at me, losing his footing and sliding under my attack.

I turn to face him. I can't think of the new debris surrounding us. The stone shards are cutting at my feet, but I don't feel them as I finally take a good look at my opponent. Older than me. Receding hairline, goatee. Short curly brown hair the colour of wet hay. The most stunning pair of blue eyes that I had ever seen. I knew this man. One side of his face was grey. Stark and solid. It was stone. Colliding with the audience earlier had chipped away at the stone and noticeable chunks were missing from his left side.

He picks something up from behind him. A stone head. The head of a woman who should never have been stone, and he tossed it to the floor.

"It's all your fault," his menacing voice laughs as I look around at the broken stone shards of the panel, the audience. Everyone who had been there before. Stone. Shattered. Silenced.

I woke up panting. I was no stranger to bad dreams or waking up to the complete and utter blackness that came upon opening my eyes, but that dream... It had been so much worse than ever before. The last time I'd had that dream of fighting the man, he'd been a faceless foe, no eyes, nose or mouth, his head rounded and bald. The audience too had been faceless, eventually walking away from me as I called after them, wanting something from them. Now, I couldn't remember what. All I could see were the stone shards.

I listened but didn't hear Aubrey breathing in the bed next to mine or her moving around our small room. Good, I had a moment to collect myself before having to face everyone else... And maybe to find my eyes... Though, I had no idea if I should put them in. What if put another dangerous one in? Obviously, there was more than one and there were so many in that case. How many different ways could I accidentally murder someone just by looking at them? I didn't want to know.

I put my hand to my heart. It was pounding. From the dream? From the exertion I thought I had put out? I sighed. No point in dwelling on bad dreams. There was nothing in dream land for me anyway. I needed to concentrate on finding Alma safely, but to do that, I would need to be able to see.

I reached out to the small table that sat between the two beds. The case was still there. How would I choose which eyes to use? I knew that they all looked different. I had seen them. I even knew that the ones that I had had in yesterday were a brilliant shade of light blue, like the sky on a sunny day. Aubrey had told me. I guessed the dark, stormy grey ones were the stone ones and I did not want them in... And that was assuming that I was right. Maybe they were something else. Maybe there was no connection between their appearance and what they did.

The curtain that covered our doorway screeched as it was pulled aside. I looked up at whoever it was, but my hand was feeling its way across the countless little eyes. A new heat filtered in with the curtain open. It must be daylight alright.

"Hey!" Aubrey beamed. "Everyone's waiting on us."

I looked in the direction of her voice. "Uh…" I said.

"Don't know which ones to wear?" She asked.

"Kinda," I agreed.

"It's like the weirdest accessory ever but hang on!" Aubrey sat down next to me. I felt her take the case. "Ooh, those yellow ones are pretty cool and oh my, what a shade of red!"

"Just something normal. Please," I begged. "I don't know what these do even."

Aubrey hummed in thought. "That's a point," she agreed. "Well, we know that the pretty blue ones turn people to ice... Do you know any others?"

I shook my head. "I lost the plain ones back at the clinic, but there has to be something in there that doesn't kill people..."

"These cat eye ones a pretty cool!" I nodded. I had seen them before. "Ooh, ooh! What about the purple swirly ones?"

"Purple swirly ones?" I asked. She went on to explain in excruciating detail the swirl and the shades of purple to black that were in the iris of the eye. "Anything that looks a little more normal and unlikely to kill anyone?" I asked.

"Well, I don't know how to determine their level of deadliness," she admitted, "but in terms of normal looking... Hmmmm... These green ones look really normal."

56

After I'd dressed, put my eyes in - normal looking as they were, Aubrey had failed to mention that they were fluro green, not a regular eye green - and reassured Aubrey that yes, despite the pain when I put the eyes in, I was alright, we finally made it out of our room. She practically dragged me to the big living area Chouette and Noah had shown us to the night before to introduce us to Emrys, Kattie and Hattie.

"Good. You're here," Noah said as soon as we entered.

Unlike the night before, the room was full. With Noah and Chouette, I counted thirteen people. All teenagers. A girl with missing eyes, a boy with some form of mechanical gadgetry set in front of… or in place of, his eyes. Everyone had oddly coloured eyes too and they were all looking at us.

A large black man walked over to us. I watched him. He was older than us, maybe not by much, but definitely older, early twenties maybe? He then stopped maybe two feet away, crossed his arms over his chest and stared at us. After a moment he looked over his shoulder at Noah.

"I thought you said that they would be useful." It was not a question. It was a statement.

"They are Cassias," Noah said.

"Come on!" A skinny girl said coming over and wrapping her arm around the big man. She was extremely pale, almost as white as paper. Her eyes were small and ice blue, and her eyebrows were just as white as her skin. "Just look at 'em, Cash!" She wore a hat atop her smooth, bald head and smiled at me with a crooked smile. Oddly though, I recognised her voice but couldn't place it.

"Get off'a me girl!" Cassias barked trying to elbow her away from him. "Ya know I can't stand that headlessness of yours."

She giggled in delight, and I realised that it was the same giggle I had heard the night before when Kattie was having his coat stolen. "Hattie?" I asked in surprise.

She looked at me in surprise. "Know any other invisible girls?" she asked.

I shook my head. "No…" I replied. "But… I can see you…"

"No way!" Kattie said, standing up from where he'd been sprawled on a couch. "Ain't nobody around here who can see Hattie but me." So, I started to describe Hattie's crooked smile and her pale blue eyes. They were so pale that it was as though I could see the blood vessels. Looking closer, I noticed that she wasn't just pale she and her skin was almost translucent, allowing blood veins to be clearly seen. There was something different about and the more I looked the more I noticed. "What's her hair like?" Kattie pressed, obviously not believing me. Hattie, bless her, took her hat off, and did a little spin as though she was showing off.

I shrugged. "She's bald, but her eyebrows are white… well, that's not right… They're almost translucent."

"Hmph," Cassias said from where he still stood. He glanced at me out of the corner of his eye, trying to ignore me, but I could see him furtively looking, so maybe I had intrigued him? "So, she can see Hattie… So what? And what about the other one?"

Hattie in turn, came over and wrapped an arm around both me and Aubrey. "She can see me and that's cool with me…" Then she trailed off, "You couldn't see me last night, right?"

I shook my head. "No," I said simply.

Hattie turned to Aubrey. "Can you see me?"

"Hat floating in thin air," Aubrey replied. Aubrey then turned to Cassias. "And as for you. Your mate Noah is only alive cause of me and Juniper. I'll have you know that I have won the last three years marksmanship competitions for my school region."

Cassias harrumphed again. "And what did you do that was so fantastic? Seeing invisible ain't all that useful unless you want to stop Hattie from snooping in your stuff!"

I took a chance. I looked Cassias in the eyes. Nothing happened. Ok, cool. Maybe seeing invisible was all this set could do. I could live with that. I looked at Aubrey. "Will you mark it down?" I asked her.

She nodded and pulled out a little notebook. We had decided to make notes on what eyes did what. It seemed like a good idea. We had noted down that the light blue ones did ice and noted that we suspected the grey ones were the stone ones that they had tried on me back at the facility.

"Lime Green ones, see invisible," she murmured as she wrote.

"Hmmmm," Hattie said looking from me to Aubrey and back again. "So, you're saying that you can change your eyes, and they all do different things?"

I nodded slowly, but it was Noah who spoke. "Cassias, to answer your question, Juniper is one of us. An experiment of Sage's. Hattie..." Then he paused. "How much can I say?"

I shrugged. "Honestly, you know about as much as I do."

Hattie, as enthusiastic as ever from what I had seen squeezed us together. "I think it's mega cool!"

"The situation is this," Noah said stepping forward to force the groups attention towards him. "Aubrey's grandmother was abducted from the eye clinic she works in."

A girl scoffed from where she was sitting on the pool table. "And since when do we help those traitorous docs?"

"Since that Doctor had taken Juniper in and got taken after someone outed her as being the one protecting her," Noah told the girl. "Aubrey's assistance was also needed when we escaped. So we, and by we, I mean Chouette and myself agreed to help them get the Doc back."

57

Later when I went looking, Noah was missing and Chouette had dragged Aubrey away to have another look at her rifle and to see what kind of ammo they had. The talk was very exuberant really. Unfortunately, most of the others had followed Cassias out to the courtyard of the camp. Emrys had vanished again, but apparently that was normal according to Hattie who had decided, since I could see her, she would follow me around. At least she was clothed currently. Apparently, she found it funny to wander around the camp, completely invisible by removing all her clothes. She would jump out at people, not only terrifying them, but also making them extremely uncomfortable.

"Oooh!" Hattie breathed when we walked onto the field. Cassias was standing there, legs spread, arms crossed. A girl was standing beside him. I had seen her earlier but didn't know her name. We were maybe the same age, and she wore an eye patch over her right eye. Her thin lips were pursed in a line, and she was mimicking Cassias's stance. "That's Sadie."

"And…?" I asked.

"Well…. Sadie's like our best fighter. Except for Noah of course. She's skilled in hand-to-hand stuff and a lot of weapons too. She also has this amazing thing she can do with her eye and ultimate control over it!" Hattie explained, a little too enthusiastically in my opinion, but oh well. "I think Cassias is gonna test ya something crazy… So, what's your superpower?"

I just stared at her. Superpower? How was I supposed to know that? I didn't even know my own name or anything about myself. "I…" I shrugged. "I don't know…" I looked around at everyone that had gathered there.

"So," Cassias said as I approached him. "What can you do?" Oh great. That question again. And Hattie had vanished to go sit with Kattie. I was on my own.

I bit my lip. Sure, I could change my eyes. Change how I looked and what the little glass things were able to do, but I had no control over them. I had no idea what most of them could do. But what the hell, I opened the case that I had gone to my room to collect, and I let them see all of the different eyes.

"Cool, right?" I heard Hattie ask loudly from the side. The other on lookers, glanced from where her hat was bobbling next to them, to me. "According to Aubrey and Juniper, each set does something different."

Kattie rolled his own eyes.

"Hmph," Cassias grumped as he stared at the collection. "But I heard that you knew nothing about them. You got lucky with that attack. Right?" He was right. It had been pure and utter luck that Aubrey and I had found one that could attack and that I had not killed Aubrey and Noah by accident. Still, if we had picked these ones that I had in today, we all would have been dead. "You're of no use to us if you have no control over your abilities, but Sadie will work with you on that later. Obviously, you're not lethal to us when you have certain ones in. So, I'll ask again. What else can you do?"

And there we were. Back to that infernal question. What could I do? Of what use was I to these people? My actions when I had first met Noah. They indicated some sort of training in something and my dream the night before seemed to reinforce that idea. What was it though? What was lurking under my memories that I couldn't see right now?

"I can fight," I said. In the dream, I had felt nervous yes, but confident in my skills and that reminder that all I needed to do was remember still lingered in the back of my mind. Remember what?

Cassias looked unimpressed though. "Uh huh." He seemed to be a master of the 'sounds of disapproval' method of communication. "Then fight," He nodded to the girl beside him. She grinned and launched herself at me. Sadie, the group's best fighter, Hattie had said. Well, crap.

"Sadie! Sadie! Sadie!" The gathered group chorused. Oh, a fan favourite to boot. Just my luck. "Sadie, the cleaning lady!" if that wasn't the weirdest moniker ever?

The girl stepped forward. She grinned at me, and it looked menacing with that patch over her eye. Oh... Flippidies... I was so screwed... I just had to remember the dream. Remember what I had done back at the clinic with Noah. My body obviously knew something. I had learned something somewhere. I moved, trying to get off the line of attack, but I must have moved too soon because she followed me, and a punch connected with my abdomen.

It was painful, but nothing like Stinky and Scratchy. They had loved to brutalize me whenever I had stepped out of line. Still, I could not get a hit in on the girl. That movement that had come to me when I had first met Noah. It failed me. The moves, the feelings, the knowledge I had felt in my dream. It failed me.

As I lay on my back, the girl, Sadie above me, displaying her killing blow, I heard one of the others call out. "She wiped the floor with you, new girl!" Oh, so that was where the nickname came from.

"I'm a gonna go see the other one shoot. Maybe there's something to actually witness there," a big guy said standing up. Several others followed him away from the seating area in the courtyard.

"Here," Sadie said, leaning over and offering me a hand. I took it. "You're still breathing and that's more than some of them," she said with a grin. "Also, Noah told me that you haven't any memory of your past life. That maybe you don't know what you know."

"And," Another girl said coming up to stand beside Sadie. "Cash, he just doesn't like nobody." She stuck her hand out to me. "Vera."

"Juniper," I replied, taking her hand.

58

People were buzzing with excitement. Unlike me, Aubrey had impressed an older girl named Cora, apparently the best shot in the camp. Everyone could fight a little, Vera and Sadie had explained to me, but some had taken to the skillset better than others. I watch Aubrey bask in her own glory, glad that people were accepting her. If they did, it would be easier to have these people help us find Alma.

I was exhausted though. After the beating from Sadie, Cassias had put me through my paces. Teaching me how to move. How to hit. How to take a hit. How to fall. I hurt, everywhere. I hurt in places that I did not know a person could hurt. Like, why did it feel like the soles of my feet were on fire? And why was it hurting to breathe? While I never complained, Cassias was hard to impress. I didn't think I ever would, especially after I tried to land a few punches on him.

"Ain't ever gonna rescue anyone like that," Cassias grunted at me. I wanted to tell him that I knew that, but I was too tired to argue. I could take almost anything Cassias threw at me. Really, I could. Stinky and Scratchy had well prepared me for such training.

"They're something else, aren't they?" Aubrey asked as she sat down across from me, a plate of food in hand.

I nodded. Then stopped. It hurt too much to even nod. "Yeah, they are."

"You know, Minnie, she grows all the food here that isn't hunted and she's completely blind and Harvey, the really tall dark kid over there by the food. He's the cook… And he heats everything with his eyes, cause they heat things up like you froze those guys the other day."

I looked over at the boy. I had seen him around, he always wore these strange dark glasses. I guess they kept his eyes in check. "Food's good," I told her.

"Yeah, those two have some serious talent. I mean, this is way better than what we got at school, and they hired actual chefs," Aubrey agreed, digging into what I now noticed was a seriously oversized plate. How obsessed was this girl with food?

"Juniper, Aubrey."

We both looked up from our food to find Noah standing behind me. "Hey," I said. I had not seen him since that morning. Him or Chouette really, but I knew that Chouette had been with Aubrey most of the day.

"What's up?" Aubrey asked him.

"We uh," Noah said sinking down to sit on the bench beside me. He looked at me almost nervously. "We wanted to uhh, maybe go through that case of yours. See what they all do and maybe document everything," he said. "Umm, you know…"

I nodded. I knew exactly what he meant. "Ok," I said, and I didn't see the relief I had expected. Instead, I was sure he still looked like he dreaded it.

"We've already started that!" Aubrey cut in. She dug into her pocket and extracted the notebook. "The lime green ones allow her to see Hattie and those ice blue ones turned the Sage Security guys to ice. We also know that there's at least one set that turns people to stone, though we don't know which ones. I'm betting on the dark grey ones."

As Aubrey rambled, I looked around at the wider group though, eating, chatting, enjoying themselves. Some were looking over at us, maybe trying to get an idea as to what we were talking about.

"We can do that, sure. Just… Not like the training… I don't want everyone there."

He nodded. "Good. I was thinking just you and me."

"You don't want any backup? I have no idea what they do. I..." Shattering people came to mind, and I saw that guard at the facility fall and break into millions of tiny pieces. "I..." I couldn't find the words to explain what I was trying to say. The nightmare had said it though. I was afraid of hurting these people.

Noah shook his head. "I'll be fine." He reassured me. "I'm going to grab some food, then we can go after we've both eaten." I nodded and watched him walk off to get his own food.

"You ok?"

I looked back at Aubrey and nodded. "Yeah. Fine."

59

Noah followed me back to my room. We left the living area in silence. He seemed like he wanted to say something but hadn't gathered the courage yet. I didn't know and I didn't want to push him. Still, at the door to the small room where Aubrey and I had taken up residence, he said nothing.

"I'll just go get them," I said in a near whisper, not entirely sure why I was whispering, but feeling as though speaking would be uncouth or even barbaric. The noise would shatter whatever was settling between us.

He nodded and I brushed the hanging cloth and beads out of the way. There were no real doors around here, but the setup provided privacy and for me, a sense that I could never be locked in. I liked that. Noah followed me in though.

"About yesterday," he said hesitantly. Had it really only been yesterday that I had met him?

"What about yesterday?" I asked.

He frowned and ran a hand through his hair. Nervous reaction? "What happens when you put the new ones in," he elaborated. "Is that every time?" I nodded. "Is it ever different? Like less with different ones?"

"No," I said picking up the case. "To date, every set I've had in have caused that reaction."

"How many times?" He asked, his voice low. I looked at him confused. Was he concerned about me?

I thought. The time at the facility... Where I had killed those people with the stone eyes... When Sebastian helped me to escape and gave me the plain sight eyes. I had worn them until my eyes bled. Not something I could apparently do. Then the ice ones at Alma's house and this morning. I relayed all that back to him. "Three... four..." I finally said. "Four times that I know about."

"You avoided it because of the pain?" he asked, crossing his arms over his chest and leaning against the doorjamb like he was trying to look as though he wasn't affected by our conversation. He wasn't, was he?

I shrugged. "That... But more because I just wanted to be normal... I didn't want Alma to think less of me because I was an Eyeless. It's apparently a huge social thing in Erihall..." I held the case of eyes close to my chest. "I also really dislike being so god damned useless," I muttered.

"Not useless, you just don't know how to operate blind," Noah corrected. "Minnie... She's completely blind. An Eyeless, but she tends our garden, plants and grows and trims and harvests everything there. She knows every single one of her plants, especially when there's something wrong with one of them. Something about the way they feel and smell... and if you believe her, the way they talk to her. I don't know about that though. Minnie's a little..." he shrugged. "She's unique. She also helps in the kitchen. Blind is not useless, you've just got to know your space."

Like I had back at the lab. I could live within my room. I had known where everything was. Out here, in the world, everything was just so big and wide and unpredictable. I stood there, the case of eyes held against me as I thought about his words. He wasn't wrong, but I had no idea what I would do if I left sightless again.

"Come on," he said after a moment. He pushed off the wall, standing straight, then held out a hand to me. "Let's go somewhere where no one will bother us."

That somewhere where no one would bother us turned out to be a small private courtyard that led out from Noah's room and a couple of others. A seniority perk or something. It was primarily made from the same stonework that made up the rest of the old base,

"We'll meet here, every night after dinner until we've been through them all," Noah said as we entered the space. "Is that alright with you?" On the far side of courtyard was an archery target. It was ratty and old, looking as though it had been scorched and had many a knife thrown at it. What did they get up to in their free time? Someone had draped second target over it, one of those paper ones with a human shape on it that the shows said the military worked with in training. It too looked as though it had been shot at, burnt, frozen, and damaged in ways I could not even begin to identify.

Noah caught me eying the target. "We bring everyone here in the beginning. We need to know what their abilities are or teach them to control it. Find out what allows them to live the most normal life possible," Noah explained.

It all seemed sensible and well thought out. "But what stops them from hurting you or whoever else is working with them?" I asked, ripping my eyes away from the disturbing sight of the target and looking back at him.

"You'll see," Noah said confidently. He led me over to a bench that was relatively clean. We sat and he waited for me. I held the case of eyes tight against my chest, trepidation making me second guess. Did I really want to do this? Noah sat patiently beside me, not saying a word, as though knowing that there were no right words for this moment. From his hesitant conversation in my room, I knew that he was no eager to ask me to do this either. With a sigh, I put the case down between us. My hands rested on it for a moment as Noah looked down at the case. With a reassuring smile from him, I opened it.

"Wow…" Noah whispered, leaning in to get a better look at the rows and rows of eyes, each pair with their startling and unique designs. He hadn't had a chance to properly see it back at Alma's, what with the gunmen trying to get into the room. The sight was impressive, even I could admit to that. Honestly, it was also pretty creepy, all those eyes looking back at you, just staring at you. "And they all do something…"

"That's what I was told."

"When I was there, I heard talk that they wanted something like this. A person with unlimited capabilities, that this was the ultimate goal of their research…" Noah shook his head in awe. "But… It never worked… Minnie is proof of that… Or at least that's what we thought."

"Apparently there was something about me…" I said, thinking back to snippets of conversation I'd overheard when I'd been nothing but a thing for Sage and his researchers to poke and prod at. "My genes or something that made it work, but it's not perfect."

"Nothing ever is… But if they're this close, we have to stop them," Noah said, "imagine what an entire army of people with this ability could do to the continent."

"Is that why you're going to help us get Alma back?"

"It doesn't diverge from our plans. Sage's people are the ones who took your friend, and they're the ones we're looking to stop. We can help each other." Noah agreed. "Now, which ones shall we try first?"

I shrugged and pointed to the first ones sitting in the case beside the empty spot for the plain eyes. "Start at the beginning, I guess."

"Sounds like a solid plan," he agreed and then sat there, waiting for something. I stared at him, then realised he was waiting for me to do something.

"Right…" I laughed nervously and reached up to my eyes to remove the ones I had in. Noah said nothing as I engaged in the process. "Can you open the compartment for them?" I asked once my world was entirely black again. Every sound seemed to become crisper, and I was conscious of Noah beside me. He must have done so, because he then guided my hand to the compartment where I placed the two eyes. Maybe he read my mind because I felt him place another one in my hand. It was cold and dry compared to the one had just put away. "What's the colour?" I asked.

"Red. Very, very red," Noah said as I put the first one in. "Probably some fire type thing like Harvey."

"Is it true? I asked, cradling the second eye in my hand. "Does he cook the food like that?"

Noah burst out laughing. "Where did you hear that?"

"Aubrey."

"Oh god, they must be still telling that to all the new arrivals," he said while gasping for breath. "It happened once. We had no fuel for the stoves, so yeah, he did… Burnt everything so bad we practically ate charcoal all night. Oh, you should have heard Minnie go off at him for ruining her vegetables… But no, he doesn't cook the food with his eyes."

I nodded. A little more satisfied with the cooking arrangement. I slid the second eye into the socket and felt the pain engulf my head, flowing from my eyes. My body seized in response to the blinding pain, and I gripped at the bench, not wanting to fall from it.

"Juniper!" He cried. I could hear the panic in his voice. Not like the absolute fear I had heard back at Alma's when I'd collapsed. Maybe the talk had helped with that, but I felt him reach out and take my hand, giving me a comforting squeeze as waves of pain wracked my body.

"I'm ok," I managed with a strangled breath. I took three, maybe four deep breaths, trying to get through the wave of pain. "Ok," I said when I had a grip on myself, and my eyes were tightly closed… "Now what?"

"Are you sure?" he breathed out, concern radiating off every word. I nodded slowly, remembering how much that could hurt. I heard him huff as though he didn't believe me, but he didn't argue. "Remember where the target is?" He asked. "Look there and see what happens."

Okie dokie. Look at the target and try not to kill anyone. I could do that right? Couldn't I? I still held my eyes tightly shut. The images of shattering stone men playing out before me.

"Juniper?" Noah asked. "You have to open your eyes."

"Yeah. Yeah," I responded, still half trapped in my thoughts.

I took a deep breath and opened my eyes. I could see again, but before I could enjoy that, the target at the other end of the courtyard burst into flames. There was nothing exciting like a line of fire going towards it. The target just erupted, almost as though it had self-combusted. But it hadn't.

Neither did the trees beside it which caught fire… From the burning target? From me? I didn't know.

I clamped my eyes back shut before anything else burst into flames. Panic filled me. Who would I hurt this time? Visions of men turning to stone flashed before me. Suddenly, I reached my hands for my eyes, ready to dig my fingers in and rip the cursed things out. As soon as my lids opened, I felt the heat on my hands. I gasped, but pushed through it, I needed them out before I hurt someone. and cried out. I scratched at my face, even as my hands seemed to burn.

"Juniper!" Noah grabbed me, roughly pulling my hands away from my face. "Juni! Stop it!" I clammed my eyes back shut even as my hands stung. I sobbed in frustration. How was I going to get them out?

"Noah?" I cried, fear engulfed me. If I couldn't even get them out, how could anyone else? I was going to kill them. I was going to kill them all!

"Look at me!" Noah said quietly, my wrists held tightly in his own hands, as to not touch the burns.

"No!" I whimpered, shutting my eyes tightly.

"Juniper, look at me!" Noah ordered, his voice more assertive than before.

I shook my head, raising my hands to also block my eyes. "No. No. No. I won't hurt you!"

The smoke of the fire was coming closer, and I could feel the heat of it against my skin. "Look at me, Juniper," Noah ordered, his hands on mine, trying to pull them away from my face. "You can't hurt me! Open your eyes!"

"Noah? Juniper?" A voice called from one of the rooms. Chouette came out from one of the doors and stared.

"Get that fire put out," Noah ordered her, still struggling with me. I could not look at him though. I would char him like barbeque if I did. I couldn't do that.

"Juniper, look at him," Chouette said. "It's ok. Just look at him," then she vanished back into the room she had come out of. She said it so confidently, so calmly, that it took me by surprise. I let Noah take my hands. A moment of weakness maybe.

"Look at me," Noah said softly. "Trust me. It's the only way to get them back out, right?"

I opened my eyes. A small bush just behind him erupted into flames, but when my eyes met his, it all stopped. No more fire. Well, except for those that were already blazing around us. Noah's eyes were white. Not the kind of white you got when your eyes were wide with fear. His eyes were all white. No iris. No pupil. Just white and I felt nothing. Nothing happened when I looked at him.

"Huh?"

He gave a weak smile. "My power…" He said stiffly. "I cancel others… Nothing works on me."

"Your eyes," I said. "They're…"

He nodded. "I wear contact lenses most of time," he held the tiny discs up in his hand. When had he taken those out? "This just looks a little bit on the creepy side." He gave a self-deprecating laugh and continued to stare into my eyes.

"Come on. We verified the fact that these are all kinds of fiery trouble. Let's take them out, huh?" He suggested.

Chouette returned with a large, dark boy.

"Again?" He groaned. "How many times are you guys gonna toast this courtyard?"

"Stop grousing and put it out," Chouette said, throwing a bucket of water over the bush behind Noah. It sizzled and smoked. I tried to lift my hands to remove the eyes, but when I did, I saw the reddened flesh that was starting to blister. I tried to flex my fingers but gasped in pain.

"I'll get the med kit," Chouette announced, before disappearing.

Noah winced, as though seeing me in pain hurt him, "Do you trust me?" What a daft question, of course I trusted him. I nodded. He motioned towards my face. "May I?" I nodded again, afraid to speak in case I broke down in wailing sobs once more. Ever so gently, he leaned forward, his calming gaze always on mine and carefully removed one eye and then then the next, leaving me in the darkness once again.

61

It was full speed ahead on Ms Reavis's project and Sebastion felt his stomach roil every time it was brought up. He needed to get his plan operational before this thing could happen. Where was she? There had been no rumoured sight of her in days, and he was beginning to wonder if she wasn't really dead after all.

No, he couldn't allow himself to think like that. She had to be out there, she had to still be alive, biding her time until... Until what? What if she never came back? Well, Sage had thought of that, hadn't he? That's why that old woman the girl had been seen with was being held, wasn't it? They expected the girl to come back for her.

Sebastian thought she would. Maybe he could use that to his advantage.

For now, all he could do was watch and learn. He looked down at the files in his hands, shuffling them to look once more at the picture of the small, blond boy and the age progressions he'd worked out on the computer. It was suspected that this boy was part of a group of renegades that often raided laboratories, liberating the test subjects and supplies. That was who he had hoped the girl had found. The boy who could cancel out all the others. With the girl and that boy, Sebastian believed he might just have what he needed to stop this whole plan from going ahead and ruining the country further. Maybe the renegade group would even help him?

"Sebastian, where are those numbers on the potential applicants?" Sage asked.

Sebastian slipped the pictures of the boy back into the sheaf of papers and lifted another. "Here, in Erihall alone we're likely to get nearly two hundred, assuming everyone eligible actually applies. They'll range from kindergarten to college aged."

Sage took the papers and skimmed over them. "Good, start putting together the names and contact details so that we can start sending out the invites as soon as the project is announced."

Sebastian nodded. "That's already happening with the older potential candidates, but the younger candidates are proving more difficult to gather information on. The clinics are being very closed lipped, especially since that raid and the disappearance of that doctor."

Sage didn't give a reaction., just nodded along to his words. "Well, keep working on them. Let it slip that something exciting is happening. Whoever we don't get now, will likely come to us after the announcement."

"How are plans for the fair going?" Sebastian asked.

"Well, everything should be ready for the end of next week."

The plan was to announce the new scheme at a huge fair in Erihall. Making the people happy with free food, games, and entertainment. Lulling them into a false sense of security more like it. Sebastian had yet to see much of the planning and had been kept busy with accumulating lists of potential candidates.

"We will turn the tide of this war," Sage assured him. "No one will ever doubt the might of Eriden ever again, especially not those Shiuran bastards."

Sebastian frowned. The longer this went on, the more fervour Sage used to talk of the war and getting one up on the Shiurans. He thought back to the diaries he'd found. Dom. He'd still not been able to figure out who Dom was., the diaries made him seem like he was Sage's brother, making him Sebastian's uncle, but he had never heard of him before. He'd also not been able to figure out where he was, what was wrong with him or what it was he had to do with the war between Eriden and Shiura. Why did Sage care so much? It couldn't only be because of the contract with the Eridenti military.

"Right," he said, plastering a smile on his face as though he approved of the sentiment. "Let's get this sorted for once and for all." And Sebastian needed to continue doing his own research to discover more about Sage's past.

62

We tested another two before I agreed to stop for the night. Noah was insistent and despite the fact that I was deathly tired, but didn't want to drag this experimentation... Exploration, out. The sooner we got through them all, the sooner we could stop altogether. My limbs felt like lead, as though the mere effort of acknowledging their existence was exhausting, let alone trying to move them and go somewhere, like my room or something.

The purple swirly ones that had intrigued Aubrey earlier that morning had turned out to hypnosis and Chouette had thought it an absolute hoot when I made the boy, apparently named Elijah, dance like a chicken for her. After coming out of it, he had sworn that we would all get our own, then stomped off in a fit, also swearing that he would never help Chouette with anything she ever asked him in the future.

Maybe if I just sat there a while longer, I would be able to move. I could wait, sit there all night if I had to.

"Are you ok?" Noah asked in a low voice.

I wanted to answer him and thought I opened my mouth to say that I was fine, but the look of concern that crossed his face as the incomprehensible garble came out had me worried. Did I look that bad?

"Chouette!" Noah called, his voice trembling slightly in what I could only assume was fear as he kept his eyes on me, only fleetingly looking in the direction of Chouette's room to see if the other girl was coming.

"Juniper?" he asked, giving me a little shake. Except it wasn't my attention that had wandered. I could see him. I could hear him, I just couldn't... move, not even enough to speak. The last pair we'd tried, ones with fluorescent green irises hadn't seemed to do anything that we could notice, so we left them listed with a question mark. I still had them in, being unable to take them out. They had the same pain effect, so we were certain that they did do something, but nothing we had done in the courtyard had given us any clue as to what their ability might be.

Slowly, I blinked up at Noah, my head tilting slightly, even as I slumped back against the wall.

"Damn it, I knew we should have stopped at the last one," he said through critted teeth. "Chouette!" he shouted again.

Chouette shoved the heavy door to her room aside and pulled a heavy, thick coat over herself as she stepped out.

"What?" she asked, swiping at her eyes. She blinked owlishly at us, trying to comprehend what she was seeing. "What are you still doing out here?" Then she caught sight of me. "Juniper!" she gasped. She stormed over to us, crouching down before me and taking my hand in hers. It was limp and almost a dead weight in her grasp. "What did you do?" she said accusingly to Noah. "Why didn't you stop after the last ones?"

"She didn't want to!" Noah cried, waving his arms almost comically in my direction.

"What do these do?" she asked, looking at my bright green eyes.

"We don't know," Noah admitted, "but I didn't want to take them out on her."

Chouette shook her head, then turned her attention back to me. She squeezed my hand, and I managed a small smile at her. "You have got to know when to say no," she said firmly. "Ok, let's get you out of here. I'm guessing you can't walk."

"Don't..." I started, surprised that words had emerged from my mouth.

"Don't what?" Chouette asked.

"Be too..." I managed slowly, "Hard..." Then I shifted my eyes so that I indicated where Noah stood.

"I'll be hard on him if I want. He's supposed to be the leader around here. When he says stop, you stop. You don't wheedle your way into a near death like state because you feel like it."

Even sighing was too much effort and nodding seemed like a dangerous idea, what if I couldn't pick my head back up again? So, I just sat there and let her continue to tell me off for not speaking up sooner. It had only been one more after the hypnosis ones and it had crept in slowly. Noah and I had talked, written our observations or lack of observations down and it had been as we'd discussed what to do next, that my limbs had filled with lead, my words had slurred, and I could no longer move.

"Not..." I tried again as Chouette turned her ire on Noah once more. "His... fault..."

"I'll be the judge of that," Chouette stated.

In the end, Chouette ordered Noah to help me up, but my legs failed to work, and he was forced to carry me through to Chouette's room. Neither thought it would be a good idea to send me back to my own room, so I was settled onto the bed and Chouette waved Noah out before slamming the door shut and turning her attention back to me. She carefully unlaced my shoes before shifting me so that I lay on the bed completely. She was surprisingly strong for her diminutive stature. Then, she pulled the blankets over me and told me to get some sleep.

And that if I ever exceeded my limit again, it would be her I had to deal with.

I was out of the way and behind Elijah before he knew what had happened. Vera appeared to my left, but she missed me. In my haste though, I missed Sadie appearing before me and her wooden knife connected with my stomach.

Yes, Cassias had decided I was too hopeless to train with live weapons, so he had insisted that everyone use the training ones. Probably a good thing, as Sadie would have gutted me where I stood with that last attack.

"Again."

I had realised pretty quickly that there was no pleasing Cassias. He was gruff and monosyllabic with all his words. He never showed joy or any sign of happiness.

I reset my stance, ready to go again. I didn't really want to, but that was the only way I was going to get better.

"This time," Sadie said. "Fight us, don't just avoid us."

"But you all have knives," I complained. It did not seem fair that I was going unarmed up against the three of them.

Vera laughed. "Disarm us then," she said it though it was as easy as pie. I was nowhere near good enough to disarm the likes of them.

"Start," Cassias ordered. His tone implying that we talked too much.

Sadie came at me first. And quite frankly she still terrified me, so I avoided her, quickly turning my attention to Vera. She tried to stab me in the neck, bringing her wooden knife down from in high.

I don't know why I did it, but I stepped forward, into her space, interrupting the attack. I used one arm to block her attack, while the other went for her face. Surprise widened her eyes before she realised that she should be the one moving now. Her head turned away just in time to stop me from sticking my fingers in her eyes. Unintentionally, of course. Then, I stepped even further into her space, and she went flying. The feeling was exhilarating. It had to have been pure luck, but I got the best of one of them.

Elijah did not let me enjoy the moment though. He was trying for the same surprise shot to my belly that Sadie had succeeded with before. I would not fall for it again. *Away from the line of attack*, the voice rang in my ears again. Sure, Sadie had said it too in practice, but this was something I could not place, just like that day at the clinic with Noah. Who was it that I kept hearing?

Off the line. Not too far though. Don't overturn. His attack passed me by, but I was behind him now. My fingers connected with the tops of his shoulders, and I stopped his forward momentum. The sudden stop challenged his balance and the slightest amount of pressure from me as I stepped backwards pulled him over into the gap where I had been standing.

"You have got to be kidding me!" Elijah cried from the ground, but I had no time for him because Sadie was still standing. I had only avoided her in the beginning.

I turned to face her, and she beamed in delight. Then she charged. I waited. Timing is your friend. *With the right timing you don't need strength.* That voice again. With the right timing, you have full control over them. I fell to my knees and curled myself into a ball. Sadie was on-top of me already, unable to stop. She collided with my side and went sprawling over the top of me. Then, apparently catching herself, she rolled until she was on her feet again facing me.

A bell rang. "Food," Elijah called out, jumping up from where I'd left him sprawled on the training ground. Was everyone obsessed with food around here?

Cassias looked ready to object, but Sadie walked over to his side and dropped her training weapon into the bucket by his feet. "Let's go eat," she announced.

"Go," Cassias finally said as Vera dropped her own in the bucket.

I grabbed my over shirt from where I had dropped it. I had been forced to take it off and train in my tank top when it had become too hot. I slipped it on.

"Not bad at all new girl," Elijah said, collecting his own belongings. "You're moving like a natural now."

I shook my head in disagreement. "Nothing like that. Just good teachers."

"It's only been a few days. No one is that good a teacher or that good a student. You're good. You're actually really good."

"I got lucky today," I said as we walked towards the living area where Harvey and Minnie would be setting out lunch. "You said so yourself. No one is that good a student."

I took a seat at the table by myself and relished the peace. The others were still ambling around camp, finishing morning chores or cleaning up after training. After spending a seemingly unending number of days alone in my room at the laboratory, being constantly surrounded by people was surprisingly exhausting. I'd had no idea how tiring it was being around so many people. I was sure that all the physical training played into that as well, but more than the rigorous training schedule, it was the people. Making nice, engaging in conversation with them, reading body language and tone and remembering your own. There was always something to remember when in a room full of people.

I caught sight of Noah talking with Cassias and Sadie. It seemed intense. I wondered what it was about and hoped that they weren't going to go back on their promise to help Alma.

"If Sadie's not careful, she's gonna lose her title." I jumped in my seat, almost falling from it as I looked around for the speaker.

Hattie stood behind me not wearing anything. "Put some clothes on!" I hissed, looking away.

"Why?" She asked. "No one can even see me."

"I can see you. Kattie can see you."

She shrugged nonchalantly. "Kattie and I been together forever and ever."

I shook my head. "Seriously Hattie." I slipped forward in my seat and shrugged my over shirt back off again and handed it to her. "Put it on." She pouted but did as I asked. I adjusted the straps on my tank top and rubbed my shoulders. It was getting chilly in the dining room, and I instantly regretted handing the garment over as goosebumps started to appear on my arms. I rubbed at them, trying to warm myself.

"Hattie!" Harvey growled seeing my floating shirt hovering behind me. "How many times have I got to tell ya? No clothes. No food."

She completed buttoning up my shirt, before looking up at him with wide, pleading eyes what could only be described as puppy dog. "I'm clothed."

"Barely," he muttered, walking past us with a tray of empty dishes. "And only cause Juniper was nice enough to freeze her own ass off and part with her own clothing."

I shrugged at Harvey as he glanced at me. Hattie continued to pout as I looked back over to where I had seen Noah. He was still standing where I had last seen him, but Cassias and Sadie had disappeared. He was now standing there, seemingly watching me. When he caught me looking at him, he looked away. I did the same.

"You and Noah are sure spending a lot of time together," Hattie ventured, resting her chin on my shoulder to see him.

"We're testing all the eyes," I said, turning so that she had to move. She stumbled slightly.

"Oh..." Hattie seemed disappointed, as though she'd been after something else. I had no idea what though.

I looked over at her, a thought occurring to me. If Noah's ability was to cancel out other abilities... Why wasn't Hattie visible when he was around. Or was it simpler than that? "Can he see you?" I asked.

"Who Noah? Nah," she said, sliding into the chair beside me.

"Not even..." I asked, motioning to my own eyes but didn't want to specify what I meant in case she didn't know what his ability was, but referring to his contact lenses all the same.

She giggled, then shook her head. "Yeah, not even then." She said. "But Kattie can't see me when he's around and has them out." I thought that that would have to be a relief for Kattie, because Hattie's antics would have to be exhausting. She was so bright and exuberant, so unashamed of anything she did that I could only imagine having to be her keeper. It was hard enough keeping myself.

I almost missed him when I entered the little courtyard. Noah was sitting on the floor by the door to his room not on the bench where we usually worked, when I arrived.

"Hey," I said softly, not sure if I should disturb him.

"Hey," he said looking up at me. Then he patted the floor beside him. "Have a seat," he said. I did as he said and sat down beside him. I put the case down in front of us and waited. He seemed in an odd mood today and I decided to wait for him and follow his lead.

When several minutes passed, I started to get worried. "Noah?" I asked.

He seemed to shake himself out of whatever cloud he was under. "Right... We're about halfway through, right?" He asked as though everything was fine.

I nodded. "Yeah," I agreed. "About that." I started to open the case. Then his hand reached out to stop me. "What?" I asked, looking at him.

"Are you sure you want to continue?"

"Of course, I am," I told him as I continued to unzip the case.

"We could just go with what we know. Not put you through anything else."

He sounded strained and I realised that I had failed to notice the strain that this process was putting on him. Each night that we had tested the eyes, he had become more and more concerned about my reaction to putting a new set in. In my opinion I was handling the pain better. Getting through it in less time, letting it affect me less each time. But maybe it didn't look like that to him.

"Noah," I said putting my free hand atop his. "I made this decision to fight. I made this decision to test each and every one of them. I can do it with you, or Aubrey and I could continue on my own." I realised that I had sounded a little harsh, especially when he looked so crestfallen at my response. "I would rather do it with you though," I added softly.

We sat there for a few more moments before he took his hand away from mine. "Ok," he said. His voice stronger now. "The next one is that one," he pointed at a particularly strange one. The pupil was black as was expected, but where the iris would have been, it was white and around that, it was red.

"It looks like it will kill someone," I said.

"No, that was the completely black one that made my heart feel as though it would stop," Noah countered. I remembered that. We had tried that one only two days earlier. I had been beside myself when Noah had collapsed, despite all efforts to counter it with his own blank white stare.

"Don't remind me," I said, clenching my fingers into a fist. I felt my fingernails dig into my palm and relished the pain. That I could take. I would take that gratefully compared to hurting Noah or anyone at Camp Sight.

He took that hand and stretched my fingers out. "Don't." With a sigh, I nodded.

I retracted my hand and took my eyes out. I was getting more comfortable with the darkness, especially when he was around now. I could sit or walk with him peacefully and confidently that nothing would happen in my unguarded moments. I even let him take the recently worn eyes from me as I took them out and hand me the new ones. I put them in, one at a time and braced myself as the second one slid in for the onslaught of pain.

I had become used to his holding my hand as the pain wracked my body, but tonight he surprised me by wrapping his arms around my shoulders and pulling me close. He was warm and comforting. Something I had not known in all my memories. Not until recently, at least. I clutched at his shirt without realising it and enjoyed the feeling of his arms around me.

As the pain subsided, far less than usual, and I pushed myself away from him, my eyes still held tightly closed. I looked towards the target. That was always the first place to look. Never at him.

Nothing happened. Another mystery set.

"Well, we're not burning," Noah said, and I could hear the smirk in his voice, even if I wasn't looking at him.

"Yeah, but what am I doing with them?"

I looked around. It was always nice when I didn't accidentally blow things up or almost kill someone. I got up and walked. It wouldn't do anything to figure out what the ability of these ones were, but after the way Noah had held me during the last seizure I needed to think. I'd been damaging various parts of the courtyard for almost a week now, but I had never really looked around the space. The back area was still charred. The target missing and the plants that had once been behind it, black. It still smelled heavily of the fire. I could feel his eyes following me as I moved. I wanted to look into the rooms. Ok, I wanted to look into one room in particular, but the doors were solid and today, his was closed.

I scuffed my foot against the charred pavers of the courtyard and noticed for the first time, writing pressed into the paver. I crouched down and brushed at it with my fingers. "What is it?" Noah asked.

"Did you know that there was something written here?" I asked.

"Yeah. But we can't read it. The language looked foreign to us."

"The Imperial Shiura Musketeers," I said, letting my fingers run across the text.

Noah had gotten up at some point and was now crouched beside me. "You can read that?" He asked. "How? The characters are all different from Eridenti."

"You do all know that this area used to be a part of Shiura, right?" Aubrey asked, almost amazed that they seemed to be surprised to find Shiuran text in the camp. After the discovery, Minnie had appeared from her room to see how the training was going, then the news of the Shiuran text had spread throughout the camp and everyone had come to look.

"I had seen maps that indicated as much, but I hadn't been able to verify them," Emrys said, pulling something up on his screen.

Aubrey walked over and had a look. "Yeah, that's it. Erihall might be a major Eridenti city now, but it was never more than a factory town and military outpost in the past. It sat on the border, a supposed barrier between the Eridenti and the Shiurans. Cause while there wasn't always a war, there has been a long-standing conflict between the two nations."

"Where does Orley fit in all this?" Elijah asked suddenly as he jotted down notes. "I'm sure I've heard parts of this story before and Orley is always a part of it, right?"

"They are," she added, animatedly pointing towards him. "The Orlese claim to be neutral on the matter, just like Eprea, Sestya, Fresil and Asnijan," Aubrey explained, ticking off on her fingers the neighbouring countries to Eriden and Shiura. "But it's actually thought that it was the Orlese government who backed the assassination of Eriden's Tagavor, their former ruler, but this was maybe two hundred years ago. There was some border fighting and towns like Erihall popped up along the borders, but it soon calmed to... I don't know, a mutually assured destruction scenario as they both kept building up their military might."

"You know a lot about this," a quiet boy who I had seen around, but never spoken to said. I might never have spoken to him myself but whenever I did see him, he always appeared to be watching Aubrey and hanging on her every word.

"School covered world history..." Aubrey said crossing her arms, defensively. "And my grandmother served in the army."

"What restarted the fighting?" I asked. "If that happened two hundred years ago and Alma served in combat, what happened?"

"Only the greatest love story ever," said Aubrey as she walked around the room, making certain that everyone's attention was on her. "It's also something of a school myth."

"Oh, this will be good," Chouette said as she watched Aubrey walk around. "What school myth?"

Aubrey finally perched herself at the edge of Emrys's desk. He stared at her, a look of mortification crossing his face, but said nothing. "So, Amorette Eriden, or Amy Nedire, as she was known at school and Iniko Shiura or Nick Shi both attended my school back in the day."

"Where on earth do you go to school?" Emrys asked, typing away at his computer.

"Eprea," Aubrey replied. "A boarding school in Eprea. It was my grandmother's idea... Anyway, Eprea has always been the place where wealthy families from across the continent send their children. This was no different for Nick and Amy. They used those assumed names in order to not draw attention from the other side... Or at least that was the claimed intention, but it had an unforeseen side effect."

Everyone was rapt with Aubrey's story. I had to admit, she had me on the edge of my seat too. "What side effect?" Minnie asked eagerly when Aubrey's pause took too long for her liking.

Aubrey chuckled, obviously enjoying being the centre of attention. "They couldn't identify each other either."

"Oh... Oh... Oh no!" Sadie gasped. "No!"

Aubrey nodded. "Yes. Nick and Amy became fast friends, not knowing that they were supposed to be enemies. It's a four-year school... and this happened back in their first year."

"What happened?" It was Sadie. I had not expected her to get so into Aubrey's story. Given how accidentally she had become involved with all this, I hadn't thought that that she would have anything to offer that would increase our knowledge of the situation.

"Well," Aubrey said dramatically. "Skip along to their final year. They're head over heels for each other. King and Queen of the senior dance, madly in love. Planning on spending their lives together."

"It's so romantic!" Vera gushed.

"Amorette returns home to Eriden to tell her parents of her plans. Iniko does the same in Shiura and that is when all hell breaks loose," she paused dramatically again. It was as though we all leaned in closer, ready to be a part of that story. "Amorette is forbidden to ever see Iniko again, with her father the Tagavor of Eriden accusing Iniko of Shiura of seducing his daughter for nefarious reasons. In response, the Arka of Shiura, Iniko's father accused Amorette of witchcraft. This goes around and round, the two fathers throwing out accusations and it spreads to the people. Shiuran men are considered a danger to women everywhere and Eridenti women across the continent are accused of witchcraft whenever a non-Eridenti man falls for them."

"All that 'cause two kids wanted to be together?" Chouette asked.

"And so much more," Aubrey replied. "Through their school friends who, of course, were on their side, rather than the political sides of their respective countries, they made a plan to run away together. Iniko made it to Sestya with his allies where he was supposed to meet with Amorette before continuing on to Tronia or Fresil, but Amorette was captured at the boarder by her father's men. Right in Erihall, I think. At this point, she was taken back to Eri-Rhou and imprisoned within the palace."

"Oh no!" Sadie gasped. "How did she get to Iniko?"

"Their friends from school, all wealthy children of high-ranking officials were still allowed into Eri-Rhou palace and so they hatched another plan. Amorette would fake her death. Her depression made it a plausible action and so she took the poison which she had been supplied after leaving a note decreeing her hatred for the war and for her father, as well as her love of Iniko."

"How would fake dying help her escape?" Harvey asked, as he walked into the room, a tray full of snacks in his arms. Aubrey snatched a little cake from the tray and grinned at him. It was Emrys who answered though.

"The Eri-Rhou cemetery is outside of the town. It would be easier to sneak her out from there, then from the palace in the middle of the city."

"Exactly," Aubrey exclaimed excitedly while pointing at him with her half-eaten cake. "Officials from far and wide came to mourn the death of Amorette, but her letter and her reasons were never made public. Not officially anyway. Anyway, the only real problem was that their messenger to Iniko was killed on the road and word of the plan never reached him. So, when Iniko heard of Amorette's death, he left his allies and went to Eri-Rhou."

Cassias, ever silent and unimpressed grunted. "Fool."

"Not knowing anything or who exactly were Amorette's allies, he avoided everyone, waiting until her body was left alone for him to finally see her," Aubrey explained. "It's said that he wept and said a whole bunch of romantic nonsense over her body, which was supposedly coming to from the poison. Her mind could hear and think, but she could not move nor speak. Iniko, so distraught at her apparent death and not noticing her slow recovery, shot himself, there beside her."

"Oh no," Sadie appeared near tears at this point. "No... No..."

"Amorette awoke finally. She was able to move and talk. Iniko's pistol was still clasped in his hand, his other around hers..."

"Amorette killed herself using Iniko's pistol," I concluded.

"Spoilsport," Aubrey complained, but she nodded all the same. "You ruined my big reveal. Anyway, you would think that after all that, that there would be some sort of reconciliation between Eriden and Shiura."

"But instead, they went to war. A grisly, gruesome war in which your grandmother served," Noah said. "And despite the ceasefire and the decrees and the treaties..."

"There are still significant tensions between the two countries," Aubrey concluded. "Significant enough, that everyone expects war to break out again at any time."

Cassias was frowning at me. That was never good. It usually meant that he wanted me to do more training or something as equally painful. He had been doing it ever since the meeting had broken up just before dinner. Aubrey's story of love and war had everyone a buzz with activity and conversation. Cassias though, was as silent as ever. I really only ever heard him speak when he was training us to fight. It was unusual though, for him to focus on any one person at any other time though.

I wanted to say something to him. Anything that would set me up for a confrontation, but before I had a chance, Vera popped up in front of me.

"C'mon," she said taking me by the arm.

"Where are we going?" I asked as I allowed her to pull me along, my gaze though, stayed with Cassias.

"Cora's getting Aubrey and we're turning you two into part of the group!" Vera said as if that explained everything. Then I thought about it. I was too clean cut compared to them. Aubrey, especially with her private school girl looks looked like she didn't belong.

"Oi, new girl," Cassias called after me. We were almost through the door when he did, and I had to pull back from Vera to make sure I got to stick around and hear what he said. "You're going with, tomorrow."

I stared at him, not one hundred percent sure what he was talking about, but then smiled. I was going with them tomorrow! Me, going with the group tomorrow when they went into Erihall! It was the best news! I had to be able to keep my promise to Aubrey and get her grandmother back. I was only able to do that if I was able to go with the group. Cassias's confidence in my ability was a reassurance that I wasn't going to be a liability as we finally started on Alma's rescue operation.

"Awesome!" I replied. "Thanks Cassias, thank you!"

He looked surprised at me, but I didn't have time to continue our conversation because Vera was getting impatient with me. She pulled and finally I relented, allowing her to drag me through the halls of the old military outpost to Chouette's room.

Everyone was there. Sadie was already waiting, Hattie perched beside her on a couch that Chouette had pushed up against the back wall of her private space. Minnie was seated on a small desk chair across from them and Cora, Aubrey and Chouette were all seated on the bed.

"I got her. Finally!" Vera said, dragging me to the centre of the room and sitting me down on the last empty chair. "Cassias chose that time to get all chatty!"

"Cash, chatty?" Cora asked. "I don't believe it."

Chouette though looked knowing. "What did he have to say?" She asked, but I could tell. She already knew.

"He said I was going tomorrow."

"Woo hoo!" Sadie cheered. "Well, he would've been a fool to say no. I mean, you've already surpassed most of us in training."

I shrugged. "I don't know about that," I said. "When we're sparring. More so then when we're just practicing, it's like... It's like everything is familiar and someone is giving me advice... Or reminding me of little things, how to move, when to move... Stuff like that..."

"Memories from your old life?" Chouette asked.

Again, I shrugged. "I don't know. I guess so..."

"Maybe you're like this great martial arts champion!" Hattie exclaimed, jumping up. I could see her, but all the others could see was her hat, tank top and jeans jumping around and kicking at the air. She threw in a few pinches for good measure. "And it's all there in you, waiting for you to unleash it upon the bad guys!"

"I wish I knew," was all I said.

"We doing this, or what?" Cora asked. "With Juniper being a recent runaway, she's so got to look different... And as much as I love my girl Aubrey here, she looks like a pretty little angel girl."

"Doesn't shoot like no angel," Hattie cut in. "Hell, she's better than you, Cor!" She pointed her fingers like little pistols and went around 'pow powing' at everyone. I just shook my head at her. Sometimes, it was the only response.

"Hey Minnie," Chouette called. "Pass the barber kit!"

The older girl who had been silent but listening to us all passed it over. "So, what are you thinking?" She asked, her voice low and I thought that she sounded distracted by something. "Nothing too unsightly like Vera's red and lilac curls I hope?"

"Huh!" Vera exclaimed. "My curls are magnificent!" For me, I had to wonder how Minnie knew what Vera's hair looked like.

After that, excited chatter of cuts, colours and styles overtook the room. Vera's outlandish suggestions, Cora's more sedate, but equally colourful ideas. Hattie's insistence on demonstrating with the hair of whomever she was near, resulting in almost everyone swatting at the invisible girl. Aubrey and I were just left in the middle of what seemed like a storm of ideas and then, hair styling as Chouette began to work on Aubrey's hair. She gasped and looked at me for help. I shrugged.

She mouthed to me. "Do something!"

I mouthed back. "Like what?"

She shrugged, which resulted in Chouette chastising her for moving while they were cutting her hair. "Turn them to stone, freeze them?"

I shook my head, but that apparently offended Sadie. "Stop moving you two!"

"Can't!" I mouthed back.

With all the focus on Aubrey and, it wasn't until the girls sat back, satisfied in their work so far, that Chouette looked around, concern plastered across her face.

Mine and Aubrey's hair was wrapped up tight, allowing dye to work its way into our strands, and Hattie was warning me not to move my head around too much. "What is it?" Vera asked.

"Where'd Minnie go?" Chouette asked. We all looked around, as though one of would magically spot something Chouette had missed, like an entire person, but Minnie wasn't there. When had she slipped out?

It was odd, this getting ready to leave Camp Sight. When I had left the facility, Sebastian had done everything for me. Aubrey was checking her rifle. She had cleaned it the night before, but now, she had dismantled it again and was checking everything over. Cora was sitting across from her at the table, doing the same thing with two pistols.

I saw Mech a quiet boy often on the sidelines, hovering in the doorway to the living area watching Aubrey as he always seemed to do. He was holding something in his hands, but from where I was, I couldn't figure out what.

"Isn't it cute?" Hattie asked. "I think Mech has a crush on Aubrey."

I glanced sideways at the invisible girl. "Or he can't figure out what it was you and the others did to her hair last night."

Hattie laughed. "Oh, don't tell me that she doesn't look so much better now! And you too for that matter." In an instant, my hand went to my hair. It had been much longer before the girls had gone at it. Now, the straight cut bob, once a solid dark blonde was streaked with lines of blue, purple, pink, and black. I barely recognised myself, which wasn't saying much as I had only started seeing myself less than a month ago. I had been very used to the long hair though. Daily brushing had been a calming routine back in the facility and I was having a hard time getting used to the different length. "Ya know who else has been staring?" Hattie asked as I played with the ends of my hair. I shook my head and for some reason, she looked exasperated with me. "Seriously?"

I just stared at her. "I don't know what you're talking about.""

She just laughed the little infuriating laugh of hers. "Noah!"

"What about Noah?" I asked, playing dumb, but Mech had finally made a move to step into the room. This should be good. He never said much when with the group and I rarely saw him interact with the others. He seemed to always prefer his own company and that of the things he created. Emrys, who definitely preferred the company of his computers, at least hung out with Elijah. Hattie was about to explain, what I'm sure were her riveting observations, but I wanted her quiet. "Shh, I want to watch this."

Surprisingly Hattie actually fell silent. Mech approached the table where Aubrey and Cora were working. He stood there, next to Aubrey and didn't say anything. I wanted to face palm. The boy was never going to get anywhere unless he actually spoke to her, as in, opened his mouth and used words.

He put the item he was carrying down on the table beside Aubrey. "Here," he said. Elaborate! I wanted to tell at him. Elaborate. Use your words! It wouldn't have mattered anyway though.

Aubrey and Cora looked up at him. I don't know how he had not expected Cora to also take notice of him, but he seemed to shrink back under both their gazes. "What is it, Mech?" Cora asked.

"I... Uh..." He looked from his mystery item to Aubrey. "It's... It's for you..." He said haltingly.

Aubrey carefully put down the pieces of her rifle and laid her hands over Mech's gift. At least, I thought it was a gift. Aubrey looked unsure about it.

"He's so totally messing this up!" Hattie whispered in my ear. I just nodded in agreement. I did not want to risk us being overheard.

Cora was looking from Mech to Aubrey and back again. The room itself had become quiet with everyone else trying to be discreet about their observations.

"Thank you," Aubrey said, looking at the item.

"It's... Umm... Well..." Mech started. "They're goggle binoculars... Cause you... Well... You're the only one who... They work kind-of like Chouette's eyes and... They'll work with your rifle in place of a scope because... Because you..."

"Because my eyes don't have any special abilities?" Aubrey questioned with a small smile. He nodded silently. Aubrey pushed her rifle back together again. "Without a scope you say?" He nodded again. She picked up the goggles and put them over her head. "Mech, would you tighten them for me?"

The boy blushed furiously, then stepped up behind her and helped her to adjust the straps. "And... I..." He slipped a hand into his pocket and pulled something out. I couldn't see what it was from where I was, but he held it out to Aubrey. "You need to put it on the end of your rifle... Then it will show you what you're targeting, no matter the distance."

Aubrey took the little device and attached it to her rifle where Mech indicated. Then, she stepped aside and put the rifle to her shoulder. "Oh, wow," she said.

"You can change the zoom like this," Mech said, reaching over and adjusting the goggles.

"Wow, I could totally hit that tree on the far end of the camp, through the window!" She exclaimed.

Cora looked where Aubrey had indicated. "What? Really? No way!"

Aubrey put the rifle down and lifted the goggles from her eyes to sit atop her head. "These are great Mech! Thank you!" Then, before the boy realised what was happening, she threw her arms around his neck and hugged him. His whole face went red, and he stood there, arms awkwardly by his side. As she pulled away from him, she kissed him on the cheek. I hadn't thought it possible, but he went an even darker shade of red.

"Mech really likes her. He doesn't make stuff for just anyone... Especially not if they don't ask and not that fast," Hattie said beside me. "Our boy is smitten!"

I chuckled and finally returned my attention to my own gear. The clothes I was wearing were different than the ones Sebastian had provided in my bag when I had escaped. Men's cargo pants, one of the pockets containing a small version of the eye case with two select choices of eyes in it aside from my standard ones that allowed me to see Hattie, which I currently had in. A thin black, hooded pullover and a jacket that held several knives that Cassias had been nice enough to lend me, at least until I completed my own ensemble of weaponry. I think I'm growing on him.

I walked past Noah as we headed out to the courtyard. I don't know, but to me, it looked like he stopped and stared. Last night when we had all gone off to do our own things, I had sported long blond hair that I had been keeping plaited back out of my way. Now, the bob that brushed the tops of my shoulders was streaked with colour. I looked like one of them now. I didn't stop though. I kept walking and made my way to Aubrey's bike. I could not drive or ride. Whatever they called it. Between everything else, learning about the eyes and the exhausted state that left me in and combat training, there hadn't been any time yet.

Noah walked past me and grabbed my bag from my hands as I was trying to put it in the saddle bags. "You're riding with me," he said and just kept walking.

"Who said?" I called, following after him. Aubrey, who was packing her own bag looked after us.

"I did," Noah said, now packing my bag into the saddle bags on his bike. "Aubrey's a shooter. We shouldn't waste her on driving."

"Hang on!" Aubrey spoke up. "This is my bike, and you think I'm letting someone else drive her?"

"You'll ride with Chouette. Sadie's driving Cora. Juniper's coming with me. It's that simple. If you don't like it, I can find someone else to come with us," Noah said. "And as for you," he turned on me. "You're stuck with me, whether you like it or not."

Aubrey came around her bike and pointed her finger at Noah, almost poking him in the chest. "How about asking next time? Or at least telling us what the deal is before you go all dictatorial on us, huh?"

Chouette put a hand on Aubrey's shoulder. "He's right. This way puts everyone in a position to best defend us on the road."

Aubrey swirled on her. "I'm not debating the logic. I'm debating his manner of giving orders. My grandmother gave me that bike. Rode it in the war and without asking, he dictates that I let someone else ride her!"

Cora and Sadie were busy packing their own belongings onto the third bike. Neither of them seemed to look in our direction. Both of them keeping their eyes firmly on their tasks. Their ears were open, that was for sure. Me? I was already peeved with him, but Aubrey was furious. "Noah," I started.

"No!" he interrupted. "You two don't understand just how dangerous it is for us to go into town. We risk everything. We're all wanted by Sage and his researchers. They could find the camp and we're not here to defend the younger kids or the non-fighters. We could be captured. They could follow us back. The decisions I make are for the good of everyone and I won't apologise for that."

"She's not asking you to apologise for that Noah," Chouette intervened. "You haven't exactly explained the details of this plan to anyone." He seemed to turn on her and she held her hands up in a surrender. "No, don't start having it out with me. What's eating at you on this one?"

Noah looked between us all, then at Chouette. "Minnie came to see me last night." That seemed to startle Chouette.

"Really? When? About what?" She asked.

Noah ran a hand through his hair. "This. Today. She said she saw something... Sage, in Erihall. She said things were going to go real bad if we weren't careful"

Cora, no longer able to pretend that she wasn't listing stood up from her pretend fussing with the bike and came over. "He's going to be there? In town? What else did Minnie say?"

"Let's get him!" Sadie added, following Cora over.

"I agree!" I had to add. I hated Nelson Sage with every fibre of my being. "Why are we standing here arguing then?"

"Because!" Noah cried. "We barely made it out of Erihall last time and that was with us four," he said, motioning towards Chouette, Aubrey, me and himself. "Now you want to get in and out of town with six, maybe even seven if we find Aubrey's grandmother. It can't work and when Minnie says that something is going to end bad, it usually does. Especially with the beefed-up security they have since Juniper's escape and now this news that he's going to be in town himself. I just…"

"You're worried," Chouette surmised. "And that's fine. Especially if Minnie says that there is something to be concerned about. But it's no reason to bite off everyone's heads and act like a jerk." She looked at the group. "How about this. You made a valid point about the chance of returning with Aubrey's grandmother. No way that can happen if we're riding with a full compliment. Why don't Cora and Sadie stay here? I'll take their bike and Aubrey can ride hers. Juniper can still go with you."

I would have rather ridden with Aubrey, but given Noah's mood, I decided that it was best not to push my luck. He was still frowning though. What had Minnie told him? And when? She had been with the rest of us girls the night before as Aubrey and I had been transformed and then I remembered. By the time the girls had announced us 'perfect' Minnie hadn't been in the room. She had left us at some point, but I couldn't pinpoint when. She had been so silent beforehand, that no one had noticed her leaving.

"Fine," Noah said begrudgingly.

Chouette nodded. "Good. Let's get on the road then."

"So, we're not coming anymore?" Sadie asked. "Why?"

"You're needed here." We all turned to see Minnie standing there, her blank, eyeless eyes looking directly at us. "Erihall will sort itself out, but you need to be here."

Cora and Sadie looked at each other, before Cora finally nodded. "Ok," she said. Then she turned to Noah. "You bring everyone back alive.

Don't even think about coming back minus anyone, cause you had the chance for backup."

70

Cora stood at the top of the watch tower, trying to look out for the bikes, but they had long ago left the sight of their binoculars. No one but Chouette would be able to spot them now and Chouette wasn't there.

"I don't like it," she said to Sadie, putting the binoculars down.

"Neither do I," Sadie agreed.

Cora went to pick up the binoculars again, growled in frustration and didn't pick them up. "I hate just standing here doing nothing!"

"So do I, but what else can we do?"

Cora looked out into the distance, then turned on her heels and headed down the narrow staircase. "We can go after them, no matter what Noah says!"

Sadie hurried after her. Cora grabbed her bag from where she'd dropped it at the bottom of tower when she'd headed up in a huff. "Wait! What about what Minnie said?"

Cora slowed only slightly before hurrying on to where her bike was still waiting. She started strapping her bag back on. Sadie grabbed her own bag and followed suit, even if a little slower.

"What's going on here?" Cassias asked, coming from inside the main living area. He stood there, arms crossed over his chest, exaggerating the size of his upper arms.

"We're going after them," Cora stated firmly.

"No, you're not," Cassias stated, glaring at her.

"Nothing's going to happen if we're not here," Cora said, "But they've all gone back into the lion's den without backup."

"Minnie says no," Cassias said, the girl in question stepping out tentatively beside him.

"Please."

"You're here, Vera's here," Cora said defensively. "You don't need us," she motioned to herself and Sadie.

"I agree that someone needs to back them up," Minnie said. "But not you."

"Then who?" Cora exploded. "You?" she asked Minnie.

"There's no need to be crass," Kattie said, his own bag in hand. Beside him, another bag floated along. "We're going."

"You? What can you do?"

"Lots of things," Hattie said. "Like get in places without being seen. Come up from behind when no one expects ya!" Her blag seemed to skip along and then it was beside the bike, the straps Cora had been working coming undone.

"You're needed here," Minnie said again. "Please."

Sadie looked from Minnie to Cassias, noting the greyish tinge to the big man's skin. "You ok?" she asked suddenly.

Cassias nodded gruffly. "Fine."

"We'll bring'em all back safe and sound," Hattie promised. "But you guys give the big guy a break. Remember, they didn't come back with his medicine last time."

"Hattie," Cassias growled.

Hattie dropped Cora's bag to the ground and attached her own to the back of the bike. Then grabbed Kattie's from his hand. "Come on, if we plan on catching up, we'd better go."

Cassias leaned back against the wall of the building as Kattie mounted up, grumbling about Hattie's lack of clothing. Cora stood there, her bag at her feet glaring at the pair, but eyeing Cassias out of the corner of her eye. He did look tired. Hopefully they thought of bringing something back for him when they got the old woman. Kattie and Hattie drove out of camp, Hattie hotting and hollering in delight as they went.

Sadie shook her head. "I guess that's that."

Cora just glowered. "Something better happen here to make this all worth it!"

71

I did not like riding any more than I had when we had fled Erihall. Noah seemed a more sedate rider than Aubrey, but whether it was the tenseness of his body, the stress of returning to town, knowing about Minnie's bad feelings, something everyone else in the group seemed to take very seriously. Riding into Erihall was no laughing matter. Something odd caught my attention as we got closer to town.

"What's that?" I asked as we passed a poster. I could have sworn that I had seen that man on it. Nelson Sage.

"What's what?" Noah asked, looking over his shoulder at me.

"Road!" I cried. "Look at the road!" Noah chuckled and kept looking at me. "The road!" I cried again. "What are you looking at me for?"

In front of us, Chouette had brought her own bike to a stop and was staring at something on a wall full of plastered posters. Noah pulled us to a stop beside her, and Aubrey came in behind us moments later. "He's going to be there. In town," Chouette breathed.

"So Minnie was right..." Aubrey said softly.

"That what you saw?" Noah asked me. I just nodded, noticing that the date for the engagement was today.

"Sage Industries is proud to announce the new Education for All Alliance, ensuring an equal education to all Erihall children, regardless of their sightedness," Aubrey read.

"Easy access to children," Noah and Chouette said at the same time.

"We have to stop this," Chouette said, clenching her fists. "There cannot be any more like us or even worse... Those that failed..."

"Part of the plan is special schools for the poorly sighted," I said reviewing the smaller text on the poster. "Special schools would mean no oversight. No protection for the children."

"Every single one of those schools would wind up being a research facility," Noah concluded. "Come on. We better be getting into town."

We rode the rest of the way in silence until Chouette drove off the main road and onto a small dirt track that went through the forest surrounding Erihall. "What is it?" Noah asked as she stopped and got off her bike.

"The blockades. We'll never make it through them. We're better off sneaking in through the tunnels."

"You don't mean the old aqueduct tunnels, do you?" Aubrey asked as she swung her leg over her bike.

Chouette nodded. "Yeah, you know them?"

"Yeah," Aubrey said. "They date back to before the first war, there's an entry way on my grandmother's land. It used to be a military base after all."

Chouette laughed. "God, you never cease to amaze me. Do you know where that one lets out?"

Aubrey looked around. "Not far from here, I think. You're better off leaving the bikes here."

We pushed the bikes into the bushes and covered what could be seen with loose branches in the hope that should anyone stumble across them, they would not see them. We then followed Aubrey as she led the way through the forest. We never left the cover of the trees, wary that Sage's security people would be walking the walls of Erihall.

A roar went up from inside the city walls. They had amassed a huge crowd from the sounds of things, and we were busy looking for a way into the town that Aubrey insisted was here.

"There!" Noah said, pointing to a bush that seemed to creep up the wall. Through it, metal grating could be seen and beyond that, complete and utter darkness.

"Yes!" Aubrey cried excitedly.

"Chouette, keep watch," Noah ordered and then he motioned for Aubrey and me to follow him.

72

Drip.

Drip.

Drip.

The tunnel was dark, and Aubrey took the lead. Apparently, the goggles Mech had given her back at the camp allowed her to see in the darkness of the tunnel. Chouette took up the rear after assuring us that she too, could see perfectly well in the darkness, if not better than the sunlight. That left me and Noah sandwiched between them.

Drip.

Another drop fell onto my head and rolled into my eyes. Ugh. Aubrey assured me that this had simply been an aqueduct, allowing water flow into and out of Erihall, but the stench told me something was not quite right with that idea anymore. It wasn't quite as bad as I imagined a sewer to smell, but I sure as hell had no intention of drinking anything that came out of this aqueduct.

Our feet were weighed down by shallow, fetid water. Flies and other little flying insects seemed to hover around us and the surface of the water. I didn't even want to consider whatever it was that brushed against my legs under the surface of the water. The hem of my pants was floating, leaving my ankles bare to the water and something soft, slimy, and squishy brushed against me. I squealed and jumped back, the water hindering my retreat from the slimy, squishy thing. I felt myself falling and I completely expected to find myself splashing into the water, likely to be consumed by the creatures that waited beneath the surface. But I stopped falling mid-air, my scream still echoing down the cave in both directions. Instead, I found myself being cradled in Noah's arms.

"Careful," he said in a soft voice, and I could imagine the look in his eyes even though I couldn't see him in the dark. It would be similar to those concerned eyes that would always watch me during our explorations of the case of eyes.

"Thanks," I replied. My voice equally soft. He slowly returned me to a standing position, and I could have sworn I saw Chouette smirking at me, but it was so dark that I was sure I had imagined it.

"We're almost at the house," Aubrey added, "Maybe a little quiet?"

I shot her a dirty look. It was not my fault that whatever it was swirling around in the water had terrified me. Absolutely not. That was not what had happened. I could convince myself that the water had tripped me up and that that was why I had screamed. Right? Believable?

Probably not.

Drip.

Frustration flooded through me as another drop seemed to locate me and fall exactly where I happened to be, missing Aubrey and falling before Noah walked beneath it. I wiped the water from my eye but managed to not express my frustration. I was sure that the others were getting dripped on too, and that I just could not see it.

"We're here," Aubrey said. "This ladder leads into Grandma's yard." She put her foot on the first rung, ready to climb.

Noah pushed past me and put a hand on her shoulder. "I'll go first."

Oh boy. I sensed another argument between the two. They had been chilly towards each other ever since the argument over who was riding what back at Camp Sight. Were Minnie's words still bothering Noah? Or was it because the rest of us were…

I never got to finish the thought as Chouette interrupted. "Scouting actually happens to be my job. I'll go." Maybe she had sensed the upcoming argument too. Surprisingly, Noah stepped aside to let her reach the ladder. Aubrey also reluctantly agreed.

We watched as Chouette ascended the ladder. At the top, a heavy cap seemed to block her access to the outside and we could hear her fumbling around trying to locate a lock or latch or something that she could dislodge to open it.

"What does this open up to?" She asked Aubrey.

"Interior of a well," Aubrey responded. "You should be able to open the cap without being seen."

"Good to know," Chouette said. "Now, quiet you three." She pushed the cap up and sunlight flooded the tunnel. Aubrey pulled the googles up from her eyes, the bright light not agreeing with the night sight mode she had been using, while Noah and I covered our eyes, having not expected so much light to filter down to us.

"Crap!" Chouette exclaimed ducking back down into the tunnel by a few rungs.

"What do you see?" I asked. I could not wait to get out of this damned tunnel. Something else brushed past my ankle and this time, I had to will myself not to look down, because with all that sunlight flooding our immediate area, I would be able to see exactly what was down there. I did not want to know what was down there with us!

"Guards!" She hissed. "Sage's men are everywhere!"

Aubrey looked at us and motioned for Chouette to come back down to us. "It's my grandmother's house. I have every right to be there. They'll check my ID papers, hassle me a bit about Grandma's connection to Juniper and what happened last we were here." She looked down to where the others waiting. "We didn't leave anyone that saw us left to report back, did we?"

Noah shook his head. "I don't think so."

Aubrey nodded hesitantly. "Ok… I'll keep them distracted while you three get out of the yard. I can prove that I wasn't here when Juniper was, because I only arrived in town that day. They can even check with school. I had to lodge my travel plans with them."

"Aubrey!" I said. "No. What if we're wrong and someone did see you?"

"It actually works," Chouette said. "As long as she can get out of the well without being seen. It works. Regardless of what happened before. Blame it on an intruder if anyone questions you about it."

"Make some statement to them on how to you came to hear Sage speak. They'll like that," Noah added, surprising us all as he agreed to the plan.

"I'll meet you guys in the town square where he's giving his speech," Aubrey agreed, then climbed up the ladder. We watched her go, Chouette following her up in order to keep watch. Then we heard it.

"You! Halt!" A scramble of boots all descended in one direction, closer to the house and away from the well. More angry men called for Aubrey to stop.

"Crap! They're all pointing guns at her!" Chouette hissed down to us.

"Trust her," I said, hoping that Aubrey's plan would work. "She's right. She has every right to be here." I gritted my teeth as Chouette reported back what she was seeing. I just hoped that I was right.

"They're hauling her into the house…" Chouette whispered, and I could hear the concern in her voice. I was not going to say I wasn't concerned, but I had to have faith that Aubrey, the only one of us with ID papers could pull this off, regardless of the role she had played in getting us out of town before.

"Let's go then," Noah said. "Up you go," he motioned to me to take the ladder ahead of him. This was going to be so much fun with those wet, slippery shoes. I wrapped my fingers around the rung that was at my eye height and pulled myself up. My feet slipped on the lower rungs, but I kept my hand grips tight. I would not fall off this ladder.

Above me, Chouette hauled herself over the side of the well and maybe I should not have let that distract me, because as she went over the side of the well, my foot slipped. My grip was still tight, but Noah had to fall to one side, hanging off the ladder by one hand to keep from being kicked in the face by me. Me? I was hanging from both hands, my feet scrabbling to find a ladder rung.

"Crap," I muttered, kicking my feet almost wildly to find a rung to set my feet upon.

"Stop it!" Noah hissed. "I'll help you find one." I looked down at him. Big mistake. Down was a long way and while I didn't think that I was afraid of heights. I did recall the soft, slimy and squishy things down there in the water, ready, I was sure, to devour me. I saw him hanging there, one arm holding him up, but I noticed, that while he had swung out to the side, one foot also remained on a rung. Ok. He wasn't going to fall for helping me get back up.

A shadow fell over us, "What's taking you so long?" Chouette hissed loudly.

"I fell!" I hissed back at her. I let my legs fall slack, then felt Noah's hand wrap around my ankle. He took it and placed the foot upon a rung. I sighed in relief as I placed my other foot beside it and relieved the pressure from my arms. I was not going to fall. I am not going to fall. Climb!

Chouette reached her hand down and helped haul me over the edge of the well. We kept low, in case someone could see us from the house. I hoped Aubrey was ok. Noah's head emerged from the well and we both offered him a hand, pulling him out from the well. Then we sat there, backs against the stone façade of the well and just breathed in the fresh air of Alma's garden.

I gave myself thirty seconds to do that. We still had to get out of here before Aubrey was hopefully released and the guards returned to their posts. "Let's go," I said standing up. Chouette nodded and pulled herself to her feet. Noah was right behind us as I led the way out of Alma's pretty garden and out into the street.

People seemed to stay away from us. We must have looked like beggars and probably smelled like it too; but that probably would work for us. No one ever took any notice of the poor. Erihall would be no different.

73

The crowds got thicker as we approached the square. Food vendors even lined the street, and the smells were so good. I wanted to eat something so bad and opened my mouth to ask.

"We can't," Chouette said as she also eyed the carts. "No money…"

"Harvey would kill us for cheating on him," Noah added, apparently also not immune to the scents that wafted our way.

"He would never know…" I said wistfully.

"He'd know!" Noah and Chouette chorused together, and I stared at them.

"How?"

"He just will," Chouette said without further explanation.

I laughed softly and together we waded into the crowd of Erihall citizens. There was a musical act on the stage. A group of small children all dressed alike in a uniform, likely from one of the local schools. They were singing a song about the glory of Eriden. I didn't recognise it, but Noah was humming along to it and most of the people we passed were singing along with the children. I eyed Noah out of the corner of my eye, but he seemed happy to continue to hum, even on occasion singing a line here or there. It was like he knew the song but could not remember all the words.

The children's song finished, and a woman came onto the stage as the children filed off in single file. She waited as the people around us applauded the young performers, then as the last child stepped off the stage, she began to speak.

"People of Erihall!" The crowd went wild with that. "Welcome! Sage Industries is so proud to be here today for this monumental and historical announcement."

Looking at the people around us, I could see many, if not most of those present had little to no eyesight. From what we had seen on the posters earlier as we had ridden towards Erihall, for them, they thought that this new plan was going to be their chance to finally get onto equal footing in Erihall society. We knew however that there was no way Sage was offering education to the unsighted masses out of the goodness of his heart.

"I would like to now welcome to the stage, the man himself. Please, a loud Erihall welcome to Doctor Nelson Sage!" the woman cried, and the crowd went wild. They cheered, they chanted his name, they even wolf whistled. Me? When my eyes fell upon that man, my blood ran cold. I stepped backwards, almost against my will as though somehow amidst this crowd he could see me with my new hair. I think I might have made a sound of fright, because suddenly Noah's hand was clasped around mine and he was beside me. I looked down at our hands, our fingers woven together. His support gave me strength, and I looked up. I could face this man as an anonymous face in the crowd. Still, the crowd went wild for him. Had they forgotten that it was his laboratory that had exploded in the centre of their town, killing hundreds of Erihall citizens, and likely releasing whatever toxin was now causing their sight problems?

Nelson Sage walked onto the stage, waving his arms at the crowd. No, only one arm, he kept the other close to his side, but he was boisterous in his movements. He was this grand celebrity who would change their lives. For better or worse, he would definitely do that.

"What's wrong with him?" Chouette asked. His neck is so still and usually, he waves both arms, eagerly trying to rile everyone up."

"I turned half his body to stone," I said without thinking. Noah's grip tightened on my hand, and I looked at him. I could sense Chouette staring at me too. I shrugged. "It was the first time I had ever had them in... and I got free... I... I don't know exactly what happened. My memories of that day are fuzzy..."

"Only half his body?" Noah asked. "What about anyone else?"

I shook my head. "I don't know exactly. One man turned to stone completely, and stone just seemed to come out of anything. I was scared and in pain and I broke my restraints.... I had no control over anything I did." Images of Stinky shattering to tiny pieces filled my mind again. "Three... I think I killed three."

"The time has come for all of Erihall to be as one," Sage was saying. "And the best way to start this journey is for there to be access to education for all. For too long, those who have suffered from poor to no eyesight have been kept from the classroom. Held back, removed and discriminated against. That is why, Sage Industries is so very proud to bring to you all the Sage Institute for the Blind, a boarding school for those unable to be educated in our mainstream schools." There it was. Boarding school. Isolate these children from their parents, prevent them from reporting back whatever abuses they will be forced to endure at the hands of Sage and his researchers.

Chouette was staring at several children in the crowd, no doubt imagining her own time in the laboratories and what they would likely wind up going through. She could not move her eyes from side to side or up and down like everyone else could. To see anything not right in front of her, she had to mover her entire head. Noah had come through his experimentations with no colour in his eyes. The experiments had worked on him, leaving him with those eerie white eyeballs that he hid behind contact lenses he had stolen from a clinic. Minnie though had been left an Eyeless by their failed experiments.

Me? I had always been alone in the labs. Alone as far as I had known, but had there been other children, kept isolated in other cell like rooms near me? Had I just not known about any of the others? It seemed strange that not only were there so many others at Camp Sight, but that they had often moved through their processes in groups, that I would have been their only research subject held at the facility.

"We can't let this happen," Chouette whispered, and I almost missed it as the crowd once again started to cheer. Cheer for Sage, cheer for their children's futures, cheer for a reality they could only hope for.

"We need to find Aubrey and get to work finding where they're keeping her grandmother," Noah said, drawing our attention away from the Erihall children. We nodded in agreement and turned to make our way back through the crowd. I know I couldn't stand the idea of hearing anything else that man had to say.

74

All of Erihall was abuzz with activity. Sebastian held his clipboard, ticking off vendors as he passed by them. He'd tried to get closer to the planning of the whole thing and the overall project, but his efforts had been constantly rebuffed. Instead, he'd been given the task of managing the vendors coming to the festival. What did he give a damn about the vendors? He needed to know what his father was doing with Ms Reavis and the rest of the team. Though, at least one benefit of the, in his opinion, useless task, was that he was out in town.

He'd tried getting into town as often as he could since the last time, but he'd been given a lot of work that had kept him sequestered at the lab or tucked into offices contacting vendors for the festival. The whole thing was ridiculous, and he now had no idea where the girl was. Was she still in town? She wasn't with the old woman, not now that she was in holding, but Sebastian hadn't seen her since. He needed her to be able to stop all this. He was sure of that. But if he couldn't find her or didn't know where she was, how was he supposed to know if she'd succeeded. Would she even help him? Maybe he should have been honest with her, except everything had taken such a drastic urn after her departure. He hadn't dreamed of how the plans would be accelerated. There would be time for that later though, when he saw her, he would tell her everything.

He came to the next stall on his list. "Everything right here?" he asked, not even looking up as the man as he marked off the necessities on his clipboard.

"Does it look alright to you?" the man asked angrily. "Powered site. I paid for a powered site. I need a powered site to cook, but what have I got? He held up the end of a long extension cable and waved it in Sebastian's face. "This is not enough."

"I'll get you a power board," Sebastian said, making a note on his paperwork. A voice caught his attention, and he looked over the man's shoulder, past the end of the cable being waved before him and tried to see the owner of that voice. A spark of coloured hair drew his attention, and he almost turned away, sure he didn't know anyone with a shoulder length bob and hair coloured in pinks and purples. It wasn't a considered appropriate for the lab environment. Then a girl with wild curly hair said something and he was certain that he'd seen her somewhere before too, but the girl with the coloured hair turned her face to look at her. He felt his heart stop.

The man was saying something, his face getting redder. "I'm trying to run a business here. A power board ain't going to cut it." He droned on and Sebastian barely heard him as he watched the group.

It was her. He was sure of it. Her hair was so different as he took a closer look. It was cut shorter, in a bob that framed her face with the bright colours of her blue, purple and pink streaks. She looked so different from what he remembered. When he'd seen her at the old disaster site, she'd already looked better than in the lab, but now? Now, she looked strong, she looked confident. She looked nothing like the frightened girl he had sent out on her own after the disaster at the lab.

Sebastian smiled to himself. Yes. She had done well for herself. Now, he took a better look at the two others with her. The girl with the wild curly hair was dark skinned and so short he almost missed her in the crowd except for her mop of curly hair making her stand out. Then he realised where he'd seen her before. The experiment with the girl who could... binocular like eyes? He would need to locate her file again, check that out. He knew she was one of the missing subjects. Did that mean... Had she done what he'd hoped?

"Are you even listening to me?"

He looked to the third member of the group. He was a fair skinned boy, taller than both girls. The boy. Was that the one he had been looking for? He lifted the paper on his clipboard, tucked under the forms for the venders and all his checklists was a picture, a small boy with fair hair and a toothy grin. Beside it, was the last known picture of the boy, older than the previous picture, but as Sebastian looked from the image of the older boy to the boy that walked with the two girls, he couldn't help but smile. Had she managed to do everything he had imagined? He could barely believe what he was seeing. Sebastian dropped the clipboard to the table of the stall and stepped towards them, planning to catch her attention. It was the only way to find out if she had found the runaways.

"Hey! What about me powered site?" the stall holder bellowed, and Sebastian jumped.

He grabbed the clipboard back up. "Someone will see to it soon," he promised, then hurried after Juniper and her friends.

75

The crowd was thinning, and I could have sworn that I saw someone I recognised. A shout drew my attention over to a stall and I was confronted with that recognisable figure once more. There weren't many people in this world I recognised from before Camp Sight, but his tall, clean-cut look was telling. The cleanliness of his clothes compared to me and everyone else in the crowd.

"Sebastian!" I breathed out.

"Who?" Noah asked, looking where I was looking.

I shook my hand free from his. I don't know why, but he was still holding mine and I and I'd forgotten. How odd. "I'll be right back!" I said excitedly and took off towards the one person I could consider my oldest friend.

"Sebastian!" I cried out.

He turned to face me, a look of surprise on his face. I hugged him, not giving him time to refuse. I had my life thanks to him, and I had met all of the wonderful people at Camp Sight because of him. I had met Alma and Aubrey because of him.

"Girl- No, what do I call you?" he asked as we pushed apart, so that we were standing at arm's length apart from each other.

"Juniper," I said. "I'm called Juniper, remember?"

Sebastian nodded slowly. "Juniper..." he said slowly, as though he was tasting the name. He smiled. "You look…"

"Different right?" I asked, raising a hand to feel the ends of the bob and try to see some of the mirage of colours the girls had insisted on using. "You said that I should be careful, right?"

He nodded slowly. "Yes, to get away from here," he hissed.

"I know," I said, "but..." I bit my lip and looked over to where Chouette and Noah were watching us. I quickly looked back at him, hoping that he hadn't noticed. "Things happened."

"Your friends?" He asked motioning towards them. I paused. Had I not been discreet enough or had he seen me with them before I approached him. He had been surprised to see me, right?

I smiled happily though. "Good people," I said.

He nodded. "Good," he said, "I'd like to talk more Juniper, but I can't now and here is too dangerous. Can we meet tonight? Maybe after the evening meal?"

I nodded. "Yeah, of course!" I probably should have checked that with Noah first, but Sebastian had an in with Sage and his goons. He would totally be able to help us find Alma. This was a good move. I was sure of it. He gave me a location where he wanted to meet, and I agreed to see him there after sunset. Then, he turned and walked away. As he disappeared into the crowd, heading towards the stage area where Sage would no doubt be waiting for him, Noah and Chouette approached.

"Who was that?" Noah asked, his voice hard and tense.

"Sebastian."

"And who is Sebastian?" Noah pressed.

I turned to face the two of them. "Sebastian is the man who saved my life. He's the one who got me out of the facility."

"So, can we trust him?" Chouette asked.

Despite my happiness to see him, something niggled away at my trust. I couldn't put a finger on it though, so, I said yes. We could totally trust Sebastian.

"There you guys are!" Aubrey said, running up to us. Her rifle was in its case, strapped across her back and she was beaming. "Who was that I saw Juniper talking to?"

"Sebastian," Noah retorted with so much snark, you would have thought that he was jealous.

She raised an eyebrow at this. "Well, I'll tell you what, those guards are so gullible. I told this epic tale of coming home from school see my grandma and made them feel real sorry for me cause I couldn't find her. Not a single comment about what happened at the house when we were there before."

"Good," Chouette said. "That's really good."

We walked along the street together. "Want something to eat?" Aubrey asked. "I grabbed some cash from my grandmother's petty cash cookie jar."

We all looked at each other. "Harvey!" Noah and Chouette groaned in unison.

Aubrey looked confused at me, "Apparently, Harvey knows when they eat food made by others," I shrugged. Even from my own lips it seemed a little out there.

"But it smells so good!" Chouette pleaded.

"You explain it to Harvey then," Noah conceded.

Aubrey wore them down and after selecting several delicious smelling dishes, we sat at a table, probably way too much food between us. Aubrey had gone all out on her purchases, insisting a little something from everywhere. Not surprising though as she seemed to always be eating something. Despite his earlier reservations, Noah tucked in as eagerly as the rest of us.

I figured that this would be a good time to let everyone know about my meeting with Sebastian that night. I should have known better. Noah's mood all day should have been a warning.

"Absolutely not!" were the first words out of his mouth. He didn't even take a second to think about it.

"And why not?" I asked.

"The man works for Nelson Sage," Noah stated as though I was stupid and didn't already know that fact. "We need to be looking for Aubrey's grandmother and not be allowing you to hang out with your boyfriend!"

Fury bubbled within me. "My what?" I cried, throwing down the roll I'd been about to bite into. "You jerk. The man saved my life! He got me out of there when the others wanted to kill me. Just who do you think you are to tell me what I can and cannot do?"

"We all saw the way you ran up to him and hugged him," Noah continued. "No. You're not going!" He bit angrily into his own roll. Chouette shot me a cautious look, as if trying to warn me off.

"He'll help us find Alma," I said, ignoring her. "He's an in. That means we don't have to go sneaking around random Sage facilities looking for her. Less chance of you and Chouette getting caught."

Noah went to open his mouth, likely to argue, but Chouette interceded. "We could use the help."

"Not from him," Noah was adamant. What was his problem?

From there, we went round in circles. The conversation seemed to get nowhere. It was all, me wanting to go, Noah saying no. Aubrey and Chouette trying to placate us and find a compromise. Finally, Noah threw his hand up. "Fine. I'll go with you then," he announced when Chouette suggested that I not go alone.

"No!" I said. It was out of my mouth so fast that I barely even recognised the fact that I had spoken. "No," I said a little slower. I didn't want Noah or Chouette coming with me, and I did not know why. They were just too close to everything Sage. I couldn't let them do it.

"I'll go," Aubrey said calmly, trying to be a voice of reason amongst all the raised voices and tension. "Probably better anyway. She is my grandmother after all."

Chouette nodded eagerly. "Brilliant," she decreased.

Noah was not happy, but he reluctantly agreed, albeit with a scowl on his face. "Fine," he muttered angrily. "Aubry will go, but Chouette and I won't be far behind."

I let out a breath of relief. Or was I just letting out all the tension Noah's mood had instilled in me? I didn't know, but with everything decided, I felt light. Noah continued to eat, chewing loudly and grabbing at things angrily as he stared at me. I tried to look anywhere but at him, but Chouette and Aubrey kept shooting each other looks, like they were having a silent conversation about us. Why did everyone keep doing that? At least Hattie wasn't there. She would be making a whole lot of fuss about Noah being as stubborn and thick headed as he'd been.

Honestly, I was getting tired of Noah's bad mood. If I ignored it, I didn't have to deal with it.

76

Noah and Chouette followed us most of the way to the meeting place that Sebastian had selected. He had tried multiple times during the day to change my mind about Aubrey coming with me, but I did not want him to come. I wanted Noah as far away as possible. It wasn't because of his crappy mood. I was pretty sure about that. I couldn't explain dread feeling I had, but I just knew that I didn't want Noah and Sebastian in the same room

Finally, they left us to walk the rest of the way alone and I felt some of the tension I'd been feeling ease.

"Noah's sure in a bad mood," Aubrey whispered, probably afraid that he could still hear us.

"He's just an idiot," I commented, resisting the urge to look back in the direction Noah and Aubrey had gone.

"Sounds kinda like he's jealous," Aubrey pushed.

"Jealous of what?"

"This Sebastian guy," Aubrey said as though it should have been the most obvious thing in the world. I just shook my head and told her that Noah was not jealous. He had nothing to be jealous of and for that matter, what reason would he have to even be jealous? I could feel the disbelieving look she gave me as we walked into the office front of a clinic. It wasn't Alma's clinic, but it did smell the same, of antiseptic and despair.

"Juniper!" Sebastian said as we walked in, stopping mid step as though he'd been anxiously pacing, awaiting my arrival. He glanced towards Aubrey, a scowl forming on his face for the briefest of moments before he smoothed out his features and smiled.

"Sebastian. Uh, this is my friend Aubrey," I said, motioning towards her. "Aubrey, this is Sebastian. He saved my life." Aubrey stuck her hand out to him, and he shook it. They exchanged greetings and that was that.

"How've you been?" Sebastian asked, focusing his gaze on me, looking me over as though looking for injuries or... No... No, he was just making sure I was well. That was all.

"Good," I replied. "And you? They didn't find out it was you, did they?"

He shook his head. "They never suspected a thing. I managed to corrupt the security system, and they were clueless." I was glad. I had been worried that someone would find out what he had done and hurt him for it. But... Given all the time we had spent together, had no one really suspected him? Even spoken to him once? "So, tell me everything. Where have you been?"

I shrugged, "Here in town," I said. I caught Aubrey's look, but my urge, my need to lie to Sebastian was huge right now. Why? Maybe Noah's paranoia was rubbing off on me.

"And young Aubrey here, a friend of yours, you say."

"Yes," Aubrey said, "the best of friends now!"

"And how did the two of you meet?" Sebastian asked, pouring us both drinks. I eyed it but didn't reach for the one he passed me.

"Aubrey's grandmother is the one who took me in. She pointed a gun at me when she found me wandering the house," I said with a smirk.

Aubrey laughed. "That was good."

Sebastian nodded thoughtfully. "And your friends from earlier, at the announcement?"

Noah and Chouette. Two runaways from the laboratories. What did I say about them? "Just met them today."

Beside me, Aubrey was squirming in her seat. I knew that she wanted to say something, anything to ask me what I was doing. She knew now was not the time though.

We talked. It seemed like ages, but the clock read that barely fifteen minutes had passed since we had entered the clinic. Aubrey reached for her drink, and I wanted to slap it out of her hand, but that would be far too obvious. Why was I being so edgy around Sebastian? He was my friend. Even back at the facility, he had been the only one to be nice to me. The only one to show me any compassion.

I rested my hand on the glass. I did want a drink, but did I need one? He was watching me.

"You're not wearing the basic ones," Sebastian stated.

I nodded and maybe this would work in our favour. "I lost them."

"Lost them? I never took you for a careless girl," Sebastian said, a flicker of irritation crossing his face.

I shook my head. "It's not like that... Sage's men, they found me. Shortly after we talked, and I'd had them out because one of the Doctors was looking at my eyes. They were hurting so much, and I was bleeding..." I sighed. It had been only a week and a half since that day. "Well... Alma my friend. I told you about her, she's Aubrey's grandmother and one of the other Doctors ratted her out for being seen with me... They took her and I had to run without them."

Sebastian nodded along to what I was saying. "Sounds like something he would do."

"Well," Aubrey said tentatively. "We were hoping.... Ok, I was hoping that maybe you could help us find my grandmother."

"Since you work for Sage and all," I added. "You could find out where he's holding her."

"And what, you two girls go break her out?" Sebastian asked with a scoff. "You would not make it through the front door."

"But-." Aubrey tried.

"But," Sebastian interrupted. "If there was an exchange of information... I could find it worth my while to risk my neck again."

"What do you want to know?" I asked, that unsure feeling I'd been having growing.

He picked up a stack of papers from the seat beside him and place them on the table between us. Had he been expecting this? Or had he been always intending to ask me for this favour? "I am looking for someone." And with that he opened the file. "Please, go through them," Sebastian said.

I reached for the folder. Files and photographs of boys. Fair skinned, blond boys with varying shades of eye colour. One caught my attention. I knew that hair, the way the hair fell into his eyes. Those eerily white eyes with not colour, no definition. Aubrey gasped when seeing it and I recalled that Noah had had no reason to let Aubrey in on his secret. The pure white eyes would be startling to her, having never seen them before. I could use that.

"What happened to his eyes?" I asked, covering for her surprise. Sebastian was acting strange. I should play dumb. Sebastian already knew that I knew Noah, but he didn't know that I knew about Noah's ability.

"He's a little like you," Sebastian said. "But different. We could not recreate what he was with your eyes. Nor ever with anyone else."

"That explains nothing," Aubrey retorted.

"It explains everything," I said, and it did. Noah could cancel the abilities of anyone he looked at. He was a powerful tool. "But I've never seen him or any of the others."

"You sure about that?" Sebastian asked. "The boy you were with this afternoon looked a lot like the boy with the white eyes." So, Sebastian had gotten a good look at Noah and maybe Chouette too. What to do? What to do?

Beside me, Aubrey yawned. "Wow... I can't believe how tired I am," she said with a dramatic show of stretching. "I think I ate way too much."

"You always eat too much," I said dryly, thinking that her attempted ploy was way too obvious, but I had nothing better to work with. "But with that, we should probably be going," I said, starting to get up.

"Already?" Sebastian asked. "But I want to hear everything about what you've been up to."

"Maybe next time," I said. Sebastian also got up. He followed us to the door. He said goodbye to Aubrey, and she stepped outside.

Sebastian gripped my upper arm though. I was so tempted to do something to him in that moment for laying a hand on me, but I couldn't show my hand. Cassias's training had started to awaken something in me, and I still didn't know exactly what I could do.

77

I went to follow Abrey out, but the door slammed shut in my face. Aubrey was outside, me still inside, Sebastian's grip on my arm tightening as I tried to struggle.

"Juniper… ring me the boy. I know you know him. That you know about him. You have to, it's the only reason that you would be wearing those see invisible eyes. To see the invisible girl. Bring me the boy and we can stop him. I'll make sure you get Doctor Corbyn-Fisher back."

My blood went cold. We had never mentioned Alma's name. And he knew about Hattie. How on earth could he know about Hattie? And what did he want with Noah? Was Noah the boy he was talking about? Of course, Noah was the boy he was talking about. What was going on right now? His voice was sinister, it was the only way to describe it.

"Sebastian," I whimpered as his grip tightened. It was just like Stinky and Scratchy. Why was he being like this? What was he doing?

Then he smiled, that sweet, serene smile I'd seen for the first time the day he'd helped me escape. He opened the door and released me as though he hadn't done anything to me at all. I stood there, outside the door and heard the locks click into place. Sebastian, my friend… Was not… Had he only helped me escape so that I would find the others? No, he was my friend. He'd been worried about me… Right?

"Juniper?" Aubrey asked, but I just stood there, staring at the sealed door. When I didn't respond, she tapped me on the shoulder. "Juniper?"

I startled slightly and took a moment to take a deep breath before I looked at her. "Let's go."

We started walking, it didn't really matter where to, as long as we did not go straight back to where Noah and Chouette were waiting for us.

I walked in silence, by head reeling with Sebastian's words, but they were interspersed with Noah's arguments about going. What did Sebastian know about Alma? Did he simply have access to her by virtue of his employment with Nelson Sage or had he had something to do with her abduction?

"Bring me the boy."

As wonderful as Emrys and Mech and Kattie and Cassias and Harvey were... Noah was the one that could stop us all in our tracks. What did Sebastian want from him? I should have asked more questions.

"I know you know him." He'd seen Noah, recognised him. How was I going to get Alma back and protect Noah?

Aubrey walked silently at my side, ever so often shooting me furtive glances, especially when we turned away from the meeting point, we'd selected with Noah and Chouette earlier. Out of the corner of my eye, I saw her biting her lip, warding off her urge to ask what was going on with me. I had to give her something.

"You've found the entire lot of them, it's the only reason that you would be wearing those see invisible eyes. To see the invisible girl." I slowed, my steps faltering as a thought occurred to me. He knew what the eyes did. He'd told me he didn't. But now he knew that these weird fluro green eyes allowed me to see the invisible, to see Hattie. He knew about Hattie too and if he knew about Hattie, then he would know about Kattie because they had been a tandem project. Hattie invisible, Kattie the only one supposedly able to see her. He knew about Noah, he knew about Hattie and Kattie. Who else did he know about? He thought he knew that they were all together, they we were all together.

Had Sebastian been lying to me all along? What was it he wanted from me? Was he working for Sage... Well, of course he was, but I had thought he was my friend, that he had my best interests at heart. What I wrong? Was my escape all part of some plan to find Noah and the others? My thoughts wouldn't stop whirling around in my head.

I didn't know what to do.

We had finally circled back around to where we had left Chouette and Noah. But when Aubrey went to meet with them, I kept walking. I needed to think, and I would never be able to do that with Noah lording it over me that going to see Sebastian had been a bad idea.

Noah for Alma.

That was not a choice. Especially not a choice that could be made lightly. Hell, who was I kidding. It was not a choice that could be made at all. Alma. Noah. I had not known either of them long, but in their own ways, both of them had become so incredibly important to me. So had the people who cared about them. Aubrey, Chouette, Hattie, Cora, Sadie, Harvey, Vera, Cassias, Elijah, Emrys, Mech, Kattie…

Alma for Noah.

"Bring me the boy. I know you know him. You've found the entire lot of them, it's the only reason that you would be wearing those see invisible eyes. To see the invisible girl. Bring me the boy and I will give you Doctor Corbyn-Fisher." That cold voice echoed in my mind. It was so unlike the Sebastian I had known. The feel of that tight hand so hard around my arm, so reminiscent of Stinky and Scratchy. Which Sebastian was real? Which one was the act?

I turned at the sound of a sob. That gasping, choking breath of oncoming tears but saw nothing. No one else was around, the party of earlier in the day had died away and the city was eerily quiet. That's when I realised that it was me. I was the one who was crying. I reached my hand to my face and sure enough, hot salty tears were tacking down my cheeks. Sebastian. He was using me. He had always been using me. Ever since that very first day when he had been nice to me to that last, dreadful and final day where I thought he had helped me escape because he had cared. No, he had wanted me to find Camp Sight. To find all the other runaways.

To find Noah.

Why did he want Noah? How long had he been planning this?

The street might have been empty, but I really didn't want anyone to see me like this, so I ducked into the next alley away. The brick wall was cool against my back, and I slid down its side until I was on the floor. The shadows of the building blocked out all sight of the moon and everything was silent. Ever so blessedly silent, except for my head and the racing thoughts.

"I'll explain everything that I can in time," he had said. Well, he had yet to explain anything to me. At least nothing that had answered any of my questions. In fact, I now had even more questions.

"That was my-" He had stopped himself more than once from saying something. *"There will only be so much Doctor Sage can do to protect you."* My what? What was Sage to Sebastian?

"*Good. Just remember, you need to get out of town as soon as possible.*" He had always pushed me to leave Erihall, to get away as soon as possible. "*And I will give you Doctor Corbyn-Fisher.*" How had he known Alma's name? A sudden thought occurred to me and my chest constricted with the thought. I had met Sebastian at the old laboratory disaster site. He had expressly told me not to trust those at the Eye Clinics and one of them had tuned on Alma pretty quickly… But that had been to save himself, hadn't it? It had not sounded as though the man had called the security teams himself.

What if it hadn't been the clinic staff who had betrayed Alma? What if it had been me? What if I'd been followed? What if Sebastian had called them in order to get me to move? The thought was too terrible to consider. I buried my face in my arms.

This was all my fault.

78

Apparently though, I had underestimated Aubrey, Chouette and probably most importantly, Noah. There I was, in my little alley of self-pity and doubt and betrayal when I heard them.

"She can't have gotten much further than this," Chouette said.

"Unless we went the wrong direction," Noah complained.

"No," Aubrey interrupted. "She just kept on walking. It was this way."

I sniffled and swiped at my eyes. Chouette's eagle eyes… No, her owl eyes, would spot me easily if she looked in this direction and I did not want to explain to them my current state of mind. Sebastian's words just kept echoing in my head, but more than anything, the feel of his hand gripping my arm with a fierce ferocity that I had never known from him. I rubbed at it, almost certain that there would be a bruise. I wondered how many bruises I had had there during my time at the facility.

"There!" Yep, Chouette had found me. There had been no point in moving, the sound of me doing so would have alerted them to my presence anyway. Instead, I pushed myself to my feet and met them.

"What are you doing?" Oh great. Noah was angry. "Do you have any idea how worried we were when you didn't return with Aubrey? Anything could have happened here. Did you even stop to think?"

He was that angry that he wasn't even going to let me speak. Aubrey stood a little behind him with Chouette, neither had dared get in front of him apparently. Then his hands were on my shoulders, and he was shaking me. My feet shifted, my hands came up between his arms moved, almost on their own as I lowered my stance and propelled his grip off of me. He stumbled and I moved back several paces, out of his reach.

"Juniper?" Chouette asked softly, as she stepped forward, putting herself between Noah and myself.

I just shook my head, backing away from her. "No... No... No..." I didn't know what to do. How did I tell any of them what had happened and what was needed?

Breathing was so hard. No matter how hard I tried, getting air into my body just seemed so hard. My hand went to my chest, clutching at it as though that would alleviate the pain I was feeling. Seeing Noah's face there, Aubrey just behind him. Did I really have to betray one of them to save the other?

Bring me the boy and I will give you Doctor Corbyn-Fisher," those words, in my head again.

"I can't," I cried. "I can't do this! I just can't!"

I must have been confusing them or scaring them. Something, because Aubrey looked ready to cry herself and the look of concern on Chouette's face was almost too much to bear. I loved these people. Them and all the others, even the ones who I hadn't gotten to know so well. I wanted to. I wanted to go back to Camp Sight, but I had promised Aubrey. I had promised her that I would help her get Alma back.

I was shaking. On my own this time, not from the force of someone imparting their will on my body. "I'm sorry," and then I turned to run. As fast as my feet would take me. Anywhere my feet would take me that wasn't here. I got maybe five steps away before strong arms wrapped around me from behind.

Noah pulled me close against his body preventing me from moving away. He buried his face in my neck, his hands grasping at my shoulders in desperation rather than anger. Then I felt him shudder against me. Was he crying?

"Don't leave," he pleaded. "Whatever it is. Whatever you need. Talk to us."

I shook my head, but the fight was gone. "I can't..." I whispered.

The fight left me and while I refused to talk about the meeting with Sebastian, I followed them. I'd allowed Noah to take my hand and lead me to an abandoned house on the outskirts of Erihall where they had set up camp while Aubrey and I had been meeting with Sebastian. There was even some leftover food from our afternoon purchases. Surprising that Aubrey hadn't eaten it all.

After Aubrey had talked about what she had seen at the meeting, we had eaten in silence. The food tasted like cardboard now, where before it had been delicious and full of warmth and flavour. Everyone else ate with gusto, so I assumed it wasn't the fact that we'd had the food all day and more how I felt. Aubrey had mentioned that Sebastian had kept me, said something to me that she was not privy to and when they had looked at me expectantly to hear what they considered the rest of the story I had said nothing, concentrating on trying to chew the tasteless food that didn't seem to go anywhere no matter how hard I tried.

I listened as talk began about returning to Camp Sight. Aubrey pressed about Alma and I stared at Noah as she did.

"Bring me the boy and I will give you Doctor Corbyn-Fisher," Sebastian had sounded so cold when he had said that. *"You've found the entire lot of them, it's the only reason that you would be wearing those see invisible eyes. To see the invisible girl."*

"We can't go back," I said, finally speaking up.

Everyone looked at me. I hadn't spoken since back at the alleyway. No one had been expecting any input from me, I suppose. I got up from where I had been sitting and walked over to them.

"Why not?" Chouette asked.

I bit my lip. "Because they know."

"Know what?" Aubrey asked.

"Know about Camp Sight. They know somehow that you all congregated together. I don't think they know where it is yet, but what if someone follows us?" I explained. "We have to lose them first."

Noah nodded. "It makes sense. Aubrey mentioned that he was looking for someone. Showed you girls files from their research participants…" He trailed off.

I wanted to slap myself silly. I had forgotten about the dossiers. Aubrey had recognised Noah in them. Of course, she had. All those boys who looked like him. She must have told him and Chouette about that and I had missed it in my stupor. How stupid could I be?

"I don't know what he wants," I stated. *Bring me the boy.* I knew exactly what he wanted. He wanted Noah. I just didn't know why. Why would Sebastian want the one person who could counter the abilities of Sage's eyes? Or did Sage want him back where he could control him?

"Did your friend agree to help as find Aubrey's grandmother?" Chouette asked.

Had Sebastian agreed to help me find Alma? Not in so many words and only if I gave him Noah. Not something I could tell them. Not something that I wanted to keep reminding myself. I shook my head. "No… There's nothing he can do."

"Well," Chouette said. "That's disappointing. We'll need a new plan then."

Beside me, Aubrey yawned. "I'm flat out exhausted… This day… And tomorrow doesn't look as though it will be any better."

Chouette was nodding. Aubrey had been nodding off already at the meeting with Sebastian, so it wasn't surprising to me that she was tired. I guessed the others were too.

"Ok," Noah finally said. "Let's turn in and start this again in the morning."

79

We turned out what little light we had on and crawled into the beds that we had arranged together in one room. The old house had been abandoned fully furnished. Was I the only one wondering what had happened to the folks who had lived here?

It was only one of the thoughts that floated through my mind at that moment. Amongst that and Sebastian's words, repeating again and again, something else emerged as I stared at the ceiling of the room, Noah, asleep to one side of me and Chouette and Aubrey on the other side.

The sight of Sage that morning. The strange way he held his body. An image flashed into my mind. The left side of Sage's neck turning grey amidst the laboratory of screaming people. The greyness of his skin and clothes travelled down his arm, the one he had held tight to his body today. Then another, the floor. The floor turning grey, the greyness chasing after some anonymous man who was too slow to prevent his feet from being caught by the ever-expanding greyness. The conversation with Noah earlier.

"I turned half his body to stone. It was the first time I had ever had them in… and I got free… I… I don't know exactly what happened. My memories of that day are fuzzy…"

"Only half his body?" Noah had asked. *"What about anyone else?"*

"I don't know. One man turned to stone completely, and stone just seemed to come out of anything. I was scared and in pain and I broke my restraints…. I had no control over anything I did." As always, images of Scratchy shattering to tiny pieces filled my mind again.

That time back at Alma's house, with the ice… All the times at Camp Sight, like when I had exploded all those plants around the target. What did all these thoughts mean? What was my brain getting at?

I crawled out of my bed, carefully trying not to wake the others and found myself a private little corner of the abandoned house and slipped the mini case from my pants pocket where it had rested all day. Were we safe overnight? I wasn't entirely sure. I looked around. The others were still sleeping.

Mech had outfitted a small slim line box he had found with soft holding places similar to the large case for me to carry two sets of extra eyes. I had picked two to come with me. The sleep ones and the stone ones. My hand hovered over the two different sets.

Stone.

Sleep.

Those were the two I had chosen to take with me. Attack capabilities. A chance to defend Noah, Aubrey and Chouette. I settled on the stone ones and then, after making sure that the others were still sound asleep, I slid first my right eye out and then my left. Darkness descended upon me instantly. It had been uncomfortable trying to sleep with them in. At Camp Sight I had gotten used to sleeping without them and waking to absolute darkness. Then, each morning, putting in the fluorescent green eyes that let me see Hattie. It was so quiet without her.

I reached into the case and slipped the first of the grey eyes out of its slot. Then, I slid them in one by one. I groaned in pain, holding my mouth closed to not wake the others. It was sad to say, but I was getting used to the pain and the way my body would seize as the eyes integrated with my body, allowing me to see. Between having to put my eyes in every morning and the training with Noah, I had gone through it so many times that it was almost second nature.

I took a deep breath and focused my thoughts. I just wanted to look. I didn't want to turn anything to stone. I was just going to take a look around like any other ordinary person. I looked at everything. The old kitchen that had not been used since the people who had once lived there had abandoned the place. The table where we had eaten our dinner, the living area where we had dumped our bags and weapons. I looked back to the table and chairs. I remembered seeing a table slowly become stone during the first trial. Carefully, I looked to where the others were sleeping to make sure none of them had woken up, then walked around the room,

When I returned back to the tiny kitchen, I stared at the table once more. It was wood and so were the chairs that surrounded it. The remnants from our meal still scattered the top. A speck of grey appeared on one corner. I touched it. The speck grew and the rough wooden surface of the table was turning smooth and cold. That speck continued to grow. It ignored my hand and started to consume our dinner remnants. The dishes and the rubbish we had left sitting there, intending on disposing of it in the morning. I cocked my head to the side as I watched the grey stone engulf most of the table. Then I blinked and it stopped. The far corner, furthest from where I was still wood and when I crouched down, I saw that that back leg was still wood, and the ends of the other legs were also tipped in wood. The one nearest me was completely stone, but it made for such a weird looking table.

It had been slow, inching its way across every surface. It had not been that slow back at the facility though. People had run in fear. They had been unable to escape because the stone had come chasing after them. Maybe I had done that? Maybe I could control the speed at which the stone moves across surfaces? Similar to the way I could target some of the other abilities... I wandered over to the comfy seats and plopped down. I kind of really wanted to sleep, who knew when I would get the next chance, but it just wouldn't come. I pushed bags off and stretched myself out on the couch.

There was a small statue sitting on the mantel piece. It was such an odd piece. Something so unique and yet familiar. Feathered wings sprouted from the back of a sleek, furry animal. The long body lead into nine beautiful tails. The feet were a little odd, kind of like my own, but different... it was a startling creature, it's little rodent face looked up towards the sky, its wings outstretched, and the nine tails spread out below.

Then I thought I saw it move. Just a twitch of one of the tails and flicker of a wing. I sat up. The statue could not have moved... Right? It was a trick of the light or my sleep deprived brain?

A foot twitched. One of the many tails moved again. A wing stretched. The stone of the statue started to disappear, replaced by a magnificent coat of stripes in cream and dark brown along the body. The wings, with feathers the same shade of brown as the dark stripes of the body expanded even wider. The tails, four of the dark brown and five of the cream fell together and suddenly, the statue took flight.

The statue was flying! The large wings flapped, and it circled the ceiling of the room, then suddenly dove at me. I ducked to the side and the little thing grabbed at a cushion with its little hands. It then tossed the cushion at me before launching itself back into the air. Its large wings knocked over a few knickknacks left behind by the previous owner. They crashed to the floor taking my attention and focus towards saving items and trying to still keep everything quiet, rather than on the little beast. It took that opportunity to fly at me again, this time grabbing my hair in its tiny little hands and pulling.

I cried out in panic and shock. So much for keeping quiet. There was thudding from the sleeping area and suddenly, I spotted through feathers and fury tails, three people trying to get through the doorway all at once. Noah burst through first, Chouette and Aubrey stumbling out behind him.

"Juniper!" They cried out as after finally getting through the doorway, just stood there staring at me and the creature.

"Help!" I cried when no one seemed to move.

Aubrey disappeared back into other room and returned with one of the thin blankets that had been on the beds. "Believe it or not, my school teaches Falconry," and with that she tossed the blanket gently over the creature and my head, closing her hands gently around the creature and trying to extract it from my hair. Chouette came over and while Aubrey held the creature, Chouette untangle my hair from the creature's tiny fingers.

"What is it?" I asked as Aubrey was finally able to pull the creature away from my head.

Keeping the bundle wrapped and close to her chest, Aubrey revealed the face of the creature. "Holy moly…" she whispered.

"What?" Noah, Chouette and I chorused, all peering over her to get a look. I was rubbing at my head, but I still wanted to see it.

"No kidding!" Chouette added as she examined the little rodent like face of the creature. "Is that what I think it is?"

"A kirpuuru," Aubrey said, moving the blanket around the examine the hands and feet of the creature. "I've only ever seen them in pictures… Illustrations even… They're a mythical beast from the times of old from

Susweassau. The family who once lived here must have been from there..."

"I didn't think they existed," Chouette said, reaching out to touch the soft fur of the creature.

"Where did it come from?" Noah asked, looking at me.

I didn't look at them. I still didn't know how these eyes worked, and I wasn't going to risk looking any of them in the eyes. But hey, no one had turned to stone yet. Yay!

"Umm…" I said.

"What?" Chouette asked.

I pointed over at the mantel where nothing now stood. The statue was once there was now the creature in Aubrey's arms and everything around it had been pushed over by the massive wingspan of the creature. "I think I… Well… You see… I think it's the statue."

"What statue?" Noah asked.

"The one that was there..." I said.

"How could it be the statue?" Chouette asked, still scratching the little creature, now under its chin.

"Well…" So, I explained, about the thoughts I'd had about the stone eyes and how I didn't think that I always had to look someone in the eyes for it to work. When I pointed out the mostly stone table, Noah had gone to touch all of it. Inspecting it from top to bottom, sliding his hands over everything. The stone, where the stone turned to wood and what had once been our dinner scraps.

"That doesn't explain that," he finally said, pointing to the bundle in Aubrey's arms.

I shrugged. "I was just looking at it, trying to figure out what it was… I mean, it was pretty, but I was intrigued by the wings and the tails and trying to identify the body."

"Ferret," Aubrey said. "The body is that of a ferret. The wings are from an eagle and the tails of the Kitsune or fox. The hands and feet are those of a monkey. They're considered extremely lucky, but they're tricksters. kirpuuru are apparently considered to be little thieves."

"Anyway, I was just looking at it when it started to move and then… Well, you saw what happened…" I said motioning to the damage done around the room.

The little creature started to struggle in Aubrey's arms, and she released her hold. I hoped it wasn't about to attack again. It sat up, resting on her hand and spread its wings. Flapped once. Twice. Then took off, its nine tails flickering as it flew from Aubrey to me. It circled and landed on my shoulder. Tentatively, I raised my hand to scratch it and to my surprise, it leaned into the caress.

"Huh…" Chouette said as she watched me. "You turned a stone statue into a living thing… Bet nobody saw that coming…"

The kirpuuru was making these strange little chirping noises as it ate. I was feeding it bits of bread as it sat on my shoulder, hands tangled in my hair once more. As long as it didn't tug on me, I was ok with it. The creature was kind of cute. It would take pieces of bread from me and hold them in its little hands, then nibble at it. As it finished its current piece, Aubrey leaned over and handed it a little bit of her bread. The creature gratefully took it and started nibbling away. The tails were wriggling excitedly against my back.

"So," Aubrey said as she leaned back in her seat. "Now what? How are we going to find out where my grandmother is?"

Noah for Alma.

That thought hit me again and I realised that all the excitement around the kirpuuru had distracted me from the thoughts that had actually been keeping me awake the night before. I had to save Alma. For Aubrey at the very least. But under no circumstances could I let Noah be taken in for whatever Sebastian wanted. He was not the man I had thought he was. Nor could I expose the rest of the group.

"I'm going to go back," I said. It seemed like the best option.

"Woah!" Noah exclaimed, stopping halfway to feeding the kirpuuru himself. "Why would you do that?" The little creature stared expectantly at Noah's outstretched hand, just out of its reach with a tasty morsel of bread in it. It stretched its long body and pressed the nine tails flat against my back before flapping its wings once and leaning all the way forward to reach Noah's hands with its own. The creature's body retracted back, and it sat there, upright on my shoulder, the bread Noah had been holding out to it, grasped within its tiny hands. In my opinion, it looked really proud off itself.

No one laughed at it though as they stared at me. I shrugged, the kirpuuru nipped at my ear to show its displeasure, then went back to its bread. "Look, all this is my fault anyway. Alma would be safe and sound if she had not found me. No one would have turned her in. You guys wouldn't be at risk now."

"We've been at risk since the day we escaped those laboratories," Chouette argued.

"But not actively exposing yourself to these people. Sebastian…" I paused as I said his name. I think I was still coming to grips what had happened at that meeting and what it meant for me. "And he mentioned Hattie to me. Maybe not by name, he also indicated that he knew that you had found each other…" Noah and Chouette looked at each other. Good. They were worried about the group. "I got Alma into this mess. I'll get her out."

"She's my grandmother," Aubrey stated. "I'm with you, every step of the way."

After all the excitement of the kirpuuru's awakening, Noah had insisted that I take the stone eyes out. I couldn't have agreed more, and so, I had, but instead of changing them for my standard see invisible, I had put my other ones in. Noah had his contacts in so I knew he would be affected by them. I took a deep breath. They would never let me leave on my own, so I looked at Aubrey first, then Chouette. Maybe I should wait until Noah was distracted? Try to escape without him noticing. There was too much risk that he would stop me or not be affected. Or that he could stop me before it put him to sleep. I turned to him. I should put him to sleep first before he had a chance to realise what I was doing.

"Noah?" Chouette asked, startled as he slumped in his seat. Chouette next then, I turned my gaze on her and she too gave in to sleep. Aubrey. I had to get her too.

"What are you doing?" Aubrey asked as she scrambled to get out of her chair, her words slurred and her movements sloppy and uncoordinated.

"What I have to do," I said. "I'm sorry," and she slumped to the floor. I rushed to catch her, to make sure she didn't hit her head as she went down. Instead, I lowered her gently to the ground.

I grabbed my bag and looked at the little creature. "You stay here, ok? Watch over them." I picked it up and placed it on the back of the chair, so that it could observe all three of them. Then I walked out the door of the old, abandoned house, never noticing anyone watching me as I left.

The kirpuuru obviously had no intention of listening to instructions, because its giant wingspan created a shadow over me as I walked. Finally, it landed on my shoulder and nuzzled at the side of my face. With a sigh I gave it a scratch near its ears and kept on walking.

"I guess it's you and me little guy…"

Then I ran. I had no idea how long they would be asleep for and I did not want to be caught by them when they did wake up. What had I done? There wasn't time to think about it though. Regardless of what happened, I couldn't let Aubrey or Alma down and nor could I let Noah get taken for whatever Sebastian was planning.

The streets were starting to fill with people as they emerged from their homes, ready for their days. Going to work, playing with their children, just getting by, one day at a time. The beggars were coming out too. Most of them were Eyeless, with no other way of attaining money in this version of society where your worth was dictated by your level of sight.

I had to track down where Sage was headquartered in Erihall. That was most likely where they were keeping Alma. She wasn't important enough to them to risk moving her or to even bother. Plus, she was supposed to be a lure, right? I slowed to a walk as I found myself in the square where yesterday we had watched Sage present his great education plans for the unsighted masses. People were working hard, dismantling the stage and all the tents where vendors had yesterday sold delicious food.

I scratched at the kirpuuru's chin. It chirped in my ear as it tried to rub itself into my fingers. "You'll need a name, won't you?" I asked it. I hadn't expected a response or anything, but it chirped away happily, its nine tails spreading across my back and the shoulder it was sitting on. "How do those not get tangled?"

The square seemed odd in the morning light, with only workers dismantling everything and the occasional passer-by walking through. I got a few odd looks, well I suppose it was the kirpuuru everyone was actually looking at, but it made me nervous.

"I wish you had stayed with the others," I whispered to it. In response, it nibbled on my ear.

A woman passed in front of me, heading towards a man who was just standing there, watching the work unfold. His uniform was the same as all the workers, so I guessed that he was their supervisor or something.

"How long until we can get out of here?"

That voice. Was she the speaker from yesterday? The woman who had introduced Sage to the crowd at the festival. I ducked behind a tent that was still untouched and followed her from the other side.

"Give us a couple more hours Ms Reavis. We'll definitely be done by midday," the uniformed man replied.

"Faster," The woman, Ms Reavis ordered. "I want out of this hell hole of a town…"

"Not everyone here loves Sage Industries, Ms Reavis. You should know that."

She harrumphed like petulant child and muttered something about Erihall wanting everything. Their fortunes, their healthcare, their education. Everything. As she walked away though, the man made a comment that the woman did not hear.

"It's also your fault that half the town is blind and all them people died."

He wasn't important to me though. The woman though, she could probably lead me to Sage and by extension, Alma. So, I followed her. She made comments to a few of the workers who appeared to be taking breaks. Yelling at them for wasting Doctor Sage's time and money. Warned them that if they did not get back to work, she would ensure that their pay was docked for laziness and incompetence. They grumbled but moved. Obviously, they thought she was serious, because they shushed one of the young members of the group who argued that they had a right to their break.

I ignored them and made my way after the woman.

"Wow…" A man muttered. "Good fortune to us all…"

"What?" the younger man who had been complaining asked.

"A kirpuuru…" His voice sounded soft, reflective, as though he was imagining his mother telling him the stories of the kirpuuru as a child. "Everything will be fine. Seeing a kirpuuru is a good omen indeed."

"Nah man, they don't exist," the younger man insisted.

81

Apparently, Ms Reavis really had just walked through the square to check on the timing and to terrorise the workers, because she kept walking, down two more blocks and into an unmarked office building. It was guarded by Sage Security though, so I guessed that it had to be the right place.

I walked up to the door of the building. "Hey. You!" One of the security men called out to me.

"Yes?" I asked innocently. I looked nothing like the frightened girl who had fled their facility. Hattie and Chouette had made sure of that with the other girls. I didn't know if I'd ever met these men before. The voice of the speaker didn't sound familiar and between my hair, clothes and demeanour, I was nothing like the test subject I had been back there. I hoped.

"You can't be here."

"Why not?" I asked. "Free country, right? And I just need to have a word with Doctor Sage."

The two men looked at each other over my head as I reached for the handle on the door. Then the one to my right made a grab for me, only to find himself with a face full of angry kirpuuru. The creature's massive wings spread out as it left my shoulder and dove for the man. I turned my attention to the other one. I ducked his grab and passed by him. I turned back to face him as he did the same. I moved my feet into a stance that I could move in any direction from and waited. He charged.

"C'mere girl!" he said as he stretched both arms out towards me.

I stepped past him again and this time, put my hands on his shoulders. He gasped in surprise and then I put some pressure on, pulling him backwards. I jumped out of the way of his falling body, and he cried out as his head collided with the floor.

The other man had the kirpuuru pulling at his hair and he was flailing wildly at it, trying to rescue himself from its powerful little hands and feet. The man was wearing dark reflective sunglasses. I pointed to my eyes, then at the man. The kirpuuru released a tuft of hair and grabbed at the glasses.

"No!" The man cried, trying to snatch his glasses back from the creature. But I could see his eyes now.

Look at me, look at me. I thought, trying to will them to do as I wanted. Unlike some of the others, these eyes required eye contact. Cassias's training had allowed me to put one of the security guys down and the other… My little furry, feathered friend had managed to distract him long enough for me to not be stuck fighting two to one. The man slumped to the floor and the kirpuuru dropped the glasses from where it was hovering in the air above the fight. They shattered to pieces as they connected with the ground near the man's head.

I held my hand out to the creature. "Nicely done," I said as it flew to my hand and landed there. It walked over my arm and situated itself back on my shoulder, chirping happily. I couldn't help but scratch at its soft fur as I opened the door to the building.

A group were standing near the entrance to a staircase, Ms Reavis amongst them. Like the workers at the square, she was berating them for wasting her time. At my entrance, the people around her turned to look at me. Reavis on the other hand, had been so busy enjoying the sound of her own voice, that she had been oblivious to my appearance.

"Are you even listening to me?" She finally asked when she noticed that not one of them was looking at her.

"Who's she?" one asked, pointing at me.

"What is that thing?" The kirpuuru was stretching its wings at that moment, making it look as though I had wings coming from my head, or at least that was what my shadow looked like. Those wings were massive considering the small body... But then again, those wings did have to carry nine extremely fluffy tails...

The woman turned. "Who-" She was cut off though as I locked eyes with her, and the effect of my sleep eyes started to take effect.

"Look," I said. "Just remember you all did this to me," and I walked towards them, making eye contact with each of them. One by one, starting with Reavis, they sunk to their knees. I was taking them out and I wasn't killing them. This was good. Very good in fact. I just needed to find Alma and get back out again before any of them woke back up.

I stepped over them and went up the stairs. I just hoped Alma was here. I hoped that Sage was here. Maybe I could take him out! Maybe I could put an end to this entire nightmare for everyone! I shivered. What was I becoming? Had the eyes changed me? Had Cassias's training changed me? No, I didn't need to take Sage out. I needed to hold him accountable for what he'd done to us. We would all have to live with the consequences of his actions, so should he.

The kirpuuru chirped loudly in my ear. Not the gentle little happy chatter it had been letting off since its arrival in my life, but an angry squawking like sound. You would think, as someone who had been blind for as long as she could remember, that I would take more effort taking in my surroundings, keeping an eye on everything around me. Apparently... I was getting complacent.

Sage. Yes, the man himself. Doctor Nelson Sage stood in the far doorway to the room I had emerged into from the stairs. "So good of you to return."

"I'm not back for you. I just want Alma."

With his good arm, Sage waved at someone behind him and one of the security guys came in. The man stood behind Alma and wrapped an arm around Alma's neck, the gun in his other hand, pointed at her head. This I had not expected. They had been waiting for me. Why were they waiting for me? Nothing made any sense.

Had Sebastian told him I was coming? Wait, wasn't it Sebastian who'd taken Alma? He'd offered to return her for Noah. Was I wrong about everything. Did Sebastian just have access to Alma through Sage? Was it really Sage all along who'd taken Alma to lure me back to him? What was going on? Had someone else seen me? Maybe my entrance had been too showy, and they'd been watching on their security system. I'd made a mess of everything, and I still had no idea who was doing what.

"Alma!" I gasped.

"Juniper!" Alma's sweet, grandmotherly voice sounded strained and tired. Her neat hair was frizzy and flying all over the place. She was alive. That was all that mattered.

The first person in my remembered life to ever actively be nice to me for no ulterior motives was in trouble. What on earth was I supposed to do? The security guy holding her was wearing those reflective sunglasses and there was no way that the kirpuuru could reach him before he pulled the trigger on Alma or it. Was its body flesh that could be hurt? Was it stone under all that fur? I had no idea and no desire to see the odd little creature hurt because of me.

"Oh, how sweet," Sage spat. "A reunion of friends."

"Release her," I said staring at him. "She has nothing to do with this!"

Sage scoffed. "Oh, she has everything to do with this." He stepped forward. No matter how much I stared at him, nothing happened. Was he immune somehow? No way... "Contact lenses made specifically to protect the wearer from the likes of you." Wait, if they had something like that, why did Sebastian want Noah? I assumed he wanted Noah as a counter... but why not get the contact lenses?

"To bad I didn't shatter you that day!" I shot back at him.

Alma was struggling with her captor. "JUNI-" the rest of my name was cut off as the man muffled her and dragged her from the room. Then a crashing pain ricocheted through my head. With a gasp, I fell to one knee. The kirpuuru launched itself from my shoulder as I fell.

"Get that thing!" Sage ordered, but I wasn't able to see what was going after the little creature as my head swam and another his sent me face first into the floor.

82

I awoke with a headache that could rival being run over by a truck. I opened my eyes to find nothing but darkness. Had the hit to my head done something to my sight? No… As I blinked, trying to find the light, I could feel that both my sockets were empty. Again, they had taken my sight. I bit down on my lip to keep from crying out.

"Girl? Juniper?"

"Sebastian," I said. I had recognised the voice, and I wrestled with my restraints. Getting my hands on him seemed liked a pretty good idea.

"Here," I felt him kneel down in front of me. He placed a hand on my knee, and I tried to kick out at him, but he pressed down harder. "I can leave you in the darkness if you prefer," he said, his voice taking on a stern, almost cruel tone.

He paused and waited for me to respond. I said nothing. I was not going to dignify him with a response. Instead, I stayed still as he inserted eyes into my empty sockets. It was almost like that time when he had helped me escape. My head even hurt in the same way, except this time… This time, Sebastian was no friend. There was no escape at the end of this for me, but maybe for Alma. Maybe for Noah. The pain and the seizure hit as it always did, but I had put eyes in and out so often over the past few weeks that the pain was now manageable. Or at least, I had gotten so used to it that I didn't respond in the same way Sebastian had expected.

As the pain subsided, I breathed a sigh of relief and opened my eyes. Yeah, I could have done without seeing Sebastian again. I blinked again though. I had gotten so used to wearing what had become my 'regular' eyes, that it had never occurred to me that they cast an unusual green hue across the world. Especially since most of them seemed to do that. Everything was always sort of faded, maybe because of the abilities added to them. That was true of all of these but one.

"These are the plain ones…" I said. Stupid I know. He knew exactly what he had given me.

"Yes. I found them exactly where you told me they were." I said nothing. Sebastian stood up and walked around me. "Nice mini case. Sleep and stone. Interesting selection."

Stone. Why hadn't I used that one? That on would have taken Sage out, contact lenses or no contact lenses. It didn't need the person to be looking me in the eyes to be affected.

Oh crap! Where was that little beast, I had woken up that morning? I look around frantically. The kirpuuru was nowhere to be seen.

"After attacking everyone in sight, we finally managed to chase that mangy beast out of here," Sebastian said, somehow know what I was thinking about. *Mangy beast?* He crouched down in front of me, elbows on his knees, chin in on his clasped hands. "Juniper, we share the same goal. The end of Nelson Sage."

I shook my head. Yeah, right. Whatever it was that Sebastian wanted, I was certain that our goals did not align. Even if they both included the removal of Nelson Sage from this world.

"Come on!" Sebastian exclaimed. "Say something!"

"What do you want me to say?" I asked. "You set up Alma to be taken in by Sage, you set me up, you kidnapped me... And now you think I want to help you?"

"Juniper," Sebastian said getting in my face. "I never did anything to the old woman. She was here and her presence happened to be useful to my purpose." His hand caressed my face. I pulled back. "We were supposed to be partners."

"You're crazy!" I spat. "And I told you. Don't call me Girl! It's Juniper."

"Juniper, Juniper, Juniper," Sebastian crooned. His hand returned to my cheek and there was nowhere else for me to move. The backs of his fingers trailed down my cheek, under my chin and down my neck. "You. You were supposed to be my future. You and that boy. The others too, who hate my... Hate Sage."

I shook my head, trying to dislodge him. "You. Sage. You can't have them," I hissed. "You and that mad man ruined us."

He shook his head. "Each and every one of you was blind or steadily going blind. We gave you a chance at a life!" He stood up, paced in front of me. I was making him frustrated. "Don't you get it?"

I had to admit, that I really did not get what he was getting at. I didn't think that he would take that answer well, so I stayed silent.

Sebastian stormed out of the room and halted, trying to control his breathing. When several deep breaths failed to calm hm, he kicked at a chair, sending it skidding into the table. It shifted, screeching against the linoleum floor and into the other chairs. Why wouldn't she tell him what he wanted to know? Her lack of answering had frustrated him to the point of having to leave her presence before he'd hurt her... He never wanted to hurt her. Or at least that was what he had said before storming out of the room and calling her ungrateful. He never wanted to hurt her, but she owed him! He'd gotten her out of the lab. He'd gotten her free. It was because of him that she even had this new life. What was one boy for all of that? It wasn't like he wanted to hurt the boy either. He just needed him if any of this was going to work.

His body quaked with fury. The way she had looked at him. Like... Like she didn't trust him. After everything he had done for her, why wouldn't she trust him? Then he'd been foolish in his attempts to win her over. The way he had touched her... Trailed his fingers over her cheek. She was beautiful, there was no denying it. She always had been and the new fiery personality that he found so frustrating was... It was something wanted to see more of... Just not directed at him. Imagine what he could do with her at his side? What had he expected though? That she would be so indebted to him that she would fall madly in love with him, her so-called saviour? He was ashamed to admit it, but yes... That was exactly what he'd hoped for.

He heard her pulling at the restraints. Well, wasn't this just great? How was he going to get her to trust him like this? He needed to make amends. He was considering going back to her, talking sense into her when someone stepped into the room.

"Mr. Anson, there is somebody here to see you," the young receptionist said.

"Who?" he asked, his hand resting on the doorknob back into the holding room.

"A young lady. She refused to give her name."

"Show her in," Sebastian ordered, turning away from the door and going to tidy up the mess he'd made of the chairs around the table. Maybe it was someone who could help him stop all this madness.

"Mr. Sebastian?" He knew that voice. From where? He turned to face the young woman. And realisation came over him.

"Ahhh," Sebastian said. "You're Juniper's friend, right?" What was her name again? Aubrey! That was right. Her name was Aubrey. What was she doing here? What could this girl want from him? Sebastian glanced awkwardly to the door that hid Juniper. Was this some sort of decoy?

"Yes. That's right," Aubrey responded, watching him intently. "I was hoping that you and I might talk," she said. Her hands grasped the back of the chair before her, turning her knuckles white. She looked around the room, before settling her gaze on Sebastian, seemingly having centred herself "The woman being held by Doctor Sage is my grandmother. I will do anything to get her back."

Sebastian stood still for a moment. She was also the old woman's granddaughter. what did she want with him? Was Juniper's unwillingness to part with the boy for the wellbeing of the old woman wearing thin on this girl? "I'm so sorry for the predicament Juniper has left you and your family in," he said carefully.

"Oh, I wouldn't call it a predicament," Aubrey said, "but, I think that you and I can help each other." He couldn't believe it. Was she really... "When we met last time… You mentioned that you were after a boy… I know where to find him."

84

I seriously did not know how much more I could take of this. I could hear them in the other room, Aubrey was betraying Noah. She was betraying all of us. Sebastian must not have closed the door properly when he'd stormed out and I could hear her every backstabbing word as she offered Noh up to Sebastian. I needed to get out this damned chair. The kirpuuru was nowhere to be found, and Noah and the others would never speak to me again for not telling them Sebastian's price and leaving them behind. I needed to stop her.

There was a thud, then a crash. "Oh crap!" A voice said and I could hear the sound of thumping, like someone jumping or hopping up and down. "That hurt!" I knew that voice too.

"Hattie?" I asked. It was odd not being able to see her. "Where are you?" I asked, looking around. I knew it was useless. I didn't have the right eyes in to see her, but I did it anyway.

"The closet!" and the door of that said space opened. Nothing stepped out as far as I could see, but Hattie's feet made little impressions on the carpet.

"Hattie are you-." I started to ask, remembering her usual state of undress when she wandered about completely invisible.

"No!" Hattie replied excitedly. "Mech and Emrys… they'd apparently been working on this idea for invisible clothes for ages. I had no idea."

Well, I had not been expecting that. "So…"

"Fully clothed. Well, I mean, it's only a tank top and some bike shorts, but hey! Gotta start somewhere, right?"

"Right…" I said, watching the footprints appear in the carpet. The door opened and Sebastian appeared. Aubrey was long gone by now and I was still seething about her betrayal of Noah and the others. I had promised that I would get Alma back. I just did not want to put Noah at risk to do it. I had the feeling that Alma would agree with me on that choice. Not that I knew the old woman like her granddaughter did I suppose…

"Well," Sebastian said, entering. There was a look of manic glee on his face. "It looks like I'll get everything I want after all." He crouched down in front of me again. "See, everything has a way of working out in the end." That hand was on my cheek, and he wound his fingers around my chin. He pulled me towards him. Our faces were so close, our noses were practically touching, and our breaths mingled. Was he going to kiss me? Seriously? The thought made me shudder in disgust. While maybe… once, for a fleeting moment in time, I might have welcomed the advance, now? Not so much. Sebastian had shown his true colours, and I wanted nothing to do with him.

Behind him, a chair rose in the air like magic and as he leaned in closer, Hattie brought the chair down on Sebastian's head. "Ain't nobody kissing our Juni, 'cept Noah!" She cried as the chair collided with his head. There was nothing I could do to avoid it. A leg of the chair snapped off as it broke into pieces with the impact on Sebastian's head. Sebastian's hand fell away from my face, and he crumpled to the floor, as I shut my eyes tight, trying to avoid the incoming chair leg. It collided with my face with excruciating force. A sound of pain left my body, but I think I might have also been choking… Why was I choking when I had just been whacked in the face with the flying leg of a chair? What the hell had Hattie just said? Why on earth would Noah be kissing me? What was Hattie going on about?

"Oh my god!" Hattie cried. "Juni! I'm so sorry! Sorry, sorry, sorry!"

It had been mentioned in my presence before, mainly by Hattie, but it was total fiction. Wasn't it? "Untie me, would you?" I asked. My head was killing me. I felt her hands at my bound wrists as soon as she agreed. My issue with the whole idea that she had that Noah was interested in me, was that from what I had seen, he was always with Chouette.

"Don't act so innocent," Hattie said in a regular tone. "Everybody knows he's got eyes for you."

So, she was going to continue that ridiculous idea of hers. As my hands came free, I leaned forward to try and untie my feet. The invisible girl came around and worked on my other foot. "Chouette," I said.

"What about Chouette?" Hattie asked.

"Noah and Chouette," I elaborated.

Hattie laughed and I was quick to try and shoosh her. It was harder, not being able to see her or anything. "Noah and Chouette?" Hattie asked in a loud whisper. "Oh, you're funny!"

Noah. Aubrey had betrayed Noah. "Hattie!" I exclaimed suddenly. Maybe even a little too loud considering what we were doing. Had she heard what Aubrey had done?

"What?" She asked surprised.

"Noah!" I cried. "Noah's in danger!"

"What? How?" Hattie explained. I could see something moving through Sebastian's pockets. She pulled out the little case Mech had made up for me. "Here," she said. "Which ones are you wearing? I don't recognise them."

"They're just plain," I said. "Nothing but sight."

"Well, go put in something more useful than that. We gotta get out of here and go save Noah. Maybe it would be good if you could see me? Or maybe blow stuff up?"

I looked sideways at her as I opened the case. "What would you prefer?"

"Wait, seriously? That's a choice?"

"Not exactly. I'm not going to be blowing anything up… But… I could turn stuff to stone… or see you. Which one is it?" I couldn't see the sleep ones that I had been using when I entered. I wondered what Sebastian had done with them, but it didn't really matter. We had to get out of here.

"Ehh… See me," Hattie finally selected.

I nodded. "Ok, keep watch."

Hattie's footprints moved towards the door to the rest of the building. I imagined her nodding at me. Then I went through the process of plunging myself into darkness by removing my eyes. Gee, my face hurt… That chair leg was going to leave a bruise. I was sure of it. I slipped one of the new ones in, then braced myself for the second. Just because I seemed to be doing this frequently did not mean that I enjoyed it.

"Juni?" Hattie asked, concern in her voice.

"Fine. Fine," I croaked at her. I opened my eyes and saw her. Standing there by the door of the room and to my surprise, she was dressed. Just like she had said. A black tank top and black bike shorts. They weren't flattering in the least, they were tight, showing off her toned body, but Hattie had such a vibrant personality that the no nonsense black garb against her white, almost translucent skin just seemed so unlike her that it seemed wrong. Still, she was clothed and still invisible. "Huh…" I said. "I wonder how they did that…"

"No idea… But cool right?"

"Yeah, very cool," I said, zipping the case back up and shoving it into my pocket. "Don't suppose you saw a flying ferret on your way, did you?"

85

The kirpuuru had been sitting on the roof of the building we were in. I had no idea how it had gotten there, but I was relieved to see it unharmed. They might have kicked it out, but maybe someone had been superstitious enough to not hurt the creature. Legends and myths related to the kirpuuru were varied enough that everyone thought that the little creatures were harbingers of luck or doom. It just depended on where you were from. Harming a kirpuuru, even when known as a trickster, was said to bring bad luck down upon the perpetrator.

As soon as we exited the building, it came swooping down, screeching in delight, almost barrelling into my face in a meteor of fur and feathers. It settled on my shoulder as it calmed and began to nuzzle at my face. Its little hands held onto my cheeks, turning my face to look at it and trying to keep me close as it did so.

Hattie squealed in delight. "Oh my god! It's so cute!" Then she stopped and a silent Hattie was a Hattie worth worrying about. Looking over at her, I realised that Hattie had stopped short and was staring at the kirpuuru as it now stared at her. "That… That…" Hattie leaned over to have a look at the creature. She lifted her hand as though to touch it but hesitated. "It really is... It's a…"

"A kirpuuru," I said, stroking the creature's furry little back as it continued to stare at Hattie.

"Wow…" Hattie exclaimed in wounder. "Can I touch it?" she asked, her hand still hovering awkwardly inches away from the creature.

I shrugged. "I don't know… You can try…" In all honesty, I had no idea how or why the creature did anything. If Hattie wanted to try and pet it, who was I to stop her? It's not like the creature was mine, even as it clung to me.

"You know…" Hattie said softly as she came closer. "I'm from Susweassau… Well, my parents are… were… whatever… I grew up listening to stories of The kirpuuru…" She reached her hand out tentatively towards the creature. It nuzzled against my cheek and stared at Hattie, or maybe where it felt the disturbance coming from. I don't know if it could see Hattie, but as her fingers gently ran through the creature's fur, it leaned away from my cheek and rubbed itself against her hand. "Wow… Where… How…? Where did it come from? They're myth… aren't they?"

I bit my lip. "It was a statue… I think I turned it to flesh. It's a long story," I muttered. The problem with being able to see Hattie, was that I could see her facial expression. The shock and awe of my statement. I knew that she wanted to ask more. Hell, I wanted to know more. The fact that I had turned the statue to flesh and fur and feather still weighed on me. What did it mean in the long run? I could turn things to stone and turn things back to flesh? Could I turn the statues in the park into a random army of lumbering stone? Wouldn't that be a sight? Hattie wanted the entire story, I was sure. We just did not have the time to get into it. Or maybe we did, and I didn't want to tell it. There were more important things to do. We had to get back to the others before Aubrey did.

"Come on, let's go. We have to get back to Noah and the others. Aubrey's trying to exchange him for her grandmother."

Hattie nodded. "Right, let's go."

We took off running.

I didn't really know where we were going. For some reason, I had decided that running back to where I had left the others was the best idea. I don't know why I thought that after everything, that they would still be there. Aubrey had obviously left, so wouldn't Chouette or Noah? What if Aubrey already had Noah? What if I had been out for so long that she had already turned him over?

"Kattie and I were supposed to meet there," Hattie said pointing towards a small park. She leaned over, hands on her knees as she tried to catch her breath. I had no idea how far we'd run, but the stitch that was starting to form on my side was an indicator that I had done enough for the night. "Well, that was the plan at least." I let her take the lead. Above us, the kirpuuru flew, it's massive wings and nine fluttering tails casting a shadow over us. It was almost like we were following that shadow to salvation.

"There!" I heard a call. Chouette had spotted the kirpuuru. Kattie suddenly came around a corner and without any shame, Hattie ran right to him. I looked. Chouette appeared, but Noah did not. I came to a stop before them as Kattie released Hattie. No matter how much he grumbled about her, or she tried to set everyone else up, I knew that those two were made for each other. Maybe even literally, as he was the only one that could always see her. Something to be said about a man who always sees the real you, I think.

"Where's Noah?" I asked.

"I don't know," Chouette said hugging me. "He and Aubrey went off together stating that they had a plan."

I looked at Hattie. "Crap!" I cried.

"This is so not good!" Hattie said. Probably the most sedate that I had ever seen her.

"What's going on?" Chouette asked, looking between us.

"Aubrey's gonna turn Noah over to Sage's lot for her grandmother," Hattie said. She wrapped an arm around one of Kattie's and rested her head on his shoulder.

"Why?" Chouette turned to me. "What happened?"

The kirpuuru circled above us, before coming down and startling Kattie by sitting on Hattie's head. "Woah!"

"It's a kirpuuru," Hattie said wistfully. "They're good luck!" She reached up and scratched at its furry body.

"I'm not seeing much good luck here," Chouette shot at her. "What's going on with Aubrey and what's Noah got to do with it?"

"I didn't think Aubrey knew this… But maybe she guessed," I started. Crappy starting, I know. Almost like I was trying to make an excuse. "Sebastian wants Noah, cause of his ability. Apparently, he's the only one it's ever worked on, and he thinks that by having Noah he can take Sage down… He thought that I would do it. Thought that I would lead him to all of you and bring him Noah…"

"But you didn't," Hattie said.

"I brought him someone who was willing to," I said looking at her. "Same thing in the long run."

"And not to mention the fact that that guy was crazy obsessed with you," Hattie added. "I mean… He had so many pictures of you and then there was the fact that he tried to- "

"I remember," I interrupted. "I was there." I shivered at the thought. Then stopped short and looked back at her. "Pictures? What pictures?"

Hattie just nodded knowingly. "Like… Pictures of you in the lab… At least I think that's where they were from. You had no eyes in and there looked to be lots of different labby kind of things around you." I shivered. "Anyway, I knocked old Sebastian out pretty good… So… Where do you think they'd go?" Hattie asked.

Chouette wrung her fingers. "Ok…" She said, "we just need to find Aubrey and Noah then."

"They'll have moved Alma after what I did…" I said.

Kattie nodded. "All the Sage personnel have pretty much left town after everything was packed up. But there is another truck that's still preparing to leave."

"It's probably going to the facility in the woods," I said. "That's where I escaped from…"

Chouette nodded. "Ok… So… What are you suggesting?"

I paced. Just three steps up, three steps back. I'd paced further back in my room at the facility. I could feel their eyes on me, Chouette more obvious with her following me as her head moved with my every step to keep me in sight. Kattie's eyes moved back and forth, while Hattie kept scratching at the kirpuuru perched on her head. But it too, was following my every move.

"We use that transport to get in. The one Kattie mentioned."

"You could put some of the people to sleep…" Chouette said, her eyes staring right at me. "Like you did to us…"

I paused and looked at her. "I'm sorry… I can't…" The sorry was also about the act of putting them to sleep. I really had been trying to keep them safe. "I can't," I said again. "Sebastian has those ones…"

"So…" Chouette pressed.

Kattie cracked his knuckles. "Let's go knock some people out!"

We all nodded in agreement. Back to the Sage building in that case. Everything seemed to revolve around that place. We took off walking again, side by side. The kirpuuru spread its wings and flew up from Hattie's head as she moved. It came to land on my shoulder.

We started to jog as we neared the building, and Hattie had to be yanked back out of the way by Kattie as a truck back hurtling out of a laneway nearby. She fell back into him, and they both stumbled. The whole matter was made worse when we noticed the Sage Industries logo on the side of the truck.

"Was that our ride?" I asked Kattie. He nodded as he set Hattie straight on her feet.

"Yeah."

"Alma's place!" I exclaimed. "Are any of them still there?" Kattie shrugged. "Ok, ok. Even if they're not, from there we can get back to the bikes. Try to cut them off on the road."

"Let's go," Chouette said. We turned down the street the truck had just come out of. The town was eerily silent now that the Sage people were leaving. It was like they only came alive for Sage to have an audience to perform for. Even amongst those out and about on the street, they walked quietly. They kept to themselves. The sighted and unsighted clearly segregated by their actions and movements.

Alma's house seemed to loom in the distance. We occasionally got strange looks because of the kirpuuru, but no one stopped us and for me, that was almost even more ominous than if someone had. We were four… ok, three, because no one else but Kattie and I could see Hattie, kids walking down the street, a magical flying ferret on my shoulder and people barely looked at us.

A man lying under a bench reached out an arm, a bowl in his hands. He didn't bother speaking, but when I took a good look at him, under the filth of the street, I could see that he was an Eyeless man. I crouched down beside him. "It will get better," I said softly to him. If he had had eyes, I think he could have looked right into my soul in that moment.

"Juniper," Chouette said. I clasped the man's hand.

"I have nothing to give you. I'm sorry." It broke my heart to try and leave him, but his hand found a strength I had not thought he possessed, and he pulled me back to him. With his other hand, he motioned for me to lean in closer. I did.

"Death…." The old man croaked. "Death lies ahead… For… For you…" I clasped my other hand over his. "Run!" he gasped, before releasing me. "Run!"

He released me so suddenly that I fell backwards, falling on my butt. It hurt, but the man had startled me, chilling me to the very core of my being. Hattie helped me up and the man seemed to follow her movements, but he was as eyeless as me without my eyes in, so there was no way that he could possibly see Hattie or anyone else.

She pulled me along as I looked back at the old eyeless man. Kattie brought up our rear and I heard him mumbling something about the truly Eyeless being even scarier than anyone had thought. I wanted to ask him what he meant, but there was no time.

Alma's house was ahead of us and if Sage's people were still there, then we needed to be wary. I took the lead, taking us in via the back gate in the garden. The large trees would hide us from view from the house until we stepped out into the middle where the well was, but that wouldn't help us as a security guy stepped out from around a hedge right in front of us.

He lowered his weapon at us. Gun. Just great. The kirpuuru launched itself from my shoulder and dived at the man. A shot went off into the ground near my feet as the creature grabbed for the man's startled face. I jumped out of the way, rolling as I hit the ground. Chouette backed off.

Hattie took the time the security guy was distracted to run past him. Kattie shifted into a fighting pose and so did I as I came to my feet. Big wings flapped in the man's face as the kirpuuru held onto the weapon and kept trying to rip it from his hands. Hattie grabbed at the man, leaving him between her grip and the kirpuuru's. He screamed as the gun was ripped from his hands and Hattie's arm wrapped around his neck. Kattie came forward and punched the man straight in the nose. He crumpled in Hattie's arms. The creature dropped the gun at his feet then returned to my shoulder.

I looked around. "Chouette?" She poked her head out from behind a hedge.

"Here."

"You ok?" Hattie asked.

Chouette looked a little rattled, but she nodded. "Let's go. If there's guards here, we should take a better look inside the house I think."

We all agreed. Maybe this was where Aubrey had brought Noah for her exchange. Maybe the irony of the situation was that they had held Alma at her own house all along. That would really suck, seeing as how we came into town through this very yard.

We dragged the unconscious security guy further into the cover of the trees. "Kattie," I suggested as I looked at the uniform.

"You want me to take his uniform?" The three of us nodded at him and he sighed. "Great... Turn around at least..." Chouette and I did as asked. "You too Hattie. Not everyone is as comfortable with public nudity as you are!"

She giggled in delight but turned around. We could hear the sounds of Kattie undressing the security guy and then himself. No one said anything, but Hattie kept on giggling. Chouette and I both shushed her. It seemed to take forever, but finally Kattie emerged, dressed in the guard's uniform. In one hand, he held the weapon that the kirpuuru had dropped at his feet earlier. An idea came to me. "Kattie can walk us right in!" Chouette and Hattie both looked at me, but I pointed at the weapon. Tie our hands, or at least make it look like you did, the walk us in, that gun at our backs. Boom, we're in the front door and no one is the wiser!"

"I like it!" Hattie said. "And nobody ever sees me coming!" She said with a grin.

Chouette held her hand out towards Kattie. "Come on. Let's get this over with. We've got to find Aubrey and Noah before it's too late."

87

"Hey!" I cried. Kattie had poked me in the back with the end of the gun he was carrying, and I had stumbled slightly. "Watch where you poke that thing."

"Move," Kattie said. It sounded like he was trying to bring out his inner Cassias with that monosyllabic response.

"We're moving! We're moving," Chouette shot back.

This time, he poked at Chouette. I have to say, being able to see Hattie was not a beneficial thing. Watching her as she held her hands over her mouth trying not to laugh was starting to set me off. This whole situation was so ridiculous and her reactions so… Well, Hattie… That I was having a hard time. I envied Chouette her ignorance of the girl's antics.

We were inside and there were so many more people than we had first suspected. Security guys, researchers in their white coats and others who I for one, could not identify the purpose of. It was like they had completely taken over Alma's house since the last time we were there. Kattie walked us up the stairs in the front foyer to the second story of the house.

As soon as our feet hit the mezzanine. "Hold it there!" Oh crap. Oh crap. Oh crap. I recognised that voice and against my will I froze. Chouette turned her head to look at the speaker but didn't say anything. Hattie seemed to instantly sober up. "Where did you find these two?"

"In the gardens, sir," Kattie announced. "They were trying to break in."

The man stepped closer. Ignored Chouette and inspected my face. He came right up close, and I could smell his breath. I had never seen his face, except maybe 'that' day, but I knew his voice. I knew his smell. Stinky. The constant companion of the late and unlamented Scratchy.

"You!" He hissed, taking my chin in his hand.

"Oh boy," I mumbled. His hand left my chin and before I could react, he backhanded me. I went sprawling into Chouette and together we collapsed down to the floor.

"What the hell?" Kattie asked. "Those are my prisoners!"

Stinky stormed up to him. He easily towered over Kattie, and he looked down at him. "Don't you know who that is? That... That... That thing!" He was pointing at me with one of those stubby fingers of his that I had always felt. "She killed my mate. She ruined Doc Sage. She is a monster!"

I ripped my hands loose from the restraints and launched myself at him. "You're the monster!" I screamed. I have to admit, Cassias's training, it went right out the window. This man had made my life a living hell the entire time I had been at the facility. I collided with him and went tumbling away from Kattie.

"Juniper!" Chouette cried as she too ripped her hands loose from the ties we had used as our disguises.

I went to hit the man, but he was so much bigger. So much stronger and I had let my anger take away any sense of calm or reason. He tossed me off him. I jumped to my feet and turned instantly to find Hattie clinging to his back. He was wrestling with her, not knowing what was happening because unlike me, he couldn't see her.

The racket we were making had drawn others into the fray and Kattie fired on a group of security guys coming up the stairs. More were coming down the corridor to our left. We were totally going to outnumbered soon. One fell down the stairs, taking the guys behind him down in one big thumping mess of men and weapons.

Stinky managed to get a grip on Hattie and he tossed her off his back, but she fell to the floor, right in front of two oncoming guys who, not seeing her there, they suddenly tripped, falling over her. With Hattie struggling beneath them, they both had issues getting back up. One screamed as she bit him. His hand had wound up in her mouth somehow.

"Maybe we coulda used those stone eyes," Kattie called over his shoulder as several armed men started back up the stairs. That was probably the wrong thing to say because Stinky lost it. He roared like a mad man and charged at me.

I stepped out his way. It was a near thing too. He managed to collide with my shoulder, and I felt myself spin out of control. Stinky turned, a rage in his eyes that made Sebastian's words from that day echo in my head. *They want you dead.* Stinky was not going to let me leave here alive and he would kill all of us to ensure that that happened. He reached for Kattie, trying to take the gun with which Kattie was firing at the men coming up the stairs. Kattie hit him in the gut with the butt of the gun and a shot went wild, shattering one of Alma's second floor windows.

Stinky tried again for Kattie and I grabbed him from behind. He was big, but I was fast. He tried to turn, elbow me in the gut. I jumped away before he could connect. My aim had been accomplished though. His attention was back on me and off Kattie. Behind me, I heard a man scream as Hattie went wild at him, kicking and punching with everything she had. It might not have been any recognisable fighting style that Cassias would approve of but given the fact that the man who she had waylaid couldn't see her, it worked in her favour. I couldn't find Chouette, but I had no time to worry about her. Stinky reached for me. I dropped to my knee and swiped at the back of his knee.

His leg went flying out and he fell to the ground hard beside me. I started to stand, but he rolled over on his side, grabbing me and continuing his momentum until I was under him. I gasped as his hands went around my throat. This was it. I was done for.

Suddenly, the floor next to me exploded. Wooden splinters flew into Stinky's face and mine. Tiny, searing burns ripped across my cheek and forehead. I gasped in shock as Stinky rolled way from the shot. I craned my neck to see where the shot had come from. I grinned, crouching in the broken window was Aubrey. Her rifle pointed so that she could see using the goggles Mech had given her.

Aubrey.

That shot had been awfully close to my head. Stinky didn't give me any time to contemplate Aubrey's presence or her target. He was on his feet, and he hauled me up by the front of my shirt. I scrambled, trying to keep my feet on the ground. I kicked at him, and I felt my foot connect with something. His knee from the way he howled in pain, maybe.

And then I was falling. The backs of my knees connected with the top of the banister and my upper body started to go over, going backwards. Somewhere, I heard Chouette scream. Was it my name? I don't know. Time seemed to slow down around me and yet, there was nothing I could do to stop my backward momentum. I was falling and then I was upside down, my legs the only thing holding onto the banister, like a kid hanging from the monkey bars.

Gee… it was a really long way down to the floor…

My hands were scrambling for anything. A rung of the banister, the floor, anything that I could hold onto when the inevitable happened. I could hear Stinky. He was laughing. Another shot rang out from Aubrey's direction and Stinky howled. But the banister shook, and I felt my legs slip.

The floor was all I could see. It would come soon enough. And then he was there. Noah ran into the downstairs foyer. He looked up and he saw me. I saw his mouth form my name and the horror in his eyes. My hands went back to scrabbling for a hold.

And then he passed from my view as my legs swung down under me. The weight of my body pulled at my arms, but I was not falling. I was hanging. I was hanging and I was alive. I couldn't see anyone else, not Noah or Chouette, Hattie or Kattie. Nor could I see Aubrey, where she was likely still crouched in the broken window, her rifle poised to shoot.

But at who? Me? Stinky? Someone else?

I let out a breath I didn't know I'd been holding and suddenly, I could hear again. People shouting my name. People I knew. People I loved.

I looked up. Maybe I could pull myself up, but as I wriggled the fingers on my right hand and thought about how I would pull myself up, I saw Stinky there and his foot crashed into the railing. Pain erupted in my fingers, and I lost the grip completely with that hand. I swung. I heard someone scream. Maybe it was me. Maybe it was someone else. The powerful report of a rifle firing echoed through the room and Stinky jerked backwards as he was hit. I have no idea where, I couldn't see.

No matter how hard I tried I couldn't get my grip up. Worse than that, if there really is worse than hanging from one hand off a balcony over a marble floor, but I could not see the others. I couldn't find Kattie anymore and had not heard the sound of his gun in a while. Hattie and Chouette were completely out of my line of sight, and I had no idea what had become of Noah. Then there was the question of what Aubrey was doing.

And then the swerving, uncoordinated body of Stinking crashed into the banister just a hair's breadth beside me. The wood already strained by me gave way under the force of his impact and his weight. The whole banister shook, and he brushed past me, some part of him clipping my ankle as he went down.

My fingers. They couldn't take it anymore. I could feel them sliding from the shaking banister. I was going down too. There was no avoiding it. My heart seemed to hammer in my head, a never-ending tattoo of drums that seemed to spell my inevitable doom. I looked down and that was a huge mistake. Stinky had landed headfirst and his body was laying there, broken in the middle of the foyer floor. Oh god... Was I going to wind up like that?

A hand grasped mine. I looked up to find Noah, laying on the edge of the mezzanine, both hands wrapped around my wrist. I must have let out a sigh of relief, because I felt my entire body sag. "I've got you," Noah called down to me.

Kattie appeared beside Noah. "Give me your hand!"

I reach up, but there was no way Kattie could reach me with the distance between his position and that arm. I looked up at Noah and our eyes met. He nodded to me and with his help, I swung. Kattie's fingers brushed against mine, but I swung back in the opposite direction before he could get a grip on me.

"Again!" Noah and I said together and back I went. This time, Kattie's hand clasped around my wrist. Together, they hauled me up through the broken segment of banister. I collapsed to the floor in between the two of them, heaving for a solid breath now that it was over. The three of us lay there for a moment, before Noah sat up and then settled into a crouch. He held his hand out to me, and I took it. He helped me to my feet. I could hear Kattie behind me, also getting up. Noah pulled me into his arms. It was sudden and it was tight. It also probably hurt more than it should, but I would not complain. Not at this point in time. He held me in a bear hug, and I wrapped my arms around his waist. It was as far as I could move my arms.

"Thank you," I breathed out.

"Always," he murmured in my ear.

My heart rate was finally starting to settle, when out of the corner of my eye, I saw her. Aubrey. She was still positioned in that broken window, and she had her rifle lowered at us. "Get down!" I cried and pulled, Noah down with me. Aubrey's shot when over our heads and we both looked to see where it had landed.

One last Sage security guy had appeared. Hattie who was helping Kattie up had been too distracted to notice him and Chouette, I couldn't see her anywhere. The man had managed to make it almost all the way to Noah and me… And we had never noticed him.

I looked back at Aubrey. She still had her rifle positioned to shoot, but she looked at us with a smile. But was it a smile of comradery or something else? I didn't know what to think anymore.

"Is it safe?" Chouette was peeking her head out from behind a doorway. She saw Kattie being pulled up by nothing, and she could see Noah and me still holding each other. I swear that before I stepped out of his embrace, I saw her smirking. She could not possibly have the same thoughts as Hattie, right?

"Aubrey," Noah called out.

"Yeah?" Aubrey called from her perch.

"You coming back any time soon?"

"Yep," Aubrey responded. "Just let me come round to an actual door…"

She got up from her crouch and we could see her make her way past the neighbouring windows. It didn't take long for her to emerge from the hall that led onto the upstairs mezzanine. She walked towards us slowly, her rifle held against her shoulder. Noah was the only one who looked friendly to her. Everyone else had heard what I'd told them about her betrayal and Chouette looked as though she was shooting daggers from her eyes. It was probably a good thing that Chouette did not have one of the attack eye abilities at that moment.

"You have a lot of nerve!" Chouette hissed as Aubrey passed her.

Hattie held Kattie's arm tighter, and he looked away.

Me? I personally wanted to clock her. Knock her daylights out. I stepped towards her, ready to meet her and do exactly that. The look in her eyes as my fist raised, ready for the biggest impact I could prepare was incredibly satisfying.

But as I was propelling my fist forward, ready for the satisfaction of dealing with her a fully prepared for the impact of fist against cheek, my arm was grabbed from behind.

"Wait!" Noah cried.

I turned to him fury in my eyes. "Do you know what she was going to do to you?"

"Yeah!" Hattie cried. "That traitor was totally going to sell you out!"

"No, I wasn't!" Aubrey cried.

Noah though, had turned his attention to where he had heard Hattie's voice come from. "I should have guessed if Kattie was here, so were you. But Aubrey was not turning me in."

"She wasn't?" Chouette asked, looking between us.

"No!" Aubrey exclaimed. "It was all a ploy to get us in here."

"Aubrey explained what she thought happened at the meeting with Sebastian," Noah explained. He pushed my fist down too, keeping contact with my hand until it was by my side. "We came up with a plan to make it look like she was giving me over."

"How did you all find out anyway?" Aubrey asked.

"I was tied up in the next room when you met with Sebastian," I told them.

"Oh Juniper!" Aubrey cried, her face crumpling with grief. "I had no idea!"

"Why didn't you tell us?" Chouette asked, giving Noah a somewhat aggressive, but playful shove.

"There was no time..." Noah started.

"We had no idea how much time had passed since Juniper had left and..." Aubrey tried to explain. "It seemed like the easier route. To just go."

"Easier?" Chouette asked. "Hattie and Juniper came back to tell us you had turned traitor and that you were potentially taking Noah to his death! All that shooting back there, I for one, couldn't tell if you were trying to kill the bad guys or Juniper or Noah or both..."

I nodded. "Felt pretty daunting at times, just how close they came..."

Aubrey harrumphed. "I never miss. If I had wanted you dead, I would have hit you the first time."

Hattie raised her hand. It was a redundant move. Only Kattie and I could see her. "Yes Hattie?"

"Maybe..." She said tentatively. "We should do what we came here for..."

Noah nodded. "Agreed. Aubrey, where in this house would you store someone, you had captured?"

She has a little nervous laugh. "Umm. I don't know. I've never considered that aspect of this house... But... All the bedrooms lock. We could try her room."

"Let's go then," Noah said, brokering no argument from anyone else. We formed up. Kattie with his stolen weaponry, Hattie stalking along behind us where she could get in her surprise 'launch on the bad guys back' secret attack, Aubrey in the lead and me, Noah and Chouette in the middle. It was good to be back together. I had not liked the idea of Aubrey being my... Our, enemy.

Flapping wings and a screech erupted from a head of us. Oh no, we had left the kirpuuru outside, certain that we would not be able to sneak in under the guise of Kattie capturing us. It had listened, or so I had thought. We looked at each other.

"Where did the little beast get to?" Chouette asked.

I shook my head. "I don't know... That thing is still a mystery..."

We followed the sound of the shrieking, thumping, flapping noises until we saw it. The little ferret head was head butting a door, thumping its wings against it and shrieking. I ran for it. It was going to hurt itself with that behaviour. I grabbed at it, pulled it to me, despite the wild flapping and shrieking. The little ferret body was tense, and the tails had the fur standing on edge.

"What's gotten into it?" Hattie asked.

I shook my head as I stroked my fingers gently through its fur. "No idea." It didn't seem like it had injured itself, but the creature trembled in my arms.

"That's grandma's room," Aubrey said, coming forward. After hearing the kirpuuru, I had overtaken her to find out what was wrong.

"Guess there's no surprise that we're coming?" Kattie said as he moved to the door.

"It's locked," Aubrey said, trying the handle.

"Allow me," Hattie said coming forwards. I watched her put her hand into Kattie's pocket and extract something. Long, thin tools that she inserted into the lock of the door. "Juuuusssst giiiiiive meeee aaaaa," something turned in the lock, "Second!"

She looked back at us. "Going in. No one will see me coming." She stayed low, kept her hand on the door handle and turned it. The door opened a little, controlled by her grasp. No one shot at her. We waited. The door opened wide enough to let Hattie in and she slipped inside on her hands and knees. Still, nothing happened.

"Hello?" a voice asked tentatively.

"Alma!" I gasped.

"Grandma!" Aubrey cried.

"All clear except for the old lady," Hattie said, standing back up.

Aubrey stepped in ahead of everyone. "Grandma," she cried again. This time running towards where Alma was tied.

"Aubrey, sweetheart. What are you doing here?" Alma asked as I approached. I had my knife out and handed it to Aubrey. "Juniper?"

I nodded. "Yeah."

Chouette stepped into the room and eyed everything in that way she did. She paused, then walked from the windows. "We gotta move. Cut her lose."

"Working on it!" Aubrey hissed as she cut at the bonds tying Alma to the chair.

"Can we still get to the well?" I asked.

"Yeah... But with Hattie and Kattie, we don't have enough bikes," Chouette said. "We never anticipated them..."

"We can go, get back to where we left ours," Kattie said. "Meet up with you on the road."

Noah nodded. "Go, be careful."

When Hattie didn't move, Kattie took her by the arm and lead her out. "But I wanted to go with Juni!"

Alma was looking around, trying to identify where the voice was coming from. "Don't mind Hattie," Aubrey said. "You get used to her."

"Who?" Alma asked.

We laughed. I don't know about the others, but I couldn't help it. There really was no describing Hattie. Kattie left with her while Aubrey and I helped Alma to her feet.

"Let's go," Noah ordered. "Back to the well."

After a few steps, Alma stopped. "I can walk on my own," she insisted.

"Are you sure?" Aubrey asked her.

"Very." A few steps later, she stopped again when the kirpuuru flew down to land on my shoulder. "Where....a kirpuuru?"

"Long story," I said and the other chorused similar sentiments as we made our way through the house.

We ran. It was at a pace Alma could keep up with, but we ran. Chouette was certain that more security were on the way, and we still had to get out of the house, through the yard and down the well.

The house was eerily quiet now. The mezzanine and front foyer were still scattered with downed guards. Noah grabbed up a weapon of his own as we passed through. One, still had his hand wrapped around the trigger of his weapon. The shot rang out and Noah jumped. The back of his shoe showed the track of the bullet.

We stared at each other before I brought a foot down on the guy's hand and then his head. "That was close," Noah said, staring at his foot.

"Too close!" I whispered back to him. His hand clasped with mine, our fingers interlacing. I swallowed hard as my heartbeat in my chest. I thought maybe my face was flushed, but surely that was from the adrenaline of the moment rather than...

"Come on," he said, and we followed the others into the well.

The tunnel still dripped, just as it had when we first entered town. Aubrey had slipped her goggles back on as soon as she had dropped down into the tunnel and was the first one in. We heard the splash as she slid down the ladder.

"Great," I muttered. "It's still wet. My feet only just got dry."

We had Alma go down next, then Chouette. The kirpuuru screeched in disagreement as I climbed down. It did not like where we were going. It seemed to nestle deeper in my hair and neck, its wings held in tight around its body, the tails all pressed hard into my back and the little hands held on for dear life. Noah slid down after me and Aubrey barely waited for him to have his wits about him in the darkness before she started us off.

It was slow going. The water seemed higher than when we had first taken this route. Instead of slithering around our ankles, the water had risen to nearer our knees... Well, unless you were Noah, then it was like mid-calf, but Chouette and Aubrey were struggling with the change in depth.

We were trudging along, and I was sure that the water level was rising. We needed to get out of here as soon as was humanly possible. I was about to tell Aubrey to speed up our pace a little if she could, when Chouette suddenly vanished. One second, she was in front of me and the next she was nowhere to be seen.

"Chouette!" I cried. Aubrey and Alma turned, and Noah crashed into my back when I stopped suddenly. "She went under!" I cried and then, without even thinking about it, I dropped under too. I didn't actually know if I could swim or not, but I had to find Chouette.

When I opened my eyes under the water, I couldn't see a thing. Smart move Juniper. Smart move... Not. I felt around. The current below the top of the water seemed stronger and I felt it difficult to keep my place. I could feel the water moving around beside me as well. Had Noah also dropped down? Maybe Aubrey? I couldn't find Chouette anywhere. She was so damned small.

Fabric brushed against my hand, and I snatched for it in desperation. I wanted to scream out her name but knew that I must resist the temptation. The water would consume me, and it would do no good anyway. Maybe the desire to scream came from my need to breath. I had no idea how long I had been under for. A hand grabbed me from above and I was hauled up and out of the water. I gasped for air as Noah held me up.

"Find her?" I gasped.

"Not yet," Aubrey said. "I'm going back under." Before either Noah or I could argue, Aubrey ducked under the water's surface again. Her goggles probably gave her the best chance of finding Chouette, then I had when under the water, but I was ready to join her.

Aubrey came up, splashing water all over us. "I've found her. She's stuck."

"Wait here," I said to Alma, then there was no argument this time. Noah and I went under. We followed Aubrey and found Chouette. Her clothes had caused her to get tabled in some thick wire. Aubrey still had my knife, so she cut Chouette loose while Noah and I brought her to the surface. The water seemed even higher than when we had noticed her missing. I looked up when I heard the fretful screeching of the kirpuuru. It was hovering near the roof of the tunnel, and it was not happy. It swooped at Alma as she approached us to look at Chouette.

"Hey! Stop that!" I chastised the creature.

"Any chance of a light?" Alma asked as she took Chouette's head in her hands.

"No," Aubrey said. "It was the one thing Mech left off my goggles…"

I grinned at her, knowing that she couldn't see me in the darkness. "Maybe you two can work on them together."

Noah chuckled, but Aubrey paused. "Yeah. Not a bad idea." I don't think she saw the irony of what she'd said or understood what we'd been suggesting. Maybe it was the tension of the moment, and it would come to her later.

"This water is rising too fast. We need to get out of here before I can help her," Alma said, her voice was calm, but I could detect the panic she was trying to conceal. Something was wrong. I looked at her, ready to say something, ask what it was, when she added, "And we need to move now. She's not breathing."

I heard Aubrey gasp. Noah was stoically silent, but in the darkness of the tunnel I couldn't see his expression. "Let's move," Aubrey cried, taking charge in Noah's shock. "Juniper, Noah, carry Chouette."

We hauled Chouette up between us, the kirpuuru, usually perched on my shoulder settled on the top of my head and we waded our way through the water. It was hard work, and at times, I was barely able to tell if my feet were on the floor or up floating in the water. I became certain at one point that the only reason I wasn't floating away was because of Chouette's weight. Ahead of us, Aubrey and Alma were holding on to one another, also trying to not get swept away by the current.

Then we saw the light at the end of the tunnel, literally. We were reaching the end, and it was so bright. Not the, oh crap we all slipped and have all really drowned now kind of light at the end of the tunnel. It was like we were invigorated, and we were able to move once again. Our strength and energy seemed to return, and we moved with a speed and purpose.

The water almost swept us out and into the creek by the clearing. But we were out and free from all the water now dumping on us, we were able to wade through the water to dry land. Noah and I fell to our knees, Chouette's weight, our exhaustion and the weight of our wet clothes pulling us down. The kirpuuru launched itself from my head as soon as daylight appeared. It flapped its massive wings and took to the sky, circling above us. The nine tails fluttered in the wind. Somehow, the creature had stayed dry throughout our tunnel journey, and it seemed to chatter in delight, instead of the wrenching shrieks it had emitted inside. Alma immediately came to us, and we helped her lay Chouette out. She hadn't made a move or a sound since we had found her and with everything that had happened, we hadn't even been able to tell if she was breathing.

"Is she going to be alright?" Noah asked, finally speaking. His voice was husky, like something was stuck in his throat. The way he stared at Chouette's still form was enough to tell me he was concerned about her.

Alma looked up from her examination of our friend. "You two, go do whatever it is you need to do to get us out of here. Aubrey, you help me." When we didn't move, she pointed away from Chouette, and shouted, "Go!"

The authoritative tone reminded me that this woman had once served in the military. I got up. Everything hurt and I'm pretty sure I let out a groan. Beside me, Noah stretched as he stood. As we walked away to locate where we had hidden the bikes the day before, he glanced back over his shoulder to where Alma and Aubrey were huddled over Chouette's unmoving body. I couldn't recall a time she had been so silent, so still. It was unnerving.

The day before? Had all that really happened in the span of a day, day and a half? It seemed surreal. I looked back when he kirpuuru shrieked in dismay. It circled Alma, Aubrey and Chouette, before landing on the floor beside Chouette and watching Alma work. It kept its little eyes on her, following her every move.

"Huh," I said.

"What is it?" Noah asked.

I shook my head. "Nothing... Not really, I think..."

"That makes so much sense," Noah said sarcastically as we hauled branches off the first of the three bikes. It was Aubrey's. "You had a thought. What is it?" He seemed jittery, as though needing the conversation to distract him.

I shrugged, not really sure what if the thought I'd had did make any sense. "The kirpuuru... It has liked all of us, even Hattie..." I trailed off. How did I explain?

"But it really seems to dislike Aubrey's grandmother," Noah finished for me.

I looked over at him, as we pulled the bike out from where it had been stashed. "Yes! Exactly that. And I know it can attack people it doesn't like."

Noah looked over at where Chouette was being tended to. "Maybe it has bad memories of older people."

Ok, that one made me stop. "It was a statue."

He nodded. "Yep. I know."

I laughed softly and kicked the stand on the bike down once it was free in the clearing. Together we moved over to the next one and repeated the process, this time allowing a comfortable silence to fall between us as we worked.

We were wheeling that second bike out into the clearing when we heard it. The sound of Chouette choking and gagging. It was a beautiful sound. The sound of our friend coming back to us. As soon as the kickstand was set, we ran back over.

"Chouette!" Noah cried as he fell to his knees beside her. He pulled her into his arms and hugged her close. I stood a bit more awkwardly behind him.

Chouette coughed but returned his hug and then looked at me and Aubrey. "Thank you. All of you!" The kirpuuru walked across the ground to her and bumped its head against her hand until she lifted it enough that it could slip under. She smiled as she slowly patted the little creature's head. "My good luck charm, huh?"

Relief overwhelmed us and I think we all allowed ourselves the chance to relax a little then. We were outside of the town. Chouette was going to be ok. We had Alma. We hadn't lost Noah. All that was left, was for us to return to Camp Sight and get on with our lives. We retrieved the third bike from its hiding place amongst the bushes and got ready to leave. Alma said it wasn't a good idea for Chouette to ride alone and instructed someone to ride with her. I could not drive so that left Aubrey or Alma herself, because Noah didn't put himself forward to ride with her. It was strange if you asked me, but no one else seemed to think it was odd. She wound up going with Aubrey and Alma would ride Chouette's bike.

Aubrey's had been hers anyway, so she insisted that she would be able to do so.

Almost as soon as we were on the main road, gunshots rang out, pelting the road and sending dirt and gravel spraying everywhere. I have no idea how they had known where we would be, but we were forced to floor it. I ducked, pushing Noah down low over the bike's handlebars and a bullet whizzed right over our heads. Noah looked over his shoulder at me., an unidentifiable look in his eyes.

"Take the gun, give us some cover fire!"

It had stayed strapped around his torso as we had fled through the tunnel. "What if it got wet?"

"Then throw it at them!" He cried.

Chouette was getting similar instructions from Aubrey. Her rifle was set in a special holder on the side of her bike, but driving, she had no chance to fire at our pursuers herself. For me, Noah lifted one arm, so that I could pull the step over his head and then the other. With one arm wrapped around him. We were on an almost flying death trap after all. I held the weapon, pressed against my ribs. It would hurt, but I could not afford to let go. Then... I pulled the trigger.

Nothing happened.

"Safety!" Noah called out, obviously realising what I had done.

Duh. Of course, I needed to find the safety and release that if I wanted something to happen. Finding that safety and switching it, one handed while on the back of a motorcycle was another story though. Oh, and add the fact that people were shooting at us!

A bullet flew over our shoulders. "Juniper!" Noah hissed.

"I'm trying!" I cried. "I'm trying."

I pulled the trigger again and the gun rebounded in my grasp and against my ribs. I let out a grunt of pain but kept firing. Chouette was releasing a steady stream of shots from Aubrey's rifle and maybe it was my imagination, but we seemed to be gaining some distance, getting further away from them as we fired upon them. A tire blew on their truck as either Chouette or I got them. A man seemed to fall from the window of the truck where he had been hanging. I think I had hit him!

Two more jumped from the truck as it came to a skidding halt and fired at us, but maybe we were a little giddy as we drove off laughing.

We came up alongside Alma again. I for one, was glad that she had escaped without injury or incident. I had managed to get the strap of the gun around my own torso, allowing me to wrap my arms around Noah again. My ribs hurt like hell, and I was sure that they were at least bruised. Maybe, if I was really unlucky, one or two might be broken. No way to tell though. Not at the moment and nothing we could do about it anyway.

I looked over at Aubrey and Chouette. Chouette looked a little worse for wear, exhaustion made her sag and like me with Noah, she had her arms wrapped around Aubrey. Her head also leaning against Aubrey, as though she was having trouble keeping it up.

Thankfully, the rest of the ride back to Camp Sight was peaceful. We continued to ride like we were being chased, but no one else appeared and we were able to ride into camp without further incident... At least until we went to dismount and Chouette fell from the back of the bike, only to be caught by Cassias, who managed to make his way from the door of the common area to the side of Aubrey's bike in the nick of time.

FLIGHT

91

Sleep, it was an elusive thing that night. Something kept rattling around in my head that I just could not place. Maybe it was he pain in my ribs, or the fact that the room was completely silent. Aubrey was not there, instead deciding to stay with Alma, who was sitting with Chouette. Then there was the worry for Chouette. We could have lost her that day and I didn't think anyone at Camp Sight would have recovered from that.

No matter the reason though, sleep was not coming for me. I'd been up and down several times already, pottering around my room, not wanting to stray out and disturb anyone else, but so hyped up that I'd even out my eyes back in so that I wasn't wandering around aimlessly. The kirpuuru had also abandoned me, instead going with Aubrey to watch over Chouette. The weird little creature had been acting weird since our return and that was saying a lot for a mythical creature that used to be a statue only twenty-four hours earlier. Well, if it were a symbol of good luck, Chouette could use all the good luck we could throw at her.

So, when the sound of a loud, and somewhat angry vehicle was heard, I was wide awake enough to get up and able to go look. I pulled on a hoodie and padded downstairs on bare feet to see what was going on. I obviously wasn't the only one who couldn't sleep, because Noah was there and a few seconds later Harvey and Mech appeared. Mech had his toolbox in hand, while Harvey and Noah were armed.

We stepped out into the courtyard and watched as the passenger side door of a truck I'd never seen before opened and for the others with me, it looked as though no one stepped out. For me though, it was a different story.

"Hattie!" I cried, stepping in front of the guys who were aiming guns at the driver. The invisible girl ran over to me and hugged me.

"You made it back!" Hattie said excitedly, then surprised Noah, when she grabbed him around the neck and hugged him close. He had never seen her coming.

"Uh…" Noah groaned. "Yeah…" He squirmed awkwardly, trying to disentangle himself from all her limbs.

I laughed and heard Kattie jump down from the driver's side of the truck. "What happened to you guys?" I asked. "We expected you back long before us."

"Mech's bloody bike stalled after several pieces fell off," Kattie hissed.

Mech glowered back at Kattie. "It stalled? What the hell did you do to it?" It was rare to hear him speak and now, it was even odder to hear his usually shy and tentative voice so low and dangerous.

"Tossed it in the back like the trash it is!" Kattie shot back. "And all the debris too! Took us forever to find something we could take. Eventually we settled on this thing."

Mech, took off towards the truck, muttering about no one ever appreciating his all his hard work and didn't we know that if it was not for him, we wouldn't have the bikes or the generators or anything?

"Kattie was so mad when it broke down!" Hattie explained, "should've seen the way that he went about hotwiring that truck!"

We laughed and it was good. The ability to poke fun at Kattie and his impatience, Hattie's antics, and each other. Things had been so serious since we had returned… And even before that. In Erihall everything had changed, and I had no idea how to make it better. With everything that had happened, with Sebastian's betrayal and the fight at Alma's and Chouette's near drowning… The stakes of this fight had become very real.

92

We stepped into Chouette's room quietly. Aubrey was asleep on the couch, her head on Minnie's lap. Minnie looked towards us when we entered, her ears ever focused on what was happening around her. Alma was seated on the desk chair, that had been pulled close to Chouette's bed.

"Any change?" I asked softly, walking over to stand beside Alma at Chouette's bedside.

"Her breathing is laboured, and she has not woken up yet," Alma said, her voice equally as soft. "Nothing was exactly ideal with our departure from Erihall. I..." Alma's words trailed off and her eyes widened when she looked up. I glanced over my shoulder and had to bite back a smirk. Hattie stood behind me and she was actually wearing clothes for once, so her hat moved around seemingly in thin air for everyone else, while her jacket seemed to erratically gesticulate as Hattie rushed over to sit by Chouette's bed.

"Alma, this is Hattie," I said, coming up behind the invisible girl. "Remember?" Hattie had been in the room when we'd rescued Alma, but so much had happened in the interim and she'd met so many people, I had no idea what she recalled, especially with all her focus on Chouette. Last time though, Hattie had been completely invisible and perhaps the oddity of the girl had been easier to ignore... Or pretend that it had been imagined.

Alma nodded slowly, "Oh... Right..." she said, staring at the seemingly empty, but moving outfit of clothes. Chouette's hand raised oddly and while I could see that Hattie was holding it between both of her own hands, all Alma saw was the small, limp hand was taken up by thin air at the end of sleeves that looked empty but were filled.

"You were saying? I asked, trying to pull Alma back to the conversation about Chouette.

"Oh?" She pulled her gaze away from where Hattie sat beside the bed and looked at me. "Right... Yes, I... I would have preferred a greater chance to work on Chouette there and then, ensure that all the water was removed from her lungs before we raced on. And well... The bikes weren't ideal for the situation either."

"Will she be alright?" Hattie asked tentatively.

Alma sat there pensively for a moment. "I believe she has every chance of being fine."

I could see Hattie frown, as though trying to decipher Alma's cryptic answer. "She'll be fine," I assured Hattie, even as Alma frowned at me in return. I was taken aback. Was Chouette's condition worse than we knew?

We talked a little longer about Chouette and I was about to leave, head back to my room and try to get an hour or two more of sleep when Minnie cried out.

"Minnie?" Hattie exclaimed, jumping up and rushing to the girl. Minnie stood up suddenly, ignoring Hattie even as Aubrey tumbled from her lap to land unceremoniously on the floor. "Minnie," Hattie cried again, reaching for the older girl as she tried to flee the room. Aubrey gave a shriek of surprise and thudded with an exclamation of pain. Hattie fumbled, changing directions to help Aubrey up. "Minnie, what is it?"

I rushed over to Minnie, concerned as she seemed to sway on her feet unsteadily. "Minnie, talk to us!"

"Somethings wrong!" Minnie said, her voice almost hollow as she spoke, like sleepwalker. Had she even heard Hattie and me? "I have to find Noah." Minnie made to leave the room, but I gripped her shoulders, trying to... I don't know, wake her up?

"It's a vision," Hattie said, "Minnie's having one of her visions."

"Visions?" Alma asked. "The girl has no..."

"Except she can sometimes see snippets of the future," Hattie clarified. "Minnie, what's going to happen?"

Minnie looked up at me, her gaping empty sockets wide open in fear. If she'd have had eyes, they'd have been bulging.

"Fire. Death. Fear." She swallowed hard. "Fire... There's fire everywhere..."

"Stay here," I said, pushing her back to the couch. "You too Aubrey." The girl nodded in agreement as she stood up. "Hattie, let's go!"

While I had been with Minnie, Hattie had already disrobed, and I was very pleased to find out that she was again wearing the set that Mech and Elijah had apparently made for her. We left the room quickly. I never even looked to see that Alma was staring in shock at Hattie... Or more accurately, where Hattie had been.

We ran out into the courtyard that the lower rooms all lead out to. Noah was there sparring with Sadie, who wrestled him to the ground and had her legs wrapped around his neck. Noah tapped out. Vera, who was sitting on the benches nearby spotted us... Well... Me...

"What's up?" she asked. "You look like you seen a ghost, Juniper."

"Minnie says something is wrong," Hattie said, making herself known.

Sadie released Noah and stood up. She offered he hand to him, which he accepted. They walked over to us. "Any idea?"

I shook my head. "She didn't say. But she was spooked."

"I'll go find Cora. See if she's spotted anything," Noah said. "Someone find Emrys. He has all those doo-dads that are supposed to guard the camp."

Sadie nodded. "Got it."

Vera went with Sadie, so Hattie and I went with Noah. He first went into his room though and came back out with several guns. I raised my eyebrows and shook my head. I had not liked that experience on the bike. He frowned but I placated him by picking up a long steel rod. It fitted nicely in my hands and the fact that it was thin meant that it wasn't too heavy to wield. I have no idea why, but it felt right in my hand. Right and wrong might be a better way to put it, but the length felt comfortable. I flicked it so that I was holding it lengthwise, the tip hiding behind my shoulder and the rest of the length running down the length of my body.

"Hattie's terrifying when you can only see a gun," Noah said, watching the other girl check for the ammunition in the pistol he had handed her. She held her hand out to him.

"She wants a second one," I said in disbelief.

Noah rolled his eyes. "Of curse she does," he said sarcastically, reaching behind so that he could grab another pistol from the back of his waistband. He held it out to her.

"Oh goodie!" Hattie exclaimed.

"Just don't shoot us," Noah chided her. We headed for the watch tower but never made it there because an old air horn started to blare. "I guess that answers whether or not Emrys is aware of what's happening."

We ran instead of walked. A gunshot rang out from on high as we crossed into the main yard where Kattie had left the truck. Cora must have seen something.

"Hattie, go get Aubrey," I ordered.

"Right!" the girl agreed. If there was shooting, we needed Cora's equal up there with her. Noah hadn't been kidding when he told Hattie not to shoot us. Mech started to run towards us but tripped over his own toolkit. He flew back to the floor, the googles he wore, similar to the ones that he had given Aubrey seemed to slip down his face.

I started to go to him, to help him up, but Noah grabbed me back. "No!"

I stared aback at him in disbelief. "What?" I asked.

"You never asked about anyone else's abilities here," Noah said, his tone hushed. "Or why people like Mech always cover their eyes.

I looked back at the boy and was in time to see a van with men hanging out the doors come crashing into the camp. They jumped to the ground, and one started towards Mech. Wasn't that always the way? Pick on the weakest link. I was not going to let Noah stop me from helping Mech, no matter what his eyes could do. I wrenched my arms away from his and headed towards the boy. He had rolled over to see what was coming as soon as the van had crashed through the gates and was doing his best to scramble towards us backwards. I reached him and dropped the bar I had been carrying. I slipped my hands under his arms and started to drag him. The goggles fell to his lap, and he grabbed them up, but not before looking at the man who was just about on us.

93

I never got to see Mech's eyes, but the man did and what he saw there made his eyes go wide right before his head exploded into dust. His body fell to the ground, where on impact, the rest of the body collapsed in on itself, leaving nothing but a pile of dust where the man had once been. I stumbled backwards. I had not been expecting that. Ok, it wasn't improbable. I had dusted a fair few of my own things during our experimentation phase, but Mech could never stop his. I grabbed my pole up with one hand and grabbed at Mech again with my other.

"Come on!" I cried. The sudden disappearance of the guy had stopped the others in their tracks. Mech shoved his goggles against his face and ran with me to where Noah was. From above, Cora took another one out and Noah gave us the chance to tie Mech's goggles back together. Many things about him suddenly made sense and as much as I wanted to talk to him about that, now was just not the time. "Is the truck working?" I asked.

"Yeah."

"Ok, good…"

"What are you thinking?" Noah asked as he fired his shotgun.

"There's more of them!" Cora called from above. "They're circling the camp."

"Crap!" I hissed. Everything was going so horribly wrong. I looked at Noah. "We gotta go…"

He nodded. "Mech. Get that truck. Get Chouette and Minnie in first. Aubrey's grandmother too."

I saw something or someone out of the corner of my eye. I tracked it but felt that it was not the right move to let them know that I had seen them. Noah covered Mech until he made it to the truck. I hoped the boy could actually drive the thing. He was a lot shorter than Kattie was. As they made distance towards the truck, I stepped slowly back to where I was tracking my shadow to. When I was sure I had him in reach, I spun around and brought my steel rod around to catch him unawares in the back of his knees. He went down and I was on top of him. I gave him a whack to the head for good measure.

Aubrey came running in, her rifle in hand. I pointed up to the tower where Cora was, and she nodded. Right behind her, Emrys and Elijah looked shocked and half asleep. "Go," I pointed back towards where they had come from. "Mech's bringing the truck. Get Chouette and Minnie ready to move."

"Wha-." Emrys tried to speak when he caught sight of the fighting. "My computers!"

He took off running. I shook my head and hoped Elijah would do what he was told. I didn't have time to find out though, because they were swarming in now. I rushed into the melee. Probably not a smart move, but hey, I had a long metal rod to hit people with! I swung it above my head and brought it down in the middle of a crowd that had been closing in on Noah.

"Thanks!" He breathed out. We stood back-to-back as the seemed to swarm around us. There was the solid sound of guns firing from above us and occasionally someone in the crowd would fall.

Out of nowhere, one of the bikes came tearing through the yard, Harvey perched on it, a bat in hand. He drove through them, the bat taking out heads as he went. Above us, Core screamed in frustration. She was out of bullets. It probably wouldn't be long until Aubrey was as well. We were losing this thing. A burst of light erupted from the tower and several men went tumbling down the rickety stairs, causing a domino effect.

"Cora's mad," Noah yelled to me. "We've got to get to the tower. Get the girls down."

They seemed to be swarming around us, coming from everywhere. I had never imagined that Sage had this many men at his disposal. "What do you mean she's mad?" I asked as we ran.

Noah smashed one guy in the face with the butt of the gun he had been carrying. I slammed my rod into another's belly. Both went down under the swarm of their own comrades.

"She took off her eye patch," Noah explained, ducking under a right hook and coming up under his assailant's chin.

So that was what the light had been. Something to do with Cora's ability. Most of them around here seemed to hide it, try to live their lives without these things. It was slow going, as we approached the tower, but the closer we got, the thicker the crowd seemed to get. Were they really all trying to get up there?

Noah and I turned. We would hold any additional men from ascending, giving Cora and Aubrey and chance to deal with what was in front of them. Neither of them were great hand to hand fighters, but we had to hope. Harvey came racing back through the crowd on his motorbike, riding right through them with his bat. From the other side of the courtyard, another bike came flying out. And yes, it seemed to take flight, before landing in front of a group of soldiers trying to make their way through to the inner courtyard, where the others were, hopefully with the truck getting those who could not fight out of Camp Sight.

A scream, a brush of air and a thud behind me startled me. I turned to look and found what looked like a soldier who had fallen from the tower to land on one behind me. I looked up at Cora and Aubrey. They gave me a thumbs up that I returned. Some idiot thought that I was too distracted to notice him though. I pulled the rod up under my arm and without a moment's notice shot it out behind me before turning to face the onslaught again.

"Incoming!" Cora yelled from above and we could hear them thumping their way down the stairs. And then there were four of us. Cora jabbed someone in the face with the butt of her rifle and Aubrey followed suit. She obviously wasn't as used to this method of using her weapon, but it was all that was left to us without ammunition. With the two on the bikes, I think the second rider was Sadie but couldn't tell for sure as they weaved in and out of the crowd, distracting many of them from us. We made a run for it and when we reached the indoor common area, we barricaded the doors as soon as Harvey and the second rider zoomed inside.

The feeling of the doors being hammered through started almost as soon as we finished the barricade. Tables, chairs and even the couch blocked the door, but it was already obvious that it would not hold for long. We looked at each other in desperation. The realisation was clear. We had no chance of holding Camp Sight. We would have to run.

Kattie's bike breaking down on the way out of Erihall was perhaps one of the luckiest things that had ever happened to us, because without him bringing that truck back, there was no way we would be able to do this. There weren't enough bikes for everyone to leave at the same time, even riding double. And even then, everyone would have had to leave everything they owned behind. That truck would not only get everyone out but also make sure that we had supplies wherever we wound up.

Mech was loading up the truck with his tools, Emrys was carrying computer parts. Everyone was carrying stuff that was theirs. Stuff that they did not want to leave behind. It looked as though everyone had realised how dire the situation at Camp Sight was.

"Where's Cassias?" Harvey asked, walking the bike he had been riding out into the inner courtyard. "I ain't seen him anywhere."

"I haven't seen him since he caught Chouette off the bike," Noah admitted. Cassias was one of our best fighters, so it was a worry that he was nowhere to be found. "Where are the other bikes?"

"That one Kattie wrecked is a goner," Mech called out as he threw another load of tools in. "Aubrey's-."

He was cut off though. "I did not wreck it!"

"Enough!" Noah shouted over the din of the soldiers trying to make their way into the inner courtyard and the argument. "We got everything?"

"Just about," Aubrey said coming around with a pile of blankets in her hands.

"Go and get your bike," Noah told her. Mech took the pile from her and Aubrey ran off to do as instructed. It looked to me like she had been waiting for the chance. "Everyone get on." Harvey, Kattie, Elijah, Emrys, everyone started to climb aboard the truck. "Kattie, you're driving."

An arm wrapped through mine and started to drag me towards the truck. "Hattie!" I said. Not only was she the only one who engaged in such practices, but I could see her. "Hang on," I told her and looked at Noah. "I've got to get the case…"

He looked towards the upper levels of the camp where my room was. "I don't like it."

I shrugged. "I need to," I said. There hadn't been time for everyone to return to rooms and collect personal possessions. My room, the one I shared with Aubrey, was on the far side of the courtyard, upstairs. It would be a perilous journey, but I couldn't leave without the case.

He nodded, but Hattie disagreed. "No!" she cried. "You can't let her go up there!"

"Do what you need to do," Noah said though, giving my hand a reassuring squeeze, then walked off to double check that we had everyone.

"Hattie!" I told her. "I need to get them. Get on the truck!" Kattie, who had been running around the side of the truck to get into the cab looked over at us. Hattie was pulling on me, trying to drag me to the back of the truck, where everyone was getting in.

"No. If you go inside, they'll find you!" she cried. I loved this girl. I really did, but they needed to be going, and I needed to get that case before everything went wrong. I pulled back at her and extracted my arm from her grip.

"I'm sorry. I've got to do this," I said and as Kattie came up behind her to hold her back, I took off. I heard her scream my name, but I couldn't let that stop me. Kattie was ordering her to stop and as I turned the corner, I caught sight of him manhandling her into the truck, where Sadie and Cora took her into their custody.

94

I took the stairs two at a time and it was lucky that I did because the doors of the common area burst open. I was too far out of sight for any of them to see when they burst in. As I ran along the upper hallway, I heard the sound of Aubrey's bike running through them. She was doing much the same as Harvey and Sadie had earlier and was using her rifle to bludgeon people as she went.

"Move!" She screamed. "Get the truck going!"

I stopped short though when I ran into an apparent brick wall. I started to fall backwards for the impact but a vice like grip caught me and kept me on my feet. I looked at the solid chest in front of me and allowed my gaze to move upwards towards the face.

"Cassias!" I breathed. "What the hell?"

"Wha…" He looked so groggy, unbalanced on his feet, swaying slightly from side to side. His shoulder even brushed the wall as he tried to right himself. "What?" He tried again. "What happened?" His voice slurred, almost like his tongue was too big for his mouth.

I just stared at him, not able to comprehend how he was unaware of everything that had happened. He just stared back at me, his eyes clouded with what appeared to be tiredness and incomprehension. "We're… We're under attack. We're evacuating." I pointed down at the courtyard where Aubrey and Noah were trying to give Kattie space to get the truck away by attacking the hoard from their bikes.

Cassias stared at the sight in disbelief, taking far too long to connect her words and the sight out the windows to some meaningful connotation, but then some of the cloud seemed to lift from his eyes. "I can't…" he said, his usually low, strong voice still thick and slurred, and slapped himself on the cheeks several times to try and wake himself up faster. "I can't think."

I had never seen him like this, but we needed to move. "Go!" I told him. I worried that he might not be able to make it down the stairs without tripping over his own feet, but I needed to get my case of eyes. I could not afford to wait for him to figure it out. "Get down there. Help them out!" He nodded slowly and took off in the direction I had just come from. I shook my head, hoping that he would be alright and continued to the room I had shared with Aubrey. This was the first place I had ever remembered feeling safe and now they had come. I ran for the small tower of drawers between the two beds and pulled open the top one. The big case and the small one were exactly where I had left them. I shoved the small one in my pants pocket and the big one into my backpack. It had been on the floor by my bed. It still had some of the things Sebastian had given me back at the facility in it.

At the door to the room, I looked both ways and when I turned to leave, I saw the one person who did not belong there. At the end of the hall, he must have come up the stairs from the common area. I thought about it and turned in the opposite direction. There wasn't really much choice in where to go. I was glad to see the truck gone when I caught sight of the courtyard. I didn't see any sign of Noah, Aubrey or Cassias, but I hoped that they had followed the truck. No matter what that meant for me, I really hoped that they had… I also hoped that Hattie would one day forgive me.

The figure followed me. It really wasn't a surprise. I had expected him to do exactly that. There was another staircase that led up to the roof of the living quarters. I guess, I was going up.

"Juniper!"

I didn't stop when he called my name. I had lost all faith and trust in this man when he had lied to me, held me hostage and demanded that I hand over Noah to his self-possessed cause of taking down Nelson Sage. I pushed through the door and skidded onto the old metal stairs. I had no idea what marvel of the architectural world had decided that these stairs should just magically start on the second floor and lead pointlessly to the roof, but we had used it as a shooting range. It was where Cora and

Aubrey had spent most of their time while I had been with Sadie and Cassias.

By the time, I made it to the roof, Sebastian was on the stairs. "Juniper! Wait!"

Not in this life, would I wait for him to catch up to me. I broke into a run when I made it to the flat surface of the rooftop. There was a fireman's pole at the far end that I could take down to the ground. It wasn't my favourite way of getting down, but it had been a favourite among others at the camp. I remember hearing, somewhere, not that I knew where, that the key to a good escape was to do things that your pursuer was not willing to do. Like go three stories down a fireman's pole. Sebastian was a lab geek. I did not expect him to follow.

I reached the pole and looked behind. He was still behind me, calling my name I grabbed onto the pole and swung myself around. I circled around to the ground and looked up in satisfaction as Sebastian skidded to a stop at the roof's edge and stared down at me. And then he surprised me. He grasped hold of the pole and although it was halting on his descent, he followed me down.

Well, didn't that just blow?

With a sigh, I ran. I honestly had no idea where to go anymore. Everyone was gone now. Everyone but Sebastian and all those men. Feet crashed to the floor with an exclamation of pain behind me.

"Juniper!"

"Juniper!" I looked in the direction of the second voice that called my name. That voice should not have been there, but it was accompanied by the rumbling of a motorcycle engine. The bike came to a stop in front of me and I couldn't help but feel so relieved to see him. A little angry too, but so relieved that he was there. That he had come back for me.

I climbed onto the back of the bike behind Noah and wrapped my arms around him. Sebastian stopped in his tracks when he saw Noah. They stared at each other, and I have to say, it was pretty awkward.

"Juniper!" Sabastian cried. "There's a traitor!"

Noah was about to drive off, but I gave him a squeeze. He must have realised that I was asking him to wait. "Who?" I asked, not even sure why I was giving this man the time of day. Sebastian confused me and I had no idea what to do about him. Maybe he was lying, but what if he wasn't?

Sebastian shook his head. "I don't know. But my- Sage found out where you are somehow. You have a traitor." He could not keep his eyes off Noah the whole time he spoke. "No matter where you go, he'll find you! We can help each other."

"Let's go," I finally said to Noah, and he revved the bike. It took off, leaving Sebastian behind us, calling out to me. I wrapped my arms tight around Noah and rested my head against his back. I had no idea where we were going, but I was ok with that.

95

We rode like the wind. If I had hated riding on the open road, I hated the uneven forest roads even more. Every bump, every branch in the road, every hole in the ground made me think that we were going to get thrown off at any moment.

Noah slowed and brought us to a stop maybe ten minutes later. I had no idea how far we were from Camp Sight, but we couldn't hear them anymore. I could feel him breathing hard, the adrenaline starting to wear off as he sat there. He put his hands over mine and squeezed them.

"You ok?" He finally asked.

I nodded against his back. "Yeah…"

"Come on," he said, and we both dismounted from the bike. The fight, the uneven road, the adrenaline, the encounter with Sebastian. I was feeling wobbly on my feet and my legs seemed to give way beneath me when I tried to stand on solid ground. Noah caught me. He seemed to always be catching me.

"Where are the others?" I asked.

"Heading further into Shiura," Noah said.

"But most of Shiura is under Eridenti occupation…" I let him sit me under a large tree and removed my backpack before leaning back against the trunk. He sat beside me, and we stared at the path we had been following. We could see nothing but trees in every direction. "And those weren't only Sage's men…"

"I know," Noah said as he wrapped an arm around my shoulders. "The Eridenti Military were there too. It was always supposed that Sage was backed by the government."

I let my head rest on his shoulder, and we just sat there, the silence falling between us so that all we could hear were the sounds of the forest around us. "What do we do now?" I asked and I didn't like how small my voice sounded.

"I don't know," Noah admitted. "Do you think that Sebastian's telling the truth?"

I shrugged. "I don't know what to think about him anymore."

"Hattie said something..." I looked up at him and he continued. He looked as though he was trying to phrase something in his head before actually speaking. "I don't think he'll hurt you... Not on purpose..." He looked.... I don't know how to describe it, maybe sad, but he was uncomfortable talking about this. "I don't think he could hurt you."

I shook my head. "If you're talking about what I think you're talking about... He was talking nonsense. Just trying to get to me, manipulate me... Into giving him you." I said the last bit so softly, I hoped that he hadn't heard me, but who was I kidding?

Noah smiled softly at me, those eyes crinkled at the sides in amusement. His free hand brushed my hair behind my ear, and he just stared down at me. "You have no idea what you do to people do you?" I want to say something, but nothing seemed right. I mean, I barely knew who I was, let alone what I could possibly be to other people, and I didn't want to have this conversation. Having something similar with Hattie had been awkward enough, but with Noah, it was like there was an energy between us that I couldn't name.

We just sat there, looking at each other, his palm resting against my cheek. His eyes flickered across my face. I don't know what he was looking for, but I couldn't look away. I bit my lip. "Noah?" I finally said.

"What?" He asked, the moment lost, and we separated a little. I missed the warmth of his hand against my cheek.

"I'm sorry."

"For what?"

"For everything," I said. "All of this... Everything that has happened since you brought me to Camp Sight..."

"No," he said with more force than I had expected. "You are not at fault for any of this and I won't hear you say otherwise. You are one of us. You have every right to be with us, and we will fight with you and for you."

I sniffled. Oh god no. I was not... Yep, tears welled in my eyes, and I buried my face in his chest. He held me as my body shook. We sat there, probably longer than he had intended, but I was grateful for the opportunity to get that off my chest. It had been building since probably before Chouette had been hurt and now with everyone on the run, I was struggling. At least when we had been fighting, I had been doing something.

"There is something we have to do," Noah said after a while.

"What?" I asked, sitting back up and rubbing furiously at my eyes to dry them. I felt them shift and paused my movements, blinking slightly until I felt them settle back into place. I wiped at them with less vigour until I could look at him clearly.

"Destroy the camp. It has always been a part of our plan. Get everyone out, then cover our tracks. The truck will be easily followed unless we distract them."

I nodded in understanding. "Set the place on fire," I said. The idea was good, but it gnawed at me unexpectedly. It was the most logical option to distract anyone and while it seemed like a dreadful thing to do, if it spread to the surrounding forest, the fire would cover any trace of escape. But Camp Sight, that old abandoned Shiuran encampment in the middle of the forest, overgrown and filled with the mix matched group of people that had become my friends. I opened my mouth to ask him if we really had to destroy it, if we could not come back there one day, but I knew before I even said anything that I was being foolish. We had to hold back Sage's men, and this was the best way.

"Yeah. Mech's got some stuff back in his workshop and then there's the fuel for the generators."

I waved him off and reached for my bag. I unzipped it hurriedly and retrieved the case of eyes. Another zipper and it flipped open, presenting us with all the colours that we had become so familiar with. "Forget trying to get to Mech's workshop. There's too many of them. Let's just hit the generators," and I pointed at the bright red eyes that had once exploded the garden in the private courtyard behind his room.

"You can't control that one," Noah said, concern tinging his voice.

"Do you really want me to control it?" The way he smirked at me, told me everything I needed to know. I reached up to start the process, but he grabbed for my hand, lacing his fingers through mine.

"Wait until we get closer. Come on."

We rode back to Camp Sight. We probably should have done this on the way out the first time, but we hadn't had the time between Sebastian and the hoards barging down our doors. Now, we were ready.

We rode slower this time, Noah taking the time to avoid the holes and the branches and the mud slides. As a result, I didn't hang on quite as tight as I had on the way out of camp. Maybe that had been his goal.

He brought us once again to a stop on the outskirts of the camp. The place was crawling with soldiers. Sage Security and Eridenti Military alike, they were looking for a way to find us. A hint on where we would go next. They were swarming over the grounds and through the buildings, tearing things off shelves and going through everything we had once owned and couldn't bring with us, anything that would guide them to us. I hadn't asked Noah about that yet, but I suppose that in the long run, it didn't really matter where we went.

We secreted his bike and ourselves away. I kneeled on the ground, Noah across from me, and pulled the case back out. As it laid open on my lap, I looked at him. I don't know, maybe I was asking if he was still sure about this. When he nodded, I put my hand on the eyes I was going to use.

"I got it," Noah said softly. I nodded and he shifted closer. It reminded me of when we had been testing each of them to see what did what. How he had held me against him as my body seized in pain. I gave into the darkness as I pulled first my right eye and then my left out. Noah's hand would cup mine and I would transfer it to him for him to put away. Instead of the case though, I felt him reach for the smaller one in my pocket. "I want to be able to find them again," he said softly as he slipped the small case back where he had found it. I nodded and started to fiddle with the covering for the fire eyes.

Noah took my hands in his though. "Noah…" I protested.

"Hang on," he said softly. Then, without any warning, he leaned in. I wished that I could have seen him, but he squeezed my hands reassuringly before his lips met mine. It was soft and ever so tentative, like maybe he expected me to hit him, or jump up and run away. Was that why he had waited until now? Was this what he had wanted to do before? I felt my body sink into his as I kissed him back. His hands slid up my arms and around my back until I was pulled tight against him. I wrapped my own arms around his neck, and I have to admit, I loved every minute of this. I had no idea if I had ever been kissed before, but wow… That was one hell of a first kiss.

I felt him pull back. "I'm sorry… I shouldn't have done that."

I wanted to ask him if he was insane but that was so totally not the right thing to say. Instead, regretting that I could not see his face, I took my hand and felt along his cheek and eyes and nose, until I found his lips. "Don't be sorry." I leaned in and kissed him again.

This time it was me who pulled back. I lowered my arms, still shaking from the buzz that was thrilling through my body at light speed. I bit my lip, trying to bite back the grin was trying to spread. I opened my mouth to say something else, but nothing came. Nothing witty or sentimental, not much of anything. It was kind of like my brain had short circuited and all I wanted to do was kiss him again. Instead, I reached for the case. Our hands touched as we both thought the same thing. I felt one of the small glass shapes in my hand. I felt it, figuring which way it was supposed to go in and lifted it to the empty socket. Noah handed me the second one and I repeated the process.

I felt him shift until he was beside me and as the pain engulfed my head first and then the rest of my body, I felt him hold me against him. It helped. It always had. I never felt as alone when he held me during the changes.

Finally, I was able to breathe again, and I reluctantly pulled myself away from him and the comfort he gave. "Let's go blow up some stuff," I said.

I kept my eyes tightly closed as Noah helped me climb back on top of the bike. This wasn't like before. I could control opening and closing my eyes… And hopefully not burning Noah to a toasty crisp. Surely there had to be a way to do this without glasses or keeping my eyes tightly shut. Some sort of control that I could exercise. But there was no time to practice, not anymore.

"We're going straight in the middle," Noah said as he revved the bike. "When I tell you when, you open up to the left of me, kay?"

"Right!" I agreed, once again holding on to him a little too tight. Good, he'd thought to tell me exactly what, where and when. Maybe, just maybe I wouldn't barbeque him.

There were shouts and orders to stop as Noah drove us through what had probably been a half-hearted attempt at barricading us out of our own encampment. I had no idea what they'd used, maybe their trucks and crates that we'd left behind, along with the occasional bit of debris, but Noah found a gap just wide enough for the bike to fit through. I felt the brush of metal and wood against my skin as we passed the barricade. Then the shouts picked up as the thundering sound of footsteps following us, but Noah knew the way around this place like the back of his own hand. He also had the benefit of speed.

"NOW!" Noah cried. I opened my eyes, looking to the left of him as he had said, and I saw the generator. I barely even glanced at it before the metal housing seemed to bubble and ripple then break its own containment. The shockwave almost pushed us over, but Noah kept us going, despite the wobble of the bike that threatened to send us skidding to the ground. I looked backwards at the squadron of Eridenti soldiers who had tried to chase us down. While most stood staring at surprise at the generator, some had continued to chase us and when I focused on them, their uniforms caught alight. I looked away, not able to bare the sight of watching them. As I did, the bottom floor of our living quarters caught fire. Noah skidded us around at the end of the interior courtyard. "Keep going," he instructed. The common area, where we had spent so many happy nights, caught next. Men came running out and one even jumped from the second floor, landing awkwardly on the ground and crying out in pain.

Then we started back in the direction we had come and the last set of rooms, those that long ago when the Shiuran Musketeers had operated this camp, had belonged to their officers, and more recently had belonged to Noah, Chouette and Minnie went up in flames. I looked in front of us now, there were even more soldiers trying to block our way out the camp.

There was a smell I would never forget. Another generator blew. Mech's lab, Emrys's computer room, the weapons supply. It was hard to tell what it was, but a man ran in front of us, fire erupting from his clothes. He dropped to the floor and Noah swerved around him.

Suddenly the soldiers were running. An order must have been given because they let us go without further opposition. As he crossed the edge of camp, I clamped my eyes shut not wanting to spread the fire any further into the woods than I had to. I put all my faith in Noah to get us away from there before the fire caught up to us.

I had no idea how much time had passed when the bike suddenly turned. It felt as though it had been forever with me clamping my eyes shut, but it couldn't have been more than a few minutes really. Noah had wrenched the handlebars hard to the right and we were riding through underbrush rather than over road.

"What is it?" I asked. I really wanted to open my eyes but until we changed them, there was too much risk that I would set everything alight.

"I heard something," Noah said softly. He stopped the bike and seemed to turn in the seat to see where we had just come from. "A vehicle or something…"

"From Camp Sight?" I asked, tightening my grip on him. Had we been followed?

"No, the other direction."

That could be anything or anyone. One of their scouts, one of ours, anything. I clung to him shamelessly, my eyes closed against the prospect of me accidentally killing us. I needed to get my other eyes in, but we were stuck until Noah was able to ascertain the risk… And if it was trouble… I was useless once again.

Then, I heard it too. The sound of not one, but two vehicles. "Bikes," I said in Noah's ear. He nodded. I frowned, stilling myself to listen harder to the sounds coming towards us. "They sound like ours…" Nights spent in total darkness at the camp had honed my hearing and the sounds of Aubrey's bike, Chouette's and the others that were in regular use were common sounds that I had heard in my self-imposed darkness.

I felt him shift as though he was trying to look me in the face. "What do you mean?"

"I don't know… I could be wrong… But… They sound like our bikes. Not the clunky one Kattie and Hattie took Erihall, but Aubrey's and Chouette's."

"Aubrey's does sound different," Noah agreed. "You're right."

"But… Would they…" I hesitated to finish the question.

"Yes. They would. Aubrey and Cassias left on bikes behind the truck to cover their backs. They would have circled back to make sure the camp was destroyed and look for us. Cassias would have ensured it."

Cassias. Something had not been right with him when I had last seen him, but Noah said he had left on the third bike, so he must have been fine. Still, it was something I would have to talk to the big man about later.

If there was a later.

The two bikes seemed to pull to a stop close to where Noah had turned into the woods. A male voice spoke, pointing out the apparently obvious track he had made, but I felt Noah sag in relief, leaning back against me.

"It's ok!" He said, "It's Cash!"

"Noah?" the big man's gruff voice called out.

"Come on!" Noah said to me. He turned the bike, and he sort of drove, walked us back to the path he had originally been on.

"Juniper! Noah!" Aubrey cried. I heard her leap from her bike, kicking the stand down and then suddenly she was wrapped around me. It was awkward to say the least. I had to extract myself from Noah and find her, all without being able to see. Nothing I wasn't used to, I guess. But still.

"How'd you find us?" Noah asked as he clasped hands with Cassias. The slap made me think that it was one of those manly grips that seemed appropriate for all situations, but particularly when you were glad to see someone.

"The entire Camp went up in flames. It literally exploded… And you think we didn't suspect you?" Aubrey asked as she released me.

We took some time for me to change my eyes back. When I finally reopened my eyes, Noah was looking right into my eyes. It was disconcerting to see his bright white orbs staring back at me, but they were just as much a part of him as my empty sockets were a part me.

I watched as Noah slid his contacts back in and he looked at me once again with those dark blue eyes that always seemed to be watching me. "Kay, we're ready," Noah said standing up. He held a hand out to me and I took it, letting him help me back to my feet. Out of the corner of my eye I saw Aubrey watching us, a little smirk tugging on her lips.

We remounted, me taking my customary position with Noah, Aubrey on her bike and Cassias on the one he had left camp on. "They should still be moving," Cassias said. "But we should be able to catch them." I couldn't help myself though, I watched Cassias's every move. He seemed far more awake but fleeing into the night for your life had that effect on people.

Behind us we could hear the fire. It was progressing behind us. Perhaps we had spent too long at our stop. We rode like the wind again, just as we had when he had first fled the camp, but now we were fleeing a destructive force of our own making.

These paths or roads or tracks, whatever they had been in the past, were long since overgrown. Kattie could never have taken the truck through here, so I wondered which way he had taken the truck full of our friends. Cassias and Noah seemed to know exactly where they were going and either Aubrey had been read in on the plan or she was just going with the flow as I was.

We never stopped. It wasn't like there was any point in stopping. We had no supplies on us. Everything that had been gathered had gone with the truck. The track seemed endless as we bounced and swerved and slid over the mud. We couldn't even speak over the sounds of the bikes and the roar of the fire behind us. I had tried to ask Noah more about the plan he and Cassias had mentioned, but I hadn't even been able to hear his response and that was assuming he had heard me and had been trying to answer my question.

The lightening sky above the tree lines glowed orange, but was it the sunrise that was coming, or was it the fire colouring everything around us? The heat was gaining on us. What had I done? And then we were out.

Just like that the trees were no longer around us. We were able to stare up at the brightening sky, aglow from the fire at Camp Sight. Around us, open plains lay before us. Behind us, the dark line of trees with the crown of fire looked ominous.

Seemingly all at once, we all came to a stop, circling around to look at the sight for a moment. It was almost like Noah and Cassias were saying goodbye to their home. I know I was sad to see it all go, and I had not had the chance to truly make it my home. It had felt like home though. The place had been safe and the people like family.

97

It was another two hours before we found them, or at least I assumed we did, when Cassias led the way into an abandoned homestead. It looked as though it would provide a sparse shelter for a group our size. It definitely wasn't something we could live in long term, not like the old military site Camp Sight had been. We rode into the yard immediately in front of the old, decrepit house like we belonged there, Noah and I right behind Cassias and Aubrey. I saw the corner of the truck peeking out from the inside of a mostly ruined barn, so this had to be the right place. The sound of a shotgun being ratcheted made us all turn on the spot.

"Cora!" Aubrey exclaimed, waving at her excitedly.

Cora lowered the weapon and seemed to sag in relief. "Oh god… We were wondering if we were ever going to see you all again. When Cassias and Aubrey left us to go look for you…" She shook her head as though not wanting to voice the fears that had floated through the group.

She led us inside the farmhouse, and it was a sorry sight indeed, just as I had imagined. Harvey and Minnie had managed to put something together for dinner, but it seemed to not lighten anyone's mood. What did though was the sight of Chouette sitting up, with some colour in her cheeks. She was seated in one of the only armchairs available in the room and appeared to be covered in almost every blanket that had been scraped together and packed prior to their departure.

Out of nowhere, Mech seemed to burst through the crowd and wrapped his arms around Aubrey. She hugged him back, her arms wrapping around his slight frame.

"I'm so glad you're ok," he said, his face blossoming with colour. Then, as if he hadn't just done something so out of character, he disappeared, back into the crowd. I looked at her, returning the smirk I had seen her send me earlier when Noah and I had been changing eyes. It was much like Hattie's, every time she saw Noah looking at me. Aubrey flushed as red as Mech and turned away.

I let my eyes roam over the space and smiled when I saw the kirpuuru curled in Chouette's lap, enjoying its head being scratched by her idle fingers. The creature's feathers would twitch every so often in contentment and then settle. I have to admit, I had missed the little beast. Its weight on my shoulder had been a comfort, but I was glad to see that it had made it out of the camp safe and sound. When I'd decided to go back for the case of eyes, there hadn't been time for me to figure out where it had gone. Before I had a chance to make my way over to her, Harvey thrust a plate of food into my hands.

"Eat," he said gruffly.

I wanted to say no, in a minute, but damn, even cold cuts smelled so good, and I was starving. I leaned back against the wall of the little homestead, overcrowded with the sixteen of us and ate. I spotted Noah, Aubrey and Cassias doing the same. Yes, the camp may have been destroyed, but this, these people, they were home. Together, we were invincible. I had to hold onto that thought, even as my heart cried out for the camp, I had destroyed myself.

"Is it done?" Chouette finally asked. Her voice was hoarse, but as she had started to speak, the din of conversation had stopped, to ensure that everyone could hear her.

"Yeah," Noah said with a nod. "It's done."

No one had eyes like Chouette, not even me and that was saying a lot, but that was no excuse for her to be up and about on her own. I sighed when I spotted her walking around in the small yard of the homestead. I jumped down from the roof, where I had been keeping watch and landed beside her.

She jumped, hand to her chest. Yep, I was right, she was not ready to be up and about. "Juniper!" She chided me. "You startled me."

"I'm sorry Chouette," I said, but I couldn't help smirking just a little. Her response had been classic. "What are you doing out here?"

"Have you ever tried sleeping in a room with more than ten other people who are all watching you like hawks to see if you croak?"

I laughed. She was right, everyone had been watching her. Intently. Even the kirpuuru. Oddly enough, the creature had not followed her out. As we walked, I peered inside. None of the doors or the windows on the homestead had any coverings and I spotted it staring at where Aubrey and Alma lay sleeping. It watched them intently. "They're driving you crazy?"

"Yes!" She accused. "You would think that I had gone and died," she said flippantly. I stopped waking and waited until she stopped and looked at me.

"You almost did Chouette. You weren't breathing. For a really long time and then when you collapsed back at the camp… They're just worried about you."

Chouette sighed. "I know. Still… I hate everyone fussing over me…"

"Let them fuss," I said. We circled the building where everyone slept and the silence between us was comfortable. Still, there were so many things that I wanted to ask. "Do you…"

"Do I what?"

I bit my lip and looked at her. "Do you remember what happened? Back in the aqueduct?"

Chouette shook her head. "Not clearly. I mean, I think that I slipped. The water was moving so fast, and it was getting higher and higher and then... Then something crashed into my leg, and I lost my footing."

"Sounds like you remember it pretty well," I returned.

Chouette shrugged. "I guess... But to be honest..." She looked around, as though making sure no one was listening to us. "It's like... I felt as though my foot was kicked out from beneath me... But...That's not possible. I mean, it was your doctor friend who was behind me, and she's spent all this time looking after me... So, it was some sort of debris, in the water..."

Her words caught me off guard. "You think-."

"No, no. I have to be wrong about that. See what I mean. I'm just imagining things," Chouette warded me off from saying what she had tried so carefully not to say. She did not want to admit that maybe... No... The thought wasn't even tolerable.

We kept walking, even straying from the homestead in order to look out at the view. We could still see the orange glow of the fire at Camp Sight. Sage's men and the Eridenti military had simply fled the area, rather than putting it out.

"They're going to let the forest burn..." Chouette said sadly. I nodded. I felt terrible about it. I had been the one to set everything ablaze, even if it had been their plan all along but from what I had seen, it had been a pretty forest with lots of old growth, stuff that might take decades if not centuries to regrow, if it ever did. Not to mention all the animals that had called that forest home. I saw her look at me out of the corner of my eye. "Don't."

"Don't what?"

"Don't beat yourself up about it," Chouette said. "It was always in our escape plan that we would burn the camp, distract them from following us, cover our tracks. I never liked it and the way Noah had set it up with the others always sounded a little like a suicide mission to me... The fact that you were there. That you could do the things you could do..." She paused for what seemed like an eternity. "I think... I think that's what made sure that everyone is here now."

"It just seems like so many bad things have happened since I showed up here..."

Chouette shook her head. "It was always coming and if you're right, then they are actively seeking some or all of us. This way we got you and Aubrey along for the ride."

I smiled. Not a big smile, just a little curve at the corners of my mouth. "So, what now?"

"That's what we discuss today. There's been some dissent in the group and that might mean adjusting our current plans." We settled into a comfortable silence, standing there, side by side, watching the sun rise above the level of the glowing red forest.

"What's that?" Chouette pointed out into the horizon, but I couldn't see what she was seeing.

"Where?" I asked, pulling the binoculars that I had hanging around my neck up to my eyes. I looked in the direction she pointed.

"There," she said. "That vehicle has a Sage Laboratories logo on it..."

I swore angrily under my breath. "How did they find us?"

"Come on," Chouette said, tugging at my sleeve. Together, we hurried back to the homestead.

"Get up! Everyone up!" I ordered. "They've found us!"

"We've got to move!" Chouette cried, running into the house.

"Wah..." Emrys groaned as she shook him. I followed suit, waking Mech, Elijah, Cora and Sadie. Each of them had their own complaints about being woken up already.

Noah had sat up the instant we had entered. "What's going on?"

"Chouette spotted Sage's men coming for us... Or at least headed in our direction," I said, shaking Harvey awake. "Come on, up you get."

It took little more than that to get Noah moving, he in turn shook awake those closest to him, Aubrey, Cassias and Vera. "How long do we have?"

I shrugged. "No idea. Longer than if Chouette hadn't spotted them."

We gathered belongings together and tried to make sure the old homestead did not look lived in recently. Chouette went back out to watch. No one would let her do any heavy lifting anyway.

Sage's men had come around the burning forest, not through it. Therefore, to find us, they must have known where we were going. Someone had to have told them or let them know somehow. But who would have done that? I ran my mind through every person in the camp and what I knew of their movements. I didn't like the fact that I had been separated from the majority of the group for so long. The days in Erihall, the time after, but that got me thinking. Who else had been separated from the group and one name stuck out? One name of someone who was not present as we fought for our lives back at Camp Sight. Who as a result of that, had ridden separately from the main group with only one person?

I found him carrying gear to the truck. No one was around, so I fell into step beside him. He looked at me out of the corner of his eye but said nothing until we stepped into the barn.

"Yes?"

I looked around. I mean, I really did not want to have this conversation with anyone, let alone this guy. Still, if I was wrong, I had no plans of spreading dissent and mistrust throughout the main group. Everyone was scared.

"Nothing. Just wondering if there was something you wanted to say," I said.

"About what, Juniper?"

I leaned against the side of the truck as he tossed bags inside it. I could see all the way to the homestead with this vantage point, so no one would be able to sneak up on us. "About what happened at the camp."

"And what happened at the camp?" He asked. Was he trying to play stupid with me? He was our protector, and he had just slept through most of the attack and the evacuation.

"Cash... You were nowhere to be found..." I started, trying to be delicate, but who was I kidding? Cassias terrified me. Why hadn't I told someone my suspicions and brought them with me? Noah. I should have told Noah. So why hadn't I?

He stopped what he was doing and looked around, also making sure that no one was around. "Do not continue with that sentence." How did he know what was going through my head? Had the others guessed at a traitor too? Who did they suspect?

I stood up straight. There was no way I would let him menace me. "I think it's a conversation that needs to be had."

He shook his head. "I don't know what happened, alright? I left Chouette with Aubrey and her grandmother, I just… I couldn't keep my head up," he said, looking over his shoulder again to make sure no one was listening in. He looked jittery though, even as he turned back to me. The words seemed to jumble together, and I got the feeling that he was lying.

"And what about the fact that we were fighting for our lives, and you weren't there!" I exclaimed.

He poked me. I mean, he actually shoved one stubby finger into my sternum. It hurt, but I was not going to let him know that. "I was out of it. I had no power in me. When I woke up, I heard everything, and it was like the world was falling apart. You saw me. I couldn't so much as put one foot in front of the other."

"And now?" I asked. "You and Aubrey were the only ones separate from the group."

"Other than you and Noah," Cassias hissed. "But quite frankly, don't you see another common denominator between those occurrences?"

My frown deepened and I swore. He was right. *"I was hoping that you and I might talk. The woman being held by Doctor Sage is my grandmother. I will do anything to get her back."* The words hit me like a tidal wave, and it hurt. Just as it had when I had first heard them. We had Alma now, but what if Aubrey's plan with Noah hadn't been a ploy? No, not possible. Aubrey had fought with everything she had back at the Camp but there was no denying that Cassias was right. Aubrey could not always be accounted for.

"What happened when you brought Chouette to her room?"

He shrugged. "I laid her out and the old woman made me clean my hands with some stuff she had."

"Did she make Aubrey do it?"

Cassias shrugged, though now he was awkwardly running his hands down his pants as though checking his pockets for something. "I don't know, I left after that… It was dinner… And I wanted to eat… But I went back to my room instead."

I patted him on the chest. "Thanks," Then I rushed off back to the house.

He was staring at me as I ran back, "Wait!" he called after me, "Juniper! That's not…" but I was on a roll, and something was making itself clear to me.

Inside the homestead, I stopped short when I saw Aubrey slap Harvey. For a moment he stood there startled by her action. I was too, but then again, so was everyone else. They had apparently come through from one of the other rooms arguing and Harvey had pushed Aubrey until she snapped.

"Take that back!" She cried as his hand rose comically to his cheek, it was going red from the impact of her blow. He tentatively touched the tender spot as he looked back at her.

"I will not! Since you showed up, we've lost everything!" he shouted in Aubrey's face.

"Harvey!" Chouette called walking over towards him.

But he apparently had no patience for her either because he held his other hand out in her direction. She almost rebounded off it with it at the same height as her head. "No. Stay out of this Chouette. Look at the state you were in yesterday. Ever since you and Noah brought her and Juniper back, we've been in danger!"

She saw me and maybe, like for me, the words she had said to me as we walked were echoing in her own mind or maybe more vividly, the feelings of going under the water in the aqueduct. I stood there, wondering what she would do or say. If she mentioned her own fears, what she thought she remembered, it would not change Harvey's mind on culpability. "Look, all of us are running on fear-." Harvey cut her off though.

"It's not fear Chouette. It's a realisation that we let a perfectly sighted person in and then this happened!"

"You!" Aubrey cried. I could tell that she wanted to say more but was doing everything in her power to hold her tongue. Her fists clenched at her sides, and it was obvious that she was struggling to restrain herself from hitting him.

It was then that Cassias walked in. "Where have you been?" Harvey shot at him.

Cassias's eyes widened in surprise. Nobody ever spoke to him in such tones, and he stood there, startled for a moment, hand still on the door he had walked in. "Packing."

"And yesterday at the camp?" Harvey continued. "Huh? Where the hell were you?"

"Harvey," I tried, having already covered this with Cassias. "First you blame Aubrey, and now you turn on Cassias?"

He rounded on me. Maybe I should have kept my mouth shut, because he stalked over to me, brushing past Chouette and pushing Aubrey out of his way. "You brought her with you. So maybe it's you, the trojan horse with your multiple eyes meant to lure us into a false sense of security. You and her? Maybe you got to him?"

"Harvey!"

The voice was loud and cut over his rant. He stopped instantly and turned. Minnie had stood up from where she had been packing things into bags. "That is quite enough. You cannot simply point the finger everybody one by one. I suppose you're going to suspect me next?"

He stopped short for a moment. "You Minnie? No, never..." He sagged momentarily but then regained his posture. "But you can't deny everything that has happened since those two arrived and Cassias didn't help us fight at the camp! He just showed up later!"

"How do you know he wasn't fighting?" Minnie asked him. "You had your own responsibility during that."

"I..." Cassias seemed at a loss for words, which as someone who rarely spoke and when he did, spoke very little seemed like a startling occurrence for him and for us. When we had talked outside, I was pretty sure that he said more in those few minutes than he had in the entire month I had been at Camp Sight. He reached his hand into his pocket and extracted a small bottle. I had no idea what it was, but it looked like a pill bottle.

"Your meds?" Harvey asked. "What have your meds got to do with anything?"

"You wanted to know where I was," Cassias stated.

Alma pushed up from where she'd been sitting and went to stand before the big man. She took the pill bottle in her hands and looked at it. "Amastrin." She opened the bottle and looked inside. "There's only three left in here. "For how long have there been three in here?"

Cassias looked anywhere but at her, so Noah answered. "He was running low already when Chouette and I went into Erihall, the day we met Juniper and Aubrey."

"What's low?" she pressed. "What have you been doing?"

"It was a quarter full at the time," Noah replied when the big man stayed silent.

"That was over a month ago," Alma said, staring at the three remaining pills. Then she looked up at Cassias. "You've been skipping doses." He nodded. "That's why you've been tired, sluggish, unable to move."

"None of this changes the fact that everything went wrong when they showed up!" Harvey intervened, pointing at me and Aubrey. "If Noah and Chouette hadn't gotten caught up in Juniper's crap that day, Cash would've had his meds. None of this would have happened."

Alma shook her head. "No, I'm assuming you were at the clinic because you were there to steal it?" she asked, looking at them. Noah and Chouette shared a look, then nodded. "We didn't have any. The delivery was late."

"But!" Harvey cried.

"Harvey," Chouette tried again. "We are all trying our best. Juniper, Cassias and Aubrey too. Also, if what we learned in Erihall is true, then this was always coming. They want us back. Some of us more than others."

Harvey heaved in breaths. His rant, his fear, had taken more out of him than anyone had realised. It must have been building within him until he had snapped, finally lashing out at the nearest person he even remotely suspected.

I sighed. Did this explanation exonerate Aubrey? I didn't know, but with tensions running high, I would have to talk to Aubrey later. It was not a conversation I could risk having overheard by Harvey.

100

We finished packing everything back up and rode away from the old farmhouse. Cassias and Aubrey were riding ahead of the truck, while Noah and I were riding behind as the vanguard. I had asked him if I slowed him down, but he had insisted that he liked having me at his back. I flushed at that, but then, he had handed me the gun I had used earlier when we had left Erihall.

Right. That was what he meant. He needed a shooter. I looked away and almost scurried over to the bike in embarrassment before he could get a good look at my face. I needed to stop letting Hattie and Aubrey get into my head. It was just their imagination... Even if he had kissed me like our lives depended on it as we'd prepared to destroy Camp Sight. No, now was not the time to let my mind wander down that path.

Before climbing up into the truck herself, Chouette had taken Cassias, Noah, Cora and I up to the roof of the house and pointed out the convoy to us. They were hours out and if we were smart, we could likely avoid them. The group was sizable though. We just had to hope that they hadn't sent off scouts that we might have missed.

Our pace had picked up then, wanting to put as much distance between the convoy, the Eridenti behind us and our eventual destination. We hurried to clean up and make it look as though no one had been there. Mech offered a tentative hand to Alma, helping her into the back of the truck.

"Thank you dear," she said, patting his hand as she regained her balance.

Mech nodded and flushed, glancing towards where Aubrey was prepping her bike. I shook my head. The poor kid had it bad for the redheaded girl.

Then we were off. Another chance to flee potential capture, but at least this time we had a much larger head start then when they'd arrived at Camp Sight with no warning. We could choose where we would stand and fight. It would likely be the only option eventually. Crossing the Shiuran border would do nothing for us. Eriden had taken forcible control over most of Shiura and few people these days even knew where the Shiura-Eriden border was. It was unlikely that we would know it when we did cross it

"Where to?" I asked Noah as we took off.

He swerved to avoid the dust and gravel being kicked up by the truck. "We're going off course. If our escape plan has been leaked, then we need to take them by surprise," he said. "The plan we had, we all agree it's been compromised. That group Chouette pointed out, they're right in the way of where we wanted to be."

"How do you think they know?" I asked.

Noah shook his head. "I don't know. Maybe they don't and it's just our bad luck. Either way, they found camp, they're on their way here and we need to find a way through."

I wrapped my arms around him tighter, taking comfort in the feel of him against me. He started the bike and took off behind the truck as they pulled out of the old farmhouse's courtyard. The night of rest had done us good, but what had it cost us? Things were not looking good for us. We could not stay on the run forever. Not with a group this size. It would only be a matter of time before one of those oncoming forces caught up to us or worse, they would ambush us and then we would have no hope of escape.

We had been on the road maybe two hours when Chouette, seated next Kattie told us that we were being boxed in. She had spotted more vehicles coming at us.

"There's nowhere to turn!" Kattie cried. He kept on driving, because stopping was certain to be catastrophic but going forward wasn't going to end well either.

Noah came up beside Chouette's window. It didn't make for a comfortable conversation, but we could hear each other and try to plan.

"We can try and hold them off," Cassias called.

"With what?" Aubrey asked. "We're mostly out of ammo."

"We're out!" Cora shouted, poking her head out between Kattie and Chouette.

"What does that leave us?" Aubrey asked, her voice almost a panicked shriek.

"The eyes," I said. "Cora's, mine, Mech... Harvey??" I asked, trying to remember if Harvey really did set things on fire with his eyes.

Noah shook his head. "I don't like resorting to that, especially not Mech."

"If we're out of ammo and we want to make it through, do we have a choice?" I asked him, a little irritated by his choice. I couldn't do this all alone and the others had usable abilities.

"Kattie! Noah ordered. "Pull over."

"What?" he cried.

"Just do it, we've got some setting up to do."

The truck came to a stop in the middle of the road, and we dismounted the bikes. Cora jumped out of the truck, and I saw Mech cautiously poke his head around the side of the truck. He did not look eager to come out. Noah must have spotted him too because he approached the boy and said softly to him. "You don't need to fight," the boy seemed to sag in relief. "Stay with the others and only do anything if there is no other option. If we've already lost, ok?" Mech nodded vehemently at the idea, then ducked back into the truck.

Cassias strode over to Cora, and she seemed to eye him warily with her good eye. "You're going to use it?" she asked.

"Got a better idea than Juniper on how to stop what's coming?" he asked gruffly.

She shook her head. "No..."

Harvey came out, followed by Emrys. The two boys looked awkward beside Cora and Cassias. Emrys's small form and large, thick bottle-rim glasses just made him took even smaller next to Cassias.

Sadie jumped out, rubbing her hands together. "Let's do this thing," she beamed. She tapped at her eye patch gleefully.

Cora just shook her head. "Girl, calm it."

"What about the rest of us?" Vera asked.

"You stay here," Minnie said, and her tone left no room for argument. We were not going to ever go against Minnie's word. Even in the time I had been with the group, she had always been right. Her feelings or visions, whatever it was that guided her in her protection of us, it was uncanny.

I saw Hattie come up behind Emrys. "No!" I said, "absolutely not."

"What is it?" Noah asked from beside me.

"Hattie. Go back inside," I told the girl, pointing back at the truck.

"No! If Noah stays out here, so will I."

"Hattie!" Noah echoed my earlier warning. "In."

"No."

"We don't have time for your childishness, girl," Cassias growled. "Get inside the damned truck," then he looked at Noah. "You too man. Hattie's right."

He looked like he was about to argue, but I took his hand and lead him away from the group. He followed without complaint and that, more than anything else was probably what made everyone look. Their eyes followed us until we passed out of their line of sight beside the truck. I drew him to me and hugged him close.

"Juni?" He asked softly, his arms wrapping around me.

I leaned my head against his chest and sighed. "Stay with the main group," I whispered softly.

"I can't... Not if you're going to-."

"Shh," I said, looking up at him. "You were their protector before you were mine. They need you with them. Mech will need someone to tell him when, because on his own, he would rather die than unleash his ability upon those men..." Noah tried to interrupt me, but I continued. "You can't fight in what's coming. Not this time."

He took my face in his hands and stared into my eyes. It seemed to last for an eternity. I had no idea how his eyes could be so deep, so expressive with those contact lenses covering those stark white eyes, but they drew me in. Kept me trapped there for what seemed an eternity.

And then he leaned down and kissed me. Our lips met and someone wolf whistled. We broke apart, me stumbling a few feet backwards in order to put distance between myself and Noah. When we looked to where it had come from, there wasn't just one. No, everyone was standing there. Hattie, her fingers coming down from her mouth, obviously the perpetrator. Kattie slapped her playfully over the back of the head. Mech was blushing a stunning shade of red that reminded me of Minnie's tomatoes back at the camp.

"See! See! See!" Hattie cried, "I told you!"

Aubrey gave me a thumbs up. Chouette looked as though she was gushing and quite possibly planning our wedding in her head. The kirpuuru was still perched on her shoulder. I have to say, I was feeling a little abandoned by the beast. It was as though I no longer existed to it. But who could blame it for sticking with Chouette while she was injured right? I turned, almost positive that I was as red as Mech.

"Don't you all have things to be doing?" Noah said, trying not to sound as disappointed and frustrated as I felt.

"Nope!" Sadie said, leaning against the side of the truck, her arms crossed in front of her. "Carry on."

Noah growled at her, then turned me around, reaching for my backpack. He dug his hand inside and pulled out the case. "We've all got preparations to make."

With that, they all dispersed, leaving us to our own preparations. Apparently, no one liked to see me change eyes. Go figure, right? I mean, it's not like I was a fan of the process myself, but here I was about to engage in the change once again before going into combat.

Then suddenly, my name was being called. "Juni! Juni! Juni!" Hattie cried, running back from the truck.

"What is it?" I asked her.

"Chouette said she spotted that man, Sebastian with the group ahead of us and we have a plan," she dragged me towards the passenger door of the truck so that I could see Chouette.

"Use him," Chouette said. "Use what he wants from you."

I shook my head. "No. He wants Noah."

"Noah will get in and won't be seen. But if it's a choice between Sage's men behind us and Sebastian before us... We stand a better chance with the man who thinks he's in love with you."

I felt the hand on my shoulder squeeze, and I knew that it was Noah. "It's a good plan," he said softly, but I could tell that he didn't like it.

"After our show of force though," I said.

Noah nodded. "Use Cassias. That should get the message across."

101

After arranging ourselves as best as we could, we had continued on, hoping that we could bypass the upcoming confrontation, but knowing that we couldn't. We had made the decision to meet the group Sebastian was with, rather than Sage's, just as Chouette had planned. I wasn't entirely sure that Sebastian was any saner that Sage, but Aubrey had convinced them all that Sebastian was in love with me, and it was complete nonsense, but no one wanted to listen to me.

Now, I stood in the middle of the road in the middle of God only knew where, the fates of everyone in the group resting on my shoulders. What if I messed it up? I had gotten them all into this mess after all. There was no saying that this plan was any better than trying to evade both groups.

The kirpuuru was once again on my shoulder, chittering away in my ear. I was surrounded by Cassias, Harvey, Cora and Emrys, all ready and busting for a fight. They had confidence in Chouette's plan, so I had to have confidence too.

The lead vehicle came to a stop. We stood there, staring at it while we waited for something to happen. Finally, Sebastian emerged, two armed guards flanking him. Slowly, the other vehicles started to discharge their passengers. They were all armed and well armoured. We would be slaughtered if this turned into a fight. I could feel it.

Sebastian stepped forward. He waved at his men to stay put. With a glance at Cassias, I did the same. The tension in the air was thick as we slowly approached one another our gazes never straying from the other's face. He looked just as I remembered him from that first day, except something was different. Back then there had been a certain amount of insecurity about him compared to the man I now saw before me. He looked harder, more certain, like a man on am mission. We had both changed in the intervening time. Hopefully, I had changed for the better, because everyone else was counting on me to be able to fool him. And what if they were wrong? What if he wasn't as infatuated with me as they thought? Then this whole ploy was doomed to fail.

"Juniper," he said, glancing past me the others briefly. He narrowed his eyes, almost in concentration, perhaps trying to identify each one of my followers, trying to discern what abilities he would be up against.

"Sebastian."

"What do we have here?"

"Nothing of interest to you," I said as nonchalantly as I could. My palms were sweating, my heart was beating a steady rhythm of unease in my head, and I was pretty sure this whole charade was not going to work. Except it had to work. We had no other plan.

"Really?" He asked. "You're going to tell me that the boy is not in there?" He pointed towards the truck.

I clenched my fingers into fists at my side. Here we go, he wasn't going to dawdle into the demands. He was going straight for what he wanted. The whole plan would live or die on my next words. What had Chouette been thinking?

"No!" The single word caught in my throat, coming out choked. He didn't appear to believe me though. Maybe my voice hadn't been strong enough. "No…" I said again, unclenching my fingers. My voice trembled with what I hoped he thought was emotion but was really nerves. This blatant lie just didn't run off the tongue as well as Chouette had hoped. "No… We… We… lost him on the road… An injury he refused to tell anyone about. Noah's dead."

102

We stood there, a building tension evident between us and Sebastian. Behind him, men waited, anxiously adjusting their weapon grips. Sebastian stared at me, disbelief evident on his face.

The awkward silence was broken by a harsh cry. "You caused this," It was Harvey. "With your experiments and your treatment of us. We just want to be free."

"Do you have any idea how much money was put into creating you all?" Another voice said from behind us.

Could this get any worse? Behind us. Sage was behind us. He thought that he could just wander up and join the conversation.

"We don't care," Cora said turning to him. "We never wanted to be your experiments."

"Not true," Nelson Sage said walking around to stand beside Sebastian. "Each and every one of you wanted to be able to see again. You or your parents or both, all agreed when I came to make my proposal."

I shook my head. What he was saying wasn't really getting through though. I was staring at Nelson and Sebastian, side by side. I had never seen them together before and had the feeling I was missing something very important.

"That can't be," I said, trying to come back to the conversation and get out of my own head. Whatever it was that was bothering me was like an annoying gnat that kept buzzing and buzzing. "Then why don't I have any memory of my life beforehand. Everyone here has memories of homes, families, lives. Everyone except me." Even if what he said was true about us agreeing, what about me? Who was I? Where did I come from? Why was I the only one with no memory of my life before him?

Nelson approached me and it took everything in me to hold my ground. His stiff upper body movements, his arm strapped to his side and the small amount of stone peeking out from the collar of his shirt were all reminders of what I had done to him. But I had no illusions that he had some way of controlling me or the others. His good hand reached up to cup my cheek and a shiver ran down my spine. Beside me Cassias tensed, and I reached out to touch his arm. He settled, but only slightly.

"You my dear girl, were different," he said, staring into my eyes. "Everything about you was different. And then there was the fact, that my dear son was besotted with you."

SON??? Who the hell was... Oh... Him...? Sebastian was Nelson Sage's son.

And just like that, so many things made sense. So many niggling things that had been bothering me made sense just like that. I looked toward Sebastian, and I could see it. That thing I had seen but not understood when they had stood side by side. I didn't recall having ever seen them together before.

"Ohhh!" Sage exclaimed. "He never told you that he was my son, did he? No, I suppose he wouldn't have."

Finally, he released my face and looked at the others. "All of you. I gave you sight. I gave you a purpose and you threw it all away." He looked at me disdainfully. "And you worst of all," He backhanded me across the face so hard I stumbled backwards, falling to one knee.

Damn, I never knew that lab geek could hit like that. He had always had his goons, Stinky and Scratchy handle that. I heard Cassias growl as he stepped in front of me. I nodded to Harvey when I was blocked from view, and he lifted his glasses. A van in the distance, surrounded by Sebastian's men, blew up sending people flying from the force of the explosion.

Screams echoed in the aftermath as I stood up, my cheek and jaw throbbed from the force of Sage's blow. We were at a serious disadvantage in terms of numbers. We probably also had no surprise factor either. Sage created us as he had so proudly stated. He knew what each and every one of us could do. Cora lifted her eye patch, and the laser beam I had seen at the attack on Camp Sight shot out, taking out two men before hitting a second vehicle.

"Party tricks girl," Sage announced. He held his good hand out and a young woman approached him. She let his arm wrap around her shoulders. She wore glasses, dark ones that hid her eyes from view. She looked up at Sage and he nodded to her. She looked back at us and took off her glasses.

Cassias jumped in front of us. "Don't look her in the eyes!" Then, he too took off the glasses I had never seen him without. It was a combat of wills. We gathered behind his large frame, and we could hear people on the other side tripping over themselves to get escape as the fear both he and this girl could create filled the air. Emrys peaked around him, his own large, goggle like glasses hopefully protecting him from what was coming.

Things seemed to pop and sizzle around the place and those wearing electronic goggles ripped them from their faces. They were red and starting to blister where the goggles had been. Emrys smirked.

"Damned monsters," One shouted as he tossed his goggles to the floor. But then he made the mistake of looking up without them. His eyes connected with Cassias before he realised what he was doing. The man screamed. It was full of fear, and he turned to run. Several others turned to looked at what he had seen. They either saw Cassias or Sage's girl and they too let out blood curdling screams before running. The endless plains seemed to stretch out forever and soldiers just kept on running until they were specks in the distance that only Chouette would be able to see.

103

Everything was chaos. Alma Corbyn-Fisher, former Colonel of the Eridenti Military's medical corps, knew chaos, especially that caused by combat and even as the kids, oh they really were only children, weren't they? Even as they confronted the first oncoming force, she knew that they stood no chance. They needed another ace in their pockets if this wasn't going to become a bloodbath.

With everyone distracted by the confrontation Alma dropped from the back of the truck, wishing that she was at least ten years younger as the landing jarred her body, forcing her to wait as the little jolts of pain rattled their way through her old bones.

"Fifteen years younger," she muttered to herself as glanced towards where Juniper and the others were confronting Sebastian and Sage. They were surrounded and outnumbered. Alma had to move now if she had any chance of getting out of this alive.

The boy Sebastian had come with the Eridenti Military, they were her goal. Surely someone in that troop either knew her or perhaps they shared a connection. Something was happening, but she couldn't focus on the kids if the was going to make this work. She had to make it to the line of soldiers baring the way ahead and she had to do it without being seen.

"Come on."

Alma paused. That was the girl Hattie's voice.

"We can't leave them," Noah objected.

"We're not leaving them," Hattie insisted. Alma peered around the truck to see the boy's arm being pulled against his will by the invisible force of Hattie. "We're going to be their rescue, but not if they find us. Besides, they're all way too interested in you! Trying to swap the old woman for you. Come on!"

So, they'd tried to make a trade, her for the boy. What did they want from him? What was it he could do? Hattie had her invisibility, Minnie had visions of the future and Alma had heard rumblings about various other abilities. Then there was of course Juniper. If anyone, shouldn't they have wanted the girl back? They did. Nelson Sage wanted the girl, but Sebastian Anson wanted the boy. Why?

She would need to get into the records if she could. The answers would always be in the records. Hattie and Noah disappeared into the forest, even as Noah objected, not wanting to leave their friends behind. Alma understood where he was coming from, but she too had a plan, just like young Hattie.

She kept low, not wanting to attract attention.

"Halt." Alma stopped moving and put her hands in the air. She knew that kind of order. Now was when she would have to make this all work. She turned, ever so slowly to the soldier who had a weapon aimed at her. "Identification. Who are you?"

"My ID is in my pocket," Alma said, really hoping that was still true. She hadn't bothered to check that and now it was a little late. A second soldier appeared, backing up is partner. "My name is Colonel Alma Corbyn-Fisher and I've been held hostage." Not a lie... just not the whole truth.

The two young men looked at each other, conversing quietly as they kept their weapons trained on her. "ID," the first one said again.

Alma patted her pockets down, almost certain that it was gone in all the chaos. What would she do if the ID packet was gone, but she felt it in the inside breast pocket of her jacket and almost groaned in relief. It was still there.

"Hands in the air!" The jumpy soldier demanded. Alma shot her hands back into their air.

"Wyman!" his partner hissed. "She's an old lady!"

Wyman started to protest, but Alma felt her confidence raise as her luck turned for the better. "Wyman? Like Oliver Wyman?" She asked.

The jittery young soldier hesitated and looked at her. "Oliver Wyman's my father..."

"How is he?" Alma asked, relaxing her arms as her shoulders ached. "I don't think I've seen Oliver since I patched him up after that... training exercise..." She said coyly. Everyone in the Eridenti military knew about Oliver Wyman and the 'training exercise.' The young man blanched, and his partner tried his best to hide a smirk. "I'm surprised they let a Wyman carry a weapon," Alma said, letting her arms rest at her sides finally. "I mean, your father..."

"I'm not my father!" the younger man exclaimed.

"Come on, we should take her to the captain," his partner insisted, and Alma breathed a sigh of relief for the second young man and his sensible nature. Wymans. They were still letting Wymans into the military. The boy looked as jittery as his father had been arrogant with a weapon in his hand. How many unintentional shootings had this boy been a part of?

Wyman jerked the weapon. "Move!" he ordered.

And she was in.

104

From there, everything developed into a melee that we didn't stand a chance of winning. Their numbers were overwhelming and we, no matter how extraordinary our abilities were, could not keep up with the sheer number of them. Despite Cassias's training regime, we weren't as coordinated or practiced as the military men. Sage's backup from the Eridenti military was already staggering in their numbers. Then there was us. There were fifteen of us in total and only half of us had combat capabilities. When they made their way to the truck, it was over. One guy had pulled Kattie out of the driver's seat, throwing him to the ground before hauling him back up and holding a gun to his head. One by one, soldiers lead our friends out of the truck. Minnie, Aubrey, Chouette and Mech.

Mech was looking every which way wildly, trying to figure out if there was anything he could or even, if he should, do something. Taking off his goggles would help, but what damage would that do to us, to even his own psyche? I did everything I could to indicate to him not to do anything.

Vera, who was hauled out after him reached for his shoulder. The boy looked at her and she shook her head. I let out a breath I didn't realise I'd been holding. Then one of their captors brought his weapons down on her arm. It fell from Mech's shoulder as she cried out in pain, the impact sending her stumbling backwards and Mech was pushed forward, stumbling several steps forward. The boy turned on Vera's attacker and lunged at him.

They wrestled, the soldier turning from Vera to Mech. Mech was no match for the burly, well-trained soldier. He threw the small boy to the ground and at he did, Mech's goggles got dislodged and then the soldier was gone. Dusted into nothingness. The dust or ash or whatever it was shimmered to the ground like a curtain. The boy cried out in dismay. Vera reached for him, pulling him into her arms and this time no one stopped her. She reached around, cradling him against her, even as he held his hands against his scrunched-up eyes. Finally, her hand settled on the goggles, and she settled them back upon the boy's eyes and helped him to his feet.

Now, people stayed away from Mech. He positioned himself in front of the group. Sadie situated herself beside him, Vera behind. They were collecting themselves. We could survive this.

Maybe.

I couldn't find Noah anywhere. Where was he? I watched as each person was hauled out. Noah never was. Well, at least our plan wouldn't be outed as a lie, but that begged the question, where was he? No one appeared to pull Hattie out either, but she could escape almost anyone or anything. Hattie not being among them did not scare me, but Noah being missing did.

I kept staring, my eyes tracking each one of our friends. Nothing. No one else emerged.

Not even Alma.

No Noah. No Hattie. No Alma. It made no sense. I looked back to the others, hoping that someone had a clue as to what was happening, but even Chouette who seemed to always know everything was staring at the truck as though expecting Noah to emerge. When our eyes met, I could see the panic there, even as we were all marched towards another truck and loaded in.

105

The cell was crowded when I came to. Then again it would be with thirteen people sprawled on the floor of the room. When I moved my feet, a groan emanated from someone I accidentally kicked.

I opened my eyes to nothing. Everything was black and it made me sick. Being able to see was becoming or maybe I should say had become something I was used to now. My friends' faces, light, colour, the sky, trees, everything the world had to offer. Even this cell. I would have given anything to be able to see. To make sure, with my own eyes that everyone was there, that everyone was in one piece. Aside from being blind again, my hands were also tied behind my back, making it hard to move.

"Ugh..." The sound came from somewhere near my head.

"Hey!" I tried to say, but the sound that emerged from my mouth was more like a "Hugh..." Pain shot through every part of my body, and I had to wonder, what was my memory missing, because other than Sage backhanding me across my face, I did not remember being beaten.

I struggled into a position where I was sitting up. It helped little as I still could not see. I could hear the others moving around so that was good.

"I can't see!"

"Turn on the lights!"

"My head!"

"What is this?"

"They've blind-folded everyone," The voice of reason. Aubrey. They must not have any reason to blindfold her. Seeing as how she was fully sighted.

Cries and calls echoed amongst the group. It felt pretty damned terrible, sitting there in the dark. "How is everyone?" I asked her.

"Groggy mainly. I think they drugged us," Aubrey called back. "You and Mech though… You look real bad…"

"So, I look as good as I feel. Great," I muttered.

"Where are we?" the voice sounded like Chouette. Shifting sounds emanated from where I heard her voice. She too must be trying to sit up.

"Who do I have to break?" Sadie announced in all her glory.

"Shh!" I ordered. I thought I heard footsteps from outside the door. Sure enough, as the outraged chatter died down, I could hear the heavy clomp clomping of boots. Then, a key rattled in the door it swung open. A gust of air seemed to be accompanying the person who entered, bringing with it a startling and ominous chill to the room.

"Girl!" I cringed but said nothing. I was not the only girl in here. If Sebastian damn well wanted me, he could use my name. I heard him sigh. "Juniper. Come here."

"No."

"Why not?"

"I can't!" I snarled.

There was a pause and then he spoke. "You always followed instructions before."

I scoffed. "I was hauled from one place to another. I never had a choice."

"I'm not here to argue with you. Come here."

"Look around. No one around here can see. I'd never make it to you without falling over everyone. So, either say what it is you want, or come over here and haul me out yourself."

To my surprise, he did. "Sir," someone said in a gasp, but that was accompanied by the sound of Sebastian's soft soled shoes making their way over the prone bodies of my friends.

"I'll get her," Sebastian said. "You know Juniper, if you had just given me what I wanted, none of this would have happened."

"What did he want?" Elijah asked softly.

"You and all your little friends would have been able to lead happy little lives of obscurity," Sebastian said as he stood over me now. I could feel his presence; smell that scent he had always worn when I had seen him. "All you had to do was give me everything I wanted."

"I couldn't give you that."

He hauled me up. "You couldn't have stayed with me?" He asked. "Couldn't have helped me take down my father and his research projects? Since the day I saw what that one could do," he pointed somewhere, but I couldn't see him, so I had no idea whom he was referring to. "I knew that it was only going to get worse. Then the files and what he was doing to all of you. We had a chance to stop it, you and me. We could have done it together."

"What?" Minnie asked. "No. I don't believe it."

"Stop whitewashing it to sound like you just wanted me. If that was true, I'd have given you anything you damned well wanted," I shouted as he grabbed me and pulled me to my feet.

"Juniper?" Vera asked. "What's he talking about?"

"Tell them!" I shouted at him. "Tell them what you really wanted from me!"

He scoffed right back at me. "It sounds so much better this way, when I tell them that you were only let go to find them. When I tell them that you had it in your power to save them all."

"I trusted you," I whispered. I could imagine the looks on everyone's faces. They were all talking around me, trying to be heard. Questions, indignation, anger… Anger at me. For keeping secrets.

"That was the point," Sebastian said. "You and me, we were supposed to take over this little enterprise. You could have had it all, instead you threw me away for a bunch of washed up and useless brats!"

My eyes… Well, my eye sockets, widened in realisation. "It was you. You kept sending Sage after us… They had never been touched before now. No one had ever found the camp because no one even cared about them. You just wanted them out of the way… or was it more that you wanted Sage out of the way?" I asked. He was dragging me from the room. Not caring that I was being hauled over my friends. I felt them reach for me, but like me they were tied up.

"I didn't need the boy out of the way. I needed the boy to combat my father's creations! Speaking of the boy, where is he?"

"I already told you!" I spat. "Dead!" Seriously, the question was driving me crazy too. Where was Noah? I also hadn't heard Hattie at all since we had been in there. She would have been leading every conversation if she had been. I was sure of that. So, where were they?

I felt his face come in close. "And the invisible girl?"

"What invisible girl?" I spat at him.

We passed the last prone member of Camp Sight when I heard someone stand up. "Tell them how you wanted to use Noah. How you wanted him to be your secret weapon." It was Aubrey.

A series of outcries rose up around us, as well as more shuffling from those who were waking up. Sebastian thrust me into the arms of the waiting guards and spun on Aubrey. "I'd be careful who you contradict little girl. You have no purpose here." I could hear more footsteps, light and tentative, as though they were carefully trying to place their feet. Was it Aubrey still? Others attempted to shuffle out of her way.

"My purpose here is them. My purpose is the friends that risked everything to help me find my grandmother. The friend who herself got captured and beaten and quite frankly, molested, by you for my grandmother. My purpose is the boy over there who still has not woken up because your goons beat him so bad after they screwed up and removed his goggles."

"Mech!" I gasped.

"You guys created them, but when you can't control them, you beat them, you kill them, you act like gods with your toys. Well, they're people! And before you came along, they had lives. We all did. Now leave her here." And with that, she grabbed my arm and tugged me back towards the room.

I loved Aubrey at that moment. I really did. Despite being used as a tug of war toy, I really did love her at that moment. The way she spoke up not just for me, but for everyone. She had no reason to. Sebastian was right, she had no value to him or Sage. And then something boomed and echoed. I had heard enough guns in the past few weeks. The force on my arm dropped, her fingers sliding away from me in slow motion.

"AUBREY!" I screamed, but it was lost in the screams and cries from the entire group. I spun on Sebastian, wrenching myself away from his guards. I found him and I hit him. Again, and again and again. He tried to wrestle with me, but I was flailing and hitting at him wildly. "Let me go!" I cried out, wrestling myself away from his attempts to subdue me. I dropped to my knees and reached for my friend, my hands scrambling around uncertainly for her until finally, I felt the wet shirt beneath my hands. Her blood was covering everything from what I could tell. "Aubrey!"

She groaned in response. Not great, but she was responding, so that was something. I pulled her on to my lap, but someone was reaching for me non too gently.

"Let her be," Sebastian ordered. "She is of no consequence to me," and with that I was hauled back to my feet and dragged from the room. I screamed. I kicked. I bit anything that came near, until a blow to my head made me see stars in my hollow eyes.

106

I was practically rabid by the time Sebastian had me tossed in a room all of my own. I skidded across the floor, scraping up my hands, arms and clothes. The impact and everything that followed hurt my already bruised body.

"You should know this room like the back of your hand," a voice I did not recognise said. I looked up, but I needn't bother. It didn't change my views of absolute darkness. I knew where I was, but that was a mistake. They should never have brought me back here.

The door slammed shut and I was left on my own in the space that had once been my room. The only space where I had been free to roam. The man had been right. I knew every nook, every cranny, and every sound of this room. So, to say I was surprised when I sat on the bed and heard someone 'oomph' at the impact was an understatement.

I jumped back up and felt the mattress. There was no one there. "Hello?" I asked. The bed was empty except for the pillow and a thin blanket.

"Down here!" that voice. It was strong and calming and hearing it filled my heart to bursting. I knew that voice. I crouched down, then got on all fours to look under the bed. Again, a useless action but it at least felt like I was doing something. "Think you could give me a hand?"

I reached my hand under the bed, and it was grabbed forcefully by a masculine hand. I pulled and we tumbled backwards, Noah landing on top of me. I could imagine that smile of his, beaming from ear to ear, the bright blue if his contact lenses sparkling in mirth. "Found you," he said in my ear.

I rolled over, tossing him to the floor beside me, then flopped back into place. Everything hurt. I hurt in places that already hurt and prior to today, had only ever known about after beatings. "How?" I finally managed to ask.

"Hattie pulled me out just before they took the truck," Noah explained, going into detail about an outrageous plan that included something about a bag and him wearing Hattie's invisible shirt over his head.

"Where is Hattie?"

"Looking for a way to get the others out," he said sitting up beside me. "You look terrible Juni," he said brushing a lock of hair out of my face.

"They shot Aubrey and Mech's hurt bad..." I said sitting by myself, curling up as small as I could. I wanted to take the time to fall into his arms and let his presence comfort me as it had in the past, but we had no time for such self-indulgence. Our friends were in danger. Our friends were hurt. I forced myself to my feet.

"Do you..." Noah started, but I brushed past him and made my way to the door.

"This was my room," I said trying at the door much as I had every day of my captivity.

"Right..." Noah said uncertainly.

I kicked at the door futilely. Now my foot hurt but so what? I turned to Noah angrily. "Why are you here?" I cried. "They need you!" I pointed wildly at any direction that I thought was the interior of the building.

"Chouette and Mech and Aubrey and Vera and Sadie... They all need you and you're here!" I heard him move before I felt him. He came over to me, tried to wrap his arms around me, but I pushed him away. "I don't need you! I am not important. You should be with them. Or better yet, as far from this place as possible!"

Apparently, unlike when I hit at Sebastian, my wild attacks seemed to grow weaker and Noah was able to pull me to him, resting my head against his chest and tightly wrapping his arms around me. I tried a few times to push him away, but he didn't let me. Instead, we stood there, me wrapped in his strong embrace and him whispering about how everything would be fine. We would escape and we would rescue all the others. Everyone would go... Well, he didn't know where. Home was gone, blown up by our own hands, eyes. Whatever you wanted to call how we did it.

I let Noah lead me back to the bed. It was the only thing in the room to sit on, and we sat down together, me still wrapped in his arms.

"Where does it hurt?" he asked, pulling away to arm's length. I guessed that he was looking at me with that look he gets when he's inspecting something or someone.

"I'm fine."

"No, you are not. You look like crap and every time you move, you groan."

I laughed, but it was cut off when I coughed, and my abdomen hurt. "Ok, ok..." I gasped out. "Everywhere. I hurt everywhere..."

"We can't get out, right?" he asked as he sat beside me.

I shook my head. "Every way I found they fixed or changed. There won't be anything until someone opens that door."

"Ok then," Noah said, his voice sounding confident and upbeat. "Regardless of everything we have to do or should be doing, there is nothing we can do right now?"

The pause seemed to drag on until I got the hint that he was waiting for me to respond. "Right..." I finally said hesitantly.

"Good," Noah said before moving so that he was laying across my old bed. He tugged at me to lay down beside him and I did. My head rested in the crook of his shoulder, and I felt his arm wrap around my waist. I curled next to him. "Then we have nothing to do but wait and for you to rest."

I sighed. I knew that he was right, but it didn't make the thought any easier to bare. We lay there in silence for a while, just being together seemed to give me strength at least. I was eternally grateful to Hattie for getting him out of the truck before the soldiers had found him, but now that he was here, I had no idea how I would prevent him from being discovered.

"I'm scared," I finally said. It was soft and part of me wished that he would not hear it.

No such luck. "Me too," came his reply. "None of us ever wanted to come back here or to any of the labs... But we are stronger together."

I wanted to look into his face, to see that earnest look that I loved, but all I was seeing was darkness. "But we're not together with the others... And you said Hattie is out on her own..."

"Don't worry about Hattie," Noah said giving me a squeeze. "She knows what she's doing."

"Mech..."

"I know... I saw how they beat him... And you..." he sighed. "I wanted to jump in and help, but Hattie held me back. Watching that... Watching everyone get rounded up..."

"But where do we go from here?" I asked. "Even if we make it out of here alive... Where do we go from here?"

I felt him shrug, "I don't know... But we will find something..."

I admired his ability to stay so positive. I nestled in closer to him and felt him hold me tighter. "I'm sorry..."

"No," his tone was firm. "Not that again. You did not cause this. Sebastian's obsession with you, Sage's desire for super soldiers, a war we had nothing to do with. They caused this."

He rolled over slightly so that he could wrap both arms around me. I held both my hands against his chest and curled against him. I had not wanted to admit it, but I was exhausted, and the soft tones of his voice were lulling me to sleep. It wasn't long until my thoughts were no longer running straight. It wasn't as though I couldn't keep my eyes open, but sleep dragged me under, wrapped in the security of Noah's embrace.

107

We must have been sleeping soundly because I never heard them come. All of the sudden I heard the door bang open, and guns being ratcheted... Was that what it was called when they all made those sounds together? I had no idea. I'd ask Aubrey when I got the chance.

Noah sat up behind me and I put myself in front of him. I hated that I couldn't see those guys, but I followed the sounds they made. If I knew any space, it was this room.

"How did he get in?" one of them asked.

There was a new sound. One I do not recall ever hearing in those halls before. High heels. The tap tapping of a woman's heels. "Where is the invisible girl?"

The world seemed to stop. The noise of the restless guards fell away as everything became hazy. My heart seemed to skip a beat and not in the good way that it did when Noah smiled at me. I tried to move, but my body seemed frozen solid. That voice... Sebastian had warned me that there was a traitor in our midst, and he'd been right. Except, we'd been so busy turning on each other to even consider the far more likely option. I didn't want to believe it though. I just couldn't. I had to be wrong.

"Alma?" I said, my voice like that of a little girl who'd woken from a nightmare and wanted her favourite teddy bear.

"Aubrey's grandmother?" Noah said at the same time.

"Don't seem so surprised Juniper, "Alma said, her footsteps coming closer, sounding as though they were echoing off the smaller space of my room rather than the hall outside. "Noah," she said to him. She kept walking, the clickety-clack of her heels coming closer until she stood before us, and I felt her take my chin in her hand. I looked away from her. "Don't be so daft, Girl," Alma chided, forcing my face back to hers. "They really roughed you up, didn't they?"

Her finger tapped gently against my cheek, a pattern of some kind. But my head was spinning. I couldn't understand. Even as I tried to speak, I couldn't come up with a coherent sentence to speak. Who was this woman? Where was the Alma who had given me my name? Made me breakfast and welcomed me into her home? This just didn't make any sense! Had I really been so wrong about her? All the while her finger continued to tap against my cheek, a little more insistently now.

"I..." What did I say? Sebastian's betrayal had hurt, but Alma's? After everything we had been through to find her and rescue her, it had all been a ploy? It didn't make any sense. I swallowed, trying to moisten my mouth and make sound come out. "I suppose you're after Noah too," I said, resigning myself to the idea that she too had used me. She had taken my Eyeless status remarkably well back in Erihall. Maybe that should have been a clue.

Alma sighed. Her hand on my face slackened. I could feel her whole body sag, as though disappointed with me. She chuckled. "Gods no girl. What Nelson has created in you and the other children is an abomination." Alma twitched, a cringe almost. Was she regretting what he was saying? I didn't know what to think. Her words and the feeling of her nearby didn't seem to match, but my head was so confused that I had no idea what was going on.

"And Aubrey?" Noah asked.

"Aubrey was never supposed to meet you. Any of you," Alma stated, her voice turning hard. She released my face finally and stepped backwards. Noah pulled me close to him in case she or anyone else tried again.

"So, is that why she's expendable now?" I asked angrily. I was so hurt. Hurt for myself. Hurt for Aubrey. "She's in the other room. They shot her! But I suppose you don't care about that." A silence I had not been expecting fell over us. It was thick with unspoken fury. Alma was still so close to me, that I was sure I could feel her body trembling in rage. I could hear the awkward shifting of feet and the heavy breathing of the panicked. The guards were afraid to move or even make a sound. "Probably one of those flat-footed brutes behind you that did it."

Alma turned sharply on her heels, the sound like a cracking whip. "Is this true?"

"Uhh... No... I mean..." The guard stammered.

"You mean what?" Alma snapped.

"She… She was interfering… And getting in Mr. Anson's way…" a second voice babbled, so the other guard.

"And that was any reason to shoot my granddaughter?" Alma hissed at them.

One of the guards tried to justify themselves, spluttering something about being told that the girl was irrelevant, but I didn't wait for him to finish his justification. I started to stand. Behind me Noah did the same. He continued to hold us close together as we shifted our weight and stepped closer to Alma. I felt a reassuring squeeze of my shoulder and nodded in understanding.

I shoved her. The woman shrieked in surprise, and I heard a shuffling commotion as people seemed to get entwined. Maybe I had pushed her into the two guards. I didn't know if I could trust her anymore and my focus had to be the others. They needed our help.

"Juniper! Noah!" Alma cried after us, "wait!"

Noah took my hand. We ran. We ran like they were chasing us to the ends of the earth. Noah's hand wrapped around my own. Unlike the last time we did this back at Alma's house, there was no uncertainty in our movements. While I couldn't see and I was reliant on him, I now trusted him. I trusted him to guide me safely and that we wanted the same things. To find our friends and get out of here. We worked well together, and my learned knowledge of the facility would guide us. Putting me back in my own room had been a stupid move.

Behind us we heard Alma and the two guards yelling at us, at each other, for someone, anyone to catch us. If we could find Hattie or the others, everything would be fine. Eventually… I had no idea how that would happen, especially not when I heard the sound of people following us. Lots and lots of thump thumping boots running down the hall after us.

Noah pulled me down on corridor then shoved open a door and pulled me in. We waited until they ran past us, not even bothering to clear each room as they went. I sighed. First Sebastian betrayed me and now Alma. Both of these betrayals hurt more than I wanted to admit. I gripped at Noah's shirt, glad for his support as these thoughts ran through me. I needed to stop thinking about them, get them out of my head and concentrate on the situation at hand if we were going to find the others and get out of here.

"I didn't see that one coming…" Noah muttered. I looked up at him. I knew it was useless, but it was habit to try and seek out his face when he spoke.

"Neither did-." What was I saying? I had suspected it. Back at the abandoned farmhouse after talking to Cassias. I had suspected Alma, but everything had moved so rapidly from that point that I hadn't been able to do anything about it. And now, here we were. "I did…" I said softly.

Noah pushed me away slightly. "What?"

I shrugged. "It only a suspicion…. After things Chouette and Cassias had said."

"What do you mean?"

We froze at the sound of a door handle rattling. Noah pulled me tight against him, then he shifted me away from the door as I heard it open. Noah froze a second time and grunted in surprise.

"What is it?" I asked, my lips against his ear so I could barely whisper.

"The door... it... it opened-" then he stopped and let his head fall against my shoulder in what might have been resignation.

"By itself?" I asked him and he nodded against my shoulder. "Hattie?" I asked louder, looking around aimlessly as though that would allow me to see the errant girl.

"Oh God! It is you guys!" The invisible girl exclaimed before we felt ourselves being pulled to her. With a laugh, I wrapped an arm around her and the other around Noah. The group hug was exactly what I had needed. It seemed to perk Noah up too from the way the tension in his shoulders seemed to slip away beneath my hand. "I've been looking everywhere for you! I found the others… Aubrey's in a bad place, so is Mech."

"I know," I said to her. "We've got to get out of here."

"Let's go!"

"Hattie, scout for us?" Noah asked.

"D'uh! Of course!" Then she poked her head out of the doorway. She popped right back in straight away.

"What is it?" Noah asked softly."

"I just saw two women in lab coats walk by," Hattie explained. Noah touched my arm then gripped at my shirt and wriggled it. I grinned as I got what he meant and nodded. Hattie giggled, apparently seeing us out of the corner of her eye. Or maybe more. It was disconcerting not being able to see her. But then again, I wasn't seeing much of anything.

The two lab coated women stopped walking at the sound of Hattie's giggle.

"Did you hear that?" one of them asked. The second one said something in a soft voice, and we couldn't hear her response. Neither would be able to see anything, but Hattie stepped deeper into the room with us and giggled again. The women followed, their footsteps getting closer. As soon as they crossed the threshold of the room Noah shut the door, trapping them inside with us. I reached for the one that had brushed past me and hit her in the back of the head. She crumpled to the ground. Hattie and I removed her lab coat and ID badge. I put the coat on and waited for Noah.

He grumbled. "Couldn't she have been a little bigger…"

Hattie laughed, unrestrained now. "Oh boy… That so does not fit!"

"It will have to do," Noah grumbled.

"Come on," I said, and we left the two unconscious women behind. We would hopefully be gone long before they could raise the alarm. This time Hattie seemed to guide me. It would probably look better than Noah and I walking hand in hand through the halls of the lab, but I missed his touch. We moved at a fast pace, Hattie leading me in what we hoped was the right direction and Noah following.

108

Alma called after them again, but she didn't think that the girl had understood what she'd been trying to say. If only those guards hadn't been in the room, she could have actually talked openly to the girl. Instead, she'd had to try for something discreet, and it had backfired.

She didn't have time to deal with Juniper now though. She had to get to Aubrey. Surely Juniper had simply been trying to scare her, hurt her the way she felt as though she'd been hurt by Alma, but the guards... They hadn't denied it, no, they'd tried to justify their actions. She pushed against one that was tangled with her and used the bed to haul herself to her feet. She felt wobbly as she stood. Perhaps this had not been the greatest plan she'd ever thought up.

She moved unsteadily towards the door, but the heels on her shoes wobbled. Without even thinking about it, she reached down and pulled the shoes off. The heel on her left shoe was broken, just about ready to snap off completely. She tossed the useless shoes to the floor and ran from the room to the cell next door.

She pushed against it, but it wouldn't open. The keypad beside the door blinked at her mockingly. She groaned in frustration and ran back to Junipers room. The two guards had picked themselves up. Alma stepped up to the closest one, grabbing the weapon from his hands. His surprise froze him to the spot and using the large gun to knock him out. She turned the weapon on his compatriot.

"Drop it," she said motioning to his own weapon. The gun clattered to the floor, and he held his hands up.

"The cell next door, open it," she demanded.

"Don't hurt me!" He whimpered. "My parents! They rely on me! I'm all they've got."

"Move!" Alma demanded, pointing the gun from him to the door. The guard scurried from the room, Alma right behind him. "Stop there," she said outside the other cell. "Open it."

The guard and he was little more than a boy really, looked at her uncertainly, but he was looking down the barrel of a gun rather than at a little old lady. She motioned to the keypad, and he turned to it slowly, his hand shaking as he attempted to enter the code. It beeped angrily and flashed red.

"I... I..." he stuttered.

"Get that door open!" she demanded, stepping closer.

Shaking harder, the young guard entered a second code into the door, and it beeped agreeably, flashing green as it did so. The door also let out a click and Alma pushed it open.

Conversation ceased immediately, and Alma was thrust against the wall, Cassias's big arm against her throat.

"Aubrey...." She breathed out before her airway was cut off.

"Cassias!" Chouette hissed. "Let her go!"

Cassias stepped back and glared at her. "Where've you been?" he growled.

"Where's my granddaughter?" she choked out, glaring at the big man.

Cassias crossed his arms over his chest and stared right back at her, his stony gaze forcing her to look away.

"Over here!" Chouette said, breaking the tension and drawing Alma over to where Aubrey lay beside Mech.

"What happened?" she asked, falling to her knees to inspect the two injured teenagers. Cora sat beside Aubrey, a bloodied cloth in hand as she tried to staunch the bleeding.

"The guards wanted revenge for what Mech did to their mate back on the road. Aubrey intervened when Sebastian took Juniper," Chouette explained. "We had no idea where you were," she said softly.

"Trying to get Juniper out," Alma replied hurriedly, as she lifted Cora's cloth to look at the wound. "Did it go through?" she asked.

Cora nodded. "Yes, we have a jacket underneath her trying to staunch it from the back, but we don't know what to do."

"You're doing the right thing," Alma assured her, putting her hands back where they'd been. "Keep the pressure, that's a good girl." She turned to Mech. The boy had been eaten within an inch of his life. She needed to get both of them out of here. "I need to get both of them to a medical bay or somewhere where I can help them."

109

Despite our impromptu costume change, we still tried to avoid lab techs and security guards. I still had no eyes and anyone around here would know that. They would maybe even recognise Noah depending on whether or not they had worked on him when he was held captive.

"Never thought we'd be back in one of these places," Hattie murmured as she moved.

"Neither did I," Noah replied.

"I had hoped to burn it to the ground." I was bitter about this place.

"Maybe we will," Noah said. "And maybe we'll wait and see if they have anything on who you really are," he suggested.

I looked back at him in surprise. "Really?" I asked.

"We're here. It would be foolish of us to destroy the place without finding that out first. The rest of us all know who we are at least."

"Yeah," I said thoughtfully. "But did you ever try going home?"

"To what?" Hattie asked. "I'm invisible. Those who the experiments failed on are now completely or partially blind. No life for them if they're Eridenti."

"A lot of that," Noah agreed. "But mainly, the fact that Sage was right. Our parents had agreed to the treatment. They put us in his care and others wanted to protect their families from what they had become."

"Or the retribution of Sage and his men coming after them," Hattie added.

We turned a corner and Hattie shoved me back. I crashed into Noah, and we stayed still, our conversation ceasing instantly. Guards walked past, the heavy clomping of their boots and the clanking of their utility belts identifying them to my ears. I turned to look at Noah as though we were having a pause in our conversation if anyone looked at us.

"Oh." One of the guards spoke. "Doctors." I nodded in return, not looking at them.

"Yes? "Noah asked.

"Be on the lookout. The monster girl and some boy escaped." Monster girl? The name echoed in my head. That was me he was talking about. I guess the name had stuck.

"Anything we should know about her or the boy?" I asked.

The pause made me think that the man shrugged or something, but Noah spoke up. "Speak up man, we're busy here."

"The girl is eyeless, but I remember now, she bites!" the second guard said. "The boy, no one seems to know what he can do. But... It's probably bad."

"Yeah, like that brat that dusted Sully," the first guard said. "Put him out good though!"

Rage built in me, but Hattie lost it. I heard her move, her bare feet padding against the ground before her body thudded into the man. She wrestled with him and must have grabbed the man's weapon right from his hands because there was the sound of his nose cracking and it sounded like the butt of a gun against flesh and bone.

"That was Mech!" she cried. "And that was your fault! Mech doesn't wanna hurt nobody!" she kept hitting him, the sound of the weapon against his skull was like a wet thuds made me cringe with every impact.

The other guard must have been staring at the gun in thin air, hammering at his partner because it didn't seem as though he did anything until he came out of whatever stupor he'd been in.

"Monster!" he cried out. I turned, using the sound of his voice to locate him. I could hear him launch his body towards where he must have thought Hattie was. I'd been practicing this, so using the sound of his movement to locate him, I grabbed him and swung him around, his own momentum propelling him forwards. I was relieved when I heard and felt him crash into a wall with a resounding crash.

"Hattie!" Noah's voice was strained, as though he was now the one trying to wrestle with her, but she wasn't having any of it. "Enough!" he ordered. "Enough Hattie!"

"He's the one who hurt Mech!" she screamed.

"He's one of them," I told her. "They're too cowardly to go at us alone."

We were a fine team at that moment. Both Noah and I wanted to comfort Hattie, but we couldn't. Not there, not then. I hit the guard I had slammed into the wall once more then turned to where I had heard their voices. "We need to get out of here if we want any chance of surviving this."

Noah's hand took mine and led me over to him. Together we got a hold on Hattie and moved her away from the downed guard. "Where are the others?" Noah asked her and the question did seem to focus her because I felt her start to lead us.

"Here," she said hitting a door.

Noah let me go and I guessed from the sounds that he was unlocking the door. It swung open and there was a roar as someone charged out of the room and Noah was hauled off his feet and into the room.

"CASSIAS!" Hattie screamed. "Cassias! It's us!"

Everything became silent and all movement stopped for a moment. Except for a grunt from Noah. Cassias must have been waiting for a guard when he attacked.

"Noah!" Sadie cried excitedly. "And was that, Hattie?"

"Yeah, yeah!" Hattie greeted and then she let out an oomph of surprise. "Kattie!" she exclaimed.

"You're ok," he gasped. "You're ok."

"Finally," I said. "Someone who can see her!"

"Juniper?" Chouette asked. Suddenly, I too was engulfed in a hug, and I smiled. I hugged her back, trying to hold back any winces of pain. I wanted to relish this moment.

"I'm here, "I said softly. "Where's Aubrey," I asked her softly.

Chouette pulled back slightly. "I don't know… Alma burst in here like a bat out of hell a little while ago and took them. She needed to get them to a med bay or something."

"Alma can't be trusted," I said, hoping my voice didn't crack as I spoke. The betrayal was still too new, too raw. "She betrayed us."

"We gotta find them and get out of here," Cora declared hesitantly.

"No," Noah said.

"What?" I don't know who it was that spoke. It sort of sounded like everyone speaking at once. The excited, but angry chatter was loud and on top of that, they all seemed to be moving in at once, closing in on us.

"Alma…" Noah paused. "Alma, Aubrey's grandmother is with them. They won't allow anything to happen to her. No matter how Alma betrayed us, she won't let anyone hurt Aubrey."

"You can't be certain of that!" Cora retorted. "And what about Mech?"

"And what are we going to do, watch her die?" Noah shot back at her. "Juniper said she was shot. Badly. We have no way of helping her. Alma is a Doctor. If we want Aubrey to live, taking her with us is the worst thing we can do. Same for Mech."

In my head, I could see their concerned faces. Everyone looking at one another, debating whether or not to argue with Noah. Deciding for themselves if this was the right move for their friends. As usual it was Chouette who settled things.

"We leave them," There were some protests at her words, but with her so close to me, I could feel her body shift as he held her hand up to settle them down. "No, I don't like it. I hate it. But Noah is right. We have no chance of ensuring that either of them survives their injuries. These people… Do…"

110

No one and I mean no one liked moving on without Aubrey and Mech, but as much as we hated the idea of leaving them behind, all of us staying there seemed worse. Even so, we ran. There was no hiding a group as large as us, so we ran. Hattie had scouted out the facility significantly before engaging in rescuing us, so she believed that she knew the way out.

"One. Two. Three. Four. Five…"

"What are you doing?" Sadie asked me.

I stumbled as I paused. I hadn't even realised I was doing it. "Counting…" I muttered.

"Each step. Each turn," Minnie added.

"Yeah," I replied. "Sorry… Habit…"

Still, in my head though, I counted every step I took. Every step we took further away from our friends and closer to freedom.

A screech echoed down the hallway and the frantic flapping of wings caught our attention. I smiled as I came to a stop. I had missed that creature. Its furry little body had been a constant source of comfort.

"Shree!" Chouette exclaimed excitedly.

"You named it?" I asked.

"Yeah… Had nothing else to do while no one would let me move and it just sat with me. I named it Shree."

"Short for Shriek?" I asked.

Chouette laughed. "Yeah. Something like that!"

The flying ferret like creature hurtled into us, colliding with of all people, me. I fell backwards, the weight of the kirpuuru colliding with my face sending me flailing backwards. From the grunts of impact, I guessed my would-be cushions to be Emrys and Elijah.

The boys stood me back up and someone must have grabbed the frantic creature. "What have you got there?" Chouette asked in a little cooing voice.

"Guys, we don't have time for this!" Noah stated.

"Hang on, hang on!" Chouette chided him. "He's got eyes!" she said excitedly. "He's got Juniper's eyes!"

"What?" I asked startled. "Which ones?"

"I have no idea."

"Let me see," Noah said. I heard his footsteps as he came to look at the eyes Chouette was holding. Then he sighed, almost as though he was disappointed. "They're the ones that let you read any language."

Pity. Could have used the fire ones or any of the attack ones, really. I held my hand out though. At least with them I would be able to see, and I would no longer be as useless as I currently felt. No one handed them to me. "Guys. Come on!"

"Juniper…" Noah started.

"No," I interrupted. "I can't see like this. I'm not as good as Minnie getting around like this. I need to be able to see. I need to be able to help you!"

I thought that it was with great reluctance that the eyes were finally handed to me. I felt the cool porcelain in my hand and felt my fingers along the first one. Without waiting for anyone to object or to try to change my mind, I slipped it into my eye socket. I was getting remarkably smooth at this. The action almost second nature now. As I moved the second one towards the other eye socket, I felt Noah or at least I assumed that it was Noah, appear beside me. His hands were on my shoulders and as the second eye slipped in, he held me up.

I felt my knees buckle as pain enveloped my head, then shot down the rest of my body. I thought I heard concern murmuring from those around me and remembered that not everyone had seen me change my eyes before. Then Noah and Chouette spoke to them, explaining the normality of this situation.

The murmuring died down but when I finally opened my eyes, I could see their concerned faces. Strength returned to my legs, and I pushed myself away from Noah, ready to stand on my own two feet.

"Woah..." I gasped, blinking several times.

"Ready?" Noah asked.

I nodded. "Yeah."

The kirpuuru, Shree, settled itself on my shoulder just as it usually did. Everything was fine. Everything would be fine.

When we came around the next bend, we found a corridor full of people blocking our way. At the centre was Alma.

"I knew we should have tied them up," Noah muttered.

They were startled to see us all. Cora stepped up beside us, her hand hovering over her eye patch, ready to unleash the laser on anyone who approached. Cassias too, hovered right behind me, his impressive height meaning that he could do what he needed to do from behind. Emrys hovered to the right of us, Harvey to the left.

Slowly, we approached the staff. "Let us pass and we won't hurt anyone," I said.

One guard scoffed. "You've killed so many already."

Had I really? There were three at the time they tested my eyes and then there was... Had I killed anyone back in Erihall? I was sure I'd only put them to sleep. Ah, the guys I'd turned to ice at Alma's house the day I met Noah and Chouette. How many had died there? And Aubrey had been shooting them too. What about our trip to Erihall? No, I had definitely only put them to sleep, but there had been the fight back at the house again... Then here were those who had died when they had raided Camp Sight, and we had been fighting for our lives. They were right. I was a monster. I did not like what I was becoming, and I could still see the look of terror on the face of the young researcher. I hadn't known him, and I hadn't known what part he had played in everything, but the fear in his eyes as his body had turned to stone had haunted my sleep. It was not something I liked to be reminded of.

"You work for a man trying to create super soldiers, what did you expect?" I asked, trying to seem nonchalant, but I thought maybe my voice might have wavered slightly.

One of the guards got twitchy his weapon aimed at us. Cora lifted her eye patch and the laser that tended to erupt from her eye did so, sending the weapon flying from the man's hands and burning both of his hands. He screamed in agony and clutched his hands to his chest. Cora eyed another one who pointed his weapon at her.

Alma held her hand up. "Enough. All of you!" Cora placed the patch back over her eye and glared at the old woman.

There was the soldier she had once been. Her presence was unmistakable. Her command was instantly listened to by people on both sides. She stepped forward, away from her guards, who now that I realised it, were Eridenti Military rather than Sage Security. Alma was not everything she had already implied. I had no idea what she was or who she really was, but it was not as simple as her tricking me or betraying us after everything we did to rescue her. I didn't know if her being there now was a good thing or a bad thing.

"Juniper, Noah," she said to us, hands held out before her, almost as though trying to placate a wild animal.

"Where's Aubrey and Mech?" I asked. Might as well get down to the point, right? And no one said that we still had to be friendly. I was in too much pain to care, and we were in the middle of the dragon's den, literally. On my shoulder, Shree… Well, Shree shrieked at Alma, just as he always had. The little bugger had never trusted Alma, always watching her, never leaving her alone with one of us, especially Chouette…

"Guess he was a better judge of character than the rest of us," Chouette mumbled, reaching up to stoke the creature's soft fur.

"I'm sorry," Alma said.

"Sorry?" I asked. "You literally, less than an hour ago called us abominations. So, excuse me if I don't care what you have to say right now," the sentiment was echoed from behind me, but I didn't look to see who it was. I know that everyone had felt Alma's betrayal. If not for themselves, then for Aubrey, who they had welcomed into their group as one of their own, who had fought for them, despite not having any reason to.

"Aubrey and the boy… Mech, you said?" She asked. I nodded. "They've been removed to a nearby medical facility," Alma said. I stared at her, silently ordering her to say more, because I was sure that like me, none of the others looked particularly impressed with her answer. Right now, I didn't trust anything this woman had to say. "They'll be safe," She assured us, but I could hear several people scoff behind me.

"Even Mech?" Emrys asked, his voice small and insecure. "Sure, Aubrey will be safe, she's your granddaughter, but what about Mech?"

"They are safe upon my orders. Your Mech too," Alma assured us.

"And when some idiot removes his goggles, and they get dusted?" Noah asked. "That's how he wound up like that."

Alma looked at him. Her expression was odd. I couldn't identify what it was she was thinking, and the silence stretched between us. Both sides were shifting uncomfortably, waiting for the other to attack. Feet shuffled, hands fluttered or gripped at clothes. "I had his eyes bound. Made a report that he had a serious eye injury and that they were not to be unbound at any point. Do you think that would be sufficient?"

I looked at Noah and Chouette. Noah shrugged, but Chouette nodded. "Why?" She asked, looking back at the old woman.

"What Nelson did to you… It was abominable… I stand by that. I also stand by the idea that what he is trying to create is wrong. Even more wrong though is the way he has gone about it. Using children, lying, steeling, killing." Nelson? Did she know Sage? Alma wasn't making much sense at the moment.

"Why are you talking with them like this?" One guard asked, coming up behind Alma. "Look what they did to Dieter."

"Perhaps Dieter should have known how to compose himself properly during a parley," Alma said, venom in her voice.

"Those things-."

"Things!" Vera hissed. "We're people you know."

"We didn't ask for this," Sadie added.

"All of this was done with the blessing of the government in order to win the war," Alma said, interrupting everyone. "But it has gone too far." So Sage was working with the Eridenti government.

111

"Mech and Aubrey are safe right?" Minnie asked, pushing past us until she stood before us, her empty eye sockets bared for everyone to see. The scars around her eyes clearer than usual in the lights of the facility. The guards reared away at the sight of her, muttering their discomfort and disgust.

"Yes," Alma said.

"And you agree that all of this, what has been done to us is too much. That it is wrong."

"You are now completely blind, young Mech can turn people to dust, the young lady there has that laser eye... These are not abilities that people should have," Alma said, her eyes searching furtively for something even as she spoke with the confidence and command of the military officer she'd once been. "Regardless of the war. Whatever happens, none of you will ever have normal lives."

Minnie nodded. She cocked her head to the side. "There is still something you are hiding. I do not know what it is, and I do not trust you. We are going to destroy this place as we leave. Emrys, blow the computers. Harvey, Cora, burn this place to the ground." I think the viciousness of Minnie words startled everyone because we just stood there. Minnie, sweet, innocent, always in her garden Minnie was giving an order like that. "Let this farce come to an end."

We were stopped from saying anything else by a group of soldiers, this time Sage's men coming up from behind. I looked at Alma. "It's time to decide what side you're really on."

"Yours," she said, then elbowed her own guard in the nose. "Always yours." The second guard tried to attack her, but Alma turned, surprising him with an uppercut to the jaw that sent him reeling backwards until he collided with the wall, sliding down it to collapse in a heap. "I tried telling you that earlier!" Alma hissed, kicking the downed guard to ensure he stayed down. In the startled silence left by her confession and the end of the fight, we could hear more guards coming from. "Run!" She ordered.

Well, another surprise from her.

"Harvey! Cora! You heard Minnie!" I shouted. The soldier Alma had elbowed in the nose was getting back up, picking up his gun. I grabbed it from him and hit him in the side of the head with it. Nearby, the man Cora had burned was whimpering. We ignored him. Harvey let everyone file past him, then he lifted his glasses and fire erupted throughout the hall. Men screamed as they were suddenly standing in the flames.

We ran. Cora shooting things at random, Harvey setting things alight. Heat pushed us forward. I pushed people past me, making sure that Minnie and Emrys and Elijah got past us to safety. Cassias had fallen into the lead, while Noah and I made sure everyone kept going, Harvey included.

"Go, go, go," I don't know how many times we repeated that. The fire seemed to catch easily, and solders were running through it in order to catch up to us. We pushed everyone past another corner.

"The door is there," I shouted, pointing down one hall. Cassias shouted that he understood and took them that way.

"What's wrong?" Noah asked, reaching for me as he tried to pass by me.

I shook my head. "Nothing." At least, I didn't think anything was wrong, but something Noah had said to me earlier rung in my head now. We were so close to getting out of there and I had no idea what would happen next, but I felt as though this was my only chance to find out. I looked at him. "There's something I have to do."

"What?" He asked.

I glanced at the others, making their way out of the facility, then at the oncoming fire that was about to destroy everything. Including my identity. "I have to find out who I am," I said suddenly.

"Juniper..." Noah said, his voice rough. He coughed, the smoke from the fire getting to him.

I took his face in my hands. Making sure that he was looking at me. "I have to. I have to find out where I came from... What made me so different..." It couldn't be denied that I was different from them. What abilities they had were only singular. They were stuck with them day and night, but me? I was something else with those interchangeable eyes. Then there was the fact that my memories had been erased. It wasn't possible that I had been raised entirely in the facility because I couldn't remember being small. I had to have an identity somewhere and if anyone knew who that was, it was Sage. He would have that information somewhere.

"I'll come with you," he said desperately.

I shook my head. "No, they need you, maybe not more than I do, but they need you. Everything is gone and that is partially my fault…"

"No!" Noah stated firmly. "We discussed that."

I cut him off. "I know, I know… But I had my part to play in everything that happened… You have yours in everything that is to happen." I kissed his cheek, and he pulled me to him, burying his face in my neck.

"Ok…" he said softly in my ear. "Go… But swear. Swear that you will come back to us… To me…"

"I…"

"Swear it Juniper, or I will haul you out of here myself. Do you understand?" His hands were holding my face, and he was staring into my eyes. "Swear it!"

"I swear it!" I breathed out. "I'll come back."

He sighed in relief and kissed me. It was rough and it was full of everything he still wanted to say, but we had no time to do so. It was a struggle to push him away, to pry myself from his grip. I turned and started down the corridor to left, away from where everyone else was going.

"Juniper…" He croaked after me and I paused my step. "I love you…" I didn't look back. I couldn't. I would have turned back and gone with them right there and then if I had.

The smoke was getting thick, but I found Sage's office easily enough. Large, ostentatious doors that would hopefully lead to my identity.

I pushed the door open with only the slightest hesitation and stepped in, quickly closing it behind me. I hoped that that would hold the heat and more importantly, the smoke off for a little longer. I looked around, taking in Sage's personal office. The space was even larger than I had expected of the man, it seemed bigger than the large living space at Camp Sight, all that for one man. Expansive bookshelves lined one wall with books and folders filling every shelf. The desk, with several filling cabinets behind it, was where I headed though. Everything I needed to know would be there. I was sure of it.

There wasn't much time until the fire would reach here, so I needed to work quickly. Harvey had done a good job setting everything on fire and I hoped that he had continued regardless of my presence. Somehow, I doubted it though. Noah would want to ensure that I had enough time to get out.

"Juniper... I love you..." had he really said that? No, I couldn't allow myself to dwell on that, even as my heart skipped a beat in delight recalling his words, spoken only moments before. I had to get through here as quickly as possible if I wanted to make it back to him. To all of them.

The computer on the desk didn't work anymore. Emrys must have gotten into the system as had been asked and short circuited everything. That was good. Kill their research. Make sure that they could never restart this project again.

I pulled open the first filing cabinet. Paper files kept in alphabetical order were neatly lined up. Shree launched from my shoulder and landed on one of the cabinets as if trying to indicate that it was the one I should be looking at. I took one more glance at the ones I was looking at.

Aharon, Elijah William

Bogdanov, Henryka Eirwen

I closed the drawer on that cabinet and opened the top drawer on the one that the kirpuuru was draping its nine tails over. It slid open and I flipped through the files, looking at names and pictures as fast as I could.

Romeijn, Cassias Mikael. I stopped at the sight of the picture. It was most definitely Cassias, our ever gruff and monosyllabic trainer. I slipped it back in and pulled out the next one. Then the next one and the next one until I found myself staring at a photo of myself. Myself before the girls had cut and coloured my hair. The me who I had been before winding up here, in this facility. My eyes had been blue. A shade bordering on grey, something reminiscent of storms and clouds. Blond hair and grey-blue eyes. What had it been like to be her? Had my personality been as unpredictable as a storm? Would I ever know who this girl had been?

I had to wrench my gaze away from the photo of the girl who might as well have been a stranger, even if we shared a face. My eyes finally flicked expectantly to the tab where the name was. Rowan. Was that my first name or my surname? I looked further.

Rowan, Shiloh May.

My surname was Rowan… Funny, being named after a tree again. I looked up at the kirpuuru. It had its head cocked to the side as though it too was trying to read and understand. "Shiloh?" I asked. "My name is Shiloh?"

The creature started to chitter in response, cocking its head to one side, but the gentle chittering turned to panicked shrieks.

"Shiloh May Rowan."

I dropped the file and whirled around. Standing the doorway, letting the smoke and heat from outside in, was Nelson Sage.

112

"You always knew," I said.

"Of course I did," he said stepping in. He didn't close the door. Why didn't he close the door? "What made you think that I didn't?" He made another step closer and the kirpuuru reared up, spreading its wings and screeching as loud as it could. "Amazing… I never thought that they existed."

"They don't," I said, reaching to scratch the creature behind its ears. It nuzzled at my hand in response. "It's a statue."

"According to my guards, it's pretty real."

I shrugged. "You're the one you did this to me."

"I think that I need you to explain," Sage said, taking a seat across from his own desk.

"I turned a statue to flesh."

His eyes widened so wide that it was almost comical. "You turned a stone statue to flesh." I could see him, trying to move his neck, but the half that had turned to stone prevented him. Instead, he used his good hand to push himself back up from the chair. I watched him, he started to move around the desk, but Shree flew towards his face. Sage back away, holding up his good arm to protect himself.

"Turn me back girl!" He cried. "Turn me back!"

It was my turn to cock my head to the side in contemplation and surprise. "Oh?"

Shree circled the room, her large wings sending huge gusts of wind through the space. Papers flew all over the place with the force of the gusts.

"Turn me back!" Sage gasped, lurching forward. Apparently, he was not going to let a flying ferret intimidate him. "I can't move half of my body!"

I laughed. "And whose fault is that?" I asked. "He bites when he doesn't like you... So... I wouldn't come any closer." I looked down to where the file had fallen and crouched down to pick it up. As expected, Shree shrieked in anger and launched himself back at Sage. I picked the file up and put it on the desk. "I'm from Obreiji... I have a mum and a dad and even a half-brother..." I looked up to see Sage fall back into the chair he had risen from.

I turned and started pulling files out of the cabinets. Cassias, Noah, Harvey, Vera, Sadie. I threw them across his desk, ensuring that he could see every picture. Other files intermingled with theirs. Children younger than us. One I thought I recognised. A girl named Henryka, but the picture of the child was of a girl maybe eight years old with white, thin, hair that framed her white face like a halo. But still... I thought maybe... That white skin...

Sage laughed. "The invisible girl."

"Hattie!" I breathed out.

"Perhaps one of my greatest creations except for you, girl."

"I apparently have an abundance of names. Try using one," I said. "None of this," I said, waving my hand over the mass of files I had scattered over his desk, "None of this tells me anything as to why you did this. Nothing here tells me why you blew up that factory in Erihall..."

"You think I blew it up?"

"Of course, I do," I said, walking around the desk to stand in front of him. "It wasn't until you did so, that people in Erihall started to go blind and have need of you. But the question still remains, why?"

He sat up straighter, crossing one leg of the other, then leaned forward, his good arm resting upon his knee and his head resting upon his hand. "We're at war Ms. Rowan."

Rowan. The name sounded strange directed at me, but then again, this man had only ever called me Girl, so any name would sound strange. There was a disconnect though. I felt no connection to it. No familiarity. What had they done to me? Beyond taking my eyes, they had destroyed my memories of my past self. Those parents, that name.

"The war is over. It has been for years. Eriden won. Subjugated Shiura… And for what? Two lovers who killed themselves?" I asked.

"They were more than that! They were the future. They could have healed this land," He cried.

"You talk as if you knew them and that Amorette and Iniko weren't just bedtime stories and excuses for a fruitless and bloody war."

That seemed to set a fire in Sage's eyes. "You know nothing. There's a part of the story that no one ever told. That no one ever dared to tell."

I raised an eyebrow at him. "Oh yeah?"

"The child they cut from her belly in the aftermath of her death," Ok. I had not been expecting that. Admittedly I didn't know the story that well, but if Aubrey had known it, she would have told us. A child. An heir to the thrones of both Eriden and Shiura. What would that mean now? What did that have to do with this? With what he had done to us? "The child their friends hid away, far away from the Shiurans and the Eridenti, who they raised to avenge the Prince and Princess."

"And what?" I asked, the disbelief obvious in my tone. "You're this child?" I wanted to laugh at the absurdity of his claim.

"You catch on quick. You always were a fast learner. Yes." I would totally have to quiz Aubrey about this. If this was true, she had left a gigantic chunk out of her story. He got up again. I got the impression that he was restless. Shree, who had been waddling over the desk, eyeing all the pictures looked up at him when he moved. It shrieked. "Shut that damned creature up," Sage said, whirling back to me and pointing at the kirpuuru. "All it does is shriek and holler at me."

"He's a good judge of character… I get the feeling that Iniko and Amorette… Assuming you really are some mystery child they had, would be so terribly disappointed in what you have become… What you have done to the people of their respective countries."

Sage paced, back and forth. His stone arm held against his side, his good arm waving all over the place as he spoke. "You, you and all those brats. You just don't get it. As the child of Amorette of Eriden and Iniko of Shiura, I am the rightful heir to both countries. Me. And yet, here I am grovelling at the feet of the Eridenti ruler. Some cousin or something, begging for more resources in order to prepare for his war!"

"And what?" I asked. "After mutilating us and our friends you were going to ask us nicely to go collect some thrones for you?"

"Gods. I made you into gods… You in particular," Sage shot back. I rolled my eyes. That was pushing it a little far. Some of us might have been sort of special, but ultimately, we were freaks. "I turned you into my greatest weapon. My greatest invention. I gave you back your sight. You were going blind, Girl. You were going to enter that world of darkness forever! The same with all of them… Except maybe the invisible girl… She really was just an experiment. With her pre-existing genetic disorder, I knew she would be different and what she became was remarkable."

"You turned us into monsters. Your own people say it. Mech can't even look a girl in the eyes without potentially turning her to dust. Harvey burns everything around him. Cora shoots lasers from her right eye. Vera only has one eye… And hey, want to explain something to me, the sight in her good eye, for both of them, is perfect, so the whole, you gave us sight thing is a load of diddly squat." I coughed. I hadn't noticed it, but the smoke was getting thicker in the room, and it was hot in there. Harvey must have done his job well.

"I am going to unite Eriden and Shiura as they should have been under Amorette and Iniko and then I'm going to destroy Orley."

"Orley?" I was flabbergasted. "Seriously? You're the quintessential mad scientist. No one is ever going to follow you… Plus, you work for the Eridenti government."

He laughed, it was rough with some and sounded somewhat unhinged. "Work for the Eridenti government?" He laughed and then broke into a cough. "Hardly girl. I work for them about as much as Alma Corbyn-Fisher does."

"What does that mean?"

"You really are just a clueless child Ms. Rowan," Sage said stopping in front of me. "This is a war. No one is who they say they are. Not even you or your little friends."

"You talk about war and taking your rightful place, yadda-yadda," I said standing up to him. He might have had a head on me height wise, but I was not intimidated. "So what? The ends justify the means?" I coughed, the smoke was getting thicker, and my throat was burning. My eyes were burning. Sweat was dripping down my face from the heat. I can't believe I hadn't noticed that.

"The ends… A unified Eriden and Shiura. Orley out of the picture. You had better believe that the ends justify the means." He stalked back to me. "Revenge for what was taken from me."

I stepped past him, avoiding having him poke me in the chest. "Revenge you say?" I asked next to his ear. "Revenge? What about our revenge on you?"

He turned "The only reason you're not already dead is that my son took a liking to you."

"Who? Sebastian?" I scoffed. "Sebastian really isn't as loyal to you as you might think."

Suddenly, he reached for me with his good hand. I don't know how I didn't see it, but there it was, wrapped around my throat. I gasped for breath. My already abused body had not been expecting that. The smoke was thick around us and my eyes moved erratically, looking for the kirpuuru. I whistled, or at least, I tried to. I hadn't heard the creature in ages. Where was it?

"That boy is a fool!" Sage gasped through the smoke. He was surprisingly strong. I seemed to recall this not being the first time I had thought this, but that didn't change the situation I was in. It was already hard to breathe and the beating I had taken from the guards was making me lightheaded. Still, he only had one usable hand. I grabbed something off the desk beside me and whacked it over his head. He grunted in pain and his hold around my neck released. He stumbled backwards a few steps, and I tried desperately to catch my breath.

The smoke was too thick. I couldn't even see two steps before me. Every breath I took burned. I coughed and through the smoke saw the shadow of Sage coming for me again. I sidestepped him, just barely. The statue I had whacked him with was still in my hand. I brandished it before me, ready to swing out if I need to. I had to get out of there. I had promised Noah that I would come back to the group, back to him and I was still in this building. I was still in here and as I scrambled past Sage, I realised that I could no longer see where the door was. Which direction was it in?

"Girl!" Sage screamed in anger.

I didn't answer. I could barely breath, let alone speak. My eyes swept the room, trying to find the way out, trying to find the kirpuuru. I had no idea if it could be hurt. It was a statue after all. Where was it? "Shree!" I called out, all the while stumbling my way through the room, my hands out before me like some kind of zombie "Shree!"

Nothing. The creature didn't let out a sound. My stomach knotted at the lack of response from the little creature. Where was it? My foot kicked something. The base of a chair maybe, I don't know, but it hurt, and I hopped two steps.

Crap!

And then suddenly, I was flat on my face. Had I tripped? I had no idea, I couldn't see a thing with all the smoke, and I realised that the floor was better, clearer than up higher. Somewhere, in the back of my head, I recalled hearing that somewhere. Get low and go, or something like that. It was good advice. The smoke was not as thick here on the floor, so aside from the fact that everything hurt, I started to crawl. I looked around me, trying to find Sage or Shree, but I still couldn't see that clearly.

I had to stop moving to cough. It was long and wracking and my whole body seemed to seize with every hacking cough. A hand grabbed my ankle as I tried to resume moving and looking back, I saw him. He had not been there a second ago, or was it more like a minute? Two? Five? I had no idea. My head was spinning. I kicked out at him, trying to dislodge his grip. I looked forward, hoping that a destination, an aim, a goal, would help me find the strength to continue, but my energy was nearly gone. Sage was holding me back though. With only one good arm, the one he was holding me with meant that he was not trying to save himself.

I kicked backwards harder, trying to dislodge his grip, but my leg felt like lead. Was it even moving or was it my imagination? Sage just gripped tighter, his fingers digging into my ankle painfully. I gave up trying to kick him free and concentrated on trying to pull myself in the direction I thought the door might be in.

Behind me, Sage coughed, his fingers digging in deeper as he did so. I strained to pull away further, tried to kick him lose but it was as though his hands were frozen in that clawlike shape around my ankle and nothing I did would dislodge him.

"Girl!" Sage choked out. "Shilo!" he attempted, coughing with the effort. "You're not going anywhere!

He was going to have me die in there with him… And there was nothing I could do about it.

113

Bright. Everything was so bright when I tried to open my eyes. It hurt. So, I clenched my eyes shut instead of opening them. Where was I? Everything smelt so… Clean… Like the facility had. I was back again, wasn't I? I was back and I was never going to escape.

Or had I never left? Had everything I had seen, everything I had done been a dream? The people… figments of my imagination? I sighed. Of course, they were… A kirpuuru… Who was I kidding? They weren't real. They were myth… And yet, I could feel that furry little body nuzzling against my cheek. I could feel the nine tails draped down my back and the feel of those feathers as it expanded its wings.

Light.

Light. I could see light. I opened my eyes. The pain be damned, and I regretted it instantly. The pain was all consuming and I shut them again. I peeked again. Yes, there really was light. This could not possibly be the facility. I could see. I could see!

A hand grasped mine eagerly as I groaned, trying once again to open my eyes and keep them open. Noah? Was Noah there? I tried to say his name, but apparently opening my eyes and speaking was too much for my brain to comprehend and I made some horrid gasping, groaning sound.

"Shh," the voice attached to the hand said. "You're ok. You're safe," I recognised the voice, but it wasn't Noah. Who was it? My head was so fuzzy that I couldn't think straight. I knew the voice. It wasn't Noah. Who else was there? "Shiloh, can you hear me?" They were calling me Shiloh.

Shiloh? Who was Shiloh? I'm Juniper. Everyone called me Juniper. I wanted to turn my head to look at the speaker. It wasn't so much of a graceful turn of the head, instead my head seemed to flop to the side on the pillow, but it achieved the same result. I laid eyes on the person holding my hand.

"Sebastian!" I gasped. Seeing him, I tried to pull my hand away, but he tightened his grip, causing me to wince in pain.

"Shhh. Shiloh, careful. You'll hurt yourself." He spoke softly, calmly. He spoke kindly. What was he doing? Why was he here? Where was Noah? Aubrey? Mech? Where were the others?

"Where...?" I tried to ask after the others, but my throat burned when I tried to speak that one word. It came out raspy and gravely.

"You're in a hospital in Erihall," Sebastian said, clasping my hand in both of his. What was he doing here? I had been trying to ask where the others were, not where I was, but that hadn't been what he heard. "Don't try to talk," He added. "Let me get you some ice chips."

His hand disappeared from mine, and I flexed my fingers gingerly. Each joint hurt. I hurt. Everywhere. I tried to track the movements of my visitor, but he ducked out of my line of sight, and it was too much effort to move my head.

Then he reappeared, a cup in his hands. This place was so sterile. A hospital he had said. Why was I in hospital? An ice chip appeared in front of me, and I accepted it. Foolish thing to do, but my throat burned, and I needed to be able to speak to him. To anyone who would listen. I did not want him here. Wherever here was...

"How...?" Again, my mouth refused to relay everything my brain told it to.

Sebastian presented another ice chip, and I took it greedily. "You were found in my father's office by the fire teams," he said.

"Ahh, Ms. Rowan, you're awake," A new voice. This one I did not recognise. "Welcome back."

My eyes met his and I could see the white coat he wore. A doctor? A scientist? I didn't know how to tell the difference. He listened to my heart and my breathing, then flashed a torch in my eyes.

"Oh, you won't get a reaction," my visitor told the doctor.

"And why not?"

"My... My Shiloh has a condition that prevents the pupils from adjusting to light in the same way a regular person's does," The doctor nodded, but looked as though he did not believe it. He checked my eyes anyway. I had been told before that my eyes did not react to sunlight, so it really came as no surprise to me when the doctor himself looked surprised.

"Shiloh?" The doctor said. I looked at him, trying to get across to him that yes, I could hear him. "I'm Doctor Akane. Can you tell me where you are?"

I looked around, I didn't think that Sebastian had been lying, but I have to admit that I wasn't entirely sure. I don't know what to do, I did not trust him or this doctor. Doctors hadn't exactly been good to me in the past. The white coat was just like 'his' and I did not want to let this man, this Doctor Akane do anything to me.

"Ho… Hop… No… Hos…" I coughed and my whole body ached with the effort. My vision went dark for a moment and Doctor Akane gently pushed me back into my pillows.

"Careful there. It's alright. You're alright. I'm just going to have a look at your throat, ok?" He asked. I nodded and the doctor used his pen light to look into my mouth. He looked concerned. "You breathed in a lot of smoke and a lot of hot air. It burned your throat and your lungs. He then handed me a pen and paper. "I don't want you talking. You need time to heal."

I looked at the pen and paper and slowly brought the two together. The pen scratched as I wrote. *Why is he here?*

Doctor Akane looked at my visitor with a smile. "Your boyfriend has been here ever since you were brought in. In fact, he was the one who raised the alarm at the research laboratory that you were still inside. I'd say you have a very special man in him."

Boyfriend? Oh puh-lease! Sebastian Anson was most definitely not my boyfriend. But then he was at my side, across from the doctor before I could dispute that, and he took my hand in his. "It's ok sweetheart. I know that you don't remember much about what happened. I'll fill you in on everything," he said.

I looked between the two. My doctor and my so-called boyfriend. I wrenched my hand back from my so-called boyfriend and wrote another question, trying to situate the pad so that only the doctor could see it. *Where are my friends?*

He shook his head. "As far as I am aware you were found alone. I'm sorry."

I looked over at Sebastian. His face was a blank mask to me. Impassive as stone. He would not tell me anything I wanted to know. He leaned over to get a better look at what I had written though, and he shook his head at me. Did he not know? Or was he telling me that he would never tell?

The doctor patted my hand, "You're in good hands with Sebastian, Shiloh. Good hands," and then he left. I did not feel as though I was in good hands.

I wanted to scream. I wanted to scream until the windows shattered and the walls fell down. I did not want to be trapped in this bed, not able to speak with Sebastian beside me.

"Noah..." I croaked out.

"Hush," Sebastian cooed, pressing tiny kisses onto my hand. My chest felt tight every time his lips touched my skin, but I just did not have the strength to pull back from him. Instead, I closed my eyes. If I didn't see him, maybe that would help.

"Noah?" I pressed. I was not going to let this go.

I felt him there, against my hand. Wrapped around my hand. He was still. So still, but I didn't open my eyes. I did not want to see the look that I knew would be there in his eyes, lurking under those chocolate brown orbs. They weren't the pale blue endless oceans of Noah's eyes.

"Aubrey?" I tried, hoping that something would get me an answer.

"I actually don't know what the old woman did with Aubrey or the boy," Sebastian said. I heard the chair he was sitting on creak, and his presence seemed to shift away from me. Suddenly I could breathe again. It had been like I was suffocating when he was close. "They were gone by the time I got there."

"Shiloh!" The door to my room seemed to crash open and a woman bustled in. I opened my eyes and once again the light blinded me, before clearing and I found myself staring at... Well... Me. Me older, but me all the same. "Oh, my girl," I flinched, but she didn't seem to notice. "My baby! You're ok. I was so worried. The trip couldn't have taken any longer," the woman just kept on rambling. "It has been so long and when I heard about the fire. Oh, I'm just so glad that you're alright."

She leaned down and kissed me on the cheek. Who was this woman? "Mrs Rowan," Sebastian said standing up. "Sebastian Anson, we spoke on the phone." He held his hand out to her over my prone body and all I could do was stare.

"Who...?" I tried.

Sebastian smiled down at me in that way he had started doing back in Erihall when he had me tied up to that chair. "I arranged for you mother to come," he said, a pep in his voice that I was sure was there for my... My mother? So... This was my mother. The woman who, if Sage was to be believed, willingly let me go with that man. Had I really been going blind as he had said? Or was I like Cora and Vera, perfectly sighted until he had come along. "Your father should be here soon too," Sebastian added. I had not stopped to contemplate my parents since I had met up with Noah and Aubrey and the others. Why was that? Why had I never wondered about them?

"Where is she?" A voice hollered down the a nearby hall. "Shiloh? Where is my daughter?"

The woman Sebastian had called my mother frowned. "You really called him too?" She asked. The cheerful, anxious demeanour she'd come in with seemed to sour as the other man's hollering seemed to come closer and closer to my room.

Sebastian nodded. "Shiloh is going to need all of us," Sebastian said, my hand still clasped within his.

The hollering man burst into my room, he had no door to crash against anything, my mother had already done that, but his presence was overwhelming when he came in. "Shiloh!" He cried. He collapsed onto the bed beside me, taking my face in his hands and kissing my forehead. I wished that I could move. All these people touching me was making me uncomfortable. Even if they were supposedly family.

114

I took a deep breath and swung my legs out from the covers. Everything still hurt and perhaps I should have taken the movement just that little bit slower, but I was tired of sitting around. I was tired of the silence that was enforced on me. I coughed and looked up at the mirror across from me.

"Hi… My name… is… Shiloh…" The name was foreign and didn't feel like me. Everyone kept calling me it, but I was Juniper. That was about the only thing I did know… didn't I? My voice was halting and slow and hard to hear. If I couldn't hear it, who else would? It didn't matter. It's not like I was going to be meeting anyone today. I repeated the name, trying to find some familiarity in it, but I didn't feel any connection to the name. Tentatively, I put my feet to the ground and allowed myself to apply pressure. Then I stood up. My head spun with the change in position, so I stayed still.

Mum… That felt weird, but everyone said that she was my mum, had set out clothes for me. Clothes that were apparently mine. This room was apparently mine, full of the things I liked. And yet, I found myself craving that tiny space with two cots crammed into it. I missed the sound of Aubrey sleeping in the cot next to mine. The sound of her breathing. The snuffling sounds and her shifting in bed. Everything had always been so clear as I had lay there, my eyes out as to avoid any of the pain that had come with wearing them too long.

It had been days, almost a week even since I had come home, longer, like a month maybe, since I had woken up in that hospital and as far as I could tell, I had had the same eyes in all along. A look in the mirror on that first day I had been allowed to walk around had shown me pale blue-grey eyes. My apparent colour according to Sebastian when he had first given them to me back when he had supposedly helped me escape from his father. Nelson Sage was Sebastian's father. I had to remember that…

I had known he was hiding something from me in the beginning But still… That realisation… That had been a surprise. I had no idea what to do with that or any idea why Sebastian hated his father so much.

"Shiloh?" I sighed. My mother was knocking on my door, and I wasn't sure if I was ready for her. "Shiloh? Are you awake?"

"Yes…" I called back. I still hesitated at calling her mum. I had no idea why, but I did.

"Your father will be here in a little while," Oh great… More pretending. This time with more people. Mum was hard enough but at least I could feign exhaustion and go to lay down. Dad, who was apparently separated from mum with a new wife and a baby son, was taking me to meet his 'other family' today. Yeah, I was totally looking forward to that.

"Ok…" I called back. I stared at myself. One thing I had not gotten used to, was my hair, or lack thereof. It was gone. Someone had shaved it all off. I ran my hand over the scraggly regrowth that had started to appear. Admittedly I had more hair than Hattie now, but I still saw her when I looked in the mirror. Had they cut it off because of the fire damage, or had it been something else? The cut and the colour that the girls had given me would have been evidence that not everything was as my parents had been told. Who does crazy hair colours while participating in a clinical trial? I missed the coloured streaks. When my hair grew back, I was going to do it again.

Better yet, Aubrey, Chouette, Cora, Vera, Minnie, Hattie, Sadie… The girls would do it for me.

Where are you guys?

I shed my night clothes for the first time in a week and dressed. Really, a dress? Mum had put out a dress for me? I sighed but dressed. Then followed that by tying a nice scarf around my scraggly head of hair. I had no interest in going out like this.

115

Again, with the hugs and kisses. I felt like I was suffocating every time someone engulfed me in their arms. My chest would seize up and feel tight and I would have to force myself to return the embrace. Dad was, in my opinion, overly affectionate with me, not in a creepy way, but in a way that made me think he was making up for something I couldn't remember. Were they this touchy feely before I forgot them? Even mum gave constant hugs, always touching me as if to see if I was real. I hated it.

"How are you today?" He asked, pulling back from the hug, hand still on my shoulders as if to hold me still as he got a look at me.

I nodded, not sure if I was trying to convince him or me. "I'm good," I said. I was. Sort of.

He smiled. "Good," he said. "I'm so glad everything worked out."

I wanted to ask him what exactly had worked out? Sage was still out there. I had no idea where my friends were. Last I'd heard, Aubrey and Mech had been seriously injured. I didn't even know if they were alive or dead. The thing that hurt the most though? Was how much I missed Noah. I couldn't even tell anyone about him, so I didn't bother to say that I was anything but alright. They had not been told the whole story. Sebastian had woven a tale that had horrified my parents but strayed so far from the truth that it didn't even belong in the same dimension. Both Mum and Dad seemed so thrilled with me and the fact that I could see that I found it hard to burst their bubble. Apparently, I had been going blind so the fact that I could see now was a blessing. For them at least. I just wanted my life back. I had no idea who any of these people were.

"Are you ready?" Dad asked.

No. I was absolutely not ready to meet his 'other family.' That much I knew for certain. I had no idea what had happened between him and Mum, but I was not ready for this. I had only had them for a week, but the idea of meeting this other woman and this other child seemed like losing him all over again. Despite his over affectionate behaviour and his suffocating hugs, I liked him. I felt closer to him than to mum and so, no, I was not ready for this. I wanted him all to myself just for a little longer.

"Yes," I said, plastering a smile to my face. I could do this.

"Great!" he said, rubbing his hands together. He turned towards the door, and I hesitantly followed him. I looked at mum and she was looking at me expectantly, I have no idea what for though. When she thought I wasn't looking, I saw her expression turn to a scowl and I quickly looked away.

"Back before dinner," she said in a pleasant voice. The smile she gave, didn't meet her eyes though. "Shiloh has a guest coming over," her smile slowly turned to a frown as I resumed following dad out of the house.

Guest? What guest? I didn't know anyone. Who would possibly be coming over? I wanted to tell her to cancel it, but knew that she would just wheedle and nag until I gave in. I guessed it was going to be a day of things I didn't want to do. Just grin and bear it.

"Right, right!" Dad called back.

"Bye," I said awkwardly with a little wave at my mother.

Everything was so clean here. People walked from one place to another. Cars drove the streets, seemingly follow rules and some sense of decorum. The buildings were intact and clean. Signs were bright, colourful, some even flashed, trying to draw your attention. There were no hulking behemoth disaster sites in the middle of town. The forest wasn't encroaching on the town and while not everyone seemed happy, everyone did seem to have a purpose to their days, people who were involved in their lives It was so different from Erihall, where everyone seemed to keep to themselves, and shame seemed to drive an entire portion of the population to extreme poverty. I hadn't seen a single beggar or homeless person since arriving in Yarm. Maybe I wasn't looking hard enough.

"You're awfully quiet," Dad said as he drove.

"Just thinking," I said, not really sure how to explain my thoughts.

"Look," Dad started. "I know… I know that all this is hard. Coming back, trying to fit back into your old life," he said cautiously.

I looked at him out of the corner of my eye. He wasn't looking at me, his gaze fixed on the road before him. He looked earnest though, as though he was certain that he was saying what he thought I needed to hear.

"I don't think any of you understand," I said carefully. I didn't want to hurt him, and I definitely did not want him to turn the car around and take me back to my mother's. Oh god... Her mystery guest. "I don't remember... I don't remember Mum... I don't remember you... Or this place... I haven't known any of the people who have come by. And there have been so many people. Family and friends and girls I apparently went to school with. I don't know any of them!"

He looked at me, apprehension, concern and maybe a dozen other emotions flickering across his face. "Shiloh-."

I shuddered. "No, I don't even remember that being my name!" I cried, the pressure reaching out through a crack in my armour. The frown lines around his eyes deepened and he looked so incredibly sad. "It's like I spend every day surrounded by strangers in a strange place where I don't know anything, and I don't know how to get back what everyone keeps telling me I've lost."

Dad looked hurt. I took a deep breath and pressed the palms of my hands against my eyes, squeezing them shut. I took another breath. It wasn't fair to put all of this on him. He'd been the epitome of caring since my return or arrival to this place. My mother though, just kept pushing so called friends at me.

He turned back to the road under the guise of concentrating on the driving, a pensive look on his face. He seemed at a loss for words, and I wanted to take back my outburst, but I was so tired of pretending that everything was so damned wonderful. It wasn't wonderful. Nothing was ever going to be wonderful ever again. Not while I was here, and they were there. I wanted to go home, my true home. Back to the girls who had taken me in hand, making me part of their group before they'd even really known me, back to Cassias's gruelling training sessions, back to Aubrey's snuffling snores in my room. Back to Noah and his eyes that just seemed to draw me in the longer he looked at me. I wanted to go back Erihall because this did not feel like home.

116

By the time Dad returned me home, I had a headache, and my body felt like lead, trying to bring me to the ground with every step I took. All I wanted to do was retreat to my bedroom and be alone. To sleep and get through another day. I could have totally used Chouette's advice right about now, but there was nothing.

I clutched the stuffed toy I had convinced my father to buy close to me. It might sound stupid at my age, but when I had seen it, I needed it. The wings, the nine tails, the face of a ferret. The plush kirpuuru reminded me of Shree. Even its colouring was similar, and my heart had broken when I had laid eyes on it. I had pulled it into my arms and hugged it close. I had barely even noticed the tears running down my face as I did.

Shree... Where are you?

In that moment, holding that little toy, well, it wasn't even that little. I had no idea how big or small actual kirpuuru were supposed to be, but this one was about the same size as the statue I had accidentally turned to flesh and fur and feathers... And claws... I could really use that little guy to hold off some of the people who kept touching me. Why did no one understand that their attempts to make me remember them were just making me want to retreat further and further away from everyone.

I started to get out of Dad's car and held the toy close to my chest. He leaned over, offering his cheek. Reluctantly, I kissed it as he expected.

"See you," I said and quickly hurried out of the car. The sooner I got into Mum's house, the sooner I could escape to my room. I hurried across the front path and used the key I had been given to enter the house.

"Shiloh? Is that you?" Mum called.

"Yeah," I replied.

She emerged from the kitchen, wiping her hands on a tea towel. "Good, good. Our visitor will be here soon. Why don't you go wash up?"

I sighed. "Mum... I'm really tired... I just..."

"You need to eat," Mum interrupted. "Go on, go wash up." She eyed the toy in my hands. "What's that?"

I smiled sadly. "It's a kirpuuru…" I said. "They bring good luck…"

She shook her head disgustedly. "Trust your father to buy you gifts totally inappropriate for your age. You're almost a grown woman. Not a small child." She reached for it, and I snatched it away from her grip.

"No," I cried. "I chose this. Don't."

Was I panicked that she was going to take this stuffed toy from me? I had spoken louder than I had intended, and I had also stepped backwards. I could tell from the look on her face that I had startled her. I hadn't shown any passion over anything since I had come to this place.

She nodded slowly. "Ok…" She replied hesitantly. She turned and walked back towards the kitchen. I took three, maybe four deep breaths trying to get myself under control. The doorbell rang startling me. I jumped. "Can you at least get the door?"

"Ok…" I said and went to open it.

My hand grabbed the knob, but instead of opening it, I leaned my head against the wood of the door and hesitated. Mum kept saying that the guest on the other side of this door was for me... But nobody knew me anymore. Unless it was Noah or Aubrey or one of the others, I didn't really care who was on the other side of this door. The doorbell rang again, and I turned the knob, hearing the click of the gears inside as I pulled my head away from the smooth surface to allow it to open.

"Shiloh!" Sebastian gushed, he held his arms out to me, trying to bring me in for a hug.

"Sebastian!" I gasped, backing away from him. What was he doing here? *"Your boyfriend has been here ever since you were brought in."* Doctor Akane's words echoed in my head. Why in the world had the doctor thought Sebastian was my boyfriend?

"I arranged for you mother to come." Sebastian's own words had followed the doctor's, like he had some sort of authority over my affairs. I hadn't seen him since the hospital, as though he had been keeping his distance. He had had contact with my parents. My mother and my father. They knew him. He'd been the one to tell them what had happened and how I'd wound up in hospital sans all my hair and suffering from burns and

severe amnesia. They knew of him, and they liked him and now he was here. Here in this house that I had been told was a safe place.

"What are you doing here?" Gods, I had hoped that I wouldn't have to see him again after I left the hospital. Why wasn't he back in Eriden?

He smiled that charming smile he had been flashing since I had woken up in the hospital. "I came to see you," he said, grabbing my waist and pulling me into his body. He hugged me close to him, and I stood there, stock still, unable to move as he gripped me with far more force than Noah ever had, even when he wanted to stop me from doing something stupid. "We have some things to discuss," Sebastian whispered in my ear as my mother returned to the living room.

Then, he kissed me. No, not on the cheek like everyone else had been doing. He kissed me square on the lips and it took everything I had in me to not push him away. When he did release me, I stepped backwards, wobbly on my feet from the shock of him and the effects of the long day. What was going on? Why was this happening? Wasn't it bad enough that everyone around me was a stranger? Why did the universe need to add Sebastian into the mix? What did he want from me?

"Ohh, dizzy from young love," Mum said, her voice gushing with admiration. "Hello Sebastian. Did you find us alright?" Had she invited him?

"Yes, thank you Mrs Rowan. Your directions were perfect," Sebastian said, slipping his hand to settle on the small of my back and lead me into the living room of my own house. My mother had invited him. She'd invited Sebastian into our home. How was I going to get rid of him?

"Come on through. Dinner's just about ready," Mum said, motioning for us to follow her into the kitchen. I was in so much shock that I let Sebastian guide my body through the house, unable to argue or resist.

"Just do as I say and everything will be fine," He whispered into my ear. That caused me to look at him. He just smiled, as though everything was perfectly normal, and he was your average boyfriend over to dinner with his girlfriend's parents.

"You are not my boyfriend," I hissed, wrenching my body away from his guiding hand.

"Try telling them that," He whispered back, pulling me into place beside him. "Everyone will just assume it's your amnesia preventing you from remembering me."

"Where are Noah and the others?" I hissed, stopping my forward momentum, and turning to look at him.

A scowl crossed his face at the mention of Noah's name and after a tense moment, he finally said, "I was telling you the truth back at the hospital. I have no idea." Then he pushed me forward into the kitchen, after my mother. "Come on, let's not keep your mother waiting."

Dinner was as awkward as I expected it to be. I felt like third wheel and Sebastian was supposed to be my boyfriend or she was supposed to be my mother... or was it both? It was hard to keep track with the way they both talked to each other, seemingly leaving me out of everything.

That was ok with me. The less I had to speak the better, especially with Sebastian here. It was bad enough waking up to find him in my hospital room, but now he was here, in my house. Talking with my mother as though they were the best of friends.

"And what are you studying?" Mum was asking him.

"Genetics," Sebastian said.

Mum looked at me. "Isn't this wonderful, that the University here accepted Sebastian's transfer. Now you two can spend all your time together."

Seriously? I wanted to scream. I did not want to spend any time with him and now he was going to be here, in town, close by. Where was the sensible mother who complained about her child's significant other monopolising all their time? I forced my mouth to twitch upwards. "Yes... Fantastic..."

I picked at my food. It all looked great, but the smell was making my stomach lurch and twist. I didn't trust myself to hold it all in if I ate. As good as it looked though, it hadn't been grown by Minnie or cooked by Harvey. Aubrey wasn't reaching over everyone trying to get a bit of everything and then seconds. Hattie wasn't trying to sneak past invisible and snatch things off everyone's plates. and Noah wasn't staring at me from across the room where he sat with Chouette and Cassias. Mech wasn't hovering at the side somewhere staring at Aubrey until she looked in his direction and he looked away.

I sighed and picked at my food some more. Nothing would ever be the same, would it?

"Are you alright honey?" Mum asked.

I nodded. "Yeah… Just tired," I replied, looking up at her. She didn't really look all that concerned. More annoyed that I was ruining her dinner.

Sebastian's hand rested upon mine, and I looked into his eyes. Those chocolate brown depths did actually show concern. As much as I despised him, in this moment, he seemed to care more than the woman they all claimed was my mother. His hand then went to my forehead.

"You're warm," he stated. "Maybe you should go and lay down.

I nodded. "I think I might," I removed my napkin from my lap. "I'm sorry Mum, it was wonderful."

And then I escaped from there as fast as I could. I scurried through the living room, pausing only long enough to retrieve the kirpuuru toy that I had picked up that day. I clutched it close to my chest for a second and then headed upstairs. Three steps later my legs were burning I really wanted to go to my room. That space that was supposedly mine. A representation of who I had been before I had been sent away supposedly to save my sight. Instead, I sunk to the stair and sat there with my back against the wall, the kirpuuru clutched to my chest.

It was hard to keep my eyes open or my head up and after struggling for a little while, trying to listen in on the conversation in the kitchen, I gave in to the darkness and let it drag me off into my dreams.

117

With dinner finished and the woman occupied, Sebastian rose from the table. "Thank you, everything was wonderful."

"You're welcome, dear."

"I think I'll just pop up and check on Ju-" No, she wasn't Juniper anymore. He had to remember that. "Shiloh, if that's alright."

"You go on, I'm sure that you have so much to talk about,"

He left the room and crossed the living room, ready to head up the stairs when he saw her. His heart thundered in his chest. She wasn't moving. She was crumpled on the third step, her back against the wall and that stupid kirpuuru toy cradled against her. He rushed up to her and reached a hand for her shoulder, gently trying to shake her awake. Her body swayed fluidly with every back-and-forth motion, and he couldn't help but smile down at her when she seemed to smile up at him languidly.

"Wakey, wakey," he cooed in her ear.

"Go away Noah..." she mumbled. Sebastian frowned. She was thinking that he was him! What else was she thinking? That they'd spent another night wrapped up in each other's arms? "I want to sleep..."

"Wake up, Shiloh," Sebastian said harshly.

"No..." She groaned. Why was she being so petulant? Angrily, he reached out for the stupid toy that looked so much like that damned creature, trying to take it away from her. Didn't she realise what was at stake? Her eyes shot open.

"No!" She hissed and he stopped pulling at the kirpuuru toy.

"Then get up," Sebastian demanded.

"Where's my mum?" Shiloh asked.

"Clearing up after dinner."

She looked around, disoriented, as if unsure of where she was. "How long have I been here?"

"About an hour I would guess," Sebastian replied. He held his hand out to her. She frowned up at him but reluctantly accepted it. He hauled her to her feet and was even gracious enough to allow her to lean on him as he helped her up the rest of the stairs.

"Where did you get that thing?' Sebastian asked as he deposited Shiloh on her bed. She kicked her shoes off and hugged that silly toy to her chest as though it would or could hold off the world.

She stared at him defiantly. "It reminds me of Shree."

Sebastian's face creased, and he leaned over her, his hands on either side of her body. His face, real close to hers. He needed her to understand. This was bigger than either of them. It was bigger than her and her friends. "This is not a game," he hissed. "None of this is a game."

"You're the one playing make believe," she shot back.

He was breathing so hard and loud. It rang in his ears and his chest heaved with every exhale. "Don't make me angry."

"What?" she asked, a coy smile on her face, "I won't like you when you're angry?"

He leaned in even closer. Their faces were touching and then he kissed her. She shoved him away. He stumbled backwards, reaching out for her as she scrambled across the bed, away from him. She almost fell off the other side reaching for something. "You don't know what you're playing with Shiloh."

"Stay away from me!" She hissed, allowing herself to slide off the other side of the bed. She grabbed for something and when she stood back up, she was brandishing a long, thin staff like weapon. She'd wielded something similar back at Camp Sight. Where had she gotten that from? "I mean it. Go away and don't come back."

Instead of showing any fear, he launched himself across the bed. He needed her to work with him, willingly or unwillingly. He needed her. She struck at him as he approached, but he anticipated the move. He grabbed the stick used it to guide her in closer to him.

She was stronger than he'd thought as he used the leverage from the weapon to shove her back against the bedroom wall. With a growl of frustration and exertion, he ripped the weapon from her hands and tossed it to the floor. It fell with a clatter, then rolled away, before being caught against the legs of the desk chair.

Weapon gone and her startled, Sebastian pressed his elbow against her neck and leaned in close to her face. "You will do as I say," he hissed. Her mouth opened and closed, trying to speak, likely to retaliate, but all that emerged were gasping, almost choked breaths. He pulled back in horror of what he was doing. "You and I," he said, his free hand coming up to caress her cheek. How to tell her that they were running out of time? That he needed her. She would never listen. She'd made it perfectly clear that she did not trust him. He would figure it out. Here in Yarm, he would have time to get her to trust him, but right now? Now he needed her to listen and do as he said. Trust would have to come later. Right now, she just needed to listen. "We're together. We have been for almost a year, and you will keep to that story… Or I'll kill you mother, and your father and his new wife. Even that adorable little baby brother of yours."

Her eyes flickered with something he'd never seen before, not directed at him and he flinched. Fear. She was afraid of him. He stumbled backwards in shock, releasing his grip on her. Sebastian stared in horror as she crumpled to the floor. He backed up further, breathing harshly before he paused in front of the mirror and composed himself. Sebastian straightened his shirt, his jacket and ran his fingers through his hair. Then he turned and looked at her, his composure restored, his mouth curling up into he hoped was his most charming smile.

"Do feel better," he said. "I'll see you later, sweetheart." And then he walked out of the room. He shut the door behind himself and leaned back against it, letting his head fall back with a thud. He was so screwed. What had he been thinking?

EPILOGUE

Life in Yarm settled into a weird sort of routine after that day in my room with Sebastian. I returned to school. Upon my request, a different school from wherever I had attended prior to going away. Mum had given in when I begged, explaining that I could not go back, repeating a year level and not knowing anyone who called me friend.

The new school... Well, I had nothing to compare it to really, but I liked it. I started there as just the new girl and while that was hard, I didn't have to explain to anyone why I had no idea who they were. Days were predictable. I would wake up, eat my breakfast, make sure I had finished my homework and then I would go to school, where one class would blend into another. My new school even had a martial arts club that I joined. I felt it in practice, it was not what I had trained in before I had gone away, but I liked the more attack-oriented nature of the style, and I often surprised my teachers and my sparring partners with things I seemed to intuit from my past life and things Cassias had taught me.

Mum had offered to bring me back to my old dojo, but I told her I wasn't ready for that yet. I wanted to learn who Shiloh May Rowan was for myself and in my own way. I would find my way back to that person, but I also had to somehow, incorporate Juniper into that equation now... And it didn't help having Sebastian at my side, following me everywhere I went after school.

"Don't you have university work to be doing?" I asked as he once again escorted me home from school.

He smiled at me and made sure that the girls nearby could hear him. "I always have time for you," Then he held his arm out and with a sigh I slipped my arm through his and allowed him to lead me home.

"You know, any one of them would date you in a heartbeat," I muttered.

"But I don't want any of them," Sebastian rebutted. I suppose that if I really cared about him, his words would be sweet and affectionate, but instead, they made my skin crawl. I never seemed to have a free moment to myself anymore. Especially not since Mum had let him move into our spare room for a modest rent.

"I have piles of homework," I finally said. "I don't have time to hang out with you tonight."

"We can study together."

Great, I thought. Just what I wanted, not. Was it too much to ask for a few moments' peace and quiet? If we were a real couple, this whole thing just seemed like too much. Too controlling. Noah had never made me feel as though I needed to watch myself every moment of every day. "Sounds great," I said instead, biting back the additional comments I wanted to make. We walked a little further on. "I have a tournament tomorrow. I need to get finished with the homework tonight. I won't have time over the weekend."

"That's fine. I'll come to cheer you on."

I still had not figured out what it was that Sebastian wanted from me or what he got from this little charade of his. Maybe he was hiding in plain sight or maybe he was keeping me within his grasp for whatever eventuality awaited me. I had tried once to track down Aubrey's school and maybe find a way to contact her, but he had found me and not believed my story about an assignment. In the aftermath of that, I had found my kirpuuru toy slashed to tatters, its stuffing pulled out and scattered across my room. I stopped trying to find any of the others after that, but Noah's words haunted me.

"Go… But swear. Swear that you will come back to us… To me…"

I had promised to return to him, and I had every intention of following through with that. When Sebastian touched me, kissed me, acted as though I was his to do with as he pleased, I pretended he was Noah. I had stopped saying Noah's name, so that was good.

"I love you." His words in my dreams kept me sane.

ABOUT THE AUTHOR

Annie Mars was born and raised in Melbourne, Victoria. From a young age, she was a voracious reader, loving anything from epic fantasy to crime thrillers and hard sci-fi. She's always had animals around her and currently enjoys the company of two cats, the grumpy Sammy and the eternally energetic Pawla.

For fun, she practices Aikido, a Japanese martial art, which sometimes makes its way into her writing.

Look into my Eyes is the first in a new series, joining the ranks of *Saga of Toserra Sorose* and *The Kahzer Chronicles*.

OTHER WORKS

The Kahzer Chronickes

Saga of Toserra Sorose

Saga of the Wild Hunt

Saga of the Tournament of Souls

Eyes of Glass

Look into my Eyes

www.ingramcontent.com/pod-product-compliance
Lightning Source LLC
Chambersburg PA
CBHW082057090726
47909CB00011B/3068